THE TRUTH ABOUT MARVIN KALISH

The Truth About Marvin Kalish

a mystery

Martin Samuel Cohen

Ben-Simon Publications
Port Angeles, Washington
Brentwood Bay, British Columbia

Ben-Simon Publications

USA: P.O. Box 2124
                Port Angeles, WA 98362

CANADA: P.O. Box 318
                Brentwood Bay, B.C. V0S 1A0

Book & jacket design by Rita Edwards
Typography by Leading Type, Victoria, B.C.
Text set in Times-Roman 11/12.5 & titles in Zapf Chancery 22
Printed on acid-free paper
Published simultaneously in Canada and USA
Acknowledgment for assistance from the EHK Memorial Fund

Library of Congress Catalog Number: 92-071041 √

Canadian Cataloguing in Publication Data

Cohen, Martin Samuel, 1953–
    The truth about Marvin Kalish

    ISBN 0-914539-05-1 (pbk.) – ISBN 0-914539-04-3 (bound)

    I. Title.
    PS8555.0545T7 1992   C813'.54   C92-091417-9
    PR9199.3.C64T7 1992

Printed and bound in Canada

1 3 5 7 9 8 6 4 2

for Joan

AUTHOR'S NOTE

The author wishes to stress that none of the characters portrayed in this book is based on a real person, living or dead, and that the entire book, including the non-Biblical epigraphs and epilogue that follows the final chapter, is a work of fiction.

The account in the first chapter of the slaughter of Jewish men at the Bucharest abbatoir follows the Jewish Telegraphic Agency dispatch from Sofia, Bulgaria of January 29, 1941; the account of the massacre of Roumanian Jews in the field outside the Jilava prison near Bucharest is based on the J.T.A. dispatch from Sofia of January 31 of that same year.

In the course of the war years, about 4,500 Jews were deported from Munich. The story told in chapter sixteen of Zelig Kropf's deportation corresponds to the basic reality of those deportations, but is in its detail the product of the author's imagination.

Yudel Wolfzahn's recollection of the events of November 9 and 10, 1938 in Hamburg are based, loosely, on the recollections of a number of former German Jews with whom the author is acquainted personally.

The Yale University Press volume mentioned in chapter twenty-two is fictitious.

Finally, the description of the Catacomb of Santa Cecilia in the twelfth chapter of this book is based loosely on the Roman Catacomb of Santa Domitilla, whose real address it bears. Aside from a few details, the entire description is the product of the author's imagination. Of the real Saint Cecilia, David Hugh Farmer assures us in *The Oxford Dictionary of Saints* (2nd edition; Oxford and New York, 1982) that almost nothing certain is known.

The ancients bequeathed their belief to all Romans that the governance of mankind lies in the shifting patterns of the zodiacal constellations. But if that be true, then it is only in this sense that it may be so: that all individuals have their private zodiacs made up of private configurations of individuals who, like the stars above, circle about them throughout their entire lifetimes, affecting them in ways which only seem magical and beyond human comprehension, but which, in reality, correspond to the principles of science we hope to set forth in these volumes. Thus is it entirely possible for an individual of indistinguished lineage and limited education to be thrust into greatness, not because of any personal merit, but merely by virtue of existing at the confluence of metaphysical vectors unknown to, and unsensed by, the individual in question...

> *– Nigidius Figulus (fl. 150 B.C.E.) ed. Warnke, fragment #318, apparently from the introduction to some lost multi–volumed philosophical rationalization of astrology*

Videbo eum sed non modo   *– Numbers*

The greatness of Liebeskind's dramatic works rests not so much in the playwright's ability to describe heroic characters who are the undisputed masters of their own fates, but rather in his singular ability to show how true greatness rests in possessing the courage to acknowledge how little in command of one's personal destiny even the strongest among us ultimately is.

> *– from the introduction to Pavel Rappaport's 'Why Not German Literature?' (3rd edition; Prague and Leipzig, 1919)*

One

"*M*aybe you should phone back, once you have your ad worded precisely," the voice said politely.

"No, no need," Bunny responded quickly. "I know just what I want to say. It's just... I... Let me start over and..."

This was the third time Bunny Luft had needed to begin reciting her advertisement from the beginning.

"I promise I'll get it straight this time. Just bear with me!" A certain tension was becoming audible in Bunny's voice as she realized that she would have to be approaching the frustration threshold of even the most indulgent of *The Times'* classified operators.

The silence on the line, however, indicated that her operator *was* still bearing with her and that she had one final chance to state her advertisement from beginning to end without any changes of style or content. It certainly wasn't the case that Bunny hadn't considered the implications of each and every word of her copy; it was precisely *because* she had devoted so much time deliberating over her text that she was so sensitive to the nuance and implication of each particular word.

Still, Bunny told herself, this wasn't a rabbinic responsum she was composing that would be studied and analyzed by generations of anxious scholars; it was a simple classified advertisement that nearly all of *The Times'* readership would gloss over without a second thought.

But it wasn't those millions of readers who concerned Bunny. The knowledge of their existence and their indifference to her words was nothing to the thought that somewhere in their midst, possibly, there was the one individual to whom her words would be anything but meaningless: a twenty-seven year old man whose life would change upon reading them if only she could manage to express herself succinctly, enticingly and clearly. Bunny felt herself rising to the challenge as she began to recite her copy a third and, she hoped, a final time.

" 'Desperately Seeking' ", she said into the receiver, "I want the words 'Desperately Seeking' on top of the box in big, black letters, then the rest in smaller letters. But not too small! Not so small someone wouldn't notice them if he were just glancing through the ads. You know what I mean?" Bunny asked, not for the first time during her phone conversation with the anonymous clerk.

"I know what you mean," the voice assured her. "Don't worry about the typeface, ma'am. Just give me the text and I'll worry about the details."

"You're a wonderful person," Bunny said. "A wonderful person for letting me be so confused and not hanging up and making me phone back later when there would be some other girl at the switchboard. Thank you very much!"

"You're welcome," came the blasé reply, followed by silence. It was, Bunny realized, now or never.

" 'Desperately Seeking'—that's on top. Then we'll say this. 'Warm, caring Jewish mother seeks…' No, I'm sorry, forget the 'warm, caring' part. Just let's say 'Jewish mother is anxious to find her little boy born May 2, 1953 and given up for adoption soon thereafter. Are you that little boy? If you are, you have a birthmark the shape of Manhattan…' Everybody said so, you know, it was exactly the shape of Manhattan! Even the doctor…"

The voice interrupted Bunny before she got too far off her track. "You don't want the ad to say 'Everybody said so, you know, it was exactly the shape of Manhattan!', do you? Let's just take it from '…a birthmark the shape of Manhattan.' "

"Okay, of course you're right. But it was exactly the shape of Manhattan, everybody *did* say so. Even Dr. Kronstadt, he should rest in peace. He was such a wonderful man—a saint!—anyway, even the doctor said so. So where were we?"

"If you are, you have a birthmark the shape of Manhattan…"

"Okay, 'the shape of Manhattan on the sole of your left foot, you have dark brown eyes and maybe you don't know this, but you were born already circumcised.' The doctor said it happens from time to time, but the rabbi—I phoned the rabbi the day I gave birth to schedule a *bris*—you know what it is, a *bris*?"

"No, ma'am." An edge of exasperation in the tired voice. "What is it?"

"A *bris*? It's when we circumcise a child. Anyway, what was I saying? Oh yes, so I was about to have the baby and I phoned the rabbi he should come and do the *bris*—I had decided to give the baby up, there wasn't any other way, really—anyway, I had decided to give the baby up, but of course I wanted the rabbi to come and give him a good send-off, especially since the agency promised he would go to Jewish people—anyway, I phoned him and told him I wanted him to come and circumcise the baby. It turned out that I must have been crazy if I had thought they'd let me keep the baby for more than a week and *then* give it up, but it didn't matter in the end because when the baby was finally born, the doctor takes a look and he tells me, 'Bunny,' he says, 'Bunny, this baby could be the *moshiach*.' "

Rose Dayton, despite her twelve years of professional service to *The Times*, could feel herself being drawn into a story she had no real desire to hear. But the thought of sicking this crazy on one of her colleagues made her feel too guilty to quit here when she could at least hope she was nearing the end of the conversation. "The what?" she asked, almost despite herself.

"The *moshiach*," Bunny Falk Luft answered immediately. "The messiah. It says somewhere that the messiah will be born already circumcised. That's one of the ways we can know who he is before he can speak up and introduce himself."

Almost against her will, Rose Dayton's mind flitted to Caravaggio's great painting of Jesus' circumcision, one she had written about in detail as part of her final examination in art history three semesters earlier. She was more than three-quarters finished with the night courses at Brooklyn College she was taking in order to finish her B.A. and had savored art history above any of her other studies.

But the operator's reverie was only a momentary respite from the reality of the speech she had for some reason committed herself to hearing through to its eventual end.

"So where were we?"

"…may not know this, but you were born already circumcised."

"That's right! It's really true. So how do we end it? '…born already circumcised. Don't be mad at your poor mother! Or at least let me tell you the whole story and then you can decide if you want to have anything to do with me. And don't think I want to come into your life and push aside the wonderful, kind woman who raised you as her own.' You think I should say she was wonderful and kind?"

"I don't know, ma'am. Why not say just 'the woman who raised you as her own'?"

"Because then he will think I am looking to take her place. Better I should say up front that I know the woman—he must call her his mother—should I say 'your mother' maybe? No, that's wrong. I mean, she's a saint for raising him, but that doesn't make her his mother, does it? I mean, he is the fruit of *my* womb, not hers."

Rose Dayton had been herself adopted in infancy and felt personally challenged to respond.

"A mother isn't a baby machine, ma'am," she ventured. "A mother is the woman who raises a child, who cares for it, who loves it, who cherishes it—not the woman attached to the womb that bore it. Motherhood is an emotional relationship, not a biological one. Ma'am." The edge of irritation in Rose Dayton's voice was rising. She believed every word of what she had said, or rather she believed that she did. But just beneath the rational surface there lay the seething sense of self-loathing and anger shared by all abandoned children, adopted or not.

Bunny could hear the edge in her unseen interlocutor's voice and knew to back off. "Let's finish this up," she said.

"Let's," agreed Rose Dayton.

"So where were we? I promise this is the end of the matter."

"We were at '…the wonderful, kind woman who raised you as her own.' "

"Okay. '…who raised you as her own. There is something important I have to tell you, something that could save your life if you only knew. So don't be afraid! Send your phone number to *Times* box whatever it is and I'll phone you as soon as I get your number.' "

Bunny could hear the clacking of Rose Dayton's computerized keyboard as she delivered her copy in as distinct syllables as she could muster.

"Shall I read it back to you?"

"Yes. No. Wait—let's add one last sentence. 'We don't have to meet even, just talk on the phone.' Add that after the box number. You have the number?"

Rose Dayton's keyboard clacked away at Bunny Luft's last sentence. "*I* assigned *you* the box number. Do you want to include your name?"

"No," Bunny answered crisply, "I don't."

"Shall I read the copy back to you?" The relief in the operator's voice was audible.

"Please."

Rose Dayton read the copy aloud in her most professional operator's voice:

Desperately Seeking

Jewish mother is anxious to find her little boy born May 2, 1953 and given up for adoption soon thereafter. Are you that little boy? If you are, you have a birthmark the shape of Manhattan on the sole of your left foot, you have dark brown eyes and maybe you don't know this, but you were born already circumcised. Don't be mad at your poor mother! Or at least let me tell you the whole story and then you can decide if you want to have anything to do with me. And don't think I want to come into your life to push aside the wonderful, kind woman who raised you as her own. There is something important I have to tell you, something that could save your life if you only knew. So don't be afraid! Send your phone number to *Times* Box 358 and I'll phone you as soon as I get your number. We don't have to meet even, just talk on the phone.

"It's too long," Bunny said immediately. "Just say, 'Were you born on May 2, 1953 and given up for adoption? Contact your birth mother for some important information.' Then give my phone number and that's enough. If he sees the ad, he'll call."

"That's all you want to say?"

Bunny's mind was made up. "That's it," she said firmly. "What more is there to say, really?"

***

Bunny Luft's classified advertisement ran in *The New York Times* on Wednesday, February 25, 1981. There were no responses, not even any false leads or idle inquiries by the usual urban pests who have nothing better to do than answer advertisements they find printed in the morning paper.

"Maybe he doesn't know he's adopted," Bunny muttered aloud on Friday morning, February 27, as she sat waiting by the telephone. "Or," came the bored response from across the breakfast table, "maybe he knows and doesn't care to hear what you have to say."

"There are other possibilities, you know. Maybe he doesn't even live in New York. Maybe he doesn't read *The Times*."

"Maybe he doesn't read at all," came the desultory response. "Maybe he's dead."

"Sha!" Bunny leapt to her son's defense before a would-be murderer. "Twenty-seven year old men don't just die. He's alive and he's somewhere. It's only a matter of finding out where my baby lives."

From across the table, silence. The pale February sunshine shone through the faded nylon curtains onto the kitchen table and somehow combined with the slightly acrid aroma of Bunny Falk Luft's coffee, the sound of rustling newsprint and the strangely irregular ticking of the timer mechanism on the Lufts' ancient toaster to create a sense of familiar well-being. That this artificial mood managed to offset the heightened sense of anxiety that was constricting her throat and making her forehead itch surprised even Bunny herself.

"He needs to know, you know," Bunny said dramatically. "This isn't some crazy idea I've suddenly had."

"I know."

"His life could depend on knowing, you know."

"I know."

"I'm not just going to forget about this."

"I know that too."

"So if you know so much, how come you don't know enough not to dip your paper in the coffee?"

Lawrence Lazar Luft lifted his section of the paper high into the air, dripping coffee as he did so all over the plastic tablecloth. "Shit on this," he said through clenched teeth.

"Shit on this, shit on that," Bunny said in her most irritating sing-song. "*Bei dir, ohn' a shit geht es nit.*"

"Shit on that too," Lawrence Lazar commented calmly. It was more than a bit true that he could hardly express himself at all without his favorite word, but Bunny's observation stung more than he chose to let on, especially when she dressed it up like a wise Yiddish proverb culled from some pre-war compendium of ancient Jewish aphorisms. 'And shit on you too,' he added soundlessly, his moving lips carefully shielded from his wife's eyes by the bottom half of the newspaper that he was still holding aloft and which was no longer dripping coffee onto the table.

The morning traffic on the Long Island Expressway seemed light for a Friday morning as it passed just beneath and beyond the Lufts' kitchen window. Lawrence Lazar looked outside as he did every morning, ostensibly to determine whether to go to work on the expressway or through city streets. But this morning, Lawrence

Lazar's gaze was not fixed on the passing cars or even on the glistening towers of Lefrak City that rose across the highway.

As Bunny cleared the breakfast dishes from the table, Lawrence Lazar stared vacantly out the window and found himself thinking about his wedding day more than a quarter of a century earlier.

He had known a lot, even then. Bunny had been smart enough to recognize that there was no point in keeping anything from him. In return, he had respected her perspicacity in understanding that eventually, husbands and wives learn all of each other's secrets. That Bunny had understood that she would only be paving the road to disaster by trying to keep something from him, especially something that dozens of people knew, had only increased her stature in his eyes. Even years later, Lawrence Lazar had never come to regret his estimation of the young Bunny's candor.

Lawrence Lazar had proposed marriage over dinner at Ratner's. It was the third night of Chanukah in 1954 and the restaurant was packed with Jewish diners searching New York for the perfectly fried *latke*.

"There's something you should know," she responded. "There's no convenient way to say this, so I'll just tell you straight out. I had a baby a year and a half ago and I gave it up for adoption."

Lawrence Lazar, who had been thinking of trying a goodnight kiss that very night *if* Bunny agreed to marry him, was more than a bit taken aback.

"A baby?" he had asked, his eyes open wide.

"Yes," Bunny had answered sadly. Her mournful, damp eyes brimmed over with regret.

"You gave a Jewish baby away to *goyim*?"

Now it was Bunny's turn to be amazed. "No," she said, "not to *goyim*, to Jewish people. I mean, I don't know who adopted him, but the agency promised that the baby would be placed with Jewish people. There are so many older couples around the neighborhood now, mostly refugees whose first families were killed by the Germans, that I've always liked to imagine he ended up living somewhere around here with some nice elderly couple who would cherish him and care for him. I mean, I don't know where he is, but I can sometimes sort of feel his presence. Just for a moment, it's true. But sometimes, sometimes in the supermarket or on line in the post office or even once or twice in the subway, I've suddenly had the sense that he was around. It's hard to describe, a certain twinge inside, a bit like a cramp, but not really a cramp—more like a stitch in your side, except inside, not outside. Anyway, I look around and..."

Lawrence Lazar cut her off in mid-sentence. "And you always see the same baby?"

"No," Bunny admitted, "I don't. Sometimes, I don't see any baby at all and other times, I see some baby, but not always the same one. Who knows what that means? Maybe he's around *somewhere*, but not right in the same room as I am or in the same car on the subway."

"Or maybe the whole thing is a crock of shit." Even as a young man, Lawrence Lazar's life-long speech patterns were in place.

"Or maybe the whole thing is a crock," echoed Bunny.

For a few minutes, there was silence at Bunny and Lawrence Lazar's table. The waiter cleared the dinner dishes and served coffee and pineapple cheese cake. Bunny looked into her boyfriend's brown eyes and wondered if she had spoken too rashly or too soon. "So?" she asked finally.

"So what?"

"So are you still interested in marrying a fallen woman."

"Fallen in what sense?"

"Well, it's one thing to have had a baby out of wedlock, you know, but to have given the child away—even animals don't give their offspring away to other animals."

"You sound as though you regret giving the baby up."

"Well, it was the right decision. I knew that then and I know it now. But it certainly doesn't make the matter any easier to think about. I mean, the child is in a wonderful, loving family now instead of having been raised by a single mother with a secretary's income and no father in sight."

"If you knew we were going to meet, would you have kept the baby?"

"Would you have raised somebody else's baby as your own?"

"You tell me first!"

Bunny thought for a moment. "If I knew I was going to meet you, I would have kept the baby."

"That's the right answer," Lawrence Lazar told Bunny, an easy smile coming to his thick lips.

"The right answer? So you still want me?"

"I do," Lawrence Lazar said, wiping his mouth with a linen napkin and placing it gently on the table next to his dessert plate. "I really do."

"Okay," Bunny said.

"Okay what?"

"Okay, I'll marry you."

"Okay."

The rest of the evening passed less eventfully. Lawrence Lazar lived with his parents on Woodhaven Boulevard in those days, not too far from the Falks' home on 97th Street in Rego Park. As they drove home along Queens Boulevard, Bunny took her fiancé's moist hand. There was, she felt, no reason not to finish the whole business that very evening rather than let any part of it fester.

"So," she said, "aren't you going to ask who the father is?"

"The father?"

"The baby's father. Babies don't only have mothers, you know. They have fathers, too."

"I know," Lawrence Lazar answered quietly.

"So aren't you going to ask?"

"No," he said firmly. "I am not."

"Because you don't want to know?"

"No, because if I know the guy, it will either ruin my relationship with him or with you. And if I don't know him, who cares?"

"How do you know I wasn't raped?"

Lawrence Lazar took his eyes off the road long enough to glance at his fianceé. "*Were* you raped?" he asked.

"No," admitted Bunny. "I was not."

Because the Falks had insisted on making the wedding at their own expense, they were given free rein to plan things as they wished. Themselves not formally affiliated with any specific Jewish community, the Falks booked the wedding for Sunday, the twenty-second of May, 1955 at four o'clock in the afternoon at Lawrence Lazar's own synagogue. Plans fell slowly into place. Cynthia Falk took care of everything, pausing only in the traditional Jewish way to allow her soon-to-be son-in-law's parents to pay for the flowers, the liquor and the band.

The ceremony and the reception were both booked into the Queens Hebrew Congregation, then a new and luxurious building standing by itself on an as yet undeveloped stretch of Queens Boulevard. At the time she booked the facility, Cynthia Falk had insisted on a private interview with the rabbi during which she revealed her daughter's secret.

"I didn't betray anybody's confidence," she argued later that evening at the Falks' dinner table. "He had to know! What if he didn't know and he decided to go on and on under the *chuppah* about the

glories of bridal virginity? There wouldn't be a person in the room—
not from our side, anyway—who wouldn't split a gut trying not to
laugh out loud. Look," Cynthia said pointedly to her daughter, "let's
not get huffy about this. You made a mistake, you dealt with it—we
all dealt with it—and now everything has worked out for the best. You
have a swell guy who'll make a great husband. You'll have all the
babies you want. He makes a decent living…"

Lawrence Lazar Luft owned a venetian blind factory in Long
Island City. His blinds were first quality, but it was only when Walter
Winchell made mention in his column of Lawrence's delivery truck's
now famous bumper sticker ("Caution: Blind Man Driving") that
business had really taken off.

"…and he comes from a nice family. And look at it this way,
honey," Cynthia Falk had continued in her most reassuring, maternal
voice, "at least you don't have to worry about whether you can have
children!"

Even years later, Bunny could recall how little reassured she was
by the fact that she, alone among her maiden friends, was entering
married life secure in the knowledge that her ovaries were in good
working order.

"But you didn't have to tell the rabbi!" she had wailed. "He'll
think I'm a whore."

"You're not a whore," Moe Falk had volunteered from behind that
evening's *Mirror*. "Whores," he added unkindly, "do it for money."

"Moe!" Cynthia Falk was not going to allow that kind of talk
about her own daughter, even from her daughter's natural father.

"And they don't usually get themselves knocked up."

"Moses Falk, you take that back."

"Okay," Moe Falk had responded with affable cruelty, "they don't
do it for money and they often get knocked up."

Silence fell like a thick fog at the Falks' dinner table. The dishes
were cleared as each of the three diners contemplated the implications
of the fact that Cynthia Falk had told her daughter's big secret to
Rabbi Weissbrot.

Rabbi Weissbrot, an older man of Roumanian origin, had seen
more than enough during the war years to know that Bunny Falk's sin
was not worth harping on.

In January of 1941, Rabbi Weissbrot had been one of the two
hundred or so Jews who had sought refuge from the fascist Iron Guard
in the Bucharest Jewish Community center. Eventually, the Green-

shirts found out where they were, and three or four five-ton trucks, all American-built and all stolen from the army, drove up to the former schoolhouse. The thirty-five or so men who couldn't be crammed onto the trucks were shot on the spot, but the others were driven outside the city to the fields near the Jilava prison. About one hundred and sixty Jews were lined up on the side of the road and shot by the fascists at point-blank range. Before they returned to the city, the Greenshirts went up and down the line shooting over and over into the crumpled corpses to make sure every single Jew was dead.

Rabbi Weissbrot was also shot, but the first bullet had somehow managed only to graze his neck; it was his good fortune to have fainted in terror and fallen backwards into the pit anyway. Because the two men directly to his right had fallen on him, he had been effectively shielded from further bullets and had somehow survived and made his way back to the city.

But his home had already been destroyed by fire and there was nothing left to return to. The rabbi, then a young man of thirty-one, had already witnessed the deportation of his parents and most of his family. He realized that he had only one single chance, and that was to escape to the Soviet Union.

Somehow, Elimelech Weissbrot made it through the Red Army lines. He eventually walked most of the way to Samarkand in distant Uzbekistan, where he spent the remainder of the war years working in a nylon factory. When the war ended, it took almost two years for the rabbi to walk back to Europe.

The rest of the story—how he came to be interred in an American D.P. camp and how he was eventually given permission to emigrate to America—was hardly unique. But his perspective on human suffering was, if not unique, then at least his own.

Rabbi Weissbrot's brother had been among the two hundred men seized by the Iron Guard a few days before the Jilava massacre and taken to the Bucharest kosher abbatoir. The men had been forced to strip naked, after which they were led to the chopping blocks where their throats were cut in a grotesque parody of the traditional Jewish method of slaughtering fowl and livestock.

The upshot of all this was that Rabbi Weissbrot knew more than enough about sin to know that Bunny Falk's wasn't worth taking too seriously in a world in which not dozens or scores or hundreds but tens of thousands of Iron Guardsmen and S.S. officers had managed to return to their former lives once the war ended, protected from prosecution by the absurd principles laid down at Nuremberg and free to tend their gardens, dandle their children on their evil knees, make love to their wives and worship God in their cozy churches. Since making love to a suitor simply couldn't qualify as transgression to a survivor of Jilava, Rabbi Elimelech Weissbrot really was the perfect man to marry Bunny Falk to Lawrence Luft.

"You know, rabbi," Cynthia had said melodramatically, "my daughter is not the chaste thing she appears now to be. She had a baby born on the wrong side of the sheets—if you know what I mean—last year. The baby was given up for adoption and everything worked out in the end."

"You needn't feel obliged to say more," the rabbi had said delicately.

But delicacy wasn't Cynthia Falk's strong suit. "But I *do* feel obliged, rabbi," she had continued. "You know what I want from you."

Rabbi Weissbrot knew. The bride's mother wanted, he presumed, two separate things. She wanted him to write up the marriage contract in the regular way, which would require referring to the never-married bride as a virgin. And she wanted him to avoid referring to anything under the wedding canopy that would lead to unnecessary sniggering among the assembled guests.

"You know the old Jewish proverb," the rabbi responded quietly, "the one according to which you aren't supposed to mention rope in the home of a hanged man? Well, don't worry, that goes for cord as well, even umbilical cord. So don't worry. And as for the *kesubbah*, that's no problem either. Let's just forget about this conversation and I'll assume as I always do that *besulah* is the Jewish word for 'unmarried girl' rather than a statement of premarital chastity. That *is* what you wanted, isn't it?"

Cynthia Falk assured him that this was precisely what she wanted. The deed done, she returned home triumphant. "Everything's taken care of," she told her astonished daughter that very evening at dinner. "After all," she added, "you know what they say—never talk about umbilical cords if you don't want the bride to hang herself."

"Hang myself? I was an unwed mother, not an S.S. officer. Honestly, mama, you've betrayed a pretty important confidence."

Cynthia was unrepentant. "I haven't betrayed anybody's confidence. He *had* to know…"

In the end, the wedding had come off without a hitch. The synagogue ballroom easily accommodated the two hundred and sixty-five guests the Falks invited and the thirty-five friends and relations of the

Lufts' who had been honored with invitations. Cynthia had commissioned tiny green-and-white forklifts as clever centerpieces for each of the twenty-eight dinner tables. "Get it?" she asked whomever she caught staring uncomprehendingly at the paper centerpieces. "It's a pun! Falk Luft! Falk-Luft! Fork lift! Her married name is going to be Fork Lift!"

'And she's going to be rich!' Cynthia Falk finished her thought silently. 'She may be Bunny Falk Luft, but she isn't going to have to lift a fork for the rest of her life. Well, maybe to eat her supper, she'll lift a fork—but not if it falls to the ground. My God, he's been mentioned in Winchell! We'll *all* be rich!'

No less predictably than if it was a sign from God Himself, an enormous green forklift was making its slow progress down the service road of the Long Island Expressway at the very moment Lawrence Lazar Luft was daydreaming about his wedding. He could practically see the paper centerpieces his mother-in-law had commissioned to give physical reality to the only pun she had ever thought of from the day she was born until the day she died.

The forklift lumbered along the service road until it passed from Lawrence's field of vision. For twenty-six years, he had dreaded the day that Bunny would seize on the idea of finding her lost baby, knowing he would have no choice but to support her when she came to her inevitable decision.

Now that the day had come; Bunny would hardly drop the project merely because her initial attempts to locate her boy had failed. It was even a bit of a relief, Lawrence Lazar discovered to his surprise: they would get things out into the open, the boy would materialize and then go back to wherever it was he came from and that, Lawrence ardently hoped, would be that.

Whether Bunny had been wise to raise the subject of a hitherto-fore unheard-of half-brother with Jeffrey and Joyce, Lawrence did not know, although he assumed he would find out. For better or for worse, though, this was his wife's ballgame and Lawrence certainly knew his wife well enough to understand that she would willingly see it through to its final inning.

The hour was getting late; the factory opened at eight o'clock sharp and the boss was supposed to be there to supervise the beginning of the work day. Grabbing his trademark black plastic sunglasses with "The Blind Man" spelled out in tiny rhinestones across the top of the frame and quickly swilling the rest of his now-tepid coffee, Lawrence Lazar was out the door.

Lawrence heard his wife's good-bye with half an ear. But Bunny's mind was not on her husband or his obsessive punctuality and neither was it on the fact that her classified advertisement had attracted no response from the public, let alone from her lost baby.

Her gaze was fixed instead on a tiny bronze mirror that lay on the kitchen windowsill in precisely the same spot it had occupied since the Lufts moved into their three-bedroom apartment in the fall of 1961.

Two

The mirror had been a wedding gift from Rabbi Weissbrot himself.

It was an inexpensive gift, but its worth in Bunny's eyes was enormous because of the symbolic importance which the rabbi had vested in it. Rabbi Weissbrot had seen enough of the world to know that what a Jewish girl needed from her rabbi on her wedding day was permission to start her life anew with neither reference to her past nor recrimination from whatever indiscretions might have flawed its smooth flow up until that auspicious date.

To his credit, Rabbi Weissbrot did not ask, not even one single time, about the baby or the circumstances of its conception.

All in all, there were three prenuptial meetings with the rabbi and at none of them did Rabbi Weissbrot even broach the topic. Bunny was more than merely grateful; she felt truly in his debt. Of course, Bunny told herself, although she knew that her mother had told the rabbi of her situation, she had to presume that the rabbi himself had no way to know that she knew; it seemed that the rabbi's promise of discretion extended even to raising the subject with the bride herself. At any rate, all the prenuptial meetings had been in the presence of Lawrence Lazar. Since the rabbi had no way to know or even to inquire regarding the degree to which the groom was in the picture, he had apparently decided to keep silent rather than risk ruining a Jewish girl's prospects for marriage.

But the reality of the situation was that the rabbi had understood that Cynthia Falk would tell her daughter that he knew about her child. And less than five minutes into their very first meeting, Rabbi Weissbrot saw clearly that Bunny Falk was not the kind of woman who would marry a man without telling him something that might otherwise destroy their marriage later on.

The rabbi kept his peace therefore neither for fear of exploding the engagement nor out of excessive modesty or reticence, but rather because he truly believed the bride to be a victim of the degree to which the Jewish world had bent itself out of shape in its relentless quest to appear normal and good to the surrounding Gentile world.

Sexuality, the rabbi knew, was a gift of God, perhaps the greatest of His gifts. That people feel desire for each other is not merely a convenient way for God to have arranged that the earth be populated; if such had been His desire, the rabbi often asked his congregants, could not the Almighty simply have created all the billions of people who live on our planet at once?

Certainly, an omnipotent God could have created an earthful of people—did He not create an ocean full of fish, as it is written, "Let the waters bring forth swarms of living creatures!" No, the rabbi would exhort his liberal congregation, the point of sexual desire is not to make babies anywhere near so much as it is to suggest to pathetically small-thinking human beings what love and passion are all about. And since God Himself wishes not merely to be loved, but to be loved passionately, does it not follow that the desire for physical love be explained as the intimation of greater things, the tease, the come-on ("the come-on, if you will" the rabbi would always say, as though to excuse his uncharacteristic vulgarity) designed to lead mankind to love God no less passionately than each individual loves his or her lover?

Decades later, these thoughts would sound ordinary. But in the early 1950's, when Rabbi Elimelech Weissbrot propounded them from the pulpit of the Queens Hebrew Congregation, they were explosive, challenging words, ideas designed to mock and denigrate the new winds blowing through post-war American society. "Let the *goyim* behave as though they have just discovered sex," the rabbi would thunder from his podium. "For us, sex is merely a tool, just as are all things that exist in this universe the Almighty has created, a tool designed to assist any individual who would take that tool in hand to fashion a relationship of intimacy with God," the rabbi would proclaim to his slightly embarrassed flock.

A confidential word from the only male member of the Hebrew School faculty convinced the rabbi that he could stop the sniggering that was wont to arise from the bar mitzvah boys' class by omitting further reference to sexuality as "a tool taken in hand," which advice the rabbi, to his credit, took graciously and entirely in the spirit in which it was offered. The ambiguous phrase was excised from further sermons and eventually forgotten.

But the rabbi's message itself was not forgotten. The age was ripe for hearing that Judaism was distinct from other religions that denigrated and distorted the meaning of the divine gift of sensual love. In an age of ever-decreasing attendance in synagogues and churches, attendance at the Queens Hebrew Congregation rose month after month until finally it became necessary to limit attendance at Sabbath morning services to members in good standing whose pledges to the Building Fund were entirely up to date.

The other half of the rabbi's message had to do with the degree to which the Jewish people had betrayed their heritage by living according to other people's standards. This message was often expressed in different contexts and with different examples, but the theme of marriage was always interlaced throughout the rabbi's remarks like a binding thread.

How could it be natural—or rather, as the rabbi often put it, how could it not be rejection of one of the Almighty's greatest gifts—for people to wait a cool ten to fifteen years after attaining physical maturity before finally marrying? Was it not absurd to expect chastity from people at the peak of their sexual powers and desires? Were we—by 'we' the rabbi always meant the Jewish people as a whole—were we not betraying our own heritage and merely aping the *goyim*—the rabbi had often said 'sucking up to the *goyim*' until warned off that expression as well—by waiting to marry until we are ready and interested in having children? Does our faith teach us that the point of human sexuality is reproduction? No, the rabbi would thunder, it does not!

Human sexuality is the key to the love of God, no less certainly so than the fear of death is the key to fearing Him. This, in a nutshell, was the essence of Rabbi Weissbrot's teaching about the nature of love.

That a pretty Jewish girl like Bunny Falk had managed to end up pregnant before getting married was no boon to her reputation, but neither was it an indelible stain on her soul. It was, to Rabbi Weissbrot's mind, merely an auspicious sign of good things to come coupled with a bit of ill-timing and unfortunate circumstance. But what a girl with passion and beauty needed was hardly a lecture on birth control! What Miss Bunny Falk needed, even as she prepared to become Mrs. Lawrence Luft, was the blessing of God. And that, Rabbi Weissbrot was more than prepared to offer her.

But during their meetings, the rabbi gave no hint of his thinking on the weighty matters of passion and faith. Instead they spoke of sundry things, of the details concerning the ceremony and the *chuppah*—the wedding canopy beneath which the groom and the bride must stand during the ceremony—and the order of the wedding procession.

"And you'll come down the aisle and when you get to the *chuppah*—the music will still be playing—you walk around your fiancé seven times."

"No one does that anymore," Bunny had pleaded.

"We do," had been the rabbi's simple answer.

"And does this ritual have any meaning?" Lawrence inquired, unaware of the rudeness conveyed by his slight, yet perceptible emphasis on the word 'this'.

"It establishes who's going to be the boss in the marriage," the rabbi had answered, no less honestly than cryptically.

"Well, then, that's not so bad," said Lawrence Lazar, who had completely misunderstood the rabbi's point, as he sat back in his chair.

"Fine," Bunny had agreed, unwilling to appear at all fractious or uncompromising lest the rabbi change the topic to whether or not the word 'virgin' should appear in the marriage document.

But Rabbi Weissbrot had no intention of raising the issue of the bride's virginity, and neither did he wish to discuss any aspect of her pregnancy.

Such exquisite reticence, however, did not mean that the rabbi had no intention to express himself on the matter. On the contrary, Rabbi Weissbrot had every intention of saying something about the bride's status. But he intended to do it with extreme tact and in such a way that only those with open, willing ears would hear and understand.

It was for that reason that Rabbi Weissbrot chose to address the matter for the first and only time under the *chuppah* and in the presence of all three hundred invited guests. The only fact which the rabbi could not know was whether the baby's father was present to hear his remarks. Well, the rabbi thought to himself, if he's around, so much the better!

"My dear Bunny," the rabbi had commenced his wedding peroration, "I stopped into the bride's room earlier this morning and found you brushing your hair as you looked at your reflection in a mirror. That mirror, combined with the sight of you adorning yourself for your wedding day, reminded me of some other mirrors from long, long ago and the message they have even today for those who care to listen to the teachings of the Torah.

"You may recall," the rabbi continued, now turning to include

the groom as well in his message, "that some of the first command-
ments addressed to the Israelites in the desert had to do with the
construction of a tabernacle, a sort of movable shrine in the desert, at
which the service of God could be carried out. The Torah goes into
great detail about this sanctuary, giving precise instructions for its
construction and the construction of the various appurtenances that
would be necessary for the divine worship to ensue.

"Of these instructions, one of the most bizarre has to do with the
kiyor, a sort of big washstand that our ancestors were bidden to use
to wash their hands and feet before approaching the holy altar.

"The Torah bids its base be decorated with mirrors of some sort
and thereby hangs the tale I wish to share with you.

"Does a mirror seem to you an odd thing to use to decorate a
washstand? Well, it seemed that way to Moses too. In fact, Moses
wished to dispense with the mirrors, not because they weren't attractive, but because they had been donated by the women to the
construction of the tabernacle—these were the ladies' make-up
mirrors, the ancient compacts they would use to adorn themselves
for their husbands. 'Instruments of vanity and puffery!' Moses com-
plained. 'These shall have no place in the tabernacle of God!'

"But Moses was wrong. Our rabbis teach us that God Himself
spoke to Moses and told him to use the mirrors, for they had their
own role in the survival of our people. In Egypt, the men were slaves
to Pharaoh. When they came home at night, they were very tired
from *shlepping* all those bricks around and building pyramids and
sphinxes and whatever else they were told to do by their wicked
taskmasters.

"How tired were they? Well, the rabbis teach that they were too
tired even to eat and drink. And if they were too tired to eat and drink,
you can imagine that they were also too tired to be with their wives..."

Rabbi Weissbrot paused for the briefest of moments after the
words 'be' and 'wives' to stress that this was a delicate euphemism
rather than a simple statement of fact.

"...to be with their wives," the rabbi repeated for emphasis.
"Anyway, what did the women of Israel do? They enticed their husbands' vanity with their own mirrors. They would look in their little
mirrors of burnished copper and coquettishly say, 'My, but don't I
look better than you do these days!' Then the Israelite ladies would
flutter their eyelashes and moisten their lips as they brushed back
their hair and pouted into their little mirrors. The husbands were
driven wild and forgot their hunger, their thirst and their fatigue—

and before you knew it, desire had arisen where only moments before there had been none.

"So anyway," the rabbi continued, "it was these little mirrors that the women of Israel offered to Moses as adornment and decoration for the Tabernacle, which Moses refused and which the Almighty Himself stepped in, so to speak, to accept.

"So why am I telling you this story? I'll tell you why. I'm telling you this story because you might misinterpret it, just as I did when I was younger. I used to think the point was that there wouldn't have been any Israelite children if the wives hadn't aroused their husbands to action and so God accepted their offering out of gratitude for preserving the Jewish people.

"But now that I'm older, I think I was wrong. After all, if God wanted there to be more Jewish people, He could just have made more like He made Adam and Eve in the first place. What God wants is to be worshipped passionately, wholeheartedly, sensually and utterly—and in a society that was too tired for sex, who could imagine what that might mean?

"So the women were rewarded for preserving the recollection in their husbands of what the worship of God is supposed to be—total, conditionless, overwhelming, passionate and exhausting."

There was a bit of nervous tittering in the back of the synagogue, but not enough to deter Rabbi Weissbrot from finishing his wedding speech with customary vigor.

"So, you two young people," he concluded hopefully, citing his favorite Biblical passage, "rejoice in your youth! Follow the desires of your heart and the glances of your eyes; banish care from you and pluck sorrow from your flesh! For youth and black hair are both fleeting!"

The point was well made and well taken by both bride and groom. Bunny had been too eager and too little chaste—but she had been obeying natural inclinations that have the most sacred purposes when correctly channeled.

The ceremony was concluded. The rabbi read the great marriage document from beginning to end in its obscure Aramaic text, pronounced the seven formal benedictions that seal the marriage, and blessed the happy couple. Lawrence Lazar broke an expensive wine goblet filched from his mother's crystal cabinet under the sole of his right foot and the couple retired for a few moments of uninterrupted seclusion before the dancing and feasting would begin.

But the seclusion was not to last as long as Bunny would have liked. After only fifteen minutes, there was a knock at the door of the rabbi's study.

"I can come in?" the unmistakable voice inquired rhetorically.

"Of course," answered Bunny. It was, after all, the rabbi's own study in which the bride and groom were being briefly sequestered. How could the rabbi himself be denied entry?

"So *mazel tov* to you both. You can stay as long as you want and when you're ready, you can greet your guests. But before you go, I have a little something for you."

The rabbi fished into his jacket pocket and produced a small box, which he handed to the bride.

"You didn't have to," Bunny stammered.

"I want you to remember what I told you under the *chuppah*."

"We will," Bunny promised. "Forever."

"Good," the rabbi answered. "And now, excuse me for not staying for the reception. I have a *shiva* this evening..." Rabbi Weissbrot's voice trailed off as he, presumably, considered how much fun it would be to stay and dance at the wedding and how little fun it was going to be to lead services at the house of mourning where he was expected.

Bunny was still holding the small package when the door closed behind the rabbi and she was suddenly left alone with her chubby husband.

***

The present turned out to be a tiny mirror of burnished bronze, a reproduction of an ancient artifact found at Mycene and sold through the Museum Shop at the British Museum. Of all the scores of wedding gifts the Lufts received, none was more precious in Bunny's eyes and even Lawrence Lazar had to admit it was a gift of exceptional thoughtfulness and kindness. Without saying a single word, the rabbi had communicated his forgiveness and understanding of Bunny's indiscretion.

Bunny had taken the mirror and placed it on her dresser where it would never be far from her sight. When the Lufts moved into their three-bedroom apartment in Rego Park in 1961, she had placed it on the kitchen windowsill, where it had sat ever since as a permanent sign of forgiveness.

After twenty years, the tiny mirror had become as much a part of the scenery as the other constants of the Luft kitchen.

Although Bunny had ceased to take notice of her rabbi's wedding gift, it was also the case that the memory of the tiny infant boy whom she had carried, birthed and given away was never far from her consciousness or conscience.

The circumstances of his conception had faded in Bunny's memory with the passing of time, as had the other dramatic moments connected with the whole episode: the hysterical scene in Dr. Kronstadt's office when the tests came back positive, the tearful announcement to the senior Falks that their baby was 'in trouble,' the secret trips to maternity shops in Gentile neighborhoods while wearing a girlfriend's borrowed wedding band, the unspeakable relief when the baby turned around by itself and thereby obviated the devastating possibility of a Caesarean delivery, the feeble attempts to explain away her morning nausea to the other girls in her office as a three-month-long siege of stomach 'flu, and the sudden discovery of a long-lost, newly deceased great-aunt whose bequest to her distant niece was now to allow Bunny to retire from the office in which she worked and take a much deserved six-month vacation in, of all places, Finland.

These details had faded, at least in their awful vividness. But the fact remained that somewhere in the world there existed a child, now long since become a man, whose mother (whose *real* mother, Bunny thought when she allowed herself a moment of internal candor) was a fifty-one year old Queens housewife with a tiny bronze mirror on her kitchen windowsill and an overweight manufacturer of venetian blinds in her twenty-one year old bed.

The thought of attempting to locate her lost child had returned to Bunny many times in the course of her married years. Once Jeffrey and Joyce were born, of course, the fantasy became more complicated, but not so impossibly as to preclude the development of a workable plan of action. Even though Bunny did not actually carry through on any of her fantasies, the indelible fact remained at the bottom of the ledger: there was a man in the world who didn't know his mother, and a woman in the same world, perhaps even in the same borough, who didn't know her son.

But now things were different! The situation was transformed from idle fantasy to urgent reality, in the regular manner of such transformations, in a single moment.

It all began on Friday evening, February 6, 1981, at approximately 8:35 p.m.

***

As a sort of wedding present, the younger Lufts had been offered a year's free membership in the synagogue with which Lawrence Lazar had been affiliated for many years as a single member. Synagogue affiliation was hardly a priority for Bunny Luft; she had insisted on discussing the matter before finally agreeing to accept the directors' generous offer.

After a year, Bunny Luft found to her great surprise that she liked being part of an organized community. When the second year's fees became due, the discussion was almost an afterthought.

"So should we join again?" Lawrence Lazar had asked.

"Of course," replied Bunny. "I like the other gals in the Sisterhood. And we're going to have someone to send to the nursery school before we know it!"

Bunny was six weeks pregnant on their first anniversary and loving every minute of it. As though to flaunt the fact that she was now doing things the right way, she wore only the most obvious maternity fashions and made a point of choosing dresses that would accentuate her bulge long before it was really necessary.

Part of this campaign involved attendance at synagogue services, a new feature in both Lawrence Lazar's and Bunny's life. The Friday evening service at the Queens Hebrew Congregation was very satisfying to them both; the ancient hymns touched a part of them that neither had known with certainty had even existed.

Rabbi Weissbrot's sermons were brief, but they always presented some aspect of rabbinic wisdom that gave Bunny food for thought and a sense of pride in her Judaism that she had never known before.

The company of the other worshippers provided a sense of community that even Bunny's own family had never been able to offer her; Bunny often remarked that affiliation with the Jewish community was a bit like having siblings without actually having to have parents as well.

Jeffrey was born on May 2, 1956, three years to the day after his unknown half-brother; Joyce—conceived following her older brother's second birthday party in an unexpectedly passionate moment while the exhausted birthday boy napped in his high chair—

followed two years and nine months later on March 9, 1959.

The years passed. The world changed and the Luft household changed with it. In 1961, when Joyce was two years old, the family moved into a splendid three-bedroom apartment overlooking the Long Island Expressway.

The elder Falks died and were buried in the Mount Hebron Cemetery overlooking the busy confluence of the Long Island Expressway and the Van Wyck Parkway. The permanent, ceaseless flow of traffic down the Expressway from beneath the Lufts' apartment to just alongside the graves of Cynthia and Moses Falk came to mean something to their daughter, who felt close to her deceased parents in a way of which most bereaved children can only dream.

The elder Lufts, Myron and Bertha, were still alive in 1981, but only barely. They had been talked into giving up their tidy home on Woodhaven Boulevard and moving to a so-called seniors' residence on Beach Nineteenth Street in Belle Harbor where the fear of death slowly replaced the fear of crime.

But although many things changed, some few details remained constant in the younger Lufts' life.

The small bronze mirror that Rabbi Weissbrot had given the couple as his personal message of forgiveness and hope sat undisturbed and mostly undusted on the white windowsill of the Lufts' kitchen overlooking the parkway.

The love that had somehow developed between Lawrence Lazar and his bride became a sustaining force in their lives.

The venetian blind business continued to flourish. By 1981, the business had about 15% of the Queens market and almost 20% of the Brooklyn trade. Plans to expand aggressively into Manhattan were afoot and there were satellite operations in six other cities along the Eastern seaboard.

The Lufts found themselves happy with their spiritual niche at the Queens Hebrew Congregation. To the surprise of their friends, they became active members, serving as directors of the synagogue and heading most of its more important committees. These special appointments had come and gone, but the Lufts' practice of attending services at eight o'clock every Friday evening had become inviolate. Except in times of illness, there was no question but that the Lufts would be in their seats at a few minutes to eight, leafing through the prayerbook, scrutinizing the announcements on the special synagogue bulletin distributed to Friday evening worshippers or discussing the outfit the mother of that Sabbath's bar mitzvah boy had chosen to wear on the eve of her son's great day.

"The point is," Bunny said to her husband when they finally returned home at about ten in the evening on February 6, 1981, "that *anyone* who knows us at all knows where to find us on Friday night at eight o'clock. It's no secret, you know."

Lawrence Lazar knew all too well that it was no secret. You can't do something every single week for twenty-five years and then be surprised that someone has observed a certain pattern to your life. "But still," he countered weakly, "the whole thing could be a prank. Some stupid practical joke."

"It's no joke," Bunny answered with uncharacteristic sharpness. "No joke at all! That woman hit you hard in the back of the head with her purse. And when we turned, we both heard her say the same thing."

"I didn't mean the whole episode was a dream, just that maybe we don't have to take it so seriously."

"Let's compromise. *You* don't take it seriously and *I* will worry about the whole thing myself."

"No," Lawrence Lazar replied. "Either we both worry about it or we both don't. I'm not sure this is such a big deal, but if you are, so be it. Where do we start?"

Bunny leaned over to her husband's side of the bed and kissed him on his forehead. "This," she said in her Marlene Dietrich voice, "is where we start."

She had more to say, but could not continue once her husband's thick lips enveloped her own; as she succumbed to one of his ardent embraces, however, her thoughts were entirely on her son. "At least," Bunny thought as she felt Lawrence Lazar beginning to caress her breasts in earnest, "I get a few minutes to think without him yammering in my face."

The incident at the synagogue hadn't lasted more than fifteen or twenty seconds. The Lufts had been seated, as they always were, in the right-hand section of the synagogue, about twelve rows from the front. Lawrence Lazar was always anxious to have an aisle seat in case he felt the need to leave the sanctuary during the service and it was an established custom of the Lufts to arrive long enough before the beginning of worship to be certain of having an aisle seat. In the days of the saintly, enormously popular Rabbi Weissbrot, this had posed a major problem; however, since the arrival of Rabbi Dornbusch, attendance had fallen off so precipitously that it was no longer actually necessary to arrive early simply to guarantee a particular seat in the sanctuary.

At any rate, Bunny and Lawrence Lazar were in their proper seats five minutes before the service began, leafing anxiously through the bulletin and whispering between themselves. The golden Ark of the Law, designed by no less an artist than the great Arthur Szyk, shimmered in the yellow electric light; the air of artistic majesty mingled with the humility of worship to create a peculiar ambience in the sanctuary that was not at all unpleasant.

Finally, it was eight o'clock; the rabbi strode forth from his private entrance to the right of the great golden Ark of the Law and took his place on the side of the *bimah*. The cantor, whose place in the synagogue hierarchy was such that he was obliged to enter the room through the front door with the rest of the congregants, found his own way to the lectern and began to chant the opening hymn, "Beloved Father of Mercy."

By the time the cantor finished the fourth and final stanza and was ready to open the introductory service with the ninety-fifth psalm, the room was utterly still. The rustling of pages ceased as the five hundred or so congregants immersed themselves in the ancient liturgy and felt the presence of God creep over their weary selves.

The service proceeded apace. Rabbi Dornbusch spoke about the final verses in the Book of Exodus, offering a sexualized homily about the great pillar of divine cloud that penetrated the holy tabernacle that would have made a psychoanalyst blush and a more traditional rabbi weep.

The part of the evening devoted to the worship service proper had just gotten underway. The cantor had just launched into "With Everlasting Love Hast Thou Loved Thy People Israel" when an older woman seated just behind the Lufts rose from her seat. Lawrence Lazar, lost in the dreamy melody and deep in meditative prayer, hardly noticed. She gathered up her things and folded back her padded seat, apparently unwilling or unable to remain for the end of the service.

As she turned to go, she managed to whack Lawrence Lazar in the back of his head with her large black patent leather purse. The blow was so heavy that even Bunny heard the thud of shiny plastic against her husband's head as Lawrence Lazar illogically raised his hands to his head to ward off a blow that had already come.

"I'm *terribly* sorry," the woman said. She was, Bunny thought, at least twenty years her senior and conservatively dressed in a black dress and a single strand of cultured pearls. 'Fakes,' Bunny thought in the split second she had to analyze the handbag's necklace. "I was only thinking about your boy," the woman added in a whisper that only Bunny and Lawrence Lazar heard.

Lawrence Lazar began to say something, but Bunny cut him off. "Sha, Larry," she hissed, knowing instinctively that this was no accident and that the message, if there *was* a message, was for her alone. "What did you say?" Bunny said to the woman.

"He's in danger," the handbag said.

"Who?"

Bunny's question hung on the air unaddressed and unanswered. The handbag turned on her high heel and made her way to the rear of the sanctuary. Bunny, unwilling to leave the matter unresolved, was on her feet only a moment later.

The woman was especially swift for someone in four-inch heels; it was only on the outer steps of the synagogue that Bunny finally caught up to her.

"Who is in danger?" Bunny demanded with all the outrage of a Queens Jewish mother investigating even the vaguest of threats against one of her children.

"Peter Stuyvesant," the woman said quietly on the second from the lowest step. Bunny, breathless, paused as a car drove up to the front entrance of the yellow stone building.

The handbag got into the car and was driven off, leaving Bunny to puzzle over what the woman could possibly have meant, if in fact she had meant anything at all.

⁎⁎⁎

"So she said four things: 'I'm terribly sorry,' 'I was only thinking about your boy,' 'He's in danger,' and 'Peter Stuyvesant.' Is that right?" Detective John Abernathy was clearly unimpressed. Vaguely wondering at what moment it would strike Mrs. Bunny Luft that he looked enough like Sidney Poitier to be his fat twin, the detective took his N.Y.P.D. mug in both hands and swirled the cold coffee around several times before lifting it to his lips. The garish neon light of the precinct house combined with the sound of Bunny Luft's shrill voice and the bitter aftertaste of the cold coffee to create the precise ambience John Abernathy hoped to be able to capture in the detective novels he planned one day to write. When he realized that his question was being answered, the detective was just making a mental note to remember the special way the hideously bright light reflected off the dirty yellow cinderblocks that served the precinct house as its interior walls when he tried to describe the special atmosphere of a New York City police station during a weekend graveyard shift. It was only to gather material for his books that Abernathy volunteered for night duty in the first place, even years after his seniority and rank would have easily combined to free him from the burden.

"That's right," Bunny answered simply.

"And you take that to be a direct threat against one of your children." A statement rather than a question.

"Yes," Bunny said defiantly, reading all the disbelief and lack of interest in Detective Abernathy's voice.

"Why?"

"Why? Because she said my boy was in danger."

"And where is your boy now?"

"You mean Jeffrey? He's home watching television. I phoned."

"Does he appear to be in danger?"

"That's just the thing," Bunny continued, "I don't think she meant my son Jeffrey. *He's* fine. I think she meant my other son."

"I thought you only had one son and one daughter."

"Well, that's almost the case. But there is a detail I've left out..."

Detective Abernathy leaned over the desk in his office at the 113th Precinct House and scrutinized the woman who was insisting with such vehement certainty that a child was in danger. "Why don't you just tell me the whole story, ma'am?"

Bunny took a deep breath and told John Abernathy the whole story. Hardly even mentioning the circumstances of the child's conception, she stressed the horror of pregnancy and the various forces that had brought her to the decision to give her baby up for adoption. She stressed that she had been guaranteed that the child was going to be adopted by deserving, decent people and that she had even been assured repeatedly that her Jewish baby was going to be placed in a Jewish home.

"And the child's name was Peter Stuyvesant?" Detective Abernathy took a stab in the dark once Bunny had fallen silent and her awful story was over.

"No, Mr. Smart-Ass Detective," Bunny snapped before she could catch herself, "I didn't name him Peter Stuyvesant. I didn't name him *anything*. But this was in 1953, remember. New York was in the middle of celebrating its Dutch heritage for some reason I can't recall anymore. Anyway, New York was having this whole Dutch thing and they figured a cheap way to start off was to rename some of the city's buildings and agencies to remind the citizens of the days of Old New Amsterdam. One office became the New Amsterdam Family Service Department, but the others got the names of different personalities from New Amsterdam days—Rip Van Winkle, Ichabod Crane, Peter Stuyvesant."

"Who was Peter Stuyvesant?" Detective Abernathy asked innocently.

"Where did you go to school? North Carolina?"

"Actually, I went to school in south Georgia," the detective admitted.

"So that explains it—you didn't have to take a semester in the history of New York City in seventh grade like you would have if you lived here."

"So who *is* this guy, this Peter Stuyvesant?"

"Who *is* he? Well, now he's a housing project and a decent city high school and a bar on Third Avenue. But once he was someone...historical."

"Someone historical?"

"He was the mayor of New Amsterdam, I think. Or maybe the governor. Or maybe he claimed New York for the Dutch. Anyway, he was somebody in history. And they named the social service agency that handled my baby's adoption after him."

Detective Abernathy began to see the light. "So the Peter Stuyvesant Agency handled the adoption?"

"Yes," Bunny said, relieved at last that he had understood, "it did."

"And you think that because this lady you'd never seen before told you that it was Peter Stuyvesant who was in danger, that she meant it was the boy you gave up for adoption twenty-five years ago?"

"Twenty-seven," came Bunny Luft's quick response.

"Twenty-seven," agreed the detective. "And what exactly do you want us to do?"

"What I want you to do? I want you to sit here all night scratching your behind. I want you to get the agency to unseal the records, find out who adopted him, trace him down and tell him he is in danger."

"Well, it isn't that simple," the detective began.

"What isn't that simple? To save a child's life? If it was your child, would it still be not that simple?"

Detective John Abernathy fell silent. You needed, he knew, a court order to force a child welfare agency to unseal files relating to matters of adoption and that that was the case even if all the parties to the adoption came forward separately to request that the files be opened.

On top of that, this case presented other difficulties. Not only had no real threat been made, but the woman who had indicated that danger existed was herself an unknown quantity. The Lufts had specifically admitted that they had never seen the woman in question before the night of the incident. If that meant that she wasn't even a regular member of the congregation, then it would only be by fluke if the police were to manage to locate her in order to ask her even the most basic questions.

Then there was the fact that the woman had referred to Bunny Luft's "son", by which expression anyone in the world would have presumed her to be speaking of Jeffrey Luft. But Jeffrey Luft was safe and sound, having spent that very evening watching television at home.

And the mysterious reference to Peter Stuyvesant could have meant anything or nothing at all. It was, Detective Abernathy reminded himself, hardly a wild guess that a woman of Bunny Luft's age seated next to her husband at Sabbath services in a large, respectable synagogue would be a mother of children, sons probably included, as well. One could hardly award the mystery woman a prize for deducing that Bunny had a son!

And yet, despite all the various reasons to ignore the information reported to him, John Abernathy felt strangely sympathetic to the request that had been laid at his night desk.

There was something convincing about Bunny Luft! She spoke with conviction—and her interpretation of the event, although hardly the only one possible, was not *that* crazy either. Perhaps there was something to what she had bothered to come to the precinct house to report—on a Friday evening, no less, when women like Mrs. Luft were generally to be found at home, fussing over their well-laden Sabbath tables.

Detective Abernathy's mother lived next door to a certain Mrs. Cohen, a pious Jewish woman who over the years had often invited her neighbor and her neighbor's son in to join her Sabbath meal. John Abernathy was a member of the Abyssinian Baptist Church of Cambria Heights, but he knew a Jewish Sabbath table when he sat down at one and he also knew Mrs. Luft's type at a glance.

"Well," he said hesitantly, "there's no reason not to do a bit of digging. I'll phone the agency Monday morning and see if there isn't something I can find out."

"Monday morning? You get a death threat against a citizen and you are going to sit on it for two and a half days before investigating? Don't be crazy! A child's life is at stake." Bunny Luft's bosom heaved at the very thought of delaying the detective's inquiries.

"Well, let's not get carried away." A certain coolness in the detective's voice. "First of all, there was hardly a death threat. And second, the child is thirty years old."

"Twenty-seven."

"Twenty-seven years old. Why not assume he can watch out for himself over the weekend, or at least until we can do some initial work?" Detective Abernathy flashed a relaxed grin to the couple leaning on his desk in hopes of persuading them that the unknown twenty-seven year old baby would be safe until Monday.

Bunny Luft leaned over the desk until her mouth almost met John Abernathy's right ear. Her bosom was pressed directly onto the detective's night book such that his nose was practically inserted between her large, speckled breasts. Detective Abernathy could actually smell the splash of Jean Naté with which Bunny had scented her bosom during her evening toilette and he could feel her hot breath on the rim of his ear.

"You must realize that this kind of laziness doesn't reflect well on your people," Bunny said in her loudest stage whisper. "Now you do your job right or I'll cancel my gift to the Negro College Fund."

In a trice, Bunny Luft lifted herself off the precinct's night desk and, Lawrence Lazar in her irresistible tow, was gone into the Sabbath night.

***

"You're back already?"

"Apparently."

"You found her?"

"I found her. And believe me, she got the message."

"How can you be so sure?"

"A woman knows these things."

"Does a woman know if *he* recognized you?"

"*Him* recognize me? All he saw were stars once I bashed him

– 31 –

with my purse. Believe me, he wouldn't have recognized his mother after that whack, much less a woman he last saw thirty years ago for five minutes."

"So how does he look?"

"Fat."

Three

"So I was finishing my next-to-last set and let me tell you the house was getting pretty antsy—I mean I had to bat clean-up after this stupid Puerto Rican telling jokes about his sister's tits—anyway I was just finishing my last set and don't get me wrong, I *was* getting somewhere, I mean, there were *some* laughs in the house, but I already knew I didn't have enough time left to really warm them up, but anyway, so where was I? Oh yeah, I was in the middle of the one about the guy with the prick named Pinocchio—it *always* gets a good laugh, you know…"

Dawn Kupchinsky had sat through Marvin's sets enough times both to know the joke and to appreciate what a good laugh it usually got. She nodded her silent affirmation as Marvin continued his story.

"…so I'm telling the Pinocchio joke and all of a sudden, this little guy comes into the room all by himself and sits down at one of the front tables. I mean, first of all, who comes to a place like Styx alone?"

Dawn, gracefully oblivious to the rhetorical tone of the question, shrugged gently.

"So anyway, as soon as he comes in, I know this is a weird dude of *some sort*. So this guy sits down and the table isn't even clean—I mean it's got some other party's glasses all over it and the ashtray's overflowing with butts and paper umbrellas and it isn't even *clear*, if you ask me, that the other party is gone for good—I mean, they could have just gone into the bar to talk until the Puerto Rican comes on again to tell more jokes about his sister's chest—but anyway, this guy sits down and it's also weird because he's still wearing his coat.

"I mean, the room is eight hundred degrees and I'm wearing a cotton shirt and *I'm* sweating to death, but this guy has an overcoat on and he sits down like he's in a deep freeze. So Marcy comes over and he orders something and she goes away and this guy is staring right at me, I mean, right at my face. So I can practically *feel* this guy's eyes boring two holes in my forehead and in the meantime,

– 33 –

I'm dying out there on stage.

"I finish the Pinocchio joke and it gets a *fair* laugh, nothing *too* great, but respectable, especially for that crowd. Anyway, so I can see Marcy bringing the guy a Mai Tai—I mean, for Chrissakes, a *Mai Tai*, like its Christmas goddam Eve at the Stork Club—anyway, she brings him the drink and he tosses the whole thing down in one swallow like she brought him a shot of booze and, like, I'm *watching* this guy because I can't take my eyes off of him. I don't know why, but I know this guy is up to something…"

Dawn sat up in bed as she opened the front of her nightgown as modestly as possible and began methodically to rub cocoa butter into the skin of her upper chest.

"So I'm finishing up. I've got three minutes to kill before I can get off stage—you know how much Manny loves it when you finish short—so anyway, I've got to kill three more minutes and I don't want to give away my best stuff in case there's somebody with a sense of humor who's there for the late set, so I figure I'll go into the thing about if teenaged boys' hormones could talk, you know the one where I pretend I'm this glob of talking testosterone…"

Dawn knew the routine all too well; she wrapped her nightgown around herself as she gave Marvin the full force of her attention now that he was approaching the climax of his story. Had he told it this same way to the police? Dawn certainly hoped not, but thought it wiser not to inquire just at this moment.

"…so anyway, I'm just getting into it—it's not my greatest material, but it was more than good enough for that morgue—so anyway, I'm actually getting some decent response and suddenly, this guy stands up at his place and starts to unbutton his coat. So he's just sort of standing there by his table opening his coat and I'm thinking to myself, holy shit, we've got another flasher. I mean, that's all this room needed was some midget waving his dick around. So anyway, I'm half thinking, well, we'll see if this crowd even *notices* and I'm sort of looking forward to the fracas that will *undoubtedly* ensue in two seconds, but then I see that his coat is open and suddenly he's got this gun in his hands…"

Dawn's eyes widened as she reminded herself that Marvin's life had truly been in danger.

"…and he's pointing it directly at me. I mean, this was some mother gun—some sort of semi-automatic rifle or something, and it's got this little barrel thing on top you look through to find your target, you know, the thing with the cross-hairs they always show in the movies. You know how you can see the guy aiming his gun at someone and moving it back and forth until the victim is precisely at the intersection of the lines? So anyway, he's got one of those things and he's aiming it at me! It's funny I can remember the whole thing now like it unfolded slowly and neatly, but the whole thing can't have taken more than ten seconds. The cops thought maybe even less, but they said it's normal to recall these things like they happened in slow motion.

"So anyway, I dive for cover, but the room is so dead—I mean it would have been more lively if they really *were* dead—they haven't even noticed this guy is aiming a *machine gun* or whatever it was at my head. I mean, this guy is about to murder me and they're sitting there over their banana goddam Daiquiris waiting for the Puerto Rican with the leather pants to come back on."

Dawn Kupchinsky moved closer to Marvin and put her arm around his waist. She hardly needed to hear the story a fifteenth time—she had missed the first recounting at the precinct house and had heard what had happened in detail only once they were on their way home, but although it was already almost four in the morning, Marvin was clearly not ready to let it go and get some sleep; he simply could not stop telling his story. But what could Dawn do but let him talk it out until even he became weary of the re-telling of it? Actually, Dawn noticed, the story *was* getting more finely honed with each re-telling. By the time the papers would start calling in the morning, Marvin would have the story down pat and ready to go.

To her considerable chagrin, Dawn suddenly realized that Marvin was *practicing* his story as though it were a new routine. But this was no routine and these details were certainly no jokes; some maniac had tried to blow her boyfriend's head off and it was only due to the strangest combination of good luck and fortunate circumstance that he had failed to do so.

But the ceaseless repetition of the story was having its effect on Dawn as well. Here it was almost time for the real dawn ("Dawn, meet dawn," Marvin had said wittily, flinging open the bedroom window to the eastern sky at sun-up on the first morning Dawn had spent the night in his bed making love until the sun had actually appeared over the Queens horizon) and there were still details Dawn hadn't heard in any of the previous re-tellings. Marvin hadn't mentioned before that the ashtray on the man's table, for example, had been overflowing with the little paper umbrellas from other people's drinks.

"So anyway," Marvin Kalish continued, his manic recitation

only fueled by the passion suggested by the feel of Dawn's rosy fingers around his neck, "this guy is aiming his gun at me and I dive for cover, but he must have just pulled the trigger before I went down and he hits one of the Klieg lights Manny has hanging from the back of the stage ever since he saw how they lighted up some comic he liked in Vegas, so anyway I'm okay, but the audience *finally* notices that there is someone waving a loaded bazooka around and these guys from table twelve lunge for the guy. It turns out they were off-duty cops—one of them was the guy who started to come on to you at the precinct house—and they knew just what to do. So they wrestle this guy down and start pounding the crap out of him, but in the meantime, someone calls the real cops—not that these guys weren't real cops, but I mean the real ones like when you call 9-1-1 and the cops come—and in three minutes, they come busting through the front door. Manny must have paid plenty for protection like that, let me tell you—anyway, they're through the door into the middle of this unbelievable *fracas*, I mean, the chairs are flying and people are screaming and everyone is looking for the gun, but the room is dark—Manny should have turned up the house lights, but he was too busy shitting in his pants in the back office—and there is all this unbelievable screaming and the cops, I mean the real guys in uniform burst in and start waving their nightsticks around and before you know it, the guy is gone.

"I mean, finally, someone *does* turn on the house lights and the scene is unbelievable. There isn't a chair or a table that is still standing up and most are broken in two and the place is a complete mess and everyone is *still* screaming their brains out and when things calm down, the guy with the gun is gone.

"I mean, the guy is gone and the gun is gone and if there weren't eighty-five witnesses, the cops would have thought we were all hallucinating. Eighty-five witnesses, I should say, and one still-breathing almost-victim and a handful of cartridges from the gun and bullet holes in Manny's precious Kliegs.

"So off we go into the police van and they take the whole story down and I called you to come and get me and the rest you know."

Marvin lay back in his bed and rolled his eyes towards the ceiling. The realization that his life had almost ended in a burst of unexpected, unwarranted gunfire was only now sinking into the less penetrable layers of the Kalish unconscious, but the effects of this sudden avowal of reality were not simple to gauge.

Marvin felt terrified *and* exhilarated *and* exhausted *and* strangely turned on by the whole incident. "Let's make love," he said to Dawn suddenly, rolling over on his right side and sliding his left hand into his friend's nightgown.

"If you promise not to talk until after we're done," came the conditional response.

"Deal," said Marvin as he switched off the light and began to massage Dawn's bare, white shoulders without saying a single word. The first faint rays of cold, yellow sunlight began to fill the room; it was Sunday morning, February 8, 1981.

***

"I'm telling you, I'm becoming obsessed."

"You're telling me you're obsessed—I have to live with you."

"Well, don't make it sound like I'm some nut case. What mother wouldn't be obsessed with finding her baby if she thought his life was in danger?"

Lawrence Lazar reached for the soy sauce as he formulated what he hoped would be a reasoned reply. "Of course any mother would obsess about her kid's safety. But this child you're talking about— let's not forget that you haven't even seen him for more than almost twenty-eight years. And when you did see him, it was for a few minutes when he was less than an hour old. Okay," Lawrence Lazar conceded, "he's still your kid. I'd feel the same way myself, I think, even without having carried the kid on the inside for nine months first. But still, to carry on as though you know for certain that someone is aiming a gun at his head just because some lunatic scared you one night in the synagogue is hardly reasonable."

Bunny weighed her husband's words. Everything he said, she knew, was entirely logical. She hadn't exactly bonded with her son—how could any two people have established much of a relationship in just a few minutes decades earlier when one was a newborn and the other an exhausted dishrag of a woman who had just completed seventeen and a half hours of labor and could hardly see straight?

And, for that matter, Lawrence Lazar's evaluation of the trustworthiness of the mysterious lady who had uttered the veiled warning was also entirely reasonable. It wasn't as though she had specifically indicated that she even knew of a son of Bunny's other than Jeffrey except for her weird reference to Peter Stuyvesant, which could, Bunny assured and reassured herself, have meant anything at all. Jeffrey, brought up to date on the events of that Friday night, had looked over his shoulder for a couple of days, then dismissed the threat as being absolute nonsense.

It was all true—true and logical and reasonable! But what did reason have to do with anything? Despite all the entirely reasonable reasons to ignore the matter, despite the desk detective's refusal to take the matter seriously, despite Lawrence Lazar's intelligent analysis of the situation—despite everything, Bunny knew how she felt and deep down, she knew that her baby boy was in danger. But from whom and for what reason, Bunny could hardly have faulted herself for not knowing.

The Lufts' return visit to the 113th Precinct House on the Monday morning following the incident in synagogue had gotten them nowhere at all.

Detective Abernathy had indicated that he would begin his investigation with a phone call to the Stuyvesant Agency the following Monday morning to see if he could find out whether the boy had even been raised in New York State. Naturally, even if he had been raised elsewhere, he could still *be* in New York now—and even if he were in some other state, how could anyone know that the death threat (if there had even been a death threat in the first place) wouldn't refer to an event about to occur somewhere other than New York?

Although the matter was, to say the very least, obscure, Detective Abernathy had found his interest piqued by the story. It sounded, for the life of him, like something out of one of the mystery novels he had read so voraciously as a teenager and which had, no doubt, been responsible for his single-minded determination to join the force. He *had* read all the books and he *had* joined the force and he *had* ended up manning the precinct walk-in desk for most nights he was on duty. Even if there were no legitimate reason for wasting N.Y.P.D. time on the case, John Abernathy was half planning to pursue the matter on his own time.

Even Bunny Luft's witless comment about the Negro College Fund had failed to put him off the scent of a good plot. The truth was that it was John Abernathy's secret plan to retire from the force after twenty years' service and write the kind of detective novels he had found so provocative as a boy. Bunny Falk would be a perfect character to use to grab the reader in an opening chapter!

The detective knew it would make far more sense to search for the mysterious woman who had accosted the Lufts than to try tracking down Mrs. Luft's long-abandoned son. If *she* could be found, she could easily be booked for assault—Lawrence Luft had the bump on his head to prove the point—and questioned.

But where to find her was another question entirely. The Lufts' accounts did not even totally agree with each other regarding her physical appearance, Mrs. Luft having described her as "an older Jewish Ann Bancroft, except much shorter and shrivelled down" and Mr. Luft having suggested her looks were closer to "a wizened, partially Jewish Ann Miller, but with Shirley MacLaine eyes and wrinkled skin." At least, the detective reassured himself, they agreed on her race.

But the New York City Police Department didn't have the kind of manpower necessary to chase down every vague threat of harm made by one citizen against another, much less a threat made against an unspecified, unidentified man by a woman who could neither be questioned nor evaluated in terms of her reliability, nor have the source of her information ascertained.

After all, if she *were* telling the truth, what would her motive have been? If she were connected with the alleged murder plot, she would hardly have blabbed to the intended victim's mother, of all people. And if she had hoped to prevent a murder, then she must have been in a position to know the whereabouts of the intended victim. And if she knew that and she wanted to stop a murder, then why wouldn't she have told Bunny Luft where to find her son and why would she have spoken so obscurely and why would she have fled the scene so quickly? And why had she bothered with Bunny Luft in the first place and not gone directly to the police?

Thinking about the mystery woman's flight turned the detective's attention to the way she had made good her escape. Someone had been driving the car into which she had jumped when she found herself pursued to the sidewalk by Bunny Falk. And yet, even though she had run out of the synagogue, she had obviously thought it at least possible that Bunny would pursue her into the street; otherwise, why would she have had a getaway car at the ready? Or, the detective asked himself, was there someone else from whom she expected she might need to escape in the course of the evening's events?

It was, John Abernathy told himself, the stuff of the kind of psychological thrillers he fully intended to become rich writing after his retirement from the force in five years' time.

But all this would have to be a private affair. If and when the detective needed the Lufts, he would simply create some pretext for calling them back in. For the moment, though, he would simply have to get rid of them.

"I called the Stuyvesant people," Abernathy told Bunny Luft at twelve minutes past ten on Monday morning, February 9, 1981.

"And?"

"And they said the records are sealed."

"So *of course* the records are sealed. You had to call them to find that out?"

"No ma'am, I knew that, but I thought I might be able to pry something out of them, even if it was only the state in which your boy was raised."

"So what happened?"

"Nothing happened. They told me that all records relating to all adoptions are absolutely sealed and that a court order is needed to unseal them."

Bunny was dismayed but not discouraged. "So we'll get a court order," she concluded logically. "Where do you go?"

"To get a court order? You go to court!" John Abernathy smiled his broad, bright smile to indicate that his joke was meant to relax rather than to insult the people on the other side of his chipped desk.

"That's it? I just go into the courthouse and ask a judge to give an order and that's the whole thing?"

"Well," the detective continued less flippantly and with greater accuracy, "not exactly. Basically, you have to sue the Stuyvesant Agency to force them to unseal your boy's records. First you have to get a lawyer and then the lawyer has to schedule a court appearance. Then you go to the judge and you tell him what you know and why you want the records opened. It isn't *that* complicated. The judge asks questions, the lawyer subpoenas me as the policeman who took the initial report and maybe a few character witnesses to prove you're peaceful citizens, the Stuyvesant people produce their own army of experts who testify that the whole adoption program will fall into complete chaos if the records of any child ever, under any circumstances and for any reason, were to be opened and their contents revealed..."

The detective's voice trailed off as he, presumably, contemplated the courtroom shenanigans of the so-called expert witnesses who would be paid to parrot the Department of Social Services' party line.

"And then what?"

"Then nothing. The judge takes it all under advisement. If he's a

– 40 –

Catholic, the Social Services people make a big deal out of the theory that any weakening of the inviolate nature of adoption proceedings will lessen public enthusiasm for adoption and lead to more abortions. If he's a Protestant, they'll make a big deal out of not wanting to send a message to horny teenagers that even if they do end up producing babies and giving them away, there's always a shot at finding the kid later on."

"And if the judge is a Jew?"

Detective Abernathy leaned back in his wooden chair. "If he's a Jew, they'll find a way to insinuate that they *know* the judge would never allow his judgment to be influenced by his own personal horror at the prospect of a nice Jewish boy having been raised by Gentiles. They won't say as much, but they'll make sure the message gets across. The judge, who probably is married to a *shiksa* anyway..."

With silent satisfaction, Detective Abernathy observed the rise his use of the Yiddish term had gotten out of the Lufts. His evenings in the company of his mother at Mrs. Cohen's Sabbath table had apparently not been entirely without value.

"...will get the message and decide against you lest anyone even *think* he might be deciding for you out of personal motives."

Bunny Luft leaned over the detective's desk for the second time in four days. "So where do we go from here?" she asked as simply and as forthrightly as she thought possible, deciding not to bother repeating that she had certainly *not* left the matter to chance and had obtained an iron-clad guarantee from the Stuyvesant Agency that her baby would go to a Jewish family.

"Where do you go from here? I'd counsel you to go home. The Stuyvesant people aren't going to open their records to anyone except God Almighty or a Queens County judge and your chances of getting a judge to see it your way are slim. So if I were you, I'd forget the whole thing. You did the right thing by reporting the incident. If a pattern emerges, I'll let you know."

"A pattern?" Now it was Lawrence Lazar's turn to ask a question.

"If more people report strange threats made against their adopted or not-adopted children during synagogue services in the next few weeks, we'll have something more to go on. But for right now, there just isn't too much."

The Lufts looked confused. "Just go home?" Bunny asked incredulously.

"Look," Abernathy sighed, "I made the call, but nothing is going to budge those people. You're highly unlikely to get a court order and you can't produce the mystery woman who warned you that your son was in danger. Without that, what are you going to do— check out every murder or attempted murder in the United States involving a twenty-eight year old man?"

"He's still twenty-seven. On the second of May," Bunny said quietly, "on May second, he's twenty-eight."

"Okay, twenty-seven. But do you really think the N.Y.P.D. has the manpower to watch the entire country—and you know it should really be the entire world!—for the unexplained murders and attempted murders of twenty-seven year old white males?"

Bunny was intrigued, oblivious to the detective's sarcasm. "Well," she opined artlessly, "there can't be *that* many murder attempts made against twenty-seven year old white males who were born on May 2 and who were given up for adoption."

"No, ma'am, there probably can't be. But what I'm telling you is that we just don't have the manpower or the ability to watch every event every place in the whole world. Look, I'm not trying to be discouraging," Detective Abernathy continued in his most discouraging voice, "but the simple truth is that I don't think there is anything you folks can do."

"Well," Bunny insisted, "there must be something. Our challenge is just to figure out what it is."

"Here, look at this," Abernathy said, now consciously working on ways to pry these people out of his office. "Some maniac took a pot-shot at a comic Saturday night not far from here. You folks know the comedy club called Styx?"

The Lufts had actually been to the club once or twice. It was located on Sixty-Third Drive in Rego Park and was widely known by its mostly Jewish clientele as Shticks. Lawrence Lazar indicated with a nod that they knew the place.

"So they have amateurs on week nights, but they have a stable of regulars they use on Friday and Saturday nights when the big crowds come in. I've been there myself and it's an okay place—no drugs, no pushy waitresses, no cover. So there's this local guy that's a regular..."

Detective Abernathy moved aside the remains of his morning's breakfast—a paper coffee cup and the wax paper in which his bran muffin, now a pile of dark crumbs, had been wrapped—to reveal a story on the inside of that morning's *Post*.

"...named Kalish, Marvin Kalish. So this guy is doing his act and suddenly some maniac pulls out a gun and starts shooting. It was just dumb luck that the guy wasn't murdered. There were some off-duty cops in the place who kept things under control until reinforcements arrived but the guy—the shooter, I mean—got away in the small riot that ensued."

"So what does this story have to do with us?" Bunny was not interested in *other* people's murders, only in her own son's.

"So the point is that there isn't any point. The point is that this guy is twenty-seven years old—see, it says so right here!" Detective Abernathy brushed a raisin off the last paragraph of the newspaper story. " 'Kalish,' it says, 'twenty-seven years of age, was unhurt.' "

"Thank God." Lawrence Lazar hardly noticed his own automatic response to the news that a Jewish boy's life had been spared.

"Thank God is right. But my point is that this guy has absolutely nothing to do with your problem. He's no one at all to you—just a twenty-seven year old who got shot at. Now it's true I could start digging with him—phone his home, see if he was born on May 2, find out if he was adopted. But tomorrow there would only be another twenty-seven year old to phone and then another and then another. And the bottom line is that I can't justify using that much public time to investigate a case that has so little to go on as an alleged death threat against your alleged son whose whereabouts are completely unknown even to you."

Bunny knew she was not going to get anything out of Detective Abernathy and that the time had come for the Lufts to go. "Okay," she said, her voice heavy with feigned dejection, "you win. We have no case and nothing to go on and we certainly don't want to waste the taxpayers' money. Look, we're taxpayers ourselves, you know. You think we want you to waste our own money? That's what they have Off Track Betting parlors for—for people to waste their money if they want. The police have other jobs, more important jobs. So forget the whole thing."

Detective Abernathy put his hands palms down at breast level, fingers slightly spread, to indicate that he wasn't irritated to have had his time wasted by the Lufts. Just the contrary, his gesture implied—he was pleased to have met such concerned citizens who didn't shirk their responsibility to come forward and report a suspicious occurrence. "No problem," he said.

"And look," Bunny said, now that the decision to do nothing had clearly been taken, "I'm sorry what I said Friday night about the Negro College Fund. In fact, I'm sorry for the whole incident. We've wasted your time and our own time and my son, if he was in any danger, isn't any safer for our efforts. And probably you're right," Bunny added in her most conciliatory tone, "that there isn't even any danger to worry about."

Her apologies made, Bunny rose to leave. She and Lawrence Lazar made a strange couple, John Abernathy thought as he watched them exit through the swinging doors that separated his office from the duty room in which he had first encountered them. "I'll be in touch if anything does develop," he called out through the swinging doors.

"You do that," came the response, but the distance from which it came made it impossible for John Abernathy to determine whether the words were meant sarcastically, gratefully or imperiously. Gravely, Abernathy turned back to his day's work even while Bunny Falk's final three words were still echoing in the stale air of the precinct house.

Four

From the station house of the 113th precinct, Bunny and Lawrence Lazar went for a late breakfast at the Hole Truth, Forest Hills' best muffin and doughnut shop.

They drank black coffee and ate Bavarian Busters as they discussed their next move; Lawrence Lazar had phoned the factory foreman early in the morning to say that it was unlikely the boss would be in until late in the afternoon, if at all.

"So?" Bunny's voice was angry.

"So what?"

"So what do we do?"

"What do we do? We don't do anything. We forget the whole thing. Wasn't the detective clear enough? If the police won't get involved, what *can* we do?" Lawrence Lazar had the unmistakable sense of being sucked irresistibly into a swirling vortex of intrigue which he felt could only lead to grief or disappointment.

"What we can do? We can get to work, that's what. That blowhard doesn't know who he's started up with!"

That much, Lawrence Lazar allowed in the privacy of his own thoughts, was entirely so.

"They can't do anything!" Bunny continued, mimicking Abernathy's self-declared impotence. "Believe you me, if it was *his* kid whose life was on the line, he'd know what to do! But it isn't his kid, it's *my* kid and he's too busy scratching his black behind to want to get more involved than he has to be."

Lawrence Lazar felt obliged at least to try to fend off his sense of impending doom. "First of all, lay off the black stuff. The fact of the matter, if you ask me, was that he was very sympathetic to the whole thing. He listened to the story, he thanked us for reporting the incident, he even phoned the adoption people..."

"He *said* he phoned," Bunny interrupted. "We'll find out later if he really phoned or not."

"Okay, he said he phoned. But if you ask me, he isn't that far off base. I mean, who knows what that weirdo at the synagogue meant. Maybe she *was* just another crazy lady—God knows they have enough of them who hang around the *shul*."

Bunny looked deep into her husband's eyes. "Listen to me," she said. "I can't say how I know and I can't even say why I am so sure that I know, but I am absolutely sure that the woman was on the level. Call it a woman's intuition or call it whatever you want, but that woman came around last Friday night to tell me my boy was in danger." Bunny's eyes were unexpectedly brimming with tears.

"So how do you know she didn't mean Jeffrey?"

"Well, don't you think I've thought of that? Of course, she might have meant Jeffrey—but she didn't. If she meant Jeffrey, she would have called him by name. Or maybe even not—but the Peter Stuyvesant line clinches it for me. I don't know what she could possibly have meant by that if it wasn't that it's my *other* son who is in danger."

"How do you even know she meant just you when she said 'your boy'—I mean, that she meant your boy, but not mine? How many people even know you have another boy aside from Jeffrey?"

"First of all, she was talking to me. So when she said 'your boy' it doesn't mean anything but my boy. And since I have two sons, it could mean either. But all this is entirely irrelevant. I'm telling you I know what she meant. And she meant that my baby boy, my twenty-seven year old baby boy, is in danger."

"And what, exactly, do you propose we do?"

Bunny looked surprised by the very question. "What I propose we do? I propose we find my boy and warn him that he is in danger."

"And how exactly do you propose we do that?"

Bunny looked dramatically over each shoulder to make sure there was no one present in the Hole Truth who might be listening in to her conversation. "I have a plan," she confided to her husband.

Lawrence Lazar pushed his rhinestone-studded black plastic sunglasses up onto the top of head and bent over the top of the formica table. When his ear was no more than six inches from his wife's mouth, she began to speak.

When Bunny and Lawrence Lazar finally left the Hole Truth, it was already early afternoon. Lawrence phoned in to tell his foreman that he wouldn't be in at all until the following day; Bunny cancelled an appointment at the Smart Set and phoned Jeffrey to tell him not to wait for dinner. His parents, she said, had decided to eat out that evening with another couple.

The calendar cleared, Bunny and Lawrence Lazar made for their lawyer's office.

Although the Degas had actually cost far more, it was always the oversized Chagall that hung behind Jack Shlonksy's desk that attracted the most attention from his clients. A large scene in vivid reds and yellows depicting three rabbis and a goose hovering over a church with a bunch of lilies lying on its gabled roof, the painting was intended to suggest culture and wealth to the lawyer's clients. But it was not to ponder the intricacies of Chagall's canvas that the Lufts had come to the offices of Shlonsky, Wimpfheimer and Fleiss. Jack Shlonsky sat back in his chair and listened closely, as he always did when his biggest clients came to him for help.

"Why not sidestep the Stuyvesant people altogether? For a lot less money than this is going to cost to pursue in court, you could take some ads in the classified sections of the biggest papers and see if the guy responds. The paper is always filled with requests from adopted kids trying to trace their birth parents; *vice versa* is more rare, but they're there too. You could at least start with some ads."

"Because no one reads the classifieds," declared Bunny, who never read the classifieds.

"Well, that's not true. First of all, people do. And second of all, it doesn't matter if people do or don't. What matters is whether your son reads them."

"So if no one reads them, he won't either."

"Well," Shlonsky countered, "if he knows he's adopted—which I would think was almost a certainty—if he knows, then maybe he does read them, just to see if his birth mother ever develops any interest in locating him."

Shlonsky's remarks were cogent, but he had not thought of his observation as being all *that* moving. It was, therefore, with some surprise that the portly lawyer noticed the tears that began to stream silently from Bunny's eyes. She wasn't exactly crying; or rather she *was* crying, but with none of the usual histrionics that generally accompany the flow of tears. Without sobs or whimpers, the tears seemed flat and inexpressive. Making a mental note not to forget the importance of the audio layer the next time he wept for a jury, Shlonsky waited for Bunny to speak.

"Look," she explained, the misery in her voice more than faintly audible, "It's not that I've been suffering over this for decades. But suddenly the thought that the matter isn't over, that it never finished—it's just too much. You have to understand, Jack, giving up a baby is the hardest thing anyone can ever do. I did it because I thought I had no choice and I still think it was probably the right decision. Anyway, right or wrong, what's done is done and there's no point in rehashing the point every time someone mentions adoption.

"But you have to understand, that as hard as it was to do, I did it. And having done it, it was necessary—absolutely necessary—to put the whole thing behind me. So I did. I don't mean it doesn't come back to haunt me. That it certainly does, but I don't suffer over it. I gave up my child to an agency that promised me he'd go to good Jewish people who for some reason couldn't have children of their own. So I considered the matter finished.

"But to tell you the truth, when I think of him, I think of a baby. I mean, I *know* that he's twenty-seven, almost twenty-eight years old. I *know* that but I don't *feel* it. It's only that when you said that—what you said about him scanning the classifieds to see if his birth mother has any interest in meeting up with him again—it suddenly struck me, I know you won't believe this, but I think for almost the first time it struck me that he is part of the whole equation by now too. I mean, he's a man who by now knows that the woman who bore him doesn't much care, or at least hasn't cared enough to seek him out, to tell him she's sorry if she's caused him pain, to check to make sure the agency people didn't lie about who'd get him..."

Bunny covered her face with her hands and collapsed in a paroxysm of self-recrimination. Lawrence Lazar reached around to embrace her shoulders. But suddenly, she sat upright again, her tears dried and her voice steady. "So," she said, "let's talk *takhlis*. How do we go about suing the Stuyvesant Agency?"

Jack Shlonsky sat back in his high-backed leather chair and looked at the moldings along the edge of his office ceiling. He wasn't paid, he knew all too well, to decide for people what legal actions they wished to undertake, merely to offer his best advice about how to proceed and then to act on his clients' behalf should they decide to go to law. On the other hand, lawyers who charge their clients by the hour can hardly determine it *not* to be in their clients' best interests to talk *takhlis*; indeed, to speak directly, even bluntly to the point—as indicated by the Yiddish expression—was probably precisely what any good lawyer should always do.

Gathering his thoughts, therefore, and skipping the lawyerly rhetoric, he replied to Bunny's question. "Well, this isn't going to be anybody's idea of a piece of cake. First of all, we have to gather the relevant materials. I have to interview the detective to whom you gave the report, then I have to see if we can't get somebody at the synagogue to I.D. the mystery lady. We have to talk to Jeffrey, since the Stuyvesant people will insist he was the boy being fingered, and we have to get a formal statement from the two of you."

"So far, so good." Bunny was encouraged.

"Well, don't get too carried away. Even after we get all that material together, you have to know that our chances of convincing a judge to order an adoptee's files unsealed are very slim. Very slim, indeed, if you ask me. After all, the bottom line is still that you don't really know that this lady wasn't nuts. And you can't say with absolute certainty that even if she *was* on the level, which the judge will doubt, she was talking about the boy you gave up. So if you want me to pursue the matter, you know I will. But I think you should know that if you weren't valued clients, I'd think twice about starting up on this one."

Bunny started to respond, then thought better of it. "Look," Lawrence Lazar interjected before his wife could decide to say anything at all, "at least Jack is being frank."

"Let him be Frank or Jack or whoever the hell he wants. What matters is that he is prepared to pursue this for us. You are prepared to represent us in this, aren't you?" Bunny looked directly at Jack Shlonsky and challenged him to say no.

"Yes," he said with only the most formal enthusiasm.

"Good."

"I'll get Evelyn to start things going in the morning."

"Also good."

"And look, I may not have my hopes too high, but that doesn't mean we won't pursue this with vigor."

"Best of all."

"So let's hope for the best."

"That's how I got pregnant in the first place."

***

Because Jack Shlonsky was able to convince Judge Barbara Stern that a young man's life might possibly be at risk, an early date on the court's overcrowded calendar was granted.

Statements were taken, subpoenas issued, relevant data gathered and pertinent interviews conducted. Eventually, everything was ready to proceed, but it was all to no avail. The Stuyvesant people won every point of every set of every match and the request to unseal the files relating to the adoption of Baby Boy F., as the infant had been formally known during the adoption proceedings in 1953, was officially turned down.

Judge Stern in her terse ruling was eloquently sympathetic about the worries of the birth mother, even going so far as to admit that an individual such as herself, who had never given up a child for adoption, could probably never imagine how difficult it must be to come to terms with that awful decision. Furthermore, the judge agreed that nothing could seem more logical to the court than that a woman, even after having given a child up for adoption, continue to worry about his or her well-being and security. Finally, the judge wrote that she could easily understand how the events of Friday evening, the sixth of February, could have left Bunny Luft in a state of extreme agitation and concern regarding her son's safety.

It was all there—official judicial concern tempered with the caring interest of a judge who was also a wife and a mother—but it was not enough. In her final analysis of the situation, Judge Stern ruled categorically against opening the records.

"You can't just accede to every request that records be opened simply because someone says something worrisome or rude to a birth mother, especially twenty-seven years after the adoption," Judge Stern said by way of judgment.

***

"You know that it's not over," Bunny said on the way home from Judge Stern's courtroom.

"I know," came the cool reply.

"I'm going to find my boy!"

"I know that too."

"And once we know he's safe, we'll just back off and let him be."

"In a pig's neck, Bunny, in a pig's neck you're going to back off and let him be. You're going to move in and reclaim him as your lost treasure. And then, after you've interfered in his life, after you've possibly wrecked his relationship with the lady who raised him *and whom he thinks of as his mother,* after you've upset Jeffrey and Joyce by *shlepping* an unwanted, unknown and unnecessary half-brother into their lives—after all that, then you will tell him that it's been grand and he should have a good life. But then, Bunny Luft, it's going to be too late. Much too late to back down; you'll satisfy your itch, but you're going to have a third child asking you for scratch for the rest of your life. So if that's not what you want, stop right here. Pay Shlonsky's bill, whatever it is, and let's just get on with our lives."

Bunny looked queerly at her husband. "Are you *meshugga*?" she asked earnestly, the Yiddish word meaning so much more to the Jewish ear than merely "crazy" or "mad."

"Apparently," came Lawrence Lazar's answer as he tried to fathom that it was not even two full weeks since the mystery lady had whacked him in the back of his head during Friday evening services at the Queens Hebrew Congregation.

Five

*W*eeks passed and as they did, the whole incident seemed less and less real to Bunny. She and Lawrence Lazar continued to attend services at the synagogue on Friday evening, coming at their appointed hour and sitting in their regular seats. They scanned the sanctuary, checked both the men's and ladies' washrooms and stayed until they were certain there were no more lonely Jews lingering around the synagogue's Sabbath dessert table.

At first, Bunny kept Jeffrey under special surveillance, requiring him to inform her of even the slightest change in his plans or his whereabouts. But even for a mother of Bunny's power and authoritarian bearing, it was not simple to keep a twenty-four year old man on such a short leash. Jeffrey hated having to check in with his parents, although apparently not enough to make him consider moving out of their home.

But the new regimen did not take and did not last. The system crumbled not so much under Jeffrey's constant chafing to be let alone as it did due to Bunny's unshakable, if inexplicable, conviction that it was not Jeffrey whose life was in danger.

As the weeks passed, the spotlight inevitably shifted from Jeffrey Luft to his missing half-sibling, the baby boy carried to term by his luckless mother in 1953 and then given up to the security and succor of someone else's bosom.

At first, Bunny wondered whether she should tell Jeffrey and Joyce about the incident of the mysterious woman at all. When finally she decided she had to say something, she was both relieved and irritated to discover that they took the whole issue with a large grain of salt.

"She's just obsessing about having dumped her kid," declared Joyce, who was a psychology major at Queens College. She and

Jeffrey were drinking Cokes at the Penguin Coffee Shop on Queens Boulevard on the Tuesday after the initial incident.

"It seems a bit long for this thing to be coming to a head only now," Jeffrey observed innocently. He too had a bachelor's degree from Queens College but had avoided the social sciences and focused on music. Knowing he was destined to inherit his father's venetian blind empire, he hadn't troubled to learn anything in particular at university, merely agreeing to please his unlettered father simply by being there and, eventually, by earning a degree of some sort.

"That is *precisely* the point," Joyce moaned in exasperation. "These things don't just *go away*! Guilt is like nuclear radiation, only without the half-life part. It's invisible, but present everywhere and all the time. And it has to either be exorcised or lived with or suppressed to be dealt with some other time. But if you ignore it, it doesn't just go off into air. It festers and becomes infected and filled with the pus of unresolved anxiety and incipient self-loathing. You either get it," she declared grandly, "or it gets you."

Guilt was something that Joyce and her friends discussed regularly and in great detail during their three-hour lunches at the Queens College cafeteria, finding in its dark crevices the demons responsible for almost all of the world's suffering. She had also discussed it with her famous therapist, Dr. Jeffrey Bleichtopf, and knew whereof she spoke. "She'll never get over it," Joyce concluded.

"Never?" Jeffrey asked with his usual lack of interest in his sister's half-baked theories of the psyche and its pathology.

"Not unless she faces it head on and annihilates it."

"You make it sound like a battle."

Joyce looked at her brother, resplendent in his $95 Florsheim wingtips and his $14 haircut. "It *is* a battle," she spat out through tight, painted lips.

"And is this whole thing her way of dealing with it?"

"Either that," Joyce suggested, "or she's *completely* nuts—or else we really do have a half-brother out there somewhere who is in some sort of danger."

Jeffrey looked at his wristwatch. "It's getting late," he said. "You want another Coke?"

"No. And I don't particularly want another brother either," she added with unexpected tenderness.

Jeffrey paid the check. They walked home along the boulevard in silence, enjoying each other's company and wondering what the next days and weeks would bring to their parents and themselves.

But there *were* no new developments. The next week, the Lufts lost their court battle to unseal Baby F.'s adoption file. Jeffrey was delighted the matter had been laid to rest so swiftly and with such apparent finality. "It's all done," he said to Joyce over lunch. Bunny had just phoned her family from the Hole Truth to announce their juridical defeat.

"Done?" Joyce asked with shrill amazement. "You think mom is just going to walk away from this because some judge told her 'no'?"

"She's not?"

"No, Sherlock, she's not. She's going to have to figure out how to go about this in a slightly different way, but she's definitely going to see this through. She's hardly the kind of woman to give up on a kid of her own just because she's hit a snag."

Jeffrey felt himself challenged. *"We're* her kids," he said quietly.

"We're apparently two of three, brother dear," Joyce responded, suddenly struck by the fact that her brother's stake in the outcome of this drama was not precisely identical to her own.

"Well, there's no reason to worry too much now. Mom isn't a private eye, you know. And this guy could be anywhere. Be anywhere and be anything. He could have died, for all we know. Or he could be in jail. Or he could be one of those nuts with bird shit painted on their noses dancing around in their yellow bathrobes in Grand Central Station."

"Or he could be a resident at Mount Sinai," Joyce countered, "or a Ph.D. in astrophysics at Yale, or a violinist with the Philharmonic."

"Or he could be a garbage man."

"Or an assistant D.A."

"Or a porn star."

"Or a Hassidic rabbi."

"Or a drug pusher."

"Or your best friend."

"My best friend?"

"Well," Joyce suggested gamely, "you did go to Forest Hills High School with a couple of thousand other boys our alleged brother's age. Some of them must have been adopted, I suppose. Maybe one of them *is* your brother."

"My brother? You mean *our* brother."

"Our *half*-brother."

"It still sounds funny, doesn't it—our half-brother. Like it's only half true."

"I know what you mean," Joyce agreed, "but it isn't half true. If it's true at all—and I'm not saying I'm sure it *is* true—but if it *is* true at all, then it's all true. He may be our half-brother, but it's all of him that is."

Jeffrey stopped to contemplate this new wrinkle in the drama. Joyce, of course, was right—he had gone to school with thousands of other boys. And he had no idea which ones were adopted—perhaps they *all* were, for all he knew. Quickly, Jeffrey made some calculations. If, as his mother had said, his half-brother was three years older than he, than he would have been a high school senior when Jeffrey was in tenth grade. That graduating class could easily have had a thousand students in it. If half were girls, that left five hundred. Subtracting at least two dozen blacks and another three or four dozen Asians, that still left well over four hundred Jewish boys with white faces and brown hair, any one of whom could have been his half-brother. And, of course, Forest Hills High School was only one of dozens of high schools in Queens and scores in the city. If the guy was even raised in the New York area… Suddenly, the vastness of the task facing his mother dawned on Jeffrey and, as it did, he smiled.

"Nothing to worry about," he told his sister. "He could be all those things, but he could also be anywhere and anything. So let her look—she'll never find him. And even if she does," he added heartlessly, "maybe the old lady with the handbag was right and he *is* in danger. She might find him and he'll already be history," Jeffrey concluded pleasantly.

"Or maybe he'll…" Joyce's voice trailed off into space, almost as though to mask the direction in which her fantasy had taken her.

"Or maybe he'll what?"

"Nothing, nothing at all. I was only thinking that if this was Shakespeare, it would turn out that our lost brother was my beloved fiancé."

"No, Joyce. If this was Shakespeare, he'd be your husband. To be your fiancé, this would have to be Gilbert and Sullivan. And he'd have to be secretly in love with our ancient wet-nurse and quite relieved to discover he couldn't marry you after all."

"Only this isn't Shakespeare *or* Gilbert and Sullivan."

"No, it isn't. It's Neil Simon, isn't it? It's like our lives have been hijacked by some alien beings and shoved into some unproduced Neil Simon play."

"Why unproduced?" Joyce asked, caught up for once in somebody else's fantasy. "Maybe *this* is the production!" Joyce began to flap her arms up and down like one of the winged monkeys in the

Wizard of Oz and to whistle the theme from the *Twilight Zone* as she encircled her bemused brother.

The spell was broken, the mood dashed. "I have to get to work," Jeffrey said finally. "Mom said that Dad isn't going in at all and *someone* has to mind the shop. And I can promise you, Julio steals more than enough without having completely free rein of the place."

"Or maybe," Joyce concluded in a stage whisper, batting her eyelashes and moving in for the kill, "our half-brother *is* Julio!"

Jeffrey closed his eyes in silent contemplation of the possibility that Julio Vega could be his secret half-brother. But there wasn't enough time to explore the thought properly; it was already almost one in the afternoon and high time Jeffrey Luft looked in on the business his father had built up and which he could now see himself having to share some day with someone other than his sister.

***

As the weeks passed, Bunny's obsession with her missing boy subsided. "Whatever they were going to do to him, they've probably already done," she said when asked if the matter was still troubling her.

"No need to be so fatalistic," Lawrence Lazar would offer by way of standard reply. "You make this sound like a mafia thing. But the mafia doesn't send ladies to victims' parents' synagogues to give them a little advance warning. They just show up one night where someone is working late, open their violin cases and blow their enemies' brains out. Don't you watch the Late Show?"

Bunny did, in fact, watch the Late Show. And Lawrence Lazar knew perfectly well that gangster movies were among her favorites. But that was hardly the point here, and both Lawrence and Bunny knew it.

For whatever reason, the fact of the matter was that a mysterious woman had appeared where anyone who had done even the most elementary research would have known to find the Lufts and told Bunny that her son was in danger. And she had given a password that could only suggest she was referring to Baby F., as the Lufts had taken to calling the missing child, rather than to Jeffrey. That was it in a nutshell. Bunny didn't understand the story and she certainly didn't like it.

Bunny was anything but flexible when it came to the safety of her children. The only solace offered her by the passage of time was the rather lame sense that whatever was scheduled to occur had probably *already* occurred and that it was therefore unnecessary to suffer over the issue.

"If they were going to kill him, he's probably already at the bottom of the East River wearing a cement *tallis*," Lawrence told his wife over the breakfast table on Monday morning, February 23, 1981. The very thought of someone floating to the bottom of the river bed wearing a cement prayer-shawl was enough to bring a smile even to Bunny's face. But the smile was short-lived as Bunny recalled almost immediately that it was her son, the fruit of her own womb of whom her husband was speaking in such a flippant matter.

"You wouldn't be so funny if this was *your* boy," she said quietly.

"I know you think that. And I think you know that I know you do. And I hope you know that it's not true. Haven't I stood by you the whole time? Have I ever suggested we not pursue this, even though finding the boy is going to complicate *my* life as much as it is going to screw around with yours?"

"Not as much," Bunny answered as though she had been awaiting the remark. "A lot, maybe, but not as much."

"So okay, Mrs. Precision in Language, maybe not quite as much—but a lot. You have to see that finding this guy is going to screw me up plenty. Not to mention what it does to our kids. You know, you've practically expected Jeff and Joyce to look forward to having this guy appear in their lives. Well, maybe you have to look into the future a bit, if you know what I mean."

"No," Bunny said quietly, surprised, "I don't know what you mean."

"What I mean is that no one lives forever. Not you and certainly not me. And one day, we'll both be gone and Jeff and Joyce are going to be left alone in this world. Except that thanks to you, they're not going to be quite alone. They're going to have a *partner*!"

Lawrence Lazar's experience over the years with partners had been so dismal that no one who knew even part of the truth could possibly wonder if he thought the sudden, unexpected arrival of a partner constituted a blessing or a curse.

"You make it sound like they'll suffer. Maybe their brother will turn out to be fabulously wealthy. Maybe *he* will be in a position to help *them*."

"Maybe. Look," Lawrence Lazar concluded, trying to make peace before having to go to his office for the day, "maybe you're right. Maybe he will be a blessing for the children. But you have to accept at least the possibility of the situation turning out less well. The point is that we are looking to buy a pig in a poke, you should pardon the expression. Who knows what we're going to find when we find him?"

"When we find him? *If* we find him is more like it. You know, I was such an innocent—I really thought we'd go to court and I'd explain the story to the judge and she'd listen and ask some pertinent questions and then tell those *shmucks* at the agency to hand over the goods and that would be that. Who knew she was going to get all technical about the whole thing? And aside from taking Shlonsky's advice about starting with ads in the paper, I don't really know what to do."

"We could hire a private investigator," Lawrence suggested.

"You'd pay for that? For a private eye to find my son, who isn't even your son?" Bunny Luft's eyes glistened with love.

"Yes, I would."

"You *are* a saint. But not yet. I still think there are things we can do to find him ourselves. Look, I know this is obsessive. I know any woman in her right mind would have let this thing go a long time ago. But there is something inside of me that knows that that lady was telling the truth. Don't ask how I know—or ask, if you want, but I still don't know. All I *do* know is that I have to find my boy. I have to find him and make sure he's safe. And it means everything that you're behind me. So let's leave the P.I. thing be for the time being—that can be our ace in the hole, what we'll do when we really have done everything else. In the meantime, let's keep looking ourselves. I'll put ads in the paper—I'll start tomorrow morning! And let's keep checking in different synagogues each Friday night.

"Don't forget—the lady behind was singing along with the congregation. You yourself remarked that that old bird certainly knew her prayers. And she didn't learn that just so she could impress me, that's for sure. She must go to synagogue *somewhere*. I'd recognize her in a minute—so let's start spreading out and see what we find."

Lawrence Lazar, already twenty minutes late to leave for work, stood up abruptly. "Okay," he said. "We'll start covering other synagogues next week. But this week, I think we should stay put."

"You mean stay home?"

"No, I mean stay at our own synagogue. In our regular seats. She could come back, you know."

"Okay, I'll put the ad in the paper tomorrow. Maybe it will be in by Wednesday already. And he'll see it and he'll phone and we'll be finished with this whole thing by Friday. Just you wait and see."

Lawrence Lazar rolled his eyes up towards the ceiling. Bunny had apparently still not quite understood that she was not going to be able to locate her missing boy, tell him that he could *possibly* be in some danger and then have him step neatly out of her life. But there was no telling her anything; her husband knew that. No matter what he would say, she was going to pursue this to the end; his only real choice was whether to go along gently or to put up a fuss. After twenty-five years of marriage, Lawrence Lazar Luft knew his options and had long since made his peace with their relative paucity.

Six

The advertisement ran in *The Times'* classified section on Wednesday morning, February 25. All day Wednesday and all day Thursday, Bunny stayed home and waited impatiently by the phone. Nothing happened; there were no responses at all.

Friday morning, Bunny and Lawrence Lazar had their conversation over the breakfast table, bid each other a pleasant day and separated until that evening. Bunny felt dejected; she had apparently invested more hope than even she had realized in the success of the classified advertisement. Its failure to produce even a single telephone call was for that reason all the more bitter.

That evening, after dinner, Lawrence Lazar and Bunny Luft walked to their regular seats at the Queens Hebrew Congregation. It was still quite chilly for the end of February and there were almost no casual strollers out for an evening's walk along Queens Boulevard. Everyone who was out seemed to be in a great hurry to get somewhere else.

In fact, the atmosphere on the street struck both Lufts as rather strange. True, the vast majority of evening strollers were not Sabbath observers and could not, therefore, be faulted for hurrying off to wherever it was they were going with such unsabbatical haste. Still, the atmosphere on Queens Boulevard seemed odd, almost ominously so, to both Bunny and Lawrence Lazar.

The pinkish-amber glow of the street lamps bathed the pedestrians in an eerie aura that suggested ill health, and the sharp February wind only added to the unpleasant ambience. As had become her usual practice, Bunny scanned every passerby lest the mystery lady cross their path again. She wouldn't escape a second time—of that much, at least, Bunny Luft was certain.

Bunny was also on the look-out for twenty-seven year old Jewish men who looked like they might be her baby grown up. Of these, there were more than a few hurrying along the boulevard, but Bunny felt unable to approach them. What would she say? That she was sorry to disturb them on a chilly evening, but would they mind telling a complete stranger if they were adopted as children, if they by any chance have a birthmark in the shape of Manhattan Island on their feet, and if they were perchance born already circumcised?

"He'll think you're out of your mind," Lawrence Lazar told his wife the very first time he caught her eyeing a young man with curly dark brown hair who did, even Lawrence had to admit, bear a striking resemblance to Bunny's Uncle Arnold or rather to how Uncle Arnold might have looked as a younger man. The young man was standing at the corner of Queens Boulevard and Sixty-Eighth Drive waiting for the Q-60 Bus into Manhattan. He had that evening's *New York Post* under his arm and was peering intently down the boulevard in the direction from which the bus would come.

"Not so!" Bunny had countered, drawing her husband under the awning of a nearby kosher take-out place, now shuttered and shut for the Sabbath. "They'll almost all think I'm crazy. But somewhere out there there's someone who won't think I'm crazy because he'll realize suddenly that I'm speaking about him. And he will be our boy."

"Your boy."

"My boy." To her credit, Bunny knew when to press a point and when to let things be.

"And you are prepared to be thought of as a crazy lady by the other 999,999 twenty-seven year olds in the world with Jewish noses and curly hair?"

Bunny looked at her husband as though she didn't quite understand his question. On either side of Lawrence Lazar's head, jars of green pickled tomatoes arrayed in the kosher caterer's window glistened in the pinkish-amber lamp light. "What mother would mind that?" she asked apparently without guile.

Lawrence Lazar thought for a moment. His own mother would certainly have risked public ridicule if she thought her son's life might possibly be in danger. Probably, he admitted to himself, Bunny was right—what mother *wouldn't* mind appearing a bit loony to safeguard one of her children? He gritted his teeth and stood close to the shop window as Bunny made her way over to the curb where the young man was standing.

"Pardon me," he could hear her say clearly, "but you're waiting for the bus?" A rhetorical question, Lawrence Lazar understood, but a plausible opening sentence.

"Yes," the man answered, "I am."

"It runs this late?"

"Sure."

Bunny appeared to join the young man in peering eastward down Queens Boulevard in search of the Q-60. "I sure wish they put benches in at these bus stops," she said pleasantly. "My feet are killing me!"

Lawrence Lazar rolled his eyes towards heaven as Bunny moved in for the kill. The young man, in the meantime, said nothing.

"It would be great if they had benches," Bunny began anew. "Not for young guys like you, but for old ladies like me. I have such old, painful feet. Of course, having painful feet isn't something new for me. Even as a child, I had terrible problems with my feet..."

The young man began to edge away from his uninvited interlocutor in the subtle manner of any savvy New Yorker when cornered at a bus stop or on a subway platform by an ambulatory schizophrenic.

"Terrible problems!" Bunny continued, unfazed by the man's pathetic attempt to escape. "I was even born with birthmarks on my feet. One was in the shape—it's funny to tell a stranger, but why not?—one was in the shape of the Statue of Liberty. You know, Lady Liberty? Anyway, it hurt like hell walking around with the Statue of Liberty sticking into my foot all day, almost like it was really made of iron or steel or whatever the Statue of Liberty is really made of. It was," Bunny concluded triumphantly, "a gift of the people of France to the people of the United States. I forget for what, but for something. I mean, you don't just give a present like that for no reason at all!"

The bus was nowhere in sight. The young man, gripping his newspaper now in both his hands, made the fatal error of nodding in tacit, unspoken agreement with Bunny's assertion.

"I think, actually, it's rather unusual to be born with birthmarks in the shape of famous places or things on your feet, don't you?"

Silence. The young man was actually wringing his paper as though it were a wet towel. He obviously needed the Q-60 a lot to put up with this, Lawrence Lazar thought from his secluded shadow. But no matter how badly he needed the bus, there would have to be some breaking point.

Bunny, as heedless as any game hunter to her prey's discomfort, moved in for the kill. "You know what would be a wonderful coincidence? The kind that belongs in books, I mean—if you were also born with some strange birthmark on your feet." Bunny took a step closer. "Were you?" she asked. "Born with a birthmark on your foot, I mean?"

The man dropped his newspaper to the ground. "No," he said, "I wasn't." His three words still hung on the night air as the Q-60 finally materialized at the bus stop as though from thin air. The man practically leapt on board, looking behind him to see if Bunny were going to follow him onto the bus and moving his lips, presumably in a brief prayer of thanksgiving, when she made no move to do so.

"Come on, let's go," Bunny said as she turned to retrieve Lawrence Lazar from his hiding place. "We'll be late altogether if we don't go now. It's already..."

Bunny looked at her wristwatch.

"...five to eight. Come on, we have just enough time."

"That guy must think you're a complete nut case," Lawrence Lazar said to his wife as he hurried down the boulevard in her irresistible wake.

"Who gives a shit about him?" Bunny answered honestly, stepping off the curb in front of the Chase Manhattan Bank. "*He's* not my boy."

Lawrence Lazar, breathing his own humble prayer of silent thanksgiving that Bunny hadn't asked the young man with the newspaper if he had by some crazy chance been born without a foreskin, stepped off the curb and hurried towards the cement island that separated the service road from the main traffic lanes of Queens Boulevard. It was already late and he could see the great doors of the synagogue in the distance opening and closing in the evening light as tardy worshippers hurried inside to their seats.

∗∗∗

Yudel Wolfzahn stirred a third teaspoon of sugar into his cold coffee and lifted the chipped mug to his lips. He could hear Clara puttering around in the kitchen and was surprised by the degree of inner comfort her artless clatter gave him. Ever since the scene at Styx, Yudel had felt uneasy. The deed itself had gone well enough, he thought. Kalish had *definitely* seen him and was therefore entirely aware that this was a matter that needed to be taken seriously. And the cops had definitely *not* seen him—he was certain he had been long gone before the first uniformed officers had arrived on the scene. The get-away had also been relatively simple; a matter of having a car in the right place at the right time that had taken off no less smoothly with Clara in the driver's seat than it had the night before when he was driving and Clara was the one doing the escaping.

And the advertisement circled in red ink that had appeared in the Wednesday newspaper now spread out on the Wolfzahns' dining room table seemed to clinch the deal: Bunny Luft was definitely seeking her son.

True, there was no particular reason to suspect that Marvin Kalish was a regular, or even an occasional reader of the *Times'* classifieds. But that didn't matter too much either, Yudel knew.

The local papers would certainly bother to pick up the story of an up-and-coming comic whom someone was trying to murder. The story would be featured on the local news and eventually force its way into *People Magazine* or perhaps even into one of the larger news weeklies.

Eventually, of course, it would dawn on Kalish that he might build his career on his misfortune. Played correctly, a series of violent, apparently senseless attacks against a handsome entertainer could easily be transformed into the type of publicity break of which less-often shot at performing artists may only dream. It might take time, but eventually some sharp P.R. man would get his claws into Marvin Kalish and make them both a great deal of money *and* a great deal of fame. If he had to, Wolfzahn thought, he'd make an anonymous phone call to some publicity people himself to get the ball rolling. But these guys were usually *very* sharp and it seemed highly unlikely they would pass up the bait being dangled before them.

Carson, Yudel Wolfzahn thought to himself, was only the tip of the iceberg. There would be gigs in Vegas, guest spots on all the best sit-coms and whatever else came with a sudden rise to fame.

But it was not with jump-starting Marvin Kalish's career that Yudel and Clara Wolfzahn were concerned. There was another side to their equation, one that focused not on the orphan comic so much as on his mother.

It was, Yudel and Clara both knew, only a matter of time before someone somewhere brought the series of strange, inexplicable assassination attempts on a twenty-seven year old Jewish boy with curly brown hair and the famous Falk nose to Bunny Luft's attention.

The beauty of the scheme lay in its utter simplicity—no matter how long it took to work, the Wolfzahns had only to continue harassing Kalish until his eventual fame came to his long-lost mother's eventual attention.

"What if she gives up the whole thing before she ever hears of Kalish?" Clara had asked her husband when he returned from his first attempt on Marvin Kalish's life.

"She won't give up. She may get discouraged—she certainly will be discouraged when the judge tells her there is no way in hell to open sealed records because someone she never heard of told her something she can't verify about someone she can't find—but she won't give up. Would you?"

"If it was *my* kid?" Clara and Yudel had one son, a boy named Sid. If she had gotten pregnant before marrying Yudel and had given the child up for adoption, how *would* she have felt about giving up the search for her child if she felt even vague suspicion that he might be in danger?

"Yes, if it was your boy."

"You bet I wouldn't give up until I found him."

"So neither," Yudel concluded grandly, "will she."

✳✳✳

It took courage, but Marvin Kalish decided finally that he would honor his commitment to finish his month at Styx. He had taken some time off, but he owed a minimum of one more evening in February. The last night in the month was, as Marvin's luck would have it, a Saturday night. He felt well, he was only moderately afraid of appearing again on stage, and he needed the money. The decision was, finally, a simple one.

"What can I tell you? We need the cash," he had offered Dawn Kupchinsky by way of explanation.

"Well," Dawn had said, "I hope no one blows you away."

"Me too."

The mood at the Kalish-Kupchinsky kitchen table was subdued as the young lovers considered whether there was foolishness, reasonableness, adolescent bravado or courage at work in the decision at hand. The bottommost line, however, as was so often the case in Marvin Kalish's life, was money.

"Look, the rent is due tomorrow and we have fifty-five dollars in checking."

"We could go to savings." Dawn Kupchinsky and Marvin Kalish had, against the advice of their parents, friends and colleagues, opened both joint checking *and* joint savings accounts when they decided to live together.

"We have ninety-five dollars in savings. Together, that is one hundred and fifty dollars and the rent is twice that. I *have* to work tonight."

"So if you have to go, why are we discussing it?" The familiar Kupchinsky pout made its persuasive way across Dawn's painted lips.

"We're discussing it so that it is a joint decision. If I get blown away tonight, I don't want you sitting at my funeral thinking I was a *shmuck* for working tonight."

"Look," Dawn began, "you yourself said there's no choice. We need the dough and that's that. I promise not to think anything bad about you if someone kills you. Or at least I promise to think I'm as much of a *shmuck* as you are for letting you go. So we'll be even."

"Now *there's* a comforting thought!"

"In this world, you take your comfort where you can."

"So we're decided? I'm going?"

"We're decided. You're going."

"And next month, we'll try to hang on to *your* pay check for more than two hours."

"Look, those bills were growing mould they were so old. The Mastercard people were breathing down my neck and threatening to do all sorts of thing to us. They can be *very* nasty if you welch on their bill, you know. I *had* to pay up—besides, the interest payments were eating us alive anyway. At least we'll save money that way."

Marvin looked at his friend and smiled. Everything she said was absolutely true. How could he argue with her for paying outstanding bills and saving them money on the interest payments? And he knew that she wasn't holding out on him—if anything, it must have taken a major loan from her mother for Dawn to cover the entire Mastercard bill, a detail Marvin was truly grateful to Dawn for omitting from their deliberations.

It was no more than he would have done for her! But still, Marvin thought to himself, it was something kind, something good that she had done for him by sparing him the discussion, by freeing him from knowing something she can't have wanted him to know and must have known he'd know anyway. It was a complicated train of thought, but the bottom line was that Dawn was not just beautiful, Marvin thought, she was also good and kind. Maybe he'd take up his father's offer of a diamond ring after all and ask Dawn to marry him.

It was hardly a new thought, but Dawn's goodness and caring gave the whole idea a sudden urgency. Marvin felt himself more in love than ever as he gazed at his friend across the formica kitchen table they had bought together at the Macy's on Queens Boulevard shortly after moving into the same apartment.

He reached for her hand and gave it a romantic squeeze. Dawn looked back at her lover across the table and felt suddenly ashamed of herself.

"Don't go," she said suddenly.

"To work?"

"To work. Don't go. Something will happen—I know it. Some guy tried to get you the last time you went and it will happen again. I just feel it in my bones. Call it woman's intuition—call it whatever you want—but I think you'll be asking for it if you step out onto Manny's stage tonight. Let it go—I'll borrow the money from Tony to cover the rent."

The outstanding money to cover the rent was far too much to borrow from the petty cash drawer at the salon; Dawn would actually have to approach Tony and ask for the cash as an advance. It wasn't *such* an absurd idea, Marvin thought. But it had a fatal flaw.

"And what happens next month?"

"Next month?"

"When the rent is due again and you've already drawn this month's salary. Are you going to ask for another advance? And then another? And then another? And then another and another and another?"

"If I have to," Dawn answered quietly. "But I *won't* have to—by then you'll have work somewhere else and we'll be on Easy Street."

"Or I won't and we won't and you will."

"Then I *will* ask for another advance. Just don't go tonight."

Marvin weighed his options. He knew it made no sense not to go—the shooting on the seventh was a fluke, a weird coincidence, the work of a maniac. Marvin had only gotten in the maniac's way—there was no way he himself could have been the intended target.

Still, Marvin reminded himself, there were all sorts of nut cases out there.

There were people who became obsessed with performers and then turned violent when their love proved unrequited.

There were people who felt the need to express their hostility to the world by focusing their rage on people who seem to them to have asked for it by the very act of stepping out onto a stage or runway.

There were deranged people who felt justified in avenging perceived injustice even in the comic arena—and jokes directed against Italians or Jews or blacks or gays or Catholics or women or cops or Hispanics were the meat of Marvin's act. All it would take would be one Catholic maniac with no sense of humor hearing the gag about the priest and the dachshund and that would be that.

A string of tiny beads of sweat formed on Marvin Kalish's forehead as he tried to recall what the man with the gun had looked like. He hadn't looked particularly Italian, Marvin thought with a sudden rush of relief as he reached for Dawn's hand and began to stroke her soft knuckles. And he certainly wasn't black or Hispanic—that much Marvin felt certain about. But that was only what the little guy *hadn't* been—what he *had* been was an entirely different question.

He could, Marvin realized with a sudden shudder, have been anything at all, including some motherless maniac out to avenge insulting remarks about *other* people's mothers. The whole thing, now that it lay open before him like a book inside his head, was simply too absurd to worry about. How, Marvin thought, could he ever feel safe on a stage anywhere if he was going to worry about the J.D.L. and the N.O.W. and the N.A.A.C.P. and a dozen other potentially hostile organizations? "Well," Marvin concluded aloud, "if they don't have a sense of humor, screw 'em."

"If who doesn't have a sense of humor?"

"Who? How should I know who? The J.D.L. or the A.D.L. or the K.K.K. or whoever. I'm going to work."

"Are you sure?"

"I'm sure."

"Can I come?"

"Why not? I'll tell you what," Marvin concluded generously, "come to the late set and we'll go out for Chinese afterwards."

"I thought we needed every penny for the rent."

"Well, maybe not every penny. And I'll ask Manny for a few bucks against next week. He'll cough it up if I ask right—he hates carrying all this Saturday cash around until the bank opens on Monday anyway. He'll be *relieved* to give some of it away, if I know him."

Dawn thought for a moment. She knew not to press Marvin too hard, especially as far as details concerning his career went. "Okay, I'll come and we'll go out to eat afterwards. And..."

"And what?"

"And if some maniac shoots you, I'll serve *real* Chinese at the *shiva*."

"That's all my mother will need," Marvin answered with a broad smile. "*Oy vey*," he continued in a falsetto meant to mimic his mother's squeaky voice, "*voos iz doos*? A *treifa* shrimp roll at my Marvindle's *shiva*. *Vere iz dot shiksa*?"

Marvin, switching back to his own persona even as he continued to cackle *"Vere iz dot shiksa?"*, lunged at his friend and pulled her down to their kitchen floor.

There was something inexplicably satisfying about making love on the kitchen floor, Marvin felt as he gave full rein to his passion. Relief, lust, determination and love mingled freely in the heady atmosphere on the kitchen linoleum. Dawn turned her head towards the white base of the stove just in time to see a cockroach expiring, its tiny legs twitching violently but ineffectively in a vain effort to escape from the sticky residue at the base of the Roach Motel hidden by the porcelain overhang of the stove's lower drawer.

Dawn screamed in horror as Marvin began his traditional pre-orgasmic moan-chant; never before had the mystic nexus between love and death seemed more real or more frightening. Whether the omen was portentous or meaningless, of course, Dawn had no way to guess as she succumbed only moments later to the waves of passion washing steadily and irreversibly over her as well.

"Shit," said Marvin, spent, only moments later as his eye drifted to the kitchen clock suspended high above the couple still intertwined on the linoleum floor, "it's after nine. I have to start the first set at ten. If we're going, we've got to move."

Marvin stood up. "I'll jump into the shower and you set up *Havdalah*, okay?"

"Okay," answered Dawn, feeling noble, pliable, exhausted and invigorated all at the same time. "We've still got plenty of time."

The ritual separating the Sabbath from the rest of the week had its usual calming effect on both Marvin and Dawn. True, their observance of the Jewish Sabbath left a lot to be desired from the vantage point of scrupulous religious law and their devotion to other parts of regular Jewish ritual was no less lax. Still, there were parts of both lovers' religious heritage neither had wished to jettison along with the rest of the baggage they had dropped along the way, and the *Havdalah* ceremony was one of them.

By the time Marvin was ready to leave for his club, the ritual was ready to be performed. Dawn Kupchinsky stood in the darkened kitchen, her face lit from below by the triple-wicked candle she held in her hands.

"Hold it the height of the man you want to marry," Marvin said with a nervous edge to his voice.

"My dream is to marry a dwarf," Dawn said, making a point of holding the candle no higher than Marvin's waist and smiling sweetly.

"As you wish," Marvin said in his friendliest voice. "I hope you two are very happy together."

"Just say the prayer," Dawn said.

Marvin launched into the ancient liturgy, proud of the fact that even fourteen years after his bar mitzvah, he could still recite the words by heart and with supreme accuracy. "Behold the God of my salvation," he sang, "I shall have faith and never fear!" As he said the words "and never fear" his gaze fixed on Dawn, who found herself staring directly into her lover's eyes. She understood the Hebrew words less well than he, but the general sense was clear: this was a man of faith whom God would protect in the coming week.

A tear formed in the corner of Marvin's right eye. He let it slide down his nose, then wiped it away and finished his prayer.

"Blessed be God, Creator of the fruit of the vine," he sang as he lifted the silver goblet.

"Amen," Dawn sang with fervor and hope.

"Blessed be God, Creator of spice." Marvin reached out to lift a small silver spice box fashioned in the shape of a medieval castle. Lifting it to his nose, he sniffed deeply the sweet mixture of nutmeg, allspice and cloves and then handed the box to Dawn. She placed it beneath her nose and inhaled the sweet scent no less deeply than he.

"Blessed be God, Creator of fire," Marvin sang, lifting his hands towards the flame and bending his fingers in towards his wrists so he could fix his gaze for a moment on his well-manicured fingernails.

"Blessed be God," he concluded, "Who separateth holy from profane, light from darkness, Israel from the Gentile nations and the Jewish Sabbath from the workaday week. Blessed be God, Creator of the sacred distinction between holy and profane."

"Amen," Dawn replied fervently. "May God grant you a good week."

"So far, so good," Marvin replied semi-lewdly as he hitched his trousers up around his slim hips. "If I get through tonight without anyone taking a shot at me, I'll be quite content."

Dawn smiled and slid her arm around his waist. "If no one takes a shot at you, I may take a shot at you myself later when we get home."

Marvin smiled back, taking her words as a compliment, a promise and an invitation all rolled into one. If she was already planning a night of renewed passion, then there really didn't seem to be any problem about going to work. He'd go, he'd come back—no one, Marvin assured himself, shoots men who have women like Dawn Kupchinsky to come home to.

Seven

Marvin saw Yudel Wolfzahn first.

"That guy," he said, "I think that's him."

"Who?" Dawn Kupchinsky craned her neck to look behind her at whomever Marvin was staring.

"Sssssssh! Don't turn around," Marvin hissed in a stage whisper. "The guy who tried to shoot me."

"Are you sure?"

"Maybe."

"Maybe? I thought you said you got a good look at him at the club."

It was true. Marvin had reported both to Dawn and to the police that he had gotten a good, long look at the man at Styx with the gun. "I did say that. And I did get a good look at him. But this guy, I don't know. He looks like him, but also not like him. Maybe he's his brother, for all I know."

Dawn twisted her head around to steal another furtive glance. "If you want to know the truth, he looks like my high school French teacher. In fact, I think it *is* him."

Without waiting for Marvin's reply, Dawn was up and on her way over to her teacher's booth. There were only a few diners at Pho-Nee's so late on a Saturday night and most of those had already gone home. In fact, in the back room of the restaurant, only two tables were still occupied at a quarter past one in the morning.

Dawn approached the little man's table, more certain with every step that she knew whom she was about to address. She spoke as soon as she was standing in front of his table.

"*Bon soir*," she said, smiling.

The remains of a large Chinese dinner littered the little man's table. He was sipping his tea and reading a copy of the *Aufbau*, from which he looked up as Dawn spoke.

"*Bon soir, Monsieur* Sztul," she said a second time.

Silence. The little man looked Dawn up and down, then, satisfied that he had seen all there was to see, he returned to his newspaper.

"*C'est moi, Aube* Kupchinsky," Dawn ventured one final time, peering intently into Yudel Wolfzahn's face as she did so. Now that she stood directly before him, it was just possible, she felt obliged to conclude, that this might *not* be her tenth and eleventh grade French teacher. The resemblance, however, was uncanny.

Somehow, Dawn knew to wait by her teacher's table, understanding that he was about to speak. She continued to peer into the little man's face and, eventually, he raised his eyes slightly and spoke.

"Bring me some more green tea," he said. "And some more fortune cookies."

Dawn could hardly think how to respond. "I'm not your waitress," she finally stammered out.

"Oh." Wolfzahn returned to his newspaper.

Dawn, realizing her error, muttered a quick apology. It wasn't *Monsieur* Sztul after all, and she regretted disturbing the little man's meal. Wolfzahn couldn't be bothered to respond or even to look up again from his magazine. Dawn, with some embarrassment, returned to Marvin and seated herself again on the Naugahyde banquette across from him.

"It's not him," she said.

"Maybe it's your *teacher's* brother. Maybe they're all brothers—the shooter, your teacher and this guy having dinner."

"I think not," Dawn conceded, cowed by the force of her lover's argument *ad absurdum*.

"Well, now I don't think he's the shooter anyway."

The sets Marvin offered the Saturday evening crowd at Styx were classic Kalish *shtick*—vulgar, clever, loud and very funny. The jokes, delivered at a supersonic pace designed to batter the audience into submission rather than to elicit their admiration in the traditional style of the genteel Jewish jokester, came off especially well. There was something in the air that acted almost like a narcotic stimulant, a certain manic energy that seemed to come directly from Marvin's sense that he could conceivably be shot to death at any moment.

The audience, which had actually risen to its feet when Marvin Kalish first walked out onto the stage for his first set after what the Queens' papers were now calling the unsuccessful assassination of the King of Shticks, was convulsed in laughter almost from the first moment Marvin opened his mouth.

As usual, the string of bag-lady jokes went well. But once Marvin launched into his character assassination material in which he savaged public figures from Nancy Reagan to Menachem Begin, the audience was no less than putty in his hands.

One woman laughed so hard that she actually fainted before she could catch her breath; a man stood up on his chair and formally apologized for leaving before the end of the set lest the steel staples holding his stomach in place pop out and cause irreparable internal bleeding.

A young man of nineteen or twenty actually vomited in the washroom, Marvin learned later, before he could calm himself down after hearing Marvin's impersonation of Ed Koch in bed with Mother Theresa and Margaret Thatcher.

Another woman stood up towards the end of the set and, brazenly opening her blouse, ripped off her brassiere and flung it at Marvin's head. It was, Marvin later had to admit, the ultimate accolade. He had lifted it from the floor, put it on around his waist by forcing his legs through the shoulder straps and pranced around the stage ad-libbing brilliantly about the soon-to-be latest trend in men's underwear fashion. The audience practically erupted in unrestrained applause and laughter.

As ever, Marvin Kalish knew to leave them wanting more.

The second set went as well as the first. Marvin had taken the precaution of planting Dawn in the audience for the midnight performance so that he could re-create the brassiere routine even if no young lady felt moved to rip her own bra off and fling it at the young comedian. But it was not necessary for Dawn to degrade herself by participating in such artificial theatrics; during the last ten minutes of the midnight set, not one but two young women felt sufficiently overwhelmed with admiration to fling their underclothing at the performer.

Wearing one of the pairs of panties on his head like a silken *yarmulke*, Marvin recreated his earlier routine and closed to applause that could only be described as thunderous.

"I should get shot at more often," Marvin said to Dawn in the tiny dressing room he was allowed to occupy for a half-hour before and after his two nightly sets.

"That's a great idea," Dawn said, picking up the sarcasm in her lover's voice and running with it. "Maybe even killed!"

"Killed," Marvin replied, "would be too much." His voice sounded strangely subdued, as though it had only just struck him that it was his own death about which he and Dawn were joking. "But almost killed is just the thing," he continued, his voice now back to being bright and happy. "Did you see that house? I could have told them 'Nurse, I said to *prick* his *boil*' stuff and they would have loved it. I'm telling you—I'm onto something. I mean they stood up and cheered before I even opened my mouth. They love me," Marvin concluded immodestly but not entirely incorrectly.

The audience *had* indeed loved him and would easily have laughed at whatever he said. But of course, the deeper truth which Marvin easily understood was that it wasn't his jokes that they were applauding or enjoying at all—it was his *chutzpah*, his indomitable spirit, the nerve of the Jewish gagman whom even bullets couldn't stop from doing stand-up. If there was anything Queens loved, Marvin knew all too well, it was indomitable spirit. "I'm the goddam Rocky of *shtick*," he added thoughtfully, as a sort of cross-cultural observation. "That's why they love me."

"That's not why I love you," Dawn said, her voice suddenly as subdued as Marvin's had briefly been.

"It's not?" Feigned surprise in Marvin's voice.

"No," Dawn answered truthfully, "it's not."

Unexpectedly moved, Marvin kissed his friend on the lips, on the forehead and in her right ear. "Not here," she said prudently.

"Why not?"

"Because I only do it on kitchen floors and in bed," she answered with a certain wistful sadness in her voice.

"So let's go home." Marvin was prepared to be flexible.

"Go home?" Mock horror in Dawn's voice. "You promised me Chinese."

"Okay, you're right. Chinese and then home to bed?"

"Deal."

"So let's go," Marvin concluded as he finished packing his few props into the cardboard box marked "Kalish" that Manny Zryb kept stored in the utility closet behind the stage on a shelf over the janitor's mops and pails. "I'm starved."

"Starved for food? I thought you were starved for sex."

Marvin reached out for a coat tree that stood by the door to his tiny dressing room and bent it over towards him as though it were a microphone stand. "I'm in the mood for love and romance," he crooned, slipping his free arm around Dawn Kupchinsky's waist.

"Okay, okay, I get the picture. But can we get something to eat first?"

"Yes."

"Chinese, like you said?"

"Yes."

"Pho-Nee's okay?"

"Yes."

"Do you know any words in English except for 'yes'?" Dawn asked, borrowing a punchline from one of Marvin's most vulgar and all-time funniest routines.

Marvin didn't answer. Instead he leaned over and kissed Dawn delicately on the cheek. "Pho-Nee's is fine," he said softly.

"So let's go," Dawn responded, a bit flustered. She could deal easily enough with Marvin the Vulgar and Marvin the Oversexed, but Marvin the Tender still threw her a bit of a curve.

In two minutes, they were out the door and onto Sixty-Third Drive. The cold night air struck them both as marvelously refreshing and invigorating. They walked to the corner of Queens Boulevard to wait for a cab at the bus stop on the chance a bus might arrive before a vacant cab drove by. This was occasionally the fortunate case, but it didn't happen very often.

No bus appeared, but within a few minutes, an empty cab drove by. Ten minutes later, they were stepping out of the taxi at Ascan Avenue only half a block from the famous Chinese restaurant.

Pho-Nee's was a phenomenon as much as it was a restaurant. Queens County's first kosher Chinese restaurant, it had actually managed to attract at least some real Chinese diners by presenting vegetarian dishes that both followed the rigid Jewish dietary laws and conformed to the canons of real Chinese cooking.

It hadn't been a simple matter. When the restaurant had first opened, rabbis across the county had denounced the phenomenon, uncertain how to react to a restaurant that catered to people *wishing* to observe the specifics of Jewish custom precisely by *appearing* to be flaunting even its most basic aspects. The rabbis understood all too well that the vast majority of people who had come to enjoy Pho-Nee braised lobster and Pho-Nee shrimp and pork rolls would simply react to the restaurant's closing by switching to real Chinese restaurants and ordering real shrimp, lobster and pork. It would be the greatest error to end up having *discouraged* Jewish people from eating vegetables instead of unkosher spring rolls and yet there was still something obnoxious, something spiritually if not precisely gastronomically *treif* about the whole enterprise.

In the end, the rabbis of the various synagogues of Forest Hills and the environs had decided more through inertia than conscious choice to keep their peace. Pho-Nee's flourished, building its clientele among Jew and non-Jew alike. When *The Times'* restaurant critic wrote the place up and offered it two stars, that clinched it for most people—the pork might have been pho-nee, but the stars were real and success was assured.

In observance of the strict Sabbath laws, Pho-Nee's was closed from an hour before sundown on Friday until an hour after sundown on Saturday evening. As a result, there was always a crush of hungry diners on Saturday night and it was often necessary for those who hadn't bothered to make reservations to wait as long as an hour at the bar until a table became available.

But by midnight, the situation was quite different. Most of the diners had finished their meals and gone home to their apartments in time for *Saturday Night Live*. There were still some people drinking at the bar and there were a number of tables still occupied in the front room. But Marvin specifically asked to be seated in the back room, and because he was considered a local celebrity whose patronage was worth cultivating, this accommodation had been granted.

It was only after he and Dawn were seated, that Marvin noticed they were not alone in the back room. There was another table still in use at which there was seated a lone man wearing a black silk skullcap and reading a German-language newspaper.

"That guy," Marvin said suddenly, "I think that's him," whereupon there followed Dawn's aborted attempt to identify the solitary diner as *Monsieur* Sztul, her former French teacher at Martin Van Buren High School, and her belated decision to accept the little man's possibly being her teacher's brother. Apparently, her teacher's twin did not share his brother's love of the French language. If they did share a last name, she had not caught even a flicker of recognition in the little man's eyes when she had pronounced it. Probably, she concluded before dismissing the matter entirely, it was the title '*monsieur*' that had thrown him, rendering him incapable of recognizing his own last name.

The meal was wonderful, as usual. They began with snow fungus and dried mushroom soup, then continued with a chili and eggplant hot-pot, plates of Pho-Nee butterfly shrimp and deep-fried taro rolls and a huge *wor* of *yee-fu* noodles. It was, as Marvin said, a feast fit for the king of the gagmen and his hairdresser-queen.

"I'm not *your* hairdresser," Dawn observed precisely. "And I'm not a queen."

"Well, you're *a* hairdresser," Marvin countered, "and you're the queen of my life. So that makes you my hairdresser-queen even if you don't actually cut my hair."

"Only because *you* won't let me," Dawn observed.

"Men go to barbers," Marvin explained patiently. "*Women* go to hairdressers."

"Wake up, fella," Dawn responded with equal patience, "this is the 1980's."

"I know."

"You do?"

"Of course I do."

"So I *can* cut your hair?"

"I suppose, if you want to."

"You know I do."

"If it makes you happy, how can I say no?"

Dawn smiled with pleasure. She had been wanting to cut her lover's hair since the day they met almost two years earlier in the Food Fair at the Queens Center. Marvin had been eating a honey-glazed doughnut and drinking black coffee and Dawn had sat down with her mother across the counter and had ordered dry toast and tea. Marvin had made a joke, later incorporated into his act, about stomach viruses and the havoc they can wreak on the digestive system and her mother had scowled and she had laughed and that was that. They had their first date the following weekend, and there had been no looking back since.

The meal concluded as usual with ice cream, green tea and a brief discussion about the plausible reasons for which a great civilization such as China, the nation that had arguably created the greatest of all cuisines, had failed so miserably to create a decent dessert menu. To the Western palate taught from childhood to evaluate a meal based on the richness of its final course, it seemed simply unthinkable that the Chinese could simply have *forgotten* about dessert. How, Marvin asked not for the first time, could the people who invented Dry Yellow Fungus Congee have forgotten to invent dessert? It simply didn't follow!

The discussion about dessert concluded and the bill paid with an overused credit card, Marvin Kalish and Dawn Kupchinsky donned their winter parkas and set forth into the chilly evening air. It was half past one in the morning on Sunday, the first of March, 1981.

Later, neither Marvin nor Dawn could recall when the little man who either was or wasn't the brother of the absent *Monsieur* Sztul had left his table. Dawn seemed to recall that he hadn't been finished with his dinner when she had approached his table, but she couldn't be certain.

They themselves had dawdled a bit over their meal and he had certainly been seated, they both agreed, when they had come in. And even if she couldn't later recall where in his meal he had been, Dawn felt absolutely certain that he had been somewhere in the midst of dinner when he and she had their brief conversation.

Hadn't he asked, after all, for more tea and some fortune cookies when he had apparently mistaken Dawn for his waitress? Once Dawn introduced that detail into the conversation, the matter seemed certain: the little man had been eating his dessert and had probably finished it when Dawn approached his table. Why else would he have asked for *more* tea and *more* cookies?

But when precisely it was that he left, neither Dawn nor Marvin could guess. At any rate, it didn't seem to matter at the moment, and the two had been lost in their own conversation.

Dawn and Marvin left the restaurant after noting that there were no more diners occupying any of the tables in the front room either. The maître d' was obviously preparing to lock up now that his last diners were leaving.

They walked out onto Ascan Avenue. The grey stone church that occupied the entire block between Austin Street and Queens Boulevard was illuminated directly before them by large flood lights placed at strategic intervals along its base. The street was still; Forest Hills was asleep.

They walked to the corner, planning to cross the boulevard and wait at a bus stop to see if perhaps a bus might arrive before the next available taxi cruised by—the same plan as earlier in the evening. Dawn put her arm through Marvin's as they walked in the cold air. "This is March?" she asked with feigned incredulity.

"Yes."

"In like a lion, out like a lamb."

"Yes."

"Do you know any words in English aside from 'yes'?"

"Yes."

Marvin stopped abruptly about ten yards from the corner. In a moment of highly uncharacteristic public passion, he leaned over and kissed his girl on her painted lips. For a moment, she resisted. But her struggle was only formal and only lasted a few moments; before she knew it, she was kissing back, kissing back and squeezing her lover's back with her arms to draw him even closer.

"Let's go home," he whispered into her willing ear.

"We need milk," the ever-efficient Dawn said, signaling with a nod of her head that the Korean grocery on the corner of Queens Boulevard and Ascan Avenue was still open.

"Then let's buy some milk," agreed Marvin affably. "And then let's go home."

"Yes," Dawn answered with a warm smile that somehow meant both friendship and love.

Silently, arm in arm, they walked to the corner store.

Inside, there was a single Korean man sitting at the cash register waiting for a customer. Marvin greeted him with a half-hearted wave as Dawn went to the back of the store to take a plastic jug of milk from a refrigerated showcase.

Later, it seemed impossible to both Dawn and Marvin that the entire incident hadn't taken minutes to unfold. But, rationally speaking, it could not have taken more than eight or ten seconds for the man from the restaurant to enter the store and walk calmly around to the baked-goods table.

Marvin had approached the Korean and had begun to chat with him while Wolfzahn walked in through the front door and around the low table directly to its left on which an array of packaged baked goods was displayed.

The storekeeper saw the gun first. Marvin had turned to see who was coming in the door when it had first opened, but although he realized that this was the little man Dawn had mistaken for her old French teacher, he still failed to recognize the shooter from the club; if anything, he was even more convinced he had been wrong when he *had* recognized him at first. Wolfzahn was dressed up in the least conspicuous outfit imaginable—an old man's old-fashioned winter coat, a felt hat of the kind favored by neighborhood Jewish men, and dark leather gloves. His face, Marvin thought later, had hardly been visible at all—but even if it had been, the truth was that Marvin had somehow failed to recognize his assailant.

"He was just so ordinary looking," Marvin later told John Abernathy at the 113th Precinct House. "He looked like a thousand other little Jewish men you see walking around Queens Boulevard."

"But he wasn't a thousand other little Jewish men, was he?" the detective asked with a sarcastic edge. "He was a man you ought to have known right away."

"Well," Marvin countered, "you can't be smart all the time. Frankly, most people aren't ever too smart, and it's probably something if you can manage to be smart even some of the time. This just wasn't that particular time, that's all."

"Well," the detective retorted, "you're lucky you are still alive to be smart again some other day."

"That," Marvin agreed wholeheartedly, "is certainly the truth."

Because Marvin was facing the counter behind which the store-keeper was sitting, he didn't see Wolfzahn at all until it was almost too late.

Yudel Wolfzahn appeared to be trying to decide between the various varieties of Entenmann's cakes. He picked up some of the shiny white boxes and jiggled them around the better to peer through their little cellophane windows at their sticky contents. He lifted up one or more of the boxes to eye level, ostensibly to read the list of ingredients. He even sniffed at the edges of one or two boxes in order, presumably to ascertain if they were as fresh as the date stamped on the side of the box indicated they were.

The Korean had looked up when he heard his pastries being jiggled, whereupon Wolfzahn stopped shaking the boxes and the Korean turned his gaze back to Marvin. Then, secure that no one was watching him, Wolfzahn strode up to the counter and positioned himself six or eight feet away from Kalish.

The shopkeeper, whose back was to the wall, was the first to see the gun Wolfzahn pulled out of his coat.

He lifted the gun to his shoulder and took aim.

"And what happened then?" Detective Abernathy was quite anxious to fix in his mind the exact order of events.

"Well, I don't really know what happened in what order," Marvin continued. "I mean, he must have shot his gun because the plaster was suddenly raining down on us all. He must have fired and hit the wall behind where the shopkeeper had been sitting."

"Had been sitting?"

"Well, either he fainted altogether when he saw the gun, or he went to dive for his alarm button or he just hit the floor, but the point is that he hit the floor. I don't know if the gun was fired at that moment or just before, but I remember thinking he had been killed. I sort of forgot that my own life was in danger and ran around, but by the time I could see that he hadn't been hit, the guy was gone."

"And he didn't make any attempt to shoot you? I thought he was hit by something your fianceé threw at him."

Marvin had elevated Dawn to the status of fianceé when they had arrived at the precinct house in order to lend more weight to their story by presenting themselves as respectable people. "Well, that is true. He must have been on the verge of shooting…"

Abernathy interrupted. "You feel certain he was about to shoot? Maybe he just wanted to scare the grocer."

"I don't know. He released the safety and he had his finger on the trigger, and then suddenly this big thing came flying at him and he must have been knocked over or at least pushed to the side as he was pulling the trigger. It all happened so fast! Anyway, the bullet hit the wall and the plaster was flying in all directions and by the time I got into the street, he was gone."

"I was coming back with the milk," Dawn told the detective in her own account of the incident, "when I saw the guy with the gun. I realized it was the guy who I had thought was *Monsieur* Sztul, my old French teacher, only it wasn't him, but anyway, this was the guy I had *thought* was him and now I saw he had a gun. Anyway, I couldn't decide if I should throw the milk at his head or at the gun, but it was too heavy anyway—I always buy the big gallon jugs because Marvin likes cereal in the morning and we use a lot of milk at home—anyway, I didn't think I could even throw the milk that far, so I looked for the biggest thing in that aisle I could find and it was this big package of disposable diapers.

"So I sort of lobbed the thing at the guy with the gun and it must have come as a surprise, I guess, because he completely missed Marvin. Or maybe I hit him just as he was already pulling the trigger—who knows?—anyway, the point is that I hit him and he didn't hit Marvin."

"Now," Detective Abernathy pulled Marvin back on track, "let's talk about the street. You just ran out into the street even though this was the guy who had just tried to kill you?"

"Well, yes," Marvin admitted, "I did. At the moment, it didn't seem like such a stupid thing to do. Anyway, I guess it was a stupid thing to do, but I sort of forgot the guy had a gun with him—I mean, I was so mad at that son of a bitch—I mean he could have *killed* me— anyway, I ran out into the street and he wasn't there. So I looked first of all to see if a bus had just come, but there wasn't one—don't forget the Q-60 doesn't run all that frequently in the daytime and this was half past one at night—anyway, there wasn't a bus, but there was a little light traffic on the boulevard and I guess he must have had a get-away car— do they really call them get-away cars in real life? I mean in the movies, they call the cars crooks get away in get-away cars, but I guess you must know that—anyway, he must have had a get-away car because I was out in the street no more than fifteen seconds after the whole thing happened—I had only taken time to see if the Korean was okay—and he was gone. I mean, the bastard who shot at me was gone and the Korean was okay. You know what I mean?"

Detective Abernathy nodded, tired both by the late hour and the manic testimony he was trying to follow.

"So I suppose you want us to protect you for the next little while?" he asked, changing the topic.

"Protect me? How the hell can you protect me? Better you should concentrate your forces on catching the bastard who shot at me twice. You can't be with me twenty-four hours a day anyway—and I am only going to be truly safe once you find him. So you let me worry about me and you worry about him."

Detective Abernathy smiled as he leaned back in his chair. Here, for once, was a sensible young man. Often when people were the victims of intended assault of one sort of another, all they wanted was to be protected by the police. The fact that eventually their protection would end and they would be as vulnerable as ever didn't seem to concern them—they wanted to be protected *now* and that was all there was to it. But rare indeed was the citizen who understood that his best hope was for the police to concentrate on catching the perpetrator, not in guarding the intended victim. Apparently Marvin Kalish was going to be one of the few.

"Very well," the detective responded. "We'll begin our formal investigation in the morning. You'll be safe until then, I'm sure."

"I certainly hope so," Marvin replied quietly.

"Me, too," added Dawn.

Despite himself, Abernathy found himself liking this young couple. He resolved to do whatever he could to help.

Naturally, he had heard the rumors that had been bandied about the precinct house after the original shooting at Styx to the effect that the whole thing was a crazy publicity stunt dreamt up by Kalish himself in order to garner a bit of free publicity. This theory, however, Abernathy dismissed out of hand. First of all, it was his experience that P.R. men, although occasionally a nasty lot, rarely used actual ammunition to get the attention of the press. Also, there had been a real chance that someone might have been killed at Styx and this seemed a crucial point.

Second, it hardly made sense for a public relations stunt to have been planned for a twenty-four hour Korean grocery in the middle of the night with no one but the victim, the victim's girl, the shooter and a shopkeeper who could hardly speak English present on the scene. It just didn't figure; Abernathy had come to the conclusion already at the very beginning of the interview, almost as soon as he gathered what had happened, that this was on the level and that someone, for some reason, was apparently bent on taking the comic out. Why, of course, was a question that would require its own answers.

But if it seemed likely that this was a real attempted crime, then that didn't mean that there weren't profound holes in the story as well. It was hardly normal procedure, for example, for professional hit men to dine in the same restaurants as their intended victims just before the shooting. And it was also highly irregular for hit men, even amateurs, to be such poor marksmen. This guy had had two chances to kill Kalish, both at relatively short range. But he had flubbed it both times and there was no obvious reason for him to have done so. True, there were the off-duties who had wrestled him to the floor at Styx and there were the flying disposables that had knocked him off balance in the grocery—but these seemed more like flimsy excuses than real reasons. The truth, Abernathy suspected, lay elsewhere. But where precisely it lay, he could not yet know.

Not an hour after they arrived at the precinct house, Marvin and Dawn were on their way home. They thanked the detective for his time and interest, promising to remain at home the following day in case the police should wish to interview them again. In the meantime, they agreed to keep press interviews to a minimum and not to reveal anything but the most basic information to any of the reporters who got wind, as they inevitably would, of the shooting.

Finally, the interview was over. Marvin stood up and shook John Abernathy's hand, as did Dawn. As he turned to leave, the detective noticed he was limping.

"You hurt your foot?"

"I twisted my ankle when I ran out of the store."

"It must hurt," the detective said, probing without even knowing why.

"It does," Marvin agreed. "I've always had problems with my feet. I was even born with this big birthmark on the sole of my foot. It was in the exact shape of Manhattan Island—I should be in the *Guinness Book of Records*."

Detective Abernathy sat down for a moment at his desk. "Tell me," he asked in as off-hand a manner as he could, "this may seem like a weird question coming out of the blue, but could you just tell me if you were adopted as a child?"

Dawn stopped and looked at her friend, who remained strangely silent.

"Tell him." A certain urgency in Dawn's voice.

"Yes."

"And you were born with a birthmark in the shape of Manhattan Island on your foot?"

"Yes, I just said so."

"And, this may seem like an *entirely* inappropriate question coming from me, but I just have to ask it. Forgive me the intrusion into your personal affairs, but were you by any chance born already circumcised? I mean, foreskinless?"

"Already circumcised? How the hell would I know? My parents only met me when I was three days old. It's funny—I never gave the matter a moment's thought, but my father did tell me once that they felt cheated out of making a *bris* for me—you know what it is, a *bris*?"

Abernathy nodded. He had just recently driven his mother to Merrick, Long Island, to attend the *bris* of Mrs. Cohen's third grandson.

"Anyway, they had expected and looked forward to making a *bris* for their baby and they were anxious for just that reason to adopt a baby less than eight days old. A Jewish baby, I mean—I mean if it wasn't a Jewish baby, they figured it wouldn't be circumcised anyway, but if it was a Jewish baby, they wanted one less than eight days old so they could make a *bris*. But they were disappointed when I came—I mean they were *ecstatic* when I came—but they were disappointed that I was already circumcised. My dad just assumed they had done it automatically in the hospital. But maybe you *are* right and I was just born that way. *Are* people ever born that way?"

Abernathy shrugged. "I don't know," he answered honestly. "I suppose someone, somewhere must have been."

For a moment, there was complete silence in the precinct house. Then, taking a step or two closer to the detective's desk, Marvin posed his fateful question. "How did you know I was adopted?" he asked.

Before Marvin and Dawn finally did go home, Abernathy had told them how he knew.

Eight

"*M*ake tea!"

"It's already boiling."

"There's some cake?"

"Some pound cake from last night. I mean from Friday night."

"The kind I like?"

"If you like it so much, how come you can't remember if I served it Friday night? Yes, the kind you like."

Clara Wolfzahn took one of her Niagara Falls souvenir trays off the top of her refrigerator and put it on her counter. On it, she placed her mother's ancient tea pot, a cup and saucer, and a dessert place. She cut two slices of yellow pound cake off the larger loaf and placed them one on top of the other on the small, white plate.

"You're not having any?" The single cup caught Yudel Wolfzahn's eye.

"I'm going to bed."

"Stay with me a while, I'm lonely."

"Stay with you? It's half past two in the morning and I'm an old, tired lady. You stay with yourself—I'm going to bed!"

"If you're too old for tea, how about a kiss?" Yudel moved closer to his wife, his arms extended like a baby asking to be lifted up.

"Kiss yourself too."

With considerable dignity, Clara placed the tray on the kitchen table in front of her husband. She poured a half-kettle of boiling water into her mother's teapot, briefly stirred the loose leaves around with a fork she'd noticed lying in the drainboard, and left the room. Although it was hardly necessary, she made a point of swinging the door to their modest bedroom shut behind her. Yudel was alone to contemplate his evening, his tea and cake, and his strange life.

The get-away was as easy as guessing that Marvin and Dawn were going to go to Pho-Nee's had been in the first place. Clara was in their 1973 Impala parked on the southwest corner of Queens Boulevard and Ascan Avenue just in front of the side door of the great stone church and about a half-block north of the front door of Pho-Nee's and directly across the avenue from the Korean grocery. She sat as she had been instructed: motor running and her eyes glued on the front door of the grocery. When Yudel came out and jumped into the car, she was away from the curb in one second. By the time the comedian was in the street, just as Yudel had predicted he would be, the Wolfzahns were across Austin Street and well within the shadow of the Long Island Railroad overhead trestle. Just as Yudel had planned, Clara parked by the side of the road and turned her lights off.

In all of Forest Hills, Yudel had observed in the course of his hundreds of evening strolls along Austin Street, there was one single parking spot that one could *always* have, regardless of the hour of day or night. This parking spot was always available because of the unbelievable mess of pigeon droppings that inevitably covered any car whose owner was foolish enough to park under the train trestle overnight and it was into that single spot that Clara pulled the Impala as she turned out the headlights to wait.

She could easily see the corner of Queens Boulevard in her side rear-view mirror. As instructed, she waited calmly until she could see that Marvin Kalish, himself convinced that his assailant had fled, had run back into the grocery, no doubt to check on his girlfriend or on the shopkeeper.

Just as Marvin disappeared into the shop, Clara fired up her engine, turned her headlights on and pulled away from the curb.

With no one to observe them, the Wolfzahns drove leisurely down Ascan Avenue until Metropolitan Avenue. At Metropolitan, they turned right, still maintaining the leisurely pace of elderly lovers returning home from a Saturday night trip to a suitable movie, and headed for Yellowstone Boulevard.

At Yellowstone, they turned right again and drove as far as the corner of Austin Street. The local Precinct House was lighted from below by large flood lights that bathed the edifice in a yellow-beige light that created a strange adobe effect on the building's green cinder-block facade. On the roof, a lone flagpole jutted out over the street like a silent aluminum sentinel, its flag safely down for the night.

"They'll bring him here," Yudel explained to his wife. "This is where they'll bring him to take his statement."

"Maybe he's there right now," Clara wondered.

"No, I don't think so. Not so fast, he couldn't be here. First he has to phone 9-1-1, then they have to verify the call, then they have to send an ambulance to see if the Chinaman is badly hurt..."

"You said you didn't even aim at the shopkeeper."

"I didn't. But when the girlfriend threw the box of diapers at me, who knows where the bullet might have gone! But I'm sure I didn't hit him. I only actually fired once and the bullet hit the wall behind the register. You could see the plaster flying."

"Thank God," Clara said fervently. "Thank God an innocent man wasn't hurt."

"You said it. Anyway, where was I? Well, he'll phone the 9-1-1 and they'll come and then they'll ask what happened and he'll tell them and then they'll ask her and *she'll* tell them and then they'll ask the Chinaman and *he'll* tell them."

"I was in there the other day for milk. He doesn't speak English too good."

"Whatever—they'll find someone, some Chinese cop even, to take his statement. And then when they've finished asking everyone what happened, they'll figure that Kalish is the main player and they'll *shlep* him down to the precinct house to take a formal statement and he'll tell the same story again. Then they'll compare the two stories, figure out what maybe really did happen and send him home. But he couldn't be there yet. They're probably still running around looking for a cop who can speak Chinese."

Clara didn't dare park her car at the station house, even though she would have dearly liked to be parked in a dark shadow when the police cruiser with Kalish and his girlfriend would drive up. But it was too dangerous! A fool might try such a stunt, but not Clara Wolfzahn! Clara drove on.

The Wolfzahn Impala made its way down Austin Street in the direction of Continental Avenue. At Continental, the Wolfzahns were obliged to wait for a red light.

"Almost home," Yudel said as the light turned green. "Another four blocks and we're back where we started out."

Clara looked at him, allowing herself to relax for the first time since her husband had jumped into the car outside the grocery. "I know where we started out," she said plainly. "It's where we're going to end up that I'd like to know."

"Well, at least for tonight, we're going to end up where we started out," Yudel answered simply.

The Wolfzahns were, in fact, home. And there was a parking spot just in front of their apartment house. "There's a spot right in front," Clara clucked, almost as though the spot itself somehow constituted an omen of divine approval.

"So park in it, my dear."

"So okay, I will."

Clara parallel-parked her car with ease; in moments, the Wolfzahns were inside their building and safely ensconced in the ancient elevator that took them up to the sixth floor.

Once inside their apartment, they were both able to relax a bit. They look off their hats and coats and Yudel turned on the television and the VCR.

"I can't believe it," he called out, "I got the timer to work. Look, I got all of *Saturday Night Live*. Come and watch with me! Look, it's Tom Selleck who's the guest host. You like him."

But Clara was not interested in watching her favorite show, even with Tom Selleck. Instead she had taken up a position at the northeastern corner of her kitchen and was peering intently at the stone church across the street and at the dark street below.

"A neighborhood of three hundred synagogues and we have to live across from the only church for miles," she said audibly, but to herself.

But it wasn't the church itself that Clara found irritating. It was that just on the other side of the church at the corner of Queens Boulevard and Ascan Avenue, there was a scene playing itself out that Clara Wolfzahn would have dearly loved to see for herself. The grocery might still be surrounded by police cars. And the Kalish boy was possibly still standing in front of the shop, talking in a low voice with the policeman taking down his story, pausing perhaps to look in on the Chinaman who had no doubt dusted himself off and was busy figuring out how much to charge the insurance company for the damage Yudel had done to his shop.

It struck Clara as funny to imagine that the police would now start searching for Yudel in every borough, at every airport, at every train station and in every adjacent county. They might even check beyond the metropolitan area, for all she knew how the police worked. But would one of the policeman stop to consider that the man he was seeking was a single block away in his own apartment in the company of his good wife of almost forty-seven years?

She was still standing at her kitchen window waiting for the kettle to come to a boil—Clara knew that Yudel would want hot tea and a piece of her pound cake as he watched the program he had for once managed to tape properly—when she heard him bellowing from the living room for tea.

***

"He didn't say it *was* the boy. So calm down—you'll only make yourself crazy." Lawrence Lazar had rarely, if ever, seen Bunny in such a state of almost hysterical excitement.

"I'm already crazy—crazy with the fact that they've found my boy."

"Whoa, Nelly!" Lawrence Lazar interjected, "Detective Abernathy didn't say he had found your boy. He said he had..."

"He did!"

"He did? He did what?"

"Say so! You said he said so!"

"I did *not* say he said so! I didn't say anything of the sort, so listen to me and I'll tell you what I said. I'll even tell you what *he* said since I took the call and whatever he said, he said to me. But don't *you* tell *me* what the man said to me. *I* will tell *you*."

"So okay, I'm sorry." Genuine regret in Bunny's voice. "Tell me exactly what he said."

It was Monday morning, the second of March, 1981. There was a light cloud cover that promised to give way to sun in the early afternoon. But it wasn't the afternoon yet—it was only five to nine in the morning. Detective Abernathy had phoned at eight o'clock promptly, as soon as he had come on shift. He had spoken clearly and with great precision, which was one of the reasons Lawrence Lazar was finding it so irritating to listen to his wife completely ignore the good detective's prudent choice of language.

"He said that he had an interesting lead on the situation that he would like to share with us. I asked him if he could elaborate on the phone and he simply said that there had been a series of violent attacks on a young man who somewhat fits the description you gave the police."

"So what else can he mean? He's found my boy!"

"*Somewhat*! He said the young man *somewhat* fits the description. But you don't forget that the description is no description at all. You haven't the faintest idea how your son looks today. All you know is that he was born without a foreskin, which he himself probably

– 89 –

doesn't know, that he had a strawberry mark on his foot in the shape of Manhattan which he also probably doesn't know anything about since it was undoubtedly removed when he was an infant and his parents probably…"

"Probably! They would have told him!"

"…and his parents *possibly* didn't tell him that either, and that he was adopted, which I grant you he probably does know about."

"Probably? You think there is even a chance he doesn't know that either?"

"How in hell should I know what his parents, whom I've never met, told their son, whom I've also never met, about the circumstances of his coming into their family, which I know nothing at all about? If you ask me, it's entirely possible your son has no knowledge at all that could ever lead us to him. The records are sealed…"

"We'll get them open!"

"Will you *stop* living in a fantasy world! We tried that and we failed. F-A-I-L-E-D," Lawrence Lazar spelled out for his wife's edification. "We failed to get the records unsealed and we are—are you listening?—we are N-E-V-E-R getting into them. So forget that! The records are sealed and it's possible your son doesn't know anything that could help him reach out to us. So don't count on anything. Possibly—probably!—this is a false alarm. I'm not saying we shouldn't go down and talk to the detective, just don't count on anything. I…I…" Lawrence Lazar lowered his voice to a whisper.

"…I don't want you to be more hurt than necessary if nothing comes of this."

Bunny, still only half-dressed in a slip and her favorite navy-blue silk blouse, came over to him and put her arms around her husband's neck. "I know you want me not to be hurt by all of this. And don't think," she continued tenderly, "that I don't know that you are one in a million for indulging me even this far. It isn't every husband," she continued, "who would—who could!—much relish the thought of his wife searching for some other guy's son who also happens to be hers. So don't you worry about me! I'll be fine. I *know* how long a shot this is and I *know* that the detective said sixteen times not to get too excited about this. I know all that and I'm still excited and I still can't believe that there is even the tiniest chance I could see my boy. So call me sentimental, call me a fool—but I want to give this thing one last chance. Mad?"

"No, I'm not mad. I…let's hope for the best."

"Sounds good," Bunny said affably as she zipped up her skirt and stepped into her navy leather pumps. "Let's go."

"No coffee?"

"Are you crazy? The cops have found my baby and you want me to start grinding beans?"

Lawrence Lazar bit off his reply. Bunny, realizing that her husband had missed her joke, came directly back down to earth. "Of course I'll make coffee," she said easily. "You finish getting dressed and I'll put up the kettle and grind some of the good beans and we'll be out of here by a quarter to ten and we'll be at the precinct by ten which is when the detective said to come anyway. Who wants to come early and sit around waiting? You even have time to shave! So shave and get dressed and I'll make the coffee and we'll go and it'll be my boy and he'll be rich as Croesus and *grateful* I gave him up and we'll all have a good cry and live happily ever after."

Bunny Luft flounced out of the room, leaving her husband to do as he had been so forcefully told. Obedient to the end, Lawrence Lazar put on a clean undershirt and went into the bathroom to plug in his electric razor.

While her husband dressed, Bunny attended to the coffee. She put up the kettle, then ground the beans, then waited for the water to boil. As she waited, she stepped over to look out the window at the constant flow of traffic on the Long Island Expressway. For the first time in years, she found herself focusing on the tiny bronze mirror Rabbi Weissbrot had given the Lufts on their wedding day as a sign of forgiveness for past sins—among which the birth, or rather the conception of the child Bunny was so anxious now to find, ranked uppermost.

She lifted up the mirror and looked into it. Because the back of the mirror had interesting engraved designs, the reflective surface was left facing down onto the sill. Bunny took a piece of paper toweling and, in the few moments she had before attending to the coffee, dusted it off and looked with surprised interest into the glass.

Later it struck Bunny odd that she had found it surprising, but she *was* strangely surprised to see her own face peering back at her. Or rather, it was vaguely surprising to see her own face as it now looked instead of the young woman's face that had looked back when Bunny had first gazed into the glass on her wedding day. She tried to remember what it was that Rabbi Weissbrot had said to her under the wedding canopy, but the words somehow escaped her.

It had been a message of warmth and reconciliation, she could easily recall; but most of all, it had been a message of forgiveness. The rabbi had bid her fast on her wedding day up until the ceremony so that the day would function for her as a sort of private Yom Kippur, a personal Day of Atonement which would erase past sins from her ledger in the great book God Himself keeps in heaven and allow her to enter her life as a married woman free from sin and guilt.

Exactly what the rabbi had said, Bunny couldn't remember clearly, but the gist of his remarks remained with her. Suddenly, Bunny had a thought. She had forgiven herself because the rabbi said it was right and appropriate for her to do so—even that it was a sort of *mitzvah* for her to forgive herself, lest any residual guilt affect and possibly even destroy the marriage upon which she and Lawrence Lazar were about to embark.

But there was someone else in the world, Bunny suddenly realized, whose forgiveness it had never struck her to seek out, and that was the one person who had *truly* been affected by Bunny's decision to give up her baby. Bunny had somehow forgotten that to achieve true forgiveness for her sins, it would undoubtedly be necessary for her to see what had happened to her little boy.

It was such a simple idea—so simple that Bunny could hardly imagine why she had failed to think of it on her own over the years. But now that she had thought it through, she knew that the woman gazing back at her out of the rabbi's tiny mirror needed to seek out her baby, or rather the man he had become. As Bunny's resolve to see the matter through to its end became even firmer, fueled as it now was by personal resolve as well as by altruistic desire, her kettle came to a boil.

Bunny ground the beans and made the morning coffee while Lawrence Lazar shaved and dressed. Breakfast at the Lufts' was always a speedy affair, but this morning not even conversation was permitted. At precisely fifteen minutes before ten o'clock, the Lufts stepped outside their apartment into the familiar hallway.

"Come on!" Bunny had showed more than enough patience by making the coffee and letting Lawrence Lazar shave; she had proven her reasonableness by agreeing to appear in the precinct house on time, but she certainly had no intention of coming late.

"Wait a minute," Lawrence said as he stooped to pick something up from the ground just in front of their door.

"It's just more junk circulars. Leave it and we can throw it out when we get home."

Ignoring his wife's advice, Lawrence picked up the envelope. "It has our name on it," he said. "Not just 'Occupant' but our real names."

"Good. Now let's go."

"No, wait. This isn't a circular. It's something someone left here for us. I think we should take it along."

"Good. Let's take it along. Now come on or I'll go by myself."

Bunny had insisted on driving and Lawrence Lazar, wary of crossing his wife when she was in one of her moods, had reluctantly agreed. It wasn't until the Lufts were out of the lobby and in their car zipping along the service road on the south side of Queens Boulevard that Lawrence Lazar remembered the mysterious envelope that he had stuck in his inside jacket pocket.

"Say, I'll open this now," he said, half to himself and half for his wife's benefit.

"Fine."

Undeterred by his wife's lack of interest, Lawrence Lazar opened the envelope. "This is really weird," he said.

Silence.

"I said, 'This is really weird.' Aren't you interested in knowing *what* is really weird?"

"Okay. Tell me," Bunny said as she stopped the car to wait out a red light.

"Well, it looks like a guide book. The kind you buy when you visit some place in Europe. In fact, it's half in Italian, half in English, half in French."

"That's three halves."

"So it has three halves. Don't you want to know what it's a guide-book to?"

For the first time, Bunny felt a twinge of interest in her husband's little find. "Okay, I'll bite. What is it a guide book to?"

"Well, if you must know," Lawrence Lazar said in his most mysterious voice, "it seems to be a guidebook to one of the catacombs in Rome."

"The catacombs? You mean where they fed people to the lions?"

"First of all, I think that was the Colosseum. And second of all, this place looks like some sort of underground cemetery." Lawrence Lazar leafed through the book as the light changed and Bunny stepped on the gas. It was eight minutes before ten.

"What is the place called?"

"Santa Cecilia," Lawrence Lazar read on the front cover. "It's a guidebook to the Roman Catacomb of Santa Cecilia."

"Great," Bunny enthused. "Next time we're in Rome, we'll know where to go if we have time to drop dead."

Nine

*T*he Lufts arrived at the precinct house at precisely one minute before ten o'clock. A different officer was sitting where Detective Abernathy had been on duty when the Lufts had first come to the police station to report the threat against Bunny's son. He acknowledged that the Lufts were expected and that Abernathy would receive them in Interview Room No. 3 on the upper level.

The door to Room No. 3 was shut.

"Knock first," Lawrence Lazar said as his wife's hand reached for the doorknob.

"And let him think *he's* allowing *us* to come in? Not for a minute—we paid the taxes that bought this door!" Bunny flung the door open and stepped into the small room.

John Abernathy was seated at a wooden table looking at some papers he had taken from a manila file that lay open in front of him. He put the papers down and rose to shake his guests' hands.

"So glad you came," he said.

"I'm so glad you're glad. Well, enough chit-chat," Bunny continued without losing a beat, "where's my boy?"

"Your boy? I didn't say I had located your boy. All I said was that there was a certain odd set of circumstances relating to a series of unexplained assaults against a certain comedian that I wanted to discuss with you."

Bunny felt deflated, but far from defeated. "So discuss," she commanded.

John Abernathy felt ill at ease. He was used to following his superiors' orders and having the men beneath him follow his. He neither wished to take orders from a citizen nor did he like the imperious attitude Bunny Luft was flinging all over his interview room.

"Look," he said, "this investigation has nothing at all to do with you. I can justify it up and down and sideways if I just treat it as though it were nothing but a vendetta being carried out by some maniac against some performer who once told a joke the guy didn't think was too funny. It is *I* who think *you* would like to be part of this, and it's *I* who invited *you* in. So you don't have to be so haughty…"

The detective's voice trailed off. He had meant to say that Bunny didn't have to be so rude, but he switched to 'haughty' at the last minute, half hoping she didn't understand quite how insulting his comment had been intended to be.

Abernathy still felt he owed Bunny Luft one for her crack about the Negro College Fund when they had first met. The detective was not especially vindictive by nature, but he didn't like people thinking they could make cracks like that and then simply apologize when they suddenly needed him on the assumption he was too dumb or too servile to take notice.

But he'd taken the right tack with Bunny. "Look," she said, switching gears almost in mid-sentence, "I didn't mean anything. I'm just very nervous. You can't imagine what I've gone through these last couple of weeks. Just the idea that you are on to something, no matter how tenuous the whole thing might be—is, I mean, how tenuous the whole thing *is*, because I completely believe you that it *is* entirely tenuous and you have no idea where my boy is except for this weird string of unexplained assaults against a twenty-seven year old comedian who was born circumcised and with a birthmark the shape of Manhattan Island on his right foot—anyway, just the idea is enough to make me crazy—and you can't even imagine the half of what we've been…"

"Whoa," Abernathy sang out in two distinct syllables, cutting Bunny off in mid-sentence. "Who told you the guy I'm talking about was born circumcised or with some birthmark on his foot?"

"Who told me? *No one* told me," Bunny answered honestly. "But I just figured why in the world would a busy man like you phone a *nudnik* like me…"

Lawrence Lazar cleared his throat significantly.

"…oh excuse me, phone *nudniks* like *us*, I mean, anyway, why in the world would you bother *shlepping* us back into the station house if you hadn't figured this guy was possibly my boy? I mean," Bunny concluded semi-triumphantly, "just being twenty-seven would hardly be enough, would it?"

Detective John Abernathy, who had felt in complete control of the interview just moments earlier, knew defeat when he experienced it. Just being twenty-seven would *not* have been enough. With no training in criminology at all, Bunny Luft had understood that Abernathy would never have started up with such irritating people—*nudnik* was just the word his mother's neighbor, Mrs. Cohen, would have used to describe Bunny Luft—if the only thing linking the alleged threat against her son to the assaults against Marvin Kalish was the fact that both Kalish and the missing son were both twenty-seven years old.

The fact was that they weren't *just* both twenty-seven; they shared a common birthday, the second of May. And Kalish had told the detective how disappointed his adoptive parents had been that they had been cheated out of fulfilling the great religious obligation of circumcising their son because he had come to them circumcised—or so they had assumed and Kalish himself had always taken for granted. But it didn't follow that he had really been circumcised at all—he could have been born without a foreskin altogether.

The detective had taken the trouble of informing himself about such an unlikely event. He had phoned his brother Calvin, a doctor at Columbia Presbyterian, to inquire whether boys are ever born without foreskins. Calvin had informed him that, although an unusual occurrence, it does occasionally happen, and certainly not *so* rarely as to make it a medical miracle or anything like that.

But, of course, it was the birthmark in the shape of Manhattan Island on Kalish's right foot that was the clincher. Foreskins and common birthdays were one thing, but the birthmark was something else entirely. The detective had never heard of anyone having such an unusual foot, but the thought that these two men had the same birthdays *and* possibly the same genital oddity of birth made it as certain as anything uncertain could possibly be that these two men were the same person.

"No," Detective Abernathy replied simply after thinking the matter through yet again, "it wouldn't be."

Bunny was magnanimous. "There," she declared in her friendliest tone, "I knew it. Is he coming today? Did you tell him *we* were coming today?"

John Abernathy drew his chair closer to the table. "I did," he said. "I asked him to come at a quarter past ten."

As though on cue, all three people in the room looked at their wrist watches. It was, in fact, precisely fifteen minutes after ten o'clock.

"He's not coming," Bunny sighed. She had known it wasn't going to be *this* easy!

"He's not even late yet," Lawrence Lazar volunteered hopefully. "It's exactly a quarter past the hour."

– 96 –

In his heart, Lawrence Lazar was experiencing a surge of almost electric ambivalence. He had played the role of supportive husband and understanding, long-suffering spouse quite long enough, he thought. He had seen the matter through as long as he felt nothing could ever come of it, and he had not even objected to standing hidden in the shadow of a kosher take-out place while his wife accosted an innocent young man at a bus stop to inquire about the most intimate circumstances of his long-forgotten birth.

But this was entirely a different matter that was unfolding around the Lufts in Interview Room No. 3. Detective Abernathy sounded rather like he had actually found Bunny Luft's missing baby.

It didn't seem possible that an overworked employee of the N.Y.P.D. could have managed such an unbelievable feat of sleuthing in just a few short weeks! Such speedy success against overwhelming odds was the arrogant fantasy of mystery writers, not the day-to-day reality of police work in the big city. Crimes far more important than the alleged threat against Bunny's alleged son had gone unsolved and forgotten for years, and the public had apparently come to accept and to half-expect such impotence from its police force.

This was, Lawrence Lazar knew all too well, a city in which people reported break-ins because their insurance companies required them to, not because they entertained even the slimmest of hopes that the police would actually locate the perpetrator. This was a city in which car theft was not even considered a serious crime, merely part of the nuisance dues owed sometime or another by anyone foolhardy enough to risk life in Gotham. Finally, this was a city in which even robbery and assault—crimes that were considered newsworthy events in other places across the United States—were not even thought of as interesting enough events to warrant mention in the daily papers. In short, Lawrence Lazar Luft knew the level of urban mayhem which was considered reasonable and not worth bothering about by the police department and could not, therefore, imagine that Detective Abernathy had been able to justify spending even thirty seconds on Bunny's strange complaint.

But all that vain theorizing was behind the Lufts now. Lawrence Lazar watched as the second hand of his watch swept around past the bottom of the dial. If the alleged young man was going to show, he had about thirty seconds to do so without being late. Incredible as it seemed, Lawrence Lazar realized he fully expected his wife's lost baby to walk through the door within the half-minute.

There was complete silence in the room. Just outside the frosted window, some early sparrows jumped from bare bough to bare bough in a tall, still entirely leafless maple tree. The traffic passing by beneath the room's window seemed distant and muted; even the occasional distant sound of an irate motorist's horn failed to affect the thick atmosphere of dread, hope and anticipation that prevailed in the narrow confines of Interview Room No. 3.

Detective Abernathy appeared to be reading some of the loose pages he had taken from the manila folder that lay open on the table before him. Bunny sat quietly, her eyes half-closed. Lawrence Lazar, his eyes darting from the detective to his wife and back again towards the door as he looked for some portent of things soon to come, displayed the most activity although he too was completely still.

One minute passed, then another. Just as Bunny was preparing herself to accept the fact that her baby was not going to show, there came a knock at the door.

All three people in the room looked up simultaneously to see a hazy head on the other side of the frosted glass. For just a second, no one spoke.

Detective Abernathy stood up and walked to the door, opening it briefly and stepping out into the hall. Bunny Luft reached over and took her husband's puffy hand in her own. "This is it," she said quietly.

"*Und hah*," Lawrence Lazar responded, for some reason choosing that moment to indulge himself in a fond memory of the way his immigrant grandmother used to try to pronounce her favorite American expression, 'And how!'

"*Und hah* is right." Bunny's grip on her husband's hand tightened. The detective appeared to be speaking at length with the person in the hallway.

"Probably he's telling him we're here."

"Or else it's not him at all."

"Or else it is him and he's preparing him to meet the woman who made him."

"Who knows?" said Lawrence Lazar. Better, he thought, to just wait patiently and see what would ensue. But even he knew better than to imagine that the detective had merely forgotten them there and gone off to attend to some other pressing matter. If the detective was standing in the hall talking with someone at length, it could only be with the coconut that had fallen so prematurely, but apparently not irretrievably, from Bunny Luft's family tree.

Only two or three minutes after he stepped into the hall, John Abernathy stepped back into the room. His shoulder holster, which

Bunny somehow managed to notice only now for the first time, was cutting into the blue shirt of his uniform on the left side of his chest just beneath his armpit. When Detective Abernathy finally spoke, Bunny had been wondering idly why the detective didn't loosen the tight leather straps when he was securely inside the precinct house. "He's here," he said simply.

"So is he going to come in?" Bunny could scarcely control the excitement in her voice.

"Of course. But before he does, I want you to promise to let me do the talking. If it turns out that this guy is your grown-up baby, you'll have time to talk privately later on. But now, it's for me to talk and for you all to answer my questions. This is a police investigation, after all, not *This Is Your Life*."

The Lufts sat quietly and said nothing.

"Agreed?" The detective was obviously unwilling to assume assent from the Lufts' silence.

"Agreed, agreed, agreed," Bunny said in tones of ever-increasing irritation, the feverish agitation in her voice a warning as much as a threat against delaying the proceedings much longer. She was willing to be patient and good, but there was a limit and the detective needed to know just how close he was coming to it.

Detective Abernathy responded by merely turning to Lawrence Lazar and waiting for his response. "Ditto," he said succinctly.

"Well then, okay."

Detective John Abernathy walked to the door and opened it. In the hallway, surprisingly, there were two people. Directly in the doorway, peering into the brightly lit room, was a man of about twenty-seven years of age.

He had short, curly hair and a distinctly Jewish look about him. He looked, both Bunny and Lawrence Lazar thought simultaneously, like a younger version of Bunny's now jowly and slightly addled Uncle Arnold. Beside him was an attractive woman, also quite Jewish-looking with a prominent bosom, dark, curly hair and healthy red cheeks. They were, Lawrence Lazar thought to himself, an attractive couple.

Bunny Luft, however, for whom this ought to have been a pivotal life moment, was distracted by an entirely unexpected circumstance: she actually *knew* the young lady in the corridor.

"Dawn?" she asked hesitantly.

The light in the corridor had been so dim, and the mixture of neon and sunlight in Interview Room No. 3 so glaring, that it took a few moments for Dawn Kupchinsky's eyes to adjust to the brightness. But even before she could see clearly, she knew that she knew that voice. But whose voice was it?

Dawn raced through the various possibilities—girlfriends, family members, customers, neighbors, relatives of Marvin's (but they would certainly have called out *his* name, not hers), former teachers, doctors, dentists—and came up short. But the fact that she couldn't immediately identify the voice didn't mean that she didn't recognize it. Even without a name to go with it, Dawn knew that she knew with certainty the voice that had called her name.

"It's me," the voice added simply.

'I know that voice," Dawn said to herself, "and it knows me."

"Bunny Luft," the voice added.

"Bunny Luft!" Dawn somehow heard herself exclaiming in feigned delight. She had considered the possibility that the voice was a customer's but she hadn't been able to place it and now it turned out that she had been right all along. Bunny Luft had been having her hair cut and styled at the Smart Set for as long as Dawn had been working there. She was a faithful customer who tipped well. But when the hairstylists vied with each other to avoid cutting Bunny Luft's hair, it was hardly the size of the expected tip that was the issue, but rather Bunny's unshakable conviction that along with the haircut and set came an unimpeachable right to interrogate her "girl," as she irritatingly referred to whichever hairstylist had ended up drawing the short straw, about even the most intimate details of her private life.

But Dawn Kupchinsky had made her special name at the salon precisely by seeking out the clients no one else wanted. She had been low woman on the totem pole when she started working for Tony Manzanilla and needed to establish a client base. The way Dawn had figured things, she could either spend three or four years waiting to develop some allegiance among ladies shunted her way due to the illness, holiday time or absence of their regular hairdressers or she could begin straight off to build her own following.

But building a following meant beating the bushes for new clients, which Dawn Kupchinsky was reluctant to do. It was only a week or two after she had begun at the salon that Tony had made his suggestion. There were, it seemed, at least two or three dozen ladies whose temperaments were so unpleasant, so presumptuous, or so arrogant or whose breath was simply so awful that none of the regular stylists would go near them.

But these ladies were paying customers as well! And they

deserved to have their hair as nicely set as the other ladies that everyone fought over. In fact, Tony had suggested slyly, perhaps they had an even greater need for good hair than their sisters with pleasant, outgoing personalities, obsequious demeanors and sweet breath. The words were hardly out of Tony's mouth before Dawn agreed.

The next morning, the sweep-up broom was handed to a newly hired Dominican lady with gold teeth and no English at all and Dawn found her card filled with appointments at half-hour intervals from opening until closing. Even her lunch hour had been trimmed to thirty minutes with the handwritten proviso on her card that she would get triple time for the half of her regular lunch hour that she would work, thereby earning eight and a half hours' salary for seven and a half hours' work. Dawn was ready!

The work turned out to be harder than she had anticipated. The most refined of Queens' ladies were tough birds, Dawn knew all too well, but these ladies were something exceptional.

Filled with venom, brimming with snide gossip and vulgar comments about anyone who had the unknowing misfortune to pop into their minds at a given moment, overcome with rage at the government, loathing for their husbands, derisive, belittling thoughts about their children and, ultimately, unbridled hatred for themselves and for both all they had become *and* all they had failed to become, these were not the little blue-haired ladies Dawn recalled fondly from her girlhood days when she would visit her mother in the salon where she had worked almost her entire life.

But life is adjustment! It took months before she could feel relaxed in the shop, but eventually she *was* relaxed with the harpies, as she called them semi-affectionately when safely out of their vengeful earshot. And the money was, as Tony Manzanilla had promised, terrific. Not only was Dawn receiving an extra seven and a half hours' pay per week against half her lunch hour, but she was earning more in tips week after week than any of the other stylists.

These clients, some veterans of more than a dozen different Queens beauty salons, knew they were lucky to have someone like Dawn Kupchinsky accept them as regulars. And they were smart enough, almost to a woman, to know that Dawn wouldn't last long without the added financial incentive of superior tipping. Tips of five and ten dollars were quite routine, but there were ladies—and plenty of them—who routinely offered Dawn ten, fifteen, or even twenty dollar gratuities.

The clients who were merely vulgar and rude were easy for Dawn to handle. It was the inquisitors, as the other stylists called them, who were the hardest to take. These were the ladies who felt that part of what they were purchasing was a complete dossier on the most intimate details of their stylists' lives. Dawn had grown used to ladies asking if she was married or if she had a boyfriend; that was almost a routine part of life in the beauty salons of Queens. But these ladies were something else! Dawn had had to parry queries about her sexual preferences, her relationship with her parents and her experience with electrolysis, not to mention questions relating to marijuana, hemorrhoids, herpes, mammograms and the degree to which she answered the question about gratuities on her income tax return honestly.

And of these regular clients, one of the ones whose appointments Dawn least looked forward to was Bunny Luft, the only woman ever to insist on sticking her fingers into Dawn's blouse to check personally for scar tissue after inquiring and receiving a negative answer as to whether Dawn's breasts had been surgically enlarged to their present size and shape with silicon implants.

Bunny Luft was a regular at the Smart Set. She was there every Friday morning at ten o'clock and was a regular feature of Dawn Kupchinsky's week. In retrospect, it seemed strange to Dawn that she had needed to hesitate for even a moment before placing Bunny's voice—but the unfamiliar context had thrown her and she hadn't been sure who the lady was until she identified herself.

All these thoughts went through Dawn Kupchinsky's mind in a matter of seconds. Bunny Luft's name was still hanging on the air in Interview Room No. 3 when its possessor rose to her feet, walked over to Dawn and kissed her warmly on the cheek.

"So who's your friend?" she asked pleasantly.

"My friend? This is my fiancé, Marvin Kalish." Marvin had specifically reminded Dawn on their drive down to the precinct house that he had introduced her to Detective Abernathy as his fiancée and it was now necessary to continue that pleasant charade if they didn't wish to make the officer suspicious. "Marvin," she added, almost as an afterthought, "this is Bunny Luft, one of my Friday regulars. She phoned a few days ago to cancel for this morning, but I certainly didn't guess it was because she was coming here."

Bunny reached out and shook Marvin's right hand. "My husband, Larry," she tossed off almost in an undertone, glancing in her husband's direction. Lawrence Lazar half stood at his place and raised his right arm in a sort of welcoming wave, whereupon he sat back down.

"So," Bunny said to Detective Abernathy, "let's begin."

"Yes, let's," Marvin Kalish said, speaking for the first time.

Bunny turned to Marvin now, facing him directly for the first time. "It's my father's voice," she said quietly.

"Holy shit," said Lawrence Lazar in an equally hushed tone.

Without taking their eyes off Bunny Luft, Marvin and Dawn sat down on the two vacant chairs around Detective Abernathy's wooden table.

The detective, his presence clearly forgotten, cleared his throat to remind everyone why they had come. "Well," he said reasonably, "I suppose I should begin at the beginning…"

Ten

$\mathcal{F}$or such a momentous tale, there wasn't actually too much to tell. Detective Abernathy started out with a bare-bones outline of the events that had led to the meeting that was now taking place.

Knowing from long experience what a disastrous mistake it would be to allow the players themselves to recount the events at hand, he himself launched into the story. He began with the earliest incident, the strange encounter between the Lufts and the mysterious lady with the large handbag in synagogue on Friday evening, the sixth of February.

He told of the event and he recounted how the Lufts had been sufficiently agitated to come directly from synagogue to the nearby precinct house—it was only one long block along Austin Street to the west of the synagogue—where they reported the incident to John Abernathy himself, who happened to be on night shift that evening.

From there, the detective moved to the first attack launched against Marvin Kalish as he was in the middle of a performance at the Styx on the following evening. At the time, naturally, the two events—the Lufts' encounter with the mystery lady at the synagogue and the assault against Kalish—had seemed unrelated, although it seemed almost eerie now to recall that the following Monday morning, Abernathy had made specific reference to the Kalish assault in an attempt to help Bunny Luft understand just how difficult it would be for her to chase down every last lead concerning twenty-seven year old white men who happened to be the victims of crime.

From the Saturday evening assault against Kalish, Abernathy proceeded to his meeting with the Lufts on Monday morning, the ninth of February. He recounted his unsuccessful attempt to pry some information from the Stuyvesant Agency regarding the baby Bunny had placed for adoption in 1953 and he repeated, almost verbatim, his advice to the Lufts regarding the folly of further inquiry.

Next, Abernathy reviewed the Lufts' brief, equally unsuccessful efforts to sue the Stuyvesant people into unsealing Baby Boy F.'s records. He hadn't had the opportunity to attend the trial, he said, but he had before him the transcript of Judge Stern's decision. It was, Bunny noted with interest, apparently that very courtroom transcript that Detective Abernathy had been perusing with such interest when the Lufts had first come into the interview room.

Marvin Kalish, who was slowly guessing precisely who he actually was in the story he was hearing, listened to John Abernathy's account of the trial with rapt interest. As he listened to the report of the trial, he stared directly at Bunny Luft, who felt obliged to avert her own eyes from the man she now believed firmly to be her son lest they end up staring directly at each other.

And now Detective Abernathy, oblivious to the various games of eye contact going on around him, was re-telling the events of the previous Saturday night, the final night of a momentous February in the lives of all the assembled. He ran through the events of the evening in order: Kalish's triumphant return to the stage of Styx, Marvin and Dawn's dinner at Pho-Nee's, the murder attempt against Kalish in the all-night Korean grocery on the corner of Ascan Avenue and Queens Boulevard.

It was, Abernathy explained, in the course of taking down Kalish's detailed statement about the assault that he had first surmised that the Lufts' mysterious encounter with the strange little lady in synagogue and the two assaults on Kalish's life might be connected.

The detective fell silent. He had finished telling the basic story, but there were still many issues to resolve. Of these, by far the most compelling was whether Marvin Kalish was or was not Baby Boy F.

Bunny Luft looked at the young man seated directly across the table from her. She knew what she wanted to ask him—about the birthmark in the shape of Manhattan, about his having been born without a foreskin, about the date of his birth (although the detective had already confirmed that Kalish's birthday was precisely the day Bunny's baby was born), about his having been adopted as an infant— but she found it difficult to find the words to begin.

Once she began, Bunny knew that her life would alter forever. Mostly, this was something she wanted—and not only wanted but had actually yearned to experience. But now that the moment was at hand, she found herself strangely reluctant. She knew she wanted to move forward, but the sudden realization that the step she was about to take was irrevocable held her back momentarily. Once she asked her initial questions, after all, there would be more questions she knew she wished to ask.

Had the agency honored her wishes and placed her baby with a respectable Jewish family? The name Kalish would suggest they had, but Bunny had to know for sure.

Did her baby harbor feelings of resentment or anger towards his birth mother for abandoning him to a family about which she had known absolutely nothing? The look in Marvin Kalish's eyes suggested that whatever adolescent resentment he might once have harbored had somehow subsided with adulthood. Bunny had occupied herself during most of Detective Abernathy's disquisition by gazing at her son when he wasn't busy staring at her and she had failed to detect even dormant dislike in his eyes.

Was her son—if Marvin *was* her son—prepared to enter into a relationship with the Lufts now that their identity had finally been revealed? Or was this to be a one-shot deal that would culminate in an uneasy dinner party to which Marvin would insist on inviting the elder Kalishes, whom he would make a point of calling Mom and Dad sixteen times a minute lest anybody present miss the point, and which would only make Bunny's sense of guilt even more burdensome?

All these questions flitted through Bunny Luft's mind as she prepared herself to speak. The detective hadn't granted her the floor, but it seemed logical that she say *something* now that Abernathy had finished talking.

For a few minutes, the room was silent. A fly buzzed around the window overlooking the intersection of Austin Street and Yellowstone Boulevard. Marvin felt that perhaps he should say something, but he too could not quite decide on what to say.

Dawn looked at Marvin and Marvin stared directly at Bunny. She finally opened her mouth as though she were about to speak, but before any words came out, Lawrence Lazar had a question.

"How come you just let the little guy your fiancée thought was her French teacher walk out of the restaurant if you thought he was the guy who had taken a shot at you at the club?" Lawrence asked out of genuine curiosity. It *was* an interesting question and all were quite relieved to have something to discuss before turning to the morning's real agenda.

The focus now shifted to Marvin Kalish. It was remarkable, Dawn thought afterwards, how calm he had been under the combined, unflinching gazes of the four others at the table; Marvin somehow either failed to notice the degree to which he had become the center of attention or else he was so dazed by the obvious possibility that he was seated in the presence of his mother—his birth mother!—that nothing else really mattered.

At any rate, he answered as though the question were an entirely normal one that had been put to him under entirely normal circumstances. "I thought it was the guy at first," he said, "but then I thought I was wrong. Or rather I guess I decided I was probably wrong after Dawn was so sure the guy was her French teacher."

Now it was Detective Abernathy's turn to interrupt. "I thought you said that Dawn actually spoke to him and decided herself that the man *wasn't* her teacher."

"Well, that's true. She thought he was, but then he wasn't. I don't know—I guess I decided that if she was wrong, I was probably wrong too. He left right after that, I guess. I mean, I don't know when he left…"

Marvin was savvy enough to realize that the guy probably *was* the shooter, that he had make a serious error by not at least engaging him in conversation while he had him, and that the precise time the guy left Pho-Nee's was obviously going to be a question of great significance to the police investigation into the attempts on his life.

"…but he was finishing his meal when Dawn went over to his table and he was gone by the time we finished ours."

"How can you be sure he was finishing his meal?" A reasonable question from Lawrence Lazar.

"Well," Marvin explained, "he mistook Dawn for the waitress and asked her for more tea and some more fortune cookies. That sounds like dessert to me!"

As he mentioned her name, Marvin looked over to Dawn and thought suddenly how remarkably little like a waitress in a Chinese restaurant Dawn looked. The man *had* asked her for more tea and cookies, but it was suddenly as obvious to Marvin as it undoubtedly was to the detective and to everyone else that he couldn't possibly have really thought Dawn was a waitress.

The atmosphere in Investigation Room No. 3 had changed since the end of the detective's tale. A fly had stopped buzzing at the window.

The pale March sunlight was making the room quite warm and one by one the room's inhabitants had shed their jackets. A certain air of forced intimacy had somehow imposed itself as well—there could be no ignoring the fact that with the obvious exception of John Abernathy, the people in the room were going to remain linked for the rest of their lives.

The discussion ended inconclusively. Now that it was obvious that the man almost certainly *was* the shooter, it did seem foolish that

Marvin had failed to recognize him.

"Look," he said finally, "now that it's obvious I was right in the first place, I guess I look pretty dumb for missing the chance to get the guy picked up. But I didn't *realize* I was right. I've been seeing guys everywhere for weeks who I've thought have been the guy. I saw a guy in Alexander's the other day who I was sure was the shooter and the day before that I saw some little pool shark at the Cue Club that I wondered about. And a few days before that there was another guy I actually followed into the men's room at Ben's Delicatessen just to get a closer look at before I decided he wasn't the right one. None of those guys was the shooter, so I just assumed my imagination was getting the better of me in the restaurant as well—and when Dawn was all wrong about the guy, I figured, so okay—I must be too."

It was the longest speech Marvin had yet given and everyone paid attention. Bunny was interested in the degree to which Marvin continued to sound like her late father. The detective, on the other hand, was far more interested in the details concerning Marvin's continuing obsession with finding the assailant, while Lawrence Lazar and Dawn were primarily focused on watching the relationship between Bunny and her son unfold.

Finally, Lawrence Lazar's question answered, the room again fell silent. Her moment, Bunny realized, had come.

"So let's get this over with quickly," she said, her voice breaking with emotion. "May 2, 1953?" she choked out as she fixed her gaze directly into Marvin's eyes.

"Check," Marvin answered briefly.

"Birthmark the shape of Manhattan?"

"Where?"

"Foot."

"Which?"

"Left."

A lone tear slipped out of Bunny's left eye and made its way down her nose almost to the outer edge of the nostril before she wiped it away.

"Double check."

"No *bris*?" Dawn turned to Detective Abernathy and soundlessly, yet somehow dramatically mouthed the word 'circumcision' directly at him so he could fully appreciate the importance of Bunny's question.

"I guess not. At least not one my parents made." A tremble crept into Marvin's voice.

"Triple check," Bunny herself said, slipping into Marvin's own idiom.

Suddenly, her emotions broke loose. Tears began to flow down either side of Bunny Luft's powdered face, each making a shallow furrow along her well made-up cheeks. She sobbed and raised her hanky to her mouth. It was simply too much to believe that this had all happened so quickly and so effortlessly. It was, she realized suddenly, not even a month since the fateful Friday evening of the initial incident with the handbag aimed at Lawrence Lazar's head.

The temperature in the room seemed to rise. Marvin felt his own emotional dike crumbling against the oncoming tsunami of hope, regret, anger and need that seemed to be coming directly towards him from the direction of the woman seated before him whom he could now recognize as his mother.

"You gave me away," he said artlessly, his voice cracking in more places that he would have thought possible for a sentence composed of only five syllables.

Bunny said nothing. Marvin's five syllables, with all their implicit shame and uncomprehending sorrow and infused with the naturally pathetic force of any abandoned child's rage against his abandoner, still hung on the warm air of the investigation room as Bunny Luft rose from her seat and approached Marvin Kalish's chair.

To everyone's complete amazement, she stopped halfway between her chair and her son's and suddenly fell to her knees.

'She's really going to beg for forgiveness,' realized Lawrence Lazar with a shock.

Like a true supplicant, Bunny covered the final inches between herself and Marvin on her knees. The room was almost completely silent; the only sound at all was gentle scraping of her nylons as she advanced.

When she was directly before him, Bunny straightened and then, unexpectedly, threw her head into Marvin's lap. Now there was only her rhythmic sobbing punctuated at irregular intervals by words of muffled supplication.

It was, Marvin later told Dawn, the single oddest moment of his life, including both instances of having been shot at.

Bunny's teased hair mushroomed out against Marvin's stomach as she buried her head even deeper into his lap. Shocked by this melodramatic display of maternal regret, all Marvin could think of was how he would have to walk out of the station house with an enormous wet patch spreading across the front of his trousers where his mother—his mother!—had buried her dyed head while she shed her copious tears and moaned her mother's lament. The whole scene was moving and embarrassing at the same time; no one, least of all Marvin, felt at all comfortable, yet none of them would have dreamt of forcing Bunny Luft to her feet or prying her head from her son's lap.

Finally, the supplication was over. Without needing to be prompted or helped to her feet, Bunny stood up and returned to her seat. She had humbled herself before someone she had wronged. She was prepared to make whatever amends her son might think necessary and could do no more. Bunny Luft was finished.

Since no one knew at all what to say, Detective Abernathy decided to take back the floor. "Let's talk *takhlis*," he said.

"America goniff!" Bunny exclaimed in wonderment. "In Poland, a Jew had to learn sixteen languages if he wanted to buy a pair of shoes from a *goyish* store and here even the *shvartzes* speak Jewish!" Suddenly, Bunny regretted her remark: after all, this detective was personally responsible for her having located her son. Bunny Luft owed a debt of gratitude to John Abernathy and she knew it.

"Pardon my French," she said sweetly, turning for a moment to the black police officer. "It just slipped out," she added, confident that no one as refined as John Abernathy would ever hold somebody responsible for a tiny slip of the tongue when no offence was meant. Besides, Bunny told herself, you can be sure they say worse things about us when we're not listening than we say about them when they are!

"That's enough," the detective said abruptly.

"So okay, who's saying no? Enough it certainly is, probably more than enough even, so yes and by all means, Mr. Detective Abernathy, let's talk *takhlis*!"

The moment had now come to turn the discussion away from the identity of Marvin Kalish's birth mother and begin discussing the next issue at hand—the attempts that had been made against his life. Mrs. Luft and Mr. Kalish, Abernathy told himself, would have to work their relationship out at some other time and in a different place. Theirs was a personal issue; the matter at hand was a police matter and urgently required resolution if Kalish's life were to be safe.

"So," he said, turning to Marvin Kalish, "let's talk about the attempts on your life. Any idea who'd want to kill you?"

Marvin had obviously pondered this question a thousand times over the previous few weeks, but still he felt obliged to feign a moment's contemplation now that the question had been formally put to him.

"No," he said after an appropriate delay, "I don't have *any* idea who'd want to take me out. I mean, there are all sorts of lunatics out there..."

John Abernathy rolled his eyes towards the ceiling: he was the very last man in New York who needed to be told that the city was filled with crazies capable of taking offence at the least slight and then taking that offence to the most outrageous limits.

Just the previous December, Abernathy had been intimately involved in the search for a man who had attempted to plunge a kitchen knife into the chest of the fruit and vegetable man at the A & P on 108th Street because his wife had reported a mildly vulgar comment the unfortunate man had made once when she had been carrying two large cantaloupes close to her own ample chest. The assailant had eventually been found and charged, but the judge, who had himself snickered as the comment was reported by the defendant, had let him off with a stern warning and thirty-five hours of community service in a woman's health clinic.

"Still," Abernathy responded after a moment's thought, "this isn't about all sorts of lunatics. It's about one particular man and it isn't as bad as it could be..."

"Isn't as bad as it could be?" Marvin's voice rose with every successive syllable as he cut off the detective in mid-sentence. "This guy is trying to *kill* me!"

"Well, that isn't what I meant. And I'm not *that* sure that he is trying to kill you either, actually. I know you're probably too close to look at this calmly, but the guy has had two excellent chances—even if you don't consider the first attempt, then he certainly had an excellent chance at the grocery to kill you. He had a gun and you were unarmed. He had plenty of time to position himself, to aim and to fire. He knew there was no one at all in the store except the shopkeeper, you and Miss Kupchinsky. All he had to do was check the street for passers-by, draw his gun, release the safety and blow your brains out. We have to consider at least the possibility that the guy's motive, whatever it *is,* isn't just to take you out."

"What other motive could somebody possibly have for shooting someone, aside from murdering them?" This was Dawn's first question and it sprang from her mouth almost before she could hold it back.

"That's the obvious question, ma'am. And I didn't say that he *wasn't* trying to murder your fiancé. All I said is that the guy had two good chances and flubbed them both. It's important to consider that he may have had *some* other motive, even if I still don't have the faintest notion what it might be."

Detective Abernathy placed a slight, almost imperceptible emphasis on the word 'still'. Dawn and Lawrence Lazar seemed to have missed it entirely, but both Marvin and Bunny looked up towards the detective to acknowledge its hopeful implication and, as they did, their eyes met.

It lasted only a moment, but in that moment, Bunny Luft and Marvin Kalish understood that they were mother and son. Nothing more needed to be said; no blood tests or DNA tests or any kind of other tests were going to be needed. In a word, Bunny and Marvin *recognized* each other; without being able to say how they knew, they both knew.

The moment passed. Marvin turned to Detective Abernathy and asked a question. "What did you mean then?"

"What did I mean when?"

"What did you mean when you said that this isn't as bad as it could be? We sort of got side-tracked into discussing if it was even possible the guy had some motive other than selling me the farm when he shot at me. But before I misunderstood, you were saying that it wasn't as bad as it could be. What did you mean?"

John Abernathy looked closely at Marvin Kalish. The young man seated before him was not only good-looking, but he also had a certain charm that Abernathy felt was the real key to his success as a performer. His curly brown hair and his dark, Jewish eyes were ordinary and his full cheeks and slightly rounded jaw suggested health and plenty rather than greed or gluttony. He looked, the detective suddenly realized, like a young, slender Bunny Luft without make-up.

"I meant," he finally said, "that we could be a lot worse off in terms of where this investigation is going. For one thing, you've seen the assailant twice now and you actually recognized him once. It doesn't matter that you changed your mind—you were distracted probably by the fact that your fiancée…"

Abernathy stole a glance at Dawn's ringless left ring finger.

"…mistook the perp, I should say the alleged perp, for her high school French teacher. But what matters is that you did recognize him. And I'll be surprised if it eventually turns out that you were wrong.

"For another," Abernathy continued, "we can make some initial deductions based on what we already know."

"We don't know much." A certain acidulous quality to Bunny's observation failed to impress the detective, who was already thinking about what he already knew.

"But we do," he answered immediately. "We know this guy

– 112 –

knows where to find Marvin—he knew to look at the Styx and he knew to look at the Chinese restaurant and he knew to find him at the grocery. Okay, maybe he was just watching to see where Marvin would go after dinner, but he knew to be there at the restaurant *before* Marvin and Dawn arrived there; they both agree he was almost finished with his dinner when they were first being seated."

"Maybe it was a coincidence. Maybe he just happened to be having dinner there?"

"It was after midnight. Most elderly men who dine alone choose an earlier dinner hour. No," Abernathy concluded decisively, "the shooter was waiting for them in the restaurant. Why he didn't assault them there and why he chose to wait until the grocery, I don't know."

"He couldn't have known they'd go anywhere," Bunny now observed. "I mean, they could have called a cab from the restaurant and gotten into it and driven away. He may not have been planning to do anything!"

It was all true. But the fact that certain questions remained unanswered didn't mean that the police knew nothing at all. "Maybe not, but I don't think so," came Abernathy's slow, professional answer. "I think he was waiting and knew them well enough to know they'd cross the boulevard and wait for a cab at the bus stop. They both say that was their normal habit. He was probably planning to accost them there when they just happened into the grocery and gave him an even better chance."

"And what else do we know?" Bunny knew when to concede a point and move along.

"Well," Detective Abernathy said with only the vaguest hint of a grin, "unless the lady who accosted your husband in the synagogue a few weeks ago was clairvoyant, we can assume fairly safely that somebody somewhere in this city…"

Detective Abernathy turned to face Bunny Luft.

"…knew who Marvin Kalish's mother was long before any of you in this room did."

"Holy shit," Lawrence Lazar murmured, almost but not quite to himself.

"Amen," agreed Bunny, her eyes glazing over with new tears of frustration, anger and regret.

Marvin reached for Dawn Kupchinsky's hand as their eyes met briefly. "Ditto," he said.

Eleven

"*I*t's him."

"It's not him."

"It *is* him. Come look in the sunlight."

"I can look in whatever light you want, but it still isn't him. It doesn't even look like him…"

Bunny Luft's voice trailed off as she stepped, almost involuntarily, into the warm sunlight. The Lufts' kitchen was neat, as it always was early in the morning; Bunny Luft could live with the busy clutter of a busy day, as she herself liked to call it, but one of her basic principles nevertheless was never to have breakfast in a messy house. Consequently, she always sat down to her morning coffee in a tidy kitchen and the morning of Friday, the sixth of March, 1981, was no exception.

Even the white plastic drain board was empty of the clean dishes with which it had been overflowing the previous night. The countertops were clean and neat and the kitchen table, usually hidden beneath a mountain of advertising flyers, unread newspapers, bills, letters, shopping lists and scratched, valueless lottery tickets, was completely free of its usual busy clutter. The tiny brown granules of coffee that invariably covered the top of the counter after Lawrence Lazar measured out the Lufts' morning coffee had been swept away; gone too, even, were the tiny black granules of roach residue that littered the kitchen floor every single morning despite the exceptional number of roach motels secreted in every corner of the Lufts' apartment—this was traditionally the first of Bunny Luft's morning chores and her least favorite.

The modest kitchen was filled with the aroma of Lawrence Lazar's strong coffee as it percolated through the tin basket of his ancient percolator, the same one that had sat for all of his childhood years on his mother's stove. The familiar scent—strong, black coffee, acrid almost to the point of bitterness, had been a feature of the Lufts' morning ritual since the day they had returned from their honeymoon at Friedman's Hotel in Loch Sheldrake, New York—filled the room, calmed morning jitters and created a sense of shared purpose based on a lifetime of common practice.

As ever, Rabbi Weissbrot's little mirror lay face down on the white windowsill.

The March sunlight streamed through the tightly shut window; advance hints of imminent spring were everywhere in Queens, but, in many ways, it was still winter. The ladies, for example, who shopped along Sixty-Third Drive were still wearing their winter coats as they progressed along the street from shop to shop. But in MacDonald Park on Queens Boulevard just across from the Post Office, the tiny tops of crocus bulbs had already been spotted poking their tiny heads through the beds of loamy soil.

Passover was still more than six weeks off, and already the Jewish wives of Rego Park and Forest Hills were discussing how warm it would undoubtedly be for the paschal week. Years in which the festival came so late as to guarantee open windows and rolled-up shirt sleeves for the traditional *seder* meals were considered bonuses in the Jewish community, one of the rare perks to derive to the Jewish people from their relentless, pre-Copernican quest to cram their lunar year into a solar calendar without doing damage to the seasonal requirements of the various festivals of the Jewish year.

***

The meeting at the precinct house had left its indelible imprint on all who had attended it. After making his observation about the probable link between the incident at the Lufts' synagogue and the two murderous attempts against Marvin Kalish, Detective Abernathy considered his work done.

From a strictly methodological point of view, there was not too overwhelming a reason to have called the interested parties together in the first place. The detective could easily have arranged for someone to take all the pertinent statements separately and to draw up a handy cross-list of points at which they coincided and at which they diverged, but John Abernathy felt that there would be purpose in having a face-to-face meeting.

More than that, he wished to see how the four parties, and especially the two central personalities, might interact with each other. It wasn't entirely clear to him that the rumors which had circulated so freely after the first attempt on Kalish's life, rumors according to which the whole affair was some sort of elaborate publicity stunt, were necessarily completely untrue. Kalish seemed nice and forthright enough, but if Abernathy forced himself to ask himself the essential '*Cui bono?*'—the first rule of all police investigation being to know who stood to benefit from the crime under scrutiny—the only person he knew who stood to achieve anything by the attacks, at least insofar as they didn't result in his death, was Kalish himself.

Abernathy could easily see that the attacks had already worked their magic. In only three or four days since the second attack, there had been coverage in all the New York dailies, including *The Times*. Based on his past experience, Abernathy could predict that the story would begin to appear in the supermarket tabloids just as it would begin to fade from the legitimate press. Precisely what the angle would be was hard to guess, but the bottom line was that Marvin Kalish's name was going to appear in print for days, probably for weeks on end and he was going to be famous.

His act would prosper; he didn't have the stature to command top dollar, but his fame would still guarantee a full house of curious patrons and that would make all the difference. There would be guest spots on local talk shows and possibly an interview in *New York Magazine*. By the time the whole thing eventually blew over, and unless somebody really did murder Marvin Kalish, his career would flourish for as long as the comedian wished to play the comedy clubs of Queens County and possibly for far longer than that.

On the other hand, motive wasn't everything. The fact that Kalish was the only obvious beneficiary of all the fuss so far hardly meant he had staged phoney assaults against himself!

Before noon, Abernathy had already concluded that Kalish was probably not behind the assaults. He thanked everyone for coming and, gathering up his papers, left the room. His four guests had been obliged to sort out their luncheon plans on their own.

It had not been possible for any of the four simply to take leave of the others. Four lives had been changed in the course of the morning in a way that could never now be undone. Even an eventual discovery that Marvin was not Bunny Luft's son would not completely undo the effect this meeting had on its participants, but simply lessen its ultimate impact.

It was obviously necessary that they leave the precinct house; if they wished to remain together, it would have to be in some other place.

Someone suggested Pho-Nee's, of all places. It was a good fifteen-minute walk directly down Austin Street to Ascan and everybody was in need of a bit of fresh air before sitting down again in an enclosed room.

More because they felt they had to than because they actually wished it, Bunny and Marvin walked together a few paces before Lawrence Lazar and Dawn. In what was intended as a gesture of closeness, Bunny actually took her son's arm and leaned towards him slightly as she walked.

"So tell me about your parents," she half-said, half-asked as they walked briskly past the back of the Queens Hebrew Congregation.

Marvin had been expecting the question. He squinted in the bright March sunlight as though he were trying to read the names of the movies listed on the marquis of the Continental Theater, but this ruse bought him only a second or two of delay. He closed his right arm a bit more tightly around Bunny's as he formulated his answer. "Well, they're nice people, good people. The Kalishes, I mean," he added nervously. "The Kalishes are good, nice people. They raised me in a traditional, decent home. We only had kosher meat, even if we only had one set of dishes, and I went to Hebrew School my whole life. Until I was bar mitzvah'ed I mean, that's when I went to the school until. I mean, until then…"

Even though Marvin's voice had trailed off into grammatical impossibility, Bunny knew better than to interrupt, but eventually her curiosity was simply too great. "I'm glad they were—are!—good people. What are their names?"

Marvin hesitated, then relented. How could he *not* tell his birth mother the names of his adoptive parents? "Alice and Ike," he said finally, simply.

"Alice and Ike Kalish?"

"That's them. My parents. Alice and Ike."

Suddenly a thought appeared to dawn on Marvin. "Look," he said, squeezing Bunny's arm even more tightly, "you understand that whatever role you end up playing in my life, my mom is still my mother. I mean, I don't know what you are—I mean, I know, but I don't know exactly what to make of it all—but whatever you are, she's my mother. If we're going to have anything between us, you've got to understand that."

Marvin knew he should leave it at that, but he felt somehow unable to hold anything back now that he had started to speak. "She'll want to meet you, you know. I mean, they've both been worried sick about the attacks. I promised I'd phone them as soon as this morning

– 117 –

was over, but they certainly aren't expecting me to tell them you've appeared, not you personally, but my real mother. I mean, she's my real mother. You are my..."

Marvin searched for the right word. "I don't know what you are. My biological mother, I guess. Birth mother is the term the detective used. That suits me, if it's okay with you—you can be my birth mother, but that doesn't make you my mom," Marvin added piously. "My mom," he concluded as the couple approached the corner of Continental Avenue, "is my mom."

Bunny leaned her head over towards Marvin as they crossed the avenue. "I don't want to take your mother's place," she said quietly. "But whatever I am to you, I need to know you forgive me for giving you up."

It was such a simple statement. Marvin knew as soon as the words were out of Bunny's mouth that he had been crazy not to have anticipated it, but the truth was that he *hadn't* expected to be asked outright to grant absolution.

In the few moments he had had to think at all about this turn of events, he had half-expected it would simply be necessary for him to find some corner of his life for his birth mother to occupy and that act itself would constitute the forgiveness Bunny needed to feel she had been granted.

But this outright request was something else entirely! To be asked to say the words was fine, but actually to mean that there remained no bitterness over having been dumped on the doorstep of some municipal agency to be farmed out to the infertile family at the top of that week's list—that was a kind of absolution Marvin Kalish did not feel certain he could give even if he *were* inclined.

***

The Kalishes were different parents to Marvin than the Lufts would have been. Marvin's father, Isaac, had been born in 1910 in Minsk into a family that was deeply observant without being particularly religious. Unlike his parents and all but one of his sisters, young Isaac (then Yitzchok, later Ike) had somehow understood that there was no future for the Jews of Byelorussia and had managed to sail out of Danzig for New York in 1928 at the age of eighteen. He never saw his parents or any of his brothers again; all were among the 25,000

Jews shot by the S.S. and their Byelorussian cohorts over the course of three days at the end of July, 1942.

By the time, however, his parents and brothers were being herded into the newly prepared execution pit on Ratomskaya Street right beside the one in which the children from the ghetto orphanage had been murdered the previous March, Ike Kalish was already a well-established New York businessman. A tailor by trade, Kalish had somehow managed to build his skill into a business that manufactured uniforms of various sorts, including the standard nurse's uniform in use in twenty-five New York area hospitals and the fireman's uniform used in Yonkers.

Even by native-born standards, Ike Kalish had become a successful, wealthy man, but in the refugee community, he was considered a titan. As he was always ready to hire another greenhorn in one of his nine factories, the word was out on the street that Ike Kalish was the ticket to ride for Jewish immigrants newly escaped from the Nazi cauldron that Europe was fast becoming.

On his thirtieth birthday, Ike Kalish married Alice Dunckelman. She was a real American, the ultimate prize for any greenhorn, no matter how well established and no matter how wealthy.

Born in Philadelphia to parents who themselves had come to North America as infants, Alice Dunckelman was as American as apple pie. She had red cheeks and high, aristocratic cheekbones, dark Jewish eyes and two rows of straight, white teeth. Her English was unaccented and entirely natural; she understood only a bit of Yiddish, which she recalled fondly from her grandparents' home, and could hardly speak a single word. Most of all, she had the refinement and ease of presence of which immigrants to any country can only dream.

They met at a Young Democrats' dance and were married twelve weeks later. The bride's family made a wonderful wedding at the Waldorf and objected when Ike insisted on paying for at least some of the cost. They countered, logically, that since he was only inviting one single table's worth of guests composed only of his sister, her husband and four or five friends from his B'nai Brith lodge, it was unreasonable for him to pay for half the wedding.

Ike's generous rejoinder—that he was half of the wedding couple and would therefore gladly accept half the bill—was received with gratitude tinged with relief and seasoned with just the faintest hint of resentment. The deal was struck and the wedding went off without a hitch.

The years passed. In 1941, both of Alice Dunckelman Kalish's parents were killed in a freak accident involving a trolley car that lost its brakes on Second Avenue just north of Sixty-first Street.

In 1942, of course, Ike Kalish's parents and brothers were murdered by the Germans and their Byelorussian collaborators. Ike was frantic with worry about his family, but as no mail at all was going in or out of the parts of the Soviet Union occupied by the Nazis, there did not seem to be much to do one way or the other. Phone contact was also impossible and there was no consulate or embassy to which one might address a request for information. The Soviet embassy in Washington merely sent a brief form letter to any who requested it stating that the government was not in control in the specific part of the Soviet Union the writer had mentioned in his or her letter and that, therefore, no information on the fate of individual civilians was available.

Ike had phoned the embassy shortly thereafter and, using the name of a well-placed senator whose brother owed him $15,000, had managed to gain access to the vice-consul in charge of dealing with the American public. He had finally agreed to take Ike's call but warned him that the price for frankness would have to be discretion: all comments were off the record and would be denied should they be thrown back in his face. "My advice to you," Vice-Consul Golyadkin said, "is to kiss them good-bye. If the Germans haven't shot them yet, then it would only be because they were able to deport them first. And deportation means death in one of the extermination camps anyway, so don't pin your hopes there. If they're still alive, it's only because they haven't been murdered yet," the emotionless voice told Ike.

"Isn't there anything I can do?" Ike had asked, dizzy with horror and disbelief, yet strangely reluctant to end the conversation.

"No, there isn't," came the immediate response. "Nothing at all."

Ike had hung up and had simply sat staring at the phone for long minutes while he tried to digest the information he had received. If only, he told himself, he could get this information to Roosevelt...

In the meantime, the Kalishes were hard at work trying to produce the children that would have to function as Ike's memorial to his murdered family. Although Alice Dunckelman had been significantly less experienced in intimate matters than her emigré husband—in the Dunckelmans' Yankee circles, a refugee with money was politely known as an emigré—she had been a fast learner. By the time their third anniversary came around in the summer of 1943, Ike had begun to wonder if something hadn't gone awry; by the summer of 1944, both Alice and Ike knew that something wasn't quite right.

The medical treatment of infertility in the mid-1940's was rudimentary when compared to the medical standards that would prevail even ten years later, and positively primitive in comparison to the techniques science would develop within two and three decades.

The long trek to various specialists commenced in the fall of 1944. As the Allied armies spread across France and prepared for the final assault against Germany, Alice Dunckelman Kalish mounted her own assault against her body's refusal to conceive a child. She spent time in dozens of doctors' offices and was admitted to hospital no less than seven times in the course of eighteen months to have various procedures attempted on her recalcitrant ovaries. Nothing helped.

The simple fact of the matter—that Alice's ovaries functioned perfectly and that she was not conceiving because of a problem of her husband's—was something both she and he were probably the better off for not fully realizing.

To his credit, Ike Kalish stood by his wife. Not once in the course of her treatments and tests did he suggest ending the marriage were it ever to become clear that they simply could not produce children.

The dramatic moment both Kalishes had been trained by Hollywood to expect—the book-lined medical study, the understanding doctor with a deep, sympathetic voice and a spotless white coat, the gentle but firm nurse waiting in the wings with strong tea and great doses of female sympathy—never came. Instead, the truth slowly began to dawn on the couple as the tests became fewer, the list of specialists remaining to consult grew shorter and the rich dollops of hope with which most of the doctors consulted had topped off their analyses of the situation grew less rich and less encouraging.

Eventually, the Kalishes understood that they would not produce children in the normal way. They began to list themselves with adoption agencies, particularly those known to specialize in the placement of Jewish babies, and even made discreet 'gifts' to a few of them.

It was slow going at first, but eventually the Kalishes hit upon an official whom they were able to impress both with their goodness and their decency and also with their willingness to honor faithful, discreet service with undeclared, untraceable gifts of hard cash. At first, Harry Emden had played hard to get, pretending to scorn Ike Kalish's generous gifts as bribes beneath contempt.

A complicated drama had ensued, as Ike was repeatedly obliged to apologize for having insulted the integrity of an honest public servant at the same time he was upping the ante to a new offer that Emden would find less of an insult. The drama continued for some months and finally took over a year; then, in the spring of 1948 an envelope filled with fifty worn twenty-dollar bills found its way onto the top shelf of Harry Emden's linen closet and a baby appeared in the files of the James Walker Agency that would be, in Emden's own words, "just perfect for the Kalishes."

The little baby, a boy only ten days old, was formally adopted by the Kalishes in April, 1948. In honor of the new Jewish state about to be proclaimed in Palestine, the Kalishes named their baby Israel. He flourished in his new home until he died of meningitis in the summer of 1952.

Alice Kalish almost died as well in the wake of her son's death, her life's purpose taken from her and her desire to live reduced to dust.

"No one can replace my baby," Alice had screamed at her husband when he first suggested that they attempt to adopt another child.

"No one ever will," he had offered as consolation. But he knew that a new baby would restore a sense of purpose to his wife's existence even if it could ever replace their missing son.

Within a few months of Israel's death, the Kalishes found themselves back in the recently retired Harry Emden's office, now occupied by one Yudel Wolfzahn. The James Walker Agency, now renamed The Peter Stuyvesant Agency in honor of one of New York's great Dutch founders, had flourished in the post-war years as New York was flooded with hundreds of thousands of older refugees who had lost their families in the Nazi debacle. The demand for healthy babies was intense and showed no particular signs of letting up; the size of the gift necessary to secure a space at the top of the perspective parents' list had risen, Ike Kalish learned to his considerable dismay, from one to three thousand dollars.

It wasn't the sum itself that disturbed Ike Kalish—in the years since he had arranged Israel's adoption he had gone from merely successful to truly wealthy—as much as the notion that he was buying for himself and his wife what others, whose suffering was as indescribable as their own, could simply not afford for themselves. These thoughts troubled Ike Kalish, but he learned not to share them with Alice even in private moments.

"You make it sound like we're buying a baby," she said in horror to her husband when he broached the reasons he hated dealing with Yudel Wolfzahn.

"What else would you call it?" Ike had asked his wife, not yet aware of the degree to which Alice had managed to insulate herself from the realities of the transaction.

The scene that had ensued stayed with Ike Kalish for the rest of his life. The crying, the wailing, the denial—it was all part, he suddenly realized, of his wife's need to forget the precise details of Israel's adoption lest she somehow come to think of him as a commodity that could be replaced. Ike Kalish never brought up the topic again; all subsequent dealings with Wolfzahn were undertaken in private and by himself.

In May, 1953, Yudel Wolfzahn phoned Ike Kalish on his private line at the office.

"I've got a baby for you if you're still interested," he said coyly.

"If we're interested?" Kalish could hardly believe his ears. "You bet we're interested! It's a healthy baby?"

"Healthy? Would I even call if the baby wasn't healthy? This baby is as good as they come—three *hundred* thousand bucks couldn't buy such good health," he declared artfully.

Ike was appalled at hearing the deal put so bluntly; he too wished to deny the reality surrounding the situation. But his desire to deny was nowhere near as strong as his desire to acquire the child. "The mother is well?" he asked no less artfully as he delicately appeared to ignore Wolfzahn's own remark.

"Healthy! Healthy and well!," Wolfzahn had replied immediately, understanding the question as well as Kalish had understood his own remark. "A fine girl, a strapping, healthy-as-a-horse *maidel*," he continued, his subtle Yiddish flourish as clear an answer to Kalish's unstated question as could be offered on a public telephone line.

"And when will the baby be available for adoption?"

"When?" Wolfzahn responded immediately, the delicate negotiations now behind him. "Right now! The baby is still in the hospital with its mother, but she is prepared to give it up as soon as an adoption can be arranged. She's a good girl," Wolfzahn added. "A fine girl from a good family!"

Kalish needed one final piece of information. "So if she's so fine and so good, how come she needs to give up her baby?" he asked bluntly.

"She got knocked up," came the simple answer.

The deal was done; the arrangements were made. On Monday morning, the eleventh of May, Ike and Alice Kalish left the Klingenstein Pavilion of Mount Sinai Hospital carrying their new son and stepped out onto New York's fashionable fifth Avenue. A car was waiting to take them home.

Alice had wanted to call the baby Israel in memory of his late brother, but Ike had objected. "Too ghoulish," he said frankly. "How about Marvin?"

"Marvin?" Alice had responded. "After who?"

"After no one," Ike explained patiently. "He'll be his own man and he'll have his own name."

Alice was too relieved and too tired to oppose her husband's wishes. By the time the hired car pulled up to the Kalish's home on suburban 112th Street in Forest Hills' best Jewish area, Marvin Kalish was fast asleep.

"We'll give him a Jewish name at the *bris*," Alice Kalish whispered to her husband as she snuggled the baby close to her breast while they were still standing on the sidewalk watching the car pull away.

Ike, who had forgotten to share one particular detail with his wife, was obliged to turn to her and to tell her what he had previously omitted. "Well," he said, "there's something I meant to tell you about having a *bris*…"

***

"I forgive you," Marvin said to his birth mother as they made their slow progress down Austin Street.

Now that he had said it, Bunny didn't much like how it sounded. On the one hand, it was she who had asked for his forgiveness. She had conceived him and carried him to parturition and then given him up to whomever the Stuyvesant Agency concluded would be the best family to raise him. In other words, she had abandoned him to his fate and contented herself with hoping for the best as far as the rest of his life was concerned. She felt guilt, she had asked for forgiveness and it had been granted.

But now that it *had* been granted, it sounded quite different to Bunny's sensitive ears. She had felt guilty, but Marvin Kalish's simple sentence sounded like more of an indictment than she had meant to elicit. 'I forgive you' was the obvious answer to her question, but it revealed in its four short syllables more about the situation than Bunny had wished to admit; she was chagrined to contemplate the harsh, stark way her son's sentence rang in her guilty ears.

Bunny grasped her son's arm all the more tightly, happier than ever that she had had the foresight not to invite Joyce or Jeffrey along to witness her reunion with their half-brother. She was about to steer the conversation into some less dark terrain when a single shot rang out from the general direction of the Farmstead Delicatessen.

Twelve

Detective Abernathy took the 9-1-1 relay call himself and was on the scene less than ten minutes after the shot rang out. He was impressed with how well the system had functioned—he arrived only minutes after the ambulance pulled up—but it was already too late; the gunman was gone!

Lawrence Lazar and Dawn Kupchinsky had been walking together about twenty-five paces or so behind Bunny and Marvin; they had been feeling at peace and increasingly relaxed in each other's company when the single shot had been fired.

There had been other pedestrians strolling along the street, but most had fled the scene even as the report was still reverberating in their ears. Some had feared for their safety or the safety of their children, but most had simply fled automatically as part of their general inclination to avoid involvement in other people's matters whenever possible.

By the time John Abernathy and his team arrived, the only people left to question were the four principals, from whom Abernathy had taken his leave less than an hour earlier, and the staff of the Farmstead plus the handful of customers who had been too slow to escape before the police arrived.

The taking down of witnesses' statements was delegated to some of Abernathy's officers as the detective himself looked around the empty street. Police barricades had been temporarily set up and a policewoman had been stationed on the corner of Continental Avenue to direct eastbound traffic on Austin Street either north to Queens Boulevard or a block south to Burns Street. Abernathy himself moved slowly across the street looking for anything he might find as he waited for the photography crew to arrive; as soon as the call had come in, he had suddenly awakened to the fact that he was in the middle of an investigation which he had been treating, he now felt, far too casually.

The witnesses all agreed that the shot had come from the elegant gourmet shop. Marvin and Bunny had been standing directly across the street from the shop and the bullet, which had missed Marvin's head by at least a foot, had ended up shattering the large show window of the clothing store in front of which he and Bunny had been walking when the shot rang out. The spent bullet had already been found lodged in the molding between the rear wall of the store and the ceiling. The apparent trajectory indicated that the shot had been fired from directly across the street.

In the Farmstead, no one had seen anything at all. The shop had been crowded with morning customers who were obliged to take numbers upon entering to guarantee that the first come were indeed the first served. Because there were only four or five countermen on duty, there had been a large number of patrons simply milling around in the shop waiting for their numbers to be called, looking at the displays and deciding what to purchase. None of the few who remained to be questioned could recall anyone unusual or suspicious in the shop.

Abernathy himself tried out Marvin's description of the man he had thought was the shooter the previous Saturday evening at Pho-Nee's on several of the customers, but to no avail—the description of a little man with a Jewish hat and an overcoat matched at least sixty-five percent of the neighborhood men and could hardly lead to any firm identification. In fact, several of the few patrons left in the shop when the police arrived themselves fit Marvin's description of the man who had shot at him at the Styx and in the Korean grocery. If the shooter was going to be apprehended, it was clear from the onset that a more precise description, perhaps accompanied by an Identikit picture, was going to be necessary.

No harm had come to the Farmstead's front window, so if the bullet was indeed fired from those premises, then it must have been fired through the open door. That much, at least, seemed certain. According to this scenario, the man had apparently simply walked up to the open door, took aim, fired and left. By the time the people in the shop realized the shot was *not* the sound of a car backfiring, the little man was long gone.

Eventually, the forensic squad arrived. They took their pictures, dusted the front door of the Farmstead for fingerprints, used fancy instruments to measure the trajectory the bullet would have had to follow to land where it did and carried away various little plastic envelopes containing samples of dust, fibers, hair and other common materials taken from the site of the crime.

While all this took place, Marvin, Dawn, Bunny and Lawrence Lazar waited safely inside a police van.

Marvin was strangely silent; he seemed lost in thought rather than terrified at the possibility that someone might eventually succeed in killing him.

Dawn, for her part, was scared enough for them both and could only imagine the day when the shooter wouldn't miss. The detective's theory that the motive of the shootings might prove to be something other than her boyfriend's murder was comforting but now appeared weak and speculative.

Bunny was in a mild state of shock; she had never been in the presence of anyone who had been shot at before. Her thoughts, perhaps as a defense against dealing with the horror of the experience, kept reverting to the Friday evening encounter in the synagogue. Had it been only a month earlier that that strange lady with the large purse had knocked Lawrence Lazar in the head and announced that Bunny's son was in some sort of danger?

Bunny, who had considered that mysterious lady's words hundred of times in the previous four weeks, found to her amazement that she could no longer recall with certainty exactly what the woman had said. But what did it matter now, she asked herself. Somehow, in only four weeks she had come from being seated in her synagogue to being seated in a mobile police van across from her baby, her beloved baby whom she hadn't seen for twenty-seven years and who had forgiven her for the sin of having given him away.

Lawrence Lazar was deep in his own thoughts, lost in regret at ever having allowed the situation to get this far and more than aware that it was precisely events like this one that cemented people to each other forever. It was his unavoidable conclusion that he was going to have Marvin Kalish and Dawn Kupchinsky as part of his family's social entourage for the rest of his life. He felt unhappy, but resigned; Bunny *had*, after all, been entirely open with him. He could still recall how she had told him about her child almost immediately after he proposed marriage, thereby offering him a polite opportunity to withdraw the offer once he knew what kind of a woman he was proposing to marry.

He had told her then that the incident didn't matter to him and he had been totally honest; it hadn't mattered a whit! But that was when he had been merely required to accept that his beloved Bunny had made an error of judgment for which she had had to pay a horrible price and there had not been any real baby waiting in the wings to step into their lives and affect their relationship with each other or with their own children.

And then, the door to the van opened and they were told they were free to go.

"Just like that?" Bunny's voice rang with skepticism and incredulity.

"Why not just like that?" The detective was obviously irritated that his men had failed to turn up any meaningful clues to the assailant's identity.

"I mean, don't we all have to do something?"

"Something?"

"Give statements or be fingerprinted or pick people out of a line-up?"

Abernathy was visibly annoyed. "This isn't a television show, ma'am," he said brusquely. "You've given your statements, the street is clear and safe, none of you is a suspect and you are free to go." The detective emphasized his last three syllables just enough to lend them an air of implicit menace. "I'll be in touch when there are further developments," he added.

"Well, that's just wonderful," Bunny countered, the sarcasm thick on her tongue. "If someone shoots my boy again, I'll give you a buzz."

"You do that."

"I will."

"Good."

Now it was Lawrence Lazar's turn. "What is this—a schoolyard? Behave like adults, both of you! You're both on the same side, you know. Not that any outside observer would think so."

Lawrence Lazar's remarks had a calming effect on both Bunny and John Abernathy. The detective stuck his hands between his belt and the top of his trousers and muttered a brief apology. Bunny too offered a few gracious words of regret for having spoken rashly.

All that done, the four stepped out of the police van onto the south side of Austin Street. For a moment, no one seemed certain what to do. It was already just a few minutes before two o'clock.

"Look," Bunny said easily as the four stood on the sidewalk contemplating their next move, "it's too late for lunch."

"Never too late," Lawrence Lazar muttered to himself.

"Well, it's too late for me," Bunny responded as though the remark had been uttered solely to solicit her reaction. "I have to get home soon and start thinking about dinner and I don't have the stomach now for a fancy meal." Bunny turned to Marvin and Dawn.

"Listen, why don't you come to our home this Friday night? We'll skip synagogue—going to *shul* is what got us into all of this trouble in the first place—and we'll have a relaxed dinner where we can all talk without anyone getting shot at or having to hurry on to his next assignment."

Bunny extended her fleshy arms to Marvin and Dawn, who were standing together just in front of the shop window that had been destroyed by the bullet aimed at Marvin's head. A man and a boy were standing in the window at that very moment using pieces of cardboard to cover the space left by the shattered pane.

"So how about it? And I'd like you to bring your parents too!" The word 'parents' stuck for a brief moment in Bunny's throat, but she managed to dislodge it effectively almost before anyone could notice her difficulty in getting the word out.

"My parents?" Marvin was nonplussed, to say the least.

"Yes, of course your parents. Who else's parents would I want to invite? I'm not trying to take your mother's place—I gave you my word before on that—but I want to meet her, and your father too."

Marvin was still amazed. "Why?" he asked simply.

"Because I want you to be part of my life," Bunny answered frankly, shielding her eyes in the sudden glare of the March sunlight. "And there will always be something strange, something odd about *our* relationship if it plays itself out against a background of missing people. If I know your parents and if they know me, our way will be clear to know each other without feeling like you are somehow betraying them by having some sort of relationship with me." It was a complicated train of thought, but Bunny felt she had expressed herself adequately. She wanted to bring the Kalishes into the picture so she could feel free to ignore them thereafter. Having said her piece, Bunny waited politely to hear her son's response.

Marvin looked at Dawn and wondered what to say. It was unthinkable that he would simply part from his birth mother with no further plans for contact and yet the very idea of dining with his own parents at the Lufts' was somehow unsettling. The Kalishes were, for one thing, significantly older than the Lufts—Ike Kalish was seventy-one years old in 1981 and Alice only a year younger, while Lawrence was sixty-one years old and Bunny a youthful fifty-one. Alice Kalish would look more like Marvin's grandmother than his mother—which she was easily old enough to be and which was precisely what Marvin feared Bunny was hoping would turn out to be the case. Even Ike Kalish was going to play into what Marvin feared was Bunny's fantasy—despite his robust good health, Ike looked his years and thus cast his own shadow on Alice's diligent efforts to look less than her actual age.

As the silence following Bunny's invitation grew embarrassingly long, Dawn jumped in to respond. "We'd love to come," she said politely. "Wouldn't we?" she asked in Marvin's general direction.

"Love to," he said succinctly and in a voice soft enough to suggest ambivalence without appearing rude or ungrateful.

"Then it's settled," Bunny announced with polite finality. "We'll see you Friday night. We're in the book. Come around seven-thirty and by all means, bring the Kalishes. I'll make sure my own kids are there too and we'll all get to know each other."

The prospect of the Luft children encountering the Kalish parents was simply too much for Marvin to fathom all at once. Possessed of an overwhelming desire to flee, he took Dawn's hand so forcefully that her shoulder bag slipped along her arm into the crook of her elbow and he began to tug her along the street back in the direction from which they had come.

"See you Friday," he called over his shoulder, anxious to disappear before there could be any more surprises. For the first time since the shooting, he felt a bit afraid that someday someone might actually kill him.

***

Yudel Wolfzahn burst into the kitchen as Clara was cutting up russet potatoes and a large yellow rutabaga into tiny pieces on her best *milichdig* cutting board. She intended to boil them until they were soft, then mash them up, cover them with a mixture of grated romano and cheddar cheese, bread crumbs and butter and bake the mixture in her oven until a thick, crispy crust formed on top. It was Yudel's favorite dish and, for once, she felt he had earned the effort it took for her to cut up the pieces of rutabaga and potato necessary to prepare it.

"You're back."

"Obviously."

"How'd it go?"

"Like clockwork. There's really nothing to it, you know. Nobody looks at anyone anymore—and the few people who may have actually seen something ran like bunny rabbits once they realized the police would want them to give statements."

"They were easy to spot?"

"The simplest. I waited in front of the precinct until they came out, then I doubled around and drove down Queens Boulevard and parked. I was window shopping on Austin Street before they were even a block from the station house. Then all I had to do was wait in the shop and watch for them. The mother was walking with him in front, just like you said she would, and all I had to do was stand there until the right moment. When they were directly across the street, I took out the gun, aimed and fired."

"And no one saw?"

"Who knows if anyone saw? I tried to hide the gun until the very last minute, but it didn't really much matter; by the time the people in the shop realized that a shot had even been fired, the gun was back in my coat and I was out on the street. I could hear the yelling and the excitement, but I just took my place in the flow of witnesses running away from the scene of the crime. I even ran a little too, but just enough to fit in with everyone else. One old lady even stopped me to ask if I saw what happened."

"And you said?"

"What do you think I said? I told her I hadn't seen a thing."

"And then? You took a while getting home."

"Well, I didn't want to look suspicious so I went into Swirsky's and bought some chopped meat." Yudel fished around in the bottom of his plastic shopping bag and produced two neatly wrapped brown paper parcels.

"We have." A note of quiet exasperation in Clara's voice; when she really did need Yudel to go out for something, he always had an excuse why it wasn't the right moment.

"So now we have more. Make hamburgers for lunch and we'll have as much as we had before I bought."

"I'm making *milichdigs*," Clara explained regretfully. She had already begun to prepare a dairy meal and could not, therefore, put any meat on her table. The Wolfzahns were careless in some areas of Jewish observance, but not having a strictly kosher kitchen was a laxness that Clara could not even begin to contemplate.

"So for dinner."

"Okay then," she answered agreeably, "for dinner. I'll buy some beer when I go out later on." Clara knew that Yudel liked his hamburgers covered with fried onions and washed down with cold Miller's beer.

Suddenly a new thought dawned on Clara. "You missed," she said.

"You're asking or you're telling?"

"I'm asking."

"So then I'm telling. I missed."

"By a lot?" It was as important that it appear that Yudel was really trying to murder Marvin Kalish as it was that he not actually end up shooting him.

"No, not by a lot a lot. But by enough—enough to shatter the front window of The Gap to smithereens."

"There's nothing in there for anyone over nineteen anyway."

"Even so—I hate destroying property when I don't have to. I mean, I don't even know who owns the shop." Yudel Wolfzahn's memories reverted momentarily to his parent's linen shop on the Rothenbaumchaussee in pre-war Hamburg. The memory of Nazi thugs smashing the shop's windows on *Kristallnacht* in 1938 and painting enormous white swastikas across the sidewalk just in front of the main entrance was bad enough, but the recollection that had made an even greater impression on Yudel had been the sight of middle-class matrons calmly reaching through the broken glass the following morning and helping themselves to whatever goods they could reach without tearing their woolen dresses on the broken glass. It had only been three weeks later that Yudel left his homeland and sailed to New York on the *S.S. Manhattan*; the vivid picture of his parents' neighbors politely waiting their turn to steal without having to jostle each other in the vicinity of so much broken glass was Yudel's final image of life in Germany. He had never forgotten.

"That's very nice—but here you had to." Clara had come to recognize the look in her husband's eyes when his thoughts returned to his life in Germany and its bitter closing chapters. Pointing out that Yudel was among the very luckiest of German Jews would hardly have been a helpful remark, but she felt obliged to say something to soothe her husband's tortured conscience. "I mean," she said, "you had to aim somewhere..." Clara's voice trailed off as she considered briefly the implication of her observation. Yudel did have to shoot somewhere and certainly the upper portion of a shop window was safer than just shooting at random into the air. And this way, Clara reminded herself, it would at least look as though he had really been aiming for Marvin Kalish and had merely pointed his weapon too high.

Clara could tell easily from the distant look that had crept over Yudel's face that her husband was deep inside his own fantasy world of Nazis and Jews. Having in any event nothing further to say, she fell silent and turned back to her casserole.

The enchanting, deeply evocative smell of baked turnips and toasted bread crumbs filled the tiny kitchen and worked its magic even on Yudel Wolfzahn's troubled soul. Feeling comforted even without realizing that it was the odor of his lunch rather than his own inner fortitude that was gently urging him out of his deepening depression, Yudel sat down at the kitchen table.

Wordlessly, Clara served her husband his lunch. He had tossed his overcoat on the armchair just inside the front door with the shotgun still inserted into its sleeve when he had come in, but he now thought better of it and retrieved the gun. Propping it up in the corner of the kitchen just behind his chair, he leaned over to inhale the fragrance of his lost childhood. For just a brief moment, he felt his mother's presence in his home.

"It smells wonderful," he said quietly, as though to underscore the rich satisfaction with which he was lifting the fork to his small mouth.

"So she's sought him and she's found him and she's saved him. That's it, isn't it?" Clara hated to spoil her husband's reverie, but she suddenly felt an overwhelming need to know exactly where they stood. She had an appointment with the dentist down the street at three o'clock and felt she would like to spend the time in Dr. Danziger's chair musing privately about her husband's strange relationship with the people he had shot at only an hour or so earlier.

"Well," Yudel answered, suddenly yanked out of his mother's kitchen and back to reality by the blunt question, "she hasn't *exactly* saved him. But we are close, I'll grant you that. Next time, she'll save him. If she had thrown him down to the street after the shot, I would have shot a second time and that would have done the trick."

"She didn't throw him down?" Clara certainly would have thrown her Sid to the ground and flung her frail body over him had anyone shot at him!

"She just froze. So there was no point to shooting again and I just left. The chopped meat tells the rest of the story!"

"So the next time she'll save him. Then what? You tell them the whole story?"

Yudel Wolfzahn looked at his wife in bemused amazement. "No," he said, "I don't just tell them the story. I don't want to end up in jail and who knows how they'll take the whole thing."

"So if you don't tell them, how do they find out?"

Yudel looked at his wife and opened his eyes wide. "I don't know," he admitted. "I mean, I left her that booklet with a good picture of the fresco from the Christian part of the catacomb. If that doesn't pique her interest, nothing will. I think that part of it has to be that she figures out for herself who she is in all of this."

"And who he is."

"And who he is."

Clara sat down at her kitchen table and poured herself a steaming cup of her own rich coffee. "Drink the coffee before it gets cold," she commanded limply, hardly bothering to invest her words with any force at all.

***

The days of the week passed slowly for Bunny Luft; by Wednesday, all that was keeping her going was the knowledge that on Friday evening, she and Lawrence Lazar would be joined at their Sabbath table not only by Jeffrey and Joyce, but also by Marvin, Dawn Kupchinsky and Alice and Ike Kalish. Eight was the perfect number for dinner, Bunny often thought. But could this eightsome get along and enjoy each other's company? That was a question to which Bunny could hardly even begin to guess the answer.

To avoid dealing with the larger questions at hand, Bunny buried herself in decisions concerning her menu.

Obviously, it would have to be a traditional Sabbath meal; that at least, Bunny felt, could be counted upon not to offend anybody before the meal would even begin. She began to shop as early as Wednesday afternoon, choosing four plump chickens from the fresh cooler at Lazar's Kosher Meat Mart and taking it by rote from there. There would be the usual trimmings that would grace any Sabbath table, but there would also be exceptions, home-made surprises calculated to impress upon Mother Kalish and the others that Bunny Falk Luft may have once been a flighty secretary who got herself knocked up, but that she had since then become an accomplished Jewish wife, a *baleboosta* in the choicest sense of that untranslatable word.

By Thursday afternoon, Bunny had already made the spicy garlic *pshcha*—her mother had always called it *fees* after its main ingredient which was, indeed, calves' foot jelly, but Bunny had opted years earlier to call the much-savored dish by its more elegant name—she would serve as her appetizer. Lawrence Lazar had wondered if everyone would like such a pungent dish, but his query had fallen on determined ears.

"Who ever heard of a Jew who didn't like *pshcha*?" Bunny had asked in total innocence, whereupon Lawrence Lazar understood the wisdom of dropping the question entirely.

Friday morning would be given over to the baking of the two traditional *challah* loaves over which Lawrence Lazar would invite Father Kalish to recite the ancient benediction and to the preparation of the carrot *tsimmes*, for which Bunny had bought an extra half-pound of blanched almonds and a full sixteen-ounce jug of Daum's honey which everyone said was the very best on the market. The chickens themselves would be roasted in the late afternoon, their completion timed precisely to coincide with the onset of the Sabbath.

Naturally, the *pièce de résistance* would be the soup and this too Bunny intended to create on Friday. Normally, one chicken made one pot of soup. But this being a special evening and Bunny so terribly wanting to put her best foot forward, she had allowed herself the luxury of using a second chicken—hence the total of four Bunny had purchased Wednesday at Lazar's. By eight in the morning, the soup was already begun and the parsnips, celery, carrots and parsley were waiting to attain room temperature in open Tupperware boxes taken from the top shelf of the Lufts' refrigerator an hour earlier before their eventual insertion into the bubbling, golden pot.

The drain board was clean and the kitchen itself was entirely spotless except for the few grains of coffee Lawrence Lazar had spilled when he had prepared his special blend of strong, rich coffee.

Bunny was looking lazily out the kitchen window at the cars on the Long Island Expressway and inhaling the restorative aroma of her own soup; Lawrence Lazar, long done with that morning's *Times*, was leafing through the guidebook to the Catacomb of Santa Cecilia he had found the previous Monday in the hallway of his apartment building as he and Bunny had been rushing to the precinct house.

The kitchen was redolent with the peculiar odor of traditional Jewish homes early on Friday mornings. The slightly sour smell of dough rising and the acrid, almost bitter smell of the strong coffee as it percolated through its little basket mingled with the smell of cut parsnips, diced carrots and boiled chicken to create a peculiar, specifically Jewish ambience Lawrence Lazar and Bunny both recalled fondly from their own mother's kitchens.

The mechanical timer that the Lufts used to signal when their morning coffee had percolated for precisely seven minutes went off;

automatically, Bunny turned from the window to take two white cups and saucers from the cupboard for the coffee.

As she opened the kitchen cabinet, however, Lawrence Lazar looked up from his little guidebook with the strangest expression on his face.

"It's him," he said distinctly.

"It's who?"

"Marvin Kalish."

"Where is Marvin?"

"In this book."

"Marvin Kalish is in your book? Marvin Kalish is in your head! What book are you reading?"

"It's that guidebook to the Catacomb of Santa Cecilia in Rome that I found in the hall."

"And Marvin is in it? What do you mean?" Bunny couldn't imagine for the moment what her husband was talking about. Marvin Kalish was a Jewish comedian from Queens, not a Roman tour guide who wrote travel brochures in his spare time.

"I mean he's here. Right here!" Lawrence Lazar's voice had a queer ring to it as he spoke. But he seemed quite certain of what he was saying and there was no obvious reason to disbelieve him. Furthermore, he was pointing vigorously to something in the book he was holding.

Bunny came around to his side of the table, the pot of hot, percolated coffee she had taken from the fire still in her right hand. "Where?" she asked, intrigued.

"Right here," Lawrence Lazar said pointing to something inside the book. "It's definitely him. Look closely!"

Bunny bent over the book to look as closely as her husband wished and, as she did, she found herself looking at what seemed to be a fresco of some sort from the ancient catacomb. "What is this?" she asked.

"Read right here," Lawrence Lazar said, pointing to the accompanying text.

Lifting the book to eye level, Bunny read the indicated passage. "The word 'catacomb' comes," she read, "from the Greek *kata kumbas* (= near the hollow) and was originally a designation only of the underground cemetery near the Church of San Sebastiano which was, apparently, situated by a pleasant hollow. Of all the catacombs of Rome the tourist may visit, however, one of the most popular and famous is the Catacomb of Santa Cecilia, Via delle Sette Chiese 282. Cecilia, a Christian convert who spent her days caring for the lepers who lounged just outside the gates of the city, was arrested during the persecutions of Diocletian and charged with spreading Christian propaganda. She was speedily tried, condemned and beheaded; only her headless body was subsequently crucified upside down and eventually released to the community. It is this headless body that the ancient faithful buried in their subterranean cemetery; the location of the head remains unknown to this very day."

Bunny cleared her throat and continued to read. "The catacomb itself is laid out as a series of large rooms, which were presumably used for the burial of bishops and communal leaders, and smaller burial chambers built around each of the larger rooms for the common folk and accessible only through a series of narrow, lightless tunnels. The occasional fissure in the rock overhead provides the barest minimum of air and, occasionally, a narrow shaft of light."

Bunny stopped reading for a moment and looked directly at Lawrence Lazar.

"Keep reading," he said simply.

Bunny lowered her eyes back to the printed page and continued in what she considered her best librarian's voice. "But," she read, "it is not because of Santa Cecilia herself that most people come to visit the catacomb today, but because of the famous fresco that graces the entrance portal."

Bunny began to scrutinize the slender volume she was holding; it was clearly weather-beaten and old. Directly across from the paragraphs she had been reading was an illustration of the aforementioned archway and it was to this glossy, color photograph that Bunny Luft now turned her attention; the photograph was the book's sole color plate.

Beneath the picture of the arch, Bunny read the following three sentences: "It was in the ancient catacombs that Christians first permitted themselves to paint portraits of the Savior. At first, these portraits portrayed Jesus as a typical Jewish man of his day, complete with beard and curly hair, or occasionally as the Good Shepherd carrying a lost lamb. Only later on was art made to serve theology as the images of Jesus became less and less Jewish and more akin to portraits of Roman nobility—by the dawn of the High Middle Ages, the rabbi of Nazareth had become, at least iconographically, a Gentile prince."

Looking at the plate carefully for the first time, Bunny saw immediately what had attracted Lawrence Lazar's attention. Wordlessly, she stared at the picture of the ancient fresco and wondered how she could possibly have come from the initial encounter with the mystery lady in the synagogue to this particular moment in less than a month.

Needless to say, Bunny's first reaction was to deny the obvious.

"It's him." Lawrence Lazar's voice had a certain firm insistence in it.

"It's not him," Bunny answered immediately.

"It *is* him. Come look in the sunlight." Bunny could hardly refuse her husband's entirely reasonable request, however little she wished to see the picture with greater clarity. But she felt she had no choice and so she stood up and stepped towards the window into the light.

"I can look in whatever light you want, but it still isn't him. It doesn't even look like him…" Her voice trailed off into convictionless silence and she stared in the pale Queens sunlight at the fresco adorning the arch leading into the tomb of some ancient somebody in the Catacomb of Santa Cecilia.

The picture featured Jesus himself surrounded by his disciples. Just as the legend stated, the picture was distinctly unlike the Renaissance masters' image of their savior as brave warrior or salvific prince, but rather portrayed a distinctly Jewish-looking young man with curly Jewish hair, dark Jewish eyes and a broad, distinctly Jewish nose.

But it was not at the depiction of Jesus at all that Lawrence Lazar's finger was pointing, but to one of the disciples pictured grouped on either side and directly behind their master.

On the left side of the fresco, three disciples over from Jesus himself, there was a picture of a young man with a rather surprised look on his face. He appeared, even after eighteen or nineteen centuries of wear, to be shocked by something he was staring out at, although it was obviously no longer possible even to guess what it might have been that so affected the ancient man.

The man seemed to be staring directly at Bunny Luft and it was that impression that was making Bunny's skin crawl and her throat constrict. Despite her insistence to the contrary, she knew immediately that her husband had been entirely right in his appraisal of the situation.

Somebody *had* left the guidebook on purpose in front of their apartment door the previous Monday, somebody who knew that Bunny Luft was the mother of Marvin Kalish and who wished, apparently, for Bunny to know that he or she knew without having actually to face her and say so.

The face of the third disciple to the left that was staring up at Bunny with such a quizzical look of surprise bordering on shock was none other than the face of Marvin Kalish himself. It could have been his twin!

"Well," she allowed finally after a moment's contemplation of the amazing photograph, "maybe a little it looks like him. A little, but not a lot. Well, maybe more than just a little, but a lot less than a lot. Like a cousin, maybe. Like a cousin..."

A dim light went on somewhere in the inner recesses of Bunny Luft's own consciousness. All her protestations to the contrary notwithstanding, Bunny *knew* that the man in the picture was Marvin Kalish as clearly as she *knew* she was stepping into something enigmatic and ancient, something troubling *and* puzzling *and* deeply alluring, all at the same time. She had gotten started with all of this to locate her son and to warn him—and that, she had already accomplished. But there was obviously more to do, and Bunny meant to see the matter through to its natural end. The picture in the book, she somehow understood, was only the beginning...

Bunny stepped out of the sunlight and opened the door of her refrigerator. Taking out a sealed plastic bag of fresh dill, she pensively dumped the bag's contents into the simmering vat of golden soup.

Thirteen

"*W*hat if they all meet coming up in the elevator?"

"So what?"

"So they'll all know each other before I can introduce them. And it's my place to introduce them—they're all related in the first place only because of me."

"Well, first of all," Lawrence Lazar said calmly, "they won't even recognize each other even if they do come up together. I mean, Marvin and Dawn are probably coming with *his* parents anyway and even if Jeffrey and Joyce *do* arrive home at precisely the wrong moment, they won't know who they are anyway. They'll only guess at each other's identity once they all get out at the same floor and start walking in the same direction. And by then, it will be too late—you'll already be out in the hall waiting and you can introduce them to each other if you think it's so important."

It was twenty past seven on Friday evening, the sixth of March, 1981. The sunny morning had given way to a cloudy, dark afternoon and the feeling of cold, dank air was clearly lingering into evening.

From the purely practical side of things, all was ready and had been for hours. The golden soup was bubbling gently in its great vat, the snippets of parsnip, carrot and celery bobbing around like tired swimmers treading water in some vast, aluminum swimming pool. The chickens were broiled to perfection, their tender, juicy flesh hidden just a millimeter beneath crispy, greaseless skin. The air in Bunny Luft's kitchen was heavy with paprika and garlic, but the sweet, subtle smell of Bunny's yellow pound cake provided a underlayer to the more dominant aroma that suggested character and integrity.

The table was set perfectly on a linen tablecloth hand-embroidered by Bunny's mother, the late Cynthia Falk. Beside each place setting was an exquisitely embroidered matching napkin Bunny herself had made in the year following her mother's death as a sort of tribute to Cynthia

Falk's talents as a homemaker and wife. The match was perfect; no one but a true expert could ever have told that the napkins and the tablecloth were made by different hands more than a decade apart.

Bunny had set out her best crystal goblets and her best Rosenthal china; her grandmother's silver glistened beside each setting, each oversized soup spoon catching the brilliance of the crystal chandelier that hung over the Lufts' dinner table.

All this was done by six in the evening; Bunny lit her Sabbath lamps, put on her triple-strand pearl necklace and sat down to read *The Times* by their flickering, yellow light.

Bunny wore black; Lawrence Lazar wore a navy blue suit he had bought wholesale from a friend's friend named Muhammed in a loft on Thirty-Second Street. If anybody asked, he would reveal how he had acquired it to accentuate the degree to which he was a complete man—*either* a wife who wore a triple strand *or* an in on Seventh Avenue was enough to suggest that a man was a *macher*, but both together were the indisputable signs of the man who had it all.

"Get someone to ask where I got the suit," Lawrence Lazar said quickly to Bunny as they both heard a quiet knock at the door; it was 7:31 p.m., time for dinner. "And *you* get the door," he added as he retreated into the bedroom. "It's your show."

The door opened and in its frame stood an older couple.

"You must be Alice and Ike," Bunny said a bit nervously.

"And you must be Mrs. Luft," came the icy reply.

"Call me Bunny," Bunny parried.

It had been Ike Kalish who had accused Bunny of being Mrs. Luft; now it was Alice whose turn it was to respond. "If you insist," she said with a defensive haughtiness born of worry and nervousness. "It's such a pleasant name," she added after a moment's pause, "it reminds me of little bunny rabbits hip-hopping around in their little cages at the Children's Zoo in Central Park. But even bunny rabbits don't throw their tiny bunny children in the garbage if keeping them at home is going to pose some sort of inconvenience in their little bunny lives. Look," she continued, her voice breaking. "I thought I could do this, but I can't. Come on, Ike, let's go home."

Bunny, generally never without a ready retort, was speechless. She had anticipated it might take some time to break the ice, but she hadn't even considered that she might encounter such inexcusable rudeness less than five minutes into the evening.

"No, wait," she said lamely. "You've gotten this far, why not just come in and have a bite. The children will be here in a moment and we can all get to know each other." Bunny was prattling on and she knew it, but suddenly she knew how to end the matter. "Besides," she said, "I'll just have to tell Marvin you didn't show when he gets here. He'll come in, he'll sit down, he'll wait... Eventually, he'll be hungry and we'll eat—we'll *all* eat except of course for you—and we'll drink and we'll talk. We'll all get better acquainted and form a wonderful friendship—all except you, of course—and Marvin and Dawn will become *our friends*. All," she concluded grandly, "without any help at all from you."

Alice stopped in her tracks; she looked shocked by Bunny's blunt forecast for the evening. Suddenly, Alice Kalish realized that by leaving she would only be paving the way for a happy friendship between her beloved son and the woman who had abandoned him at birth.

The decision was made; the Kalishes would stay. "You win," she said as she entered the apartment, the obedient Ike Kalish in her powerful wake. "We'll eat your *farshtinking* meal," she added venomously.

"We're so glad you could come," Lawrence Lazar said politely as he entered the living room to meet his guests, as yet unaware that the Kalishes were bitter, angry people more in the mood for a hanging than for a pleasant Sabbath dinner in the style of Queens County Jewry. "How about a drinky-dinky-doo?" he added pleasantly, stepping behind his rolling bar-cart and pretending to swoon with delight as he lifted a chilled glass pitcher of his best dry martinis to nose level and pretended almost to swoon as he inhaled the intoxicating fumes.

It took a long time, but eventually the evening went reasonably successfully. The Kalishes were still standing in the front foyer contemplating Lawrence Lazar's strange offer of a drink when, all at once, Marvin Kalish, Dawn Kupchinsky, and Jeffrey and Joyce Luft arrived. Their presence helped to remove the tension that had seemed almost physically oppressive only moments earlier; it was Bunny's idea to make the introductions so elaborate that they would carry over by virtue of their very detail into conversations between some of the various people meeting each other for the first time. The ploy worked; within a few minutes of their arrival, all the guests, the elder Kalishes included, were seated in the Lufts' living room chatting amiably about the weather and the Mets and the way John Lindsay had ruined New York.

"That *momzer* just gave the city to the unions, he should burn in hell," Alice Kalish opined pleasantly, now that she was committed to spending the evening at the Lufts' and felt more at home.

"Lindsay? He wasn't a mayor—he was hardly even a man. Albert Shanker was the mayor when Lindsay was in office. Shanker and Harry Van Arsdale and everybody else whose workers had the city by the shorts." Finally, Bunny thought, a subject we can all agree about.

When Ike Kalish turned the conversation to snow removal, Bunny glanced at Lawrence Lazar in undisguised triumph. "When Robert F. Wagner was mayor..." she heard her husband say as he launched into one of his favorite diatribes to the general delight of the assembled guests. Even Joyce and Jeffrey, both of whom had heard the speech scores of times before, seemed enthralled by the strange blend of personal outrage, Jewish self-pity and New York bathos that always characterized this particular soliloquy once Lawrence Lazar really got going. The evening was, Bunny thought, progressing marvelously.

The meal was well received.

"The soup is very good," Alice allowed herself to say as an act of partial reconciliation. Knowing all too well that no greater compliment can ever be paid the Jewish housewife, she meant her few words to indicate her willingness to talk peace. And besides, she rationalized privately, the soup *was* good, excellent even. Alice Kalish popped a tiny round of chicken-fat suffused parsnip into her wrinkled mouth and smiled at her hostess.

Bunny Luft smiled back, feeling the tension in her shoulders and neck ease as she did so. Things were going to be okay!

And things were okay. The *pshcha* was as well received as the soup; even the rather surly Ike Kalish, now warmed up by the soup and the general ambience of acceptance and good feeling, allowed himself to compare Bunny's *fees* to his late mother's. The appetizers gave way to the main course and, as they did, a new atmosphere seemed to fill the room.

Marvin was uncharacteristically quiet, a bit overwhelmed by the fact that he was seated at a richly laden Sabbath table in the presence of his girlfriend, his parents and his birth mother. After so many years of fantasizing about the moment that was coming to pass before his very eyes, Marvin could hardly believe how well everyone was getting along. Even the relationship between the elder Kalishes and Dawn Kupchinsky, which had never been especially warm, seemed somewhat friendlier than usual.

His eyes darted back and forth from Bunny Luft to Alice Kalish. For better or worse, Alice was his mother—of that, Marvin had no doubts at all. But it was equally impossible to deny that Bunny Luft was something to him as well and it was not as easy as an outsider might have imagined to say precisely what that something was.

She was more than the woman inside of whose uterus the fetal Marvin had grown from zygote to healthy infant. That was simple to say, but to carry on and say what she was as clearly as what she wasn't was nowhere near as simple. Marvin ate silently, his knee firmly wedged against Dawn's.

As the dinner plates were being cleared by a willing Lawrence Lazar, Bunny told the story of Marvin's birth. "I know this is an awkward moment, but I suppose everyone wants to know the circumstances of your birth," she said. "And eventually the whole story will come out, I suppose, but unless I tell it from beginning to end, it will somehow come out all cockamaimy and confused and everyone will have a different picture of what happened. So I propose we wait a few minutes until dessert and I'll tell the story once and for all and then we can have some dessert and some hot tea and we can either forget the story or discuss it or whatever you all want, but at least it won't be there lurking in the closet waiting to spring out at us at some less opportune time when we won't be all together and we won't all hear the same thing precisely."

Bunny looked around her table. Alice and Ike Kalish looked dismayed, but they were clearly staring at Marvin; this was apparently his call to make. Dawn Kupchinsky was also staring at Marvin. Bunny imagined she could see her hand grasping Marvin's right knee and quivering slightly, but whether it was the knee or the hand that was trembling, she could not tell with certainty.

She told the story, beginning with the moment she realized she was pregnant and hurrying through the details of the actual pregnancy. She dwelled at length on the wonderful way her parents behaved, offering succor and genuine support rather than pointless, after-the-fact advice. She spoke about her decision to give up the baby for adoption and, as she did so, she wept tears of genuine regret and sadness. She spoke about her marriage to Lawrence Lazar and the way he had accepted the reality of Bunny's past with neither censure nor prissy moralizing. And she spoke about the way Rabbi Weissbrot had understood that she had been careless, unwise and foolish rather than evil or depraved. Her error was merely to have taken a stupid chance, Bunny recalled the rabbi having said. " 'If you have committed sins,' " Bunny quoted, her voice fairly accurately mimicking Rabbi Weissbrot's Byelorussian accent, " 'the greatest of them lies in having brought worry and pain to your parents.' I can still hear those words like it was yesterday," Bunny repeated. "Yesterday!" And, having repeated the rabbi's single sentence of censure, Bunny Luft wept.

The tears rolled off her cheek and onto the tablecloth almost as though her make-up were completely impervious to water. She was crying without making a sound, as though her face were merely leaking. But the fact that Bunny sincerely regretted, not—God forbid!—Marvin's conception, but rather the pain and suffering his conception had brought to Cynthia and Moe Falk was obvious. Dawn herself began to cry as she watched Bunny's tears roll down her cheeks.

The mood had changed from the general sense of warmth and good feeling that had prevailed before Bunny had begun her story. There was regret in the air—regret and pity for a woman who had made a great error and never completely come to terms with its consequences.

Even Alice Kalish was moved. "Don't make such a *tsimmes*," she said quietly, "you know that all's well that ends well. You may have made your own mother sad, but you made me and my husband very happy. You missed raising a wonderful child, but he was raised anyway and Ike and I were fulfilled and happy because you gave him up. Look," she continued sensibly, "I can see how you are still suffering about this, but don't get carried away. Marvin had a wonderful childhood and a warm, loving home. True, his father used to torture him by making him do stand-up for whomever we had at the house, but that was small potatoes in the long run. What matters is that we had plenty—plenty of money and plenty of love and plenty of food. Ask Marvin if he grew up deprived or unhappy—he'll tell you!

"And another thing—I'm sorry I was so horrible when we came in. You know, most people think the worst fear an adoptive parent has is that the birth mother will have a change of heart and come back and take the baby away. There are a few months when she has the legal right, you know—of course, *you* would know—to come back and let me tell you, those months are *hell*. But then they pass and the birth mother has no more legal right to take the baby back, but you still worry. What if! What if she comes back anyway? What if she turns out to be the kid's second-grade teacher? Or his Cub Scout Troop's den mother? What if she stalks him and just introduces herself one day as the kid's *real* mother?"

"It sounds horrible," Dawn said softly as Alice caught her breath.

"Horrible?" Alice Kalish seemed surprised by Dawn's remark. "No, it's not horrible. Raising a child is wonderful. And you have a million worries and fears about the child anyway. This is just another set most people don't have. But eventually, you stop worrying. The birth mother hasn't shown up. There hasn't been any effort to contact you or the kid. Things are settled and you are at peace.

"Except for one remaining fear—and it's a big one. One day it strikes you all of a sudden that the kid's parents—his birth parents, I mean—that they're out there. They're out there and in the meantime, the kid is an adult and they have no legal constraints at all on them. They can find him if they want—you never really believe that story about how the records are sealed up forever—and they can start up a relationship and suddenly it strikes you that *that's* your real fear. Not that they would break the law and snatch the kid when he's eleven, but that they'll come back and befriend the kid when he's twenty-five. And that the kid will have two mothers—one who punished him when he misbehaved and made him go to bed early on school nights and didn't let him eat peanut brittle—and one who never once disciplined him or raised her voice, a pleasant lady, well-dressed and much closer to the kid's own age than his adoptive mom. And which do you really think the kid is going to like more? I know you're all thinking it's a crazy fear, but it's real—and I guess I just allowed myself to succumb before. I'm sorry. I'm really sorry I was rude and I'm not at all sorry you've all come into our lives. I—Marvin—well, we'll all just have to adjust a bit. I'll give it my best shot, for whatever that's worth."

Alice's speech was very well received by the assembled guests. Bunny, the last dinner dish in her hand, herself wiped a tear from the corner of her eye as she looked at Marvin. "So?" she said simply. "What do you think?"

"I think I want to know who my father was. I mean, who my birth father is, who the man was who…" Marvin's voice trailed off for a moment. "The guy who got you pregnant," he finally blurted out, his reformulation as accurate as it was inelegant. "Who was he?"

In retrospect, it seemed impossible for Bunny to have failed to anticipate this question. It was, obviously, the single most interesting fact that had yet to be revealed in the story and it was, equally obviously, the detail Marvin Kalish could have been counted on to find the most personally important. It was unthinkable that the question should have caught Bunny unawares, but it somehow had. All at the same time, she was stunned by the question's directness, appalled that it had been asked in public and uncertain whether to answer honestly or not.

She could hardly mumble that she couldn't recall who Marvin's father had been, after all—she was a foolish girl who paid the ultimate price for a momentary lapse of her usual common sense, not some sort of floozy who could actually have conceived a child without being able to say who the father was.

But the truth was that Bunny instantly realized that she had repressed even the possibility—much less the likelihood—that this question would be asked precisely because she so little liked to recall its answer.

In the meantime, as these thoughts flitted through Bunny's mind, those assembled at her dinner table turned the full force of their attention on her.

Alice Kalish looked mildly amused, almost as though she was glad that Marvin was going to acquire a birth father as well as a birth mother and that Ike would, therefore, be on as thin ice as she with respect to their son's future affections.

Ike, to whom that thought had obviously also occurred, seemed less amused than his wife, but he too was staring directly at Bunny Luft's mouth, almost as though he expected Marvin's biological father to spring forth from between her lips.

Dawn Kupchinsky, who knew all too well that the lack of information about his birth father had always been far more troubling and unsettling for Marvin than not knowing about his birth mother, also watched Bunny carefully as if afraid she might suddenly get cold feet and rush from the apartment leaving Marvin's crucial question unanswered.

Lawrence Lazar, who had managed to enjoy almost twenty-six years of marriage to Bunny Falk without even once asking about the circumstances under which she had become pregnant out of wedlock, seemed transfixed. It was obviously absurd to feel jealous of a man his wife had known more than a quarter-century earlier and whom she had, in the final analysis, *not* married, but Lawrence Lazar surprised himself by feeling intensely jealous and irritated by the prospect of having his rival's name thrust unwillingly upon him.

Jeffrey Luft stole a quick glance at his sister and turned her glance with his towards their mother. Looking forward to Bunny's answer with the same enthusiasm with which any son would anticipate learning the identity of his mother's first lover, he felt suddenly ashamed that this whole scene was playing itself out in his and Joyce's presence.

Joyce, for her part, kept still and waited; she had trained herself to think so rarely and so poorly of her mother as a sexual being in her own right, that it merely amused her to think she was about to learn the name of a human being who had, at least once, thought otherwise.

Still, of all the assembled, it was Marvin who had the most riding on the answer to his own question. He sat quietly in his chair and wondered what the name was going to be. The thought crossed harmlessly through his mind that the only, single detail about his biological father that he could state with certainty was his race. In a matter of seconds, that would shift from the sole piece of information he had to the least important detail he could possibly imagine.

The temperature seemed to climb a degree or two in the few seconds during which all these thoughts passed through the minds of the Lufts and their Sabbath guests.

After taking a deep breath, Bunny gave her answer simply and, she hoped, elegantly. "He was an older man," she said. "And his name was Wolfzahn—Judah Wolfzahn, but everyone called him Yudel. I suppose," Bunny continued, making a point of averting her eyes from her husband's as she turned to the Kalishes, "you've met."

Marvin's mouth hung open in amazement. In his mind's eye, he had always imagined his parents as young teenagers fooling around on somebody's mother's sofa and having the inestimably poor luck of actually ending up with a baby as the wages of their adolescent sin. As distraught and nearly blind with remorse as Marvin had pictured them, the randy seventh-graders would then have had no choice but to give their baby up to adults who could properly care for it!

But now it had turned out that his parents hadn't been young, foolish children at all. His mother must have been in her twenties when he was born and now he was hearing that his father was even older than that. 'An older man', Bunny had called him. That, Marvin suddenly thought, could either mean a man of thirty years of age to a twenty-three year old or else it could mean a man of sixty-five.

And on top of that, Bunny was now suggesting that his parents actually knew or had once known this Wolfzahn character, although it was entirely clear from the look on both Alice and Ike's faces that if they ever had known him, they certainly hadn't understood his relationship to their son.

The first to speak was Ike Kalish. "That son of a bitch!" he said quietly. "He sold me his own son for three goddam grand."

Suddenly, without the reason being apparent, all heads turned to Lawrence Lazar, whose brow was suddenly deeply furrowed. "That piece of shit told me you were his wife's friend, not his child's mother," he said blankly in Bunny's direction.

Marvin looked as though he might say something, but he quickly closed his mouth after having apparently changed his mind.

Fourteen

$\mathcal{A}$t the exact moment Bunny Luft was uttering his name, Yudel Wolfzahn was walking briskly down Queens Boulevard in the cool March air. As he passed the great honeystone facade of the Queens Hebrew Congregation, he checked his thin gold wristwatch; it was ten minutes before nine o'clock and he was precisely on time.

As he crossed Yellowstone Boulevard and paused only long enough to check the price of gold on the electronic sign in the window of the Bank Leumi, Yudel felt vaguely guilty about having left Clara at home to clean up their Sabbath dinner while he was out. If Clara hadn't cleaned up by the time he got home, Yudel promised himself that he would do the washing up and thank her for allowing him the privilege.

The stop at the bank's window cost Yudel a minute of his time, but it hardly mattered. It was four minutes to nine as he stepped off the curb on the south side of Queens Boulevard just in front of the great Parker Towers housing development. Yudel Wolfzahn sighed as he recalled all too well when the development had been an empty lot with a 'For Sale' sign in front of it twenty years earlier. He had thought of buying the lot and building a parking lot there, but his brother-in-law had discouraged him. It had been a bad call; the people who finally had bought the lot had become multi-millionaires by building highrise apartment towers that housed two thousand people while Yudel Wolfzahn was still clipping coupons and shopping at Waldbaum's. Yudel shuddered as he contemplated his lost riches as he crossed the final few traffic lanes of the ten-lane boulevard and stepped onto the north curb just in front of the Kropf Pharmacy.

The drugstore, of course, was closed. A red and white sign advertising the pharmacy's hours hung in the glass door; its bottom quarter was connected to the larger part of the sign with a piece of string which was twisted so that the hand-lettered word "CLOSED" faced out. A laminated paper arrow hung inside the doorway just to the right of the larger sign and pointed to a buzzer on the door's aluminum frame; inside the arrow was a hand-written message encouraging patrons in need of emergency aid to press the indicated doorbell at any hour of the day or night.

If no one should appear after a few minutes, the sign said, then the distraught patron should phone a special phone number, which was also given, which would connect him or her with a recording prepared daily by the New York Association of Professional Pharmacists. The recording, the sign continued, would indicate which NYAPP drugstores in Queens were assigned to stay open all night on any particular evening.

Yudel looked surreptitiously over his shoulder as he approached the thick glass door, but no one appeared to be anywhere near him. With a sudden, unexpected shudder, Yudel Wolfzahn pushed the buzzer and waited patiently for Zelig Kropf to appear. A cold breeze whipped down Queens Boulevard as the Q-60 bus appeared at its bus stop precisely as Yudel's finger touched the buzzer.

No one got on or off and Yudel found himself wondering why the bus driver had bothered making a stop at all. It was an idle thought, but Yudel was in a state of heightened anxiety as he waited to hear Zelig Kropf's footfalls coming down the back staircase.

"Sabbath peace, Yudel," Zelig Kropf said as he opened the door wide enough for a man to pass through.

"And to you," Yudel responded automatically.

The ease of an old, established friendship reaffirmed, there remained little to say. Zelig turned on his heel and led his friend through the drugstore and up the back stairs to his amazing apartment.

From the outside, no one would ever have guessed that anyone lived over the Kropf Pharmacy because, although the building was easily tall enough to house a second story, there were no windows at all over the large glass windows of the pharmacy itself. If anybody had ever bothered to compare the height of the pharmacy's ceiling with the height of the outer walls of the building that housed it, the obvious conclusion would have been that the building had an attic of some sort that the druggist used as a convenient, secure storeroom. To Zelig Kropf's knowledge, however, no one had ever subjected the building to such careful scrutiny.

The staircase at the back of the shop was dark, but the combination of his friend's familiar footfalls just above him and the feel of the familiar wooden bannister beneath his hand kept Yudel calm as he followed his friend upstairs.

The first moment inside the apartment was always breathtaking. With the exception of a small skylight in the kitchen which Zelig Kropf used to determine whether the sun was shining, there were no windows; all the interior illumination was by electric light. The familiar, evocative combination of yellow light and dark wood filled Yudel with the strange combination of *déjà vu,* foreboding and rich memory.

Passing quickly through the tiny foyer almost without bothering to admire the reproduction of the ancient fresco that hung over the doorway, Yudel found himself in the great salon.

The table, at which were seated a group of older and younger men, was covered with hearty Sabbath puddings, great insulated tureens of steamed vegetables, dutch ovens filled with roasted potatoes still simmering in hot olive oil and several silver platters of roasted turkey and chicken. On the wall over the Sabbath table, Kropf's specially commissioned, life-size reproduction of the great apsidal mosaic from the Church of Santa Pudenziana was hanging in its usual place. As Yudel's eyes adjusted to the striking balance of light and shadow in the room, he found his eyes automatically darting across the face of the magnificent mosaic until they came to rest on the third apostle to the left. There, looking out at him with his regular, bemused stare, was none other than Marvin Kalish.

"Stop staring!" Zelig's voice sounded a bit harsh, but the warm look of seasoned, lifelong friendship that washed over his face as he spoke belied the severity of his command.

"Sorry," Yudel responded immediately. "It's just so…"

"So what?"

"So big. So big and so lifelike. It really looks like him, you know."

"Of course it looks like him. Who else should it look like? Ronald Reagan?"

"That's not what I meant." Yudel looked directly at his friend. "You should take it down, you know," he said quietly.

"Why in the world should I do that?" Amusement and resentment mingled uneasily in Zelig Kropf's voice.

"Because," Yudel answered plausibly, "one day you're going to be waiting on line in Waldbaum's and you'll drop dead from a heart attack and the cops will come and search this place to see if you've got a will…"

"I don't have a will."

"Well, you should. But the cops won't know that. They'll just assume that a successful pharmacist like you would…"

"I'm not that successful."

"Stop being infuriating. They'll look at the store and they'll look at your pinky ring and they'll *assume* you are successful and they will *assume* that a man they *assume* to be as successful as you would have a will. And they'll break into the apartment to find the will they'll *assume* you have left because someone they *assume* to be as rich and smart as you wouldn't be so stupid as to just *assume* that his estate will just divide itself up in accordance with his wishes."

Zelig assumed an air of deep concern. "I have no wishes," he said plainly.

"They'll *assume* you do," Yudel said, barely knowing whether to be infuriated or amused. "And they'll break in here and find that thing…"

Yudel gestured vaguely towards the apsidal mosaic.

"…and then you'll have some explaining to do!"

"I thought I was going to be dead," Zelig pointed out politely.

"Okay, Mr. Wiseguy. But let's say you're not dead. Let's say you've only had a massive heart attack and you're still alive, only clinging to this life by the most slender hair and they could still ask and you could still have to answer!"

Zelig Kropf clapped his right hand around his friend's left shoulder and drew him closer. "If I'm not dead," he said softly, "they won't break in to look for my will."

The men seated at the table were still eating their dinner. The casseroles and dutch ovens were only half-empty, which led Yudel to conclude that he hadn't missed dinner after all.

"You'll eat something?"

"I've already eaten and I left Clara with the dinner dishes to prove it."

"You both could have eaten here."

"Clara says all this goyish art gives her heartburn. 'Too *oomge-patchket*,' she says, "to leave a Jewish digestive tract to do its work in peace.' I have to admit, I know what she means. And she also hates always being the only woman." Zelig Kropf's dinner guests were almost always men.

"Then I won't show you what's new."

"Show me!" The avid interest in Yudel's voice was more than perfunctory; he was clearly very anxious to see his friend's new acquisition.

As usual, Yudel marvelled at the acoustics of his friend's great loft. The men at table were no more than fifteen feet from where he and their host were standing, but no one seemed to notice his presence and not a single head turned in his direction. He could clearly see

– 153 –

them eating and he could even hear snippets of their various conversations, but it was all rather like watching people dining on a television show rather than experiencing the presence of real people.

Silently, Yudel recalled the many times he had been seated at the table lost in conversation or deeply involved in a disquisition on this or that aspect of the weekly Torah lesson. He could himself remember not noticing a new arrival until he was actually seated at the great wooden table.

As Yudel contemplated the diners at table beneath the mosaic, he recalled briefly his 1969 visit to the fifth century church on the Via Urbana. The church had been poorly lighted and less than immaculate and the sad truth was that the reproduction of the mosaic was far more impressive looking down on Zelig Kropf's dinner table than the original in the Eternal City had seemed at the time.

The reverie was pleasant, but brief. As Yudel stood in contemplation of the enormous mosaic, his friend returned with a large volume.

"You know what this is?" he asked with a sly glint in his eyes.

"It's a book."

"Very good. It's a book." Zelig seemed pleased with his friend's sarcastic answer. He opened the book to a page he had marked with a scrap of newspaper. The page was given over to a glossy plate featuring some sort of silver box.

"Can you recognize what this is?"

"No," Yudel answered thoughtfully, "I don't."

"Guess!"

"I can't guess."

"Try!"

"I don't want to try. You tell me."

"Well, I will. But you're certainly no fun today. What's your problem?"

"You're my problem. But do tell me what you've got."

Zelig Kropf ran his fingers over the shiny plate. The box in the picture was small, but with a beautifully embossed relief of Christ and his disciples on its cover. It was, Yudel thought, clearly a depiction of an ancient picnic of some sort; baskets of bread and jugs of wine were clearly visible at the base of the picture.

"The original is in a church in Milan," Zelig Kropf said proudly. "In the Church of Saint Nazaro."

"You saw it?"

"When would I have seen it? They say it was sent by some pope to Saint Ambrose as a present and he gave it to the church."

"But that's not true?" Yudel was clearly intrigued.

"How should I know if it's true? Maybe it *is* true! But what difference does that make. Late fourth century max, maybe a bit earlier."

Yudel peered at the picture of the box, but as he did so, the glossy paper reflected the strong yellow light of the overhead chandelier almost directly into his eyes. Yudel lifted his hand to his face to shield his eyes from the bright reflected light.

"Put down your hand and look closely," Zelig Kropf said quietly. "You see the error?"

Yudel looked with interest at the picture of the silver reliquary, but it gave no hint wherein its error might lie. The artist had clearly been attempting to portray the wedding at Cana as the jugs of wine and baskets full of bread at the base of the picture clearly indicated. "No," he answered.

"So why don't you count the disciples, if you're so curious?"

Yudel quickly counted. There were eleven.

"Eleven."

"One missing?"

"I suppose."

"What would you say if someone offered you this box?"

"To buy?"

"Okay, to buy."

"I'd say it's a rip-off. The artist wasn't too skilled and he couldn't count to twelve. I'd say it's a copy of some original—fair craftsmanship, lousy detail."

Zelig was clearly delighted and he clapped his friend on the back to show it. Yudel's shoulder was still smarting from the blow when he realized his friend had stepped to the far side of the room and was retrieving something from the massive oak sideboard standing there.

In the meantime, the diners were helping themselves to seconds and some few who had already finished their dinner were beginning to sing some of the traditional table songs Yudel knew from his parents' home in Jewish Hamburg and which he and Clara still sang from time to time, especially when Sid joined them for Sabbath dinner.

Yudel began to sing along with "My Soul Thirsteth for the Living God" when he realized that Zelig was already back by his side.

"Looky here," he said with relish. He was holding a silver box almost identical to the one in the picture.

Knowing entirely well what he was about to see, Yudel bent over the silver box. There, three apostles to the left, was a man with the precise face of Marvin Kalish. "It's astonishing," Yudel said quietly.

"Yes and no," Zelig answered honestly.

Yudel smiled broadly. It was the perfect answer! Yes, it was astonishing and no, it wasn't particularly astonishing at all. The perfect retort!

"Where did you get this?"

"You'd love to know!"

"I would."

"Well," Zelig admitted, laughing, "if I didn't, I would too."

"So where *did* you get it?"

"You don't want to know," Zelig said, laughing.

Although Yudel hadn't noticed anyone standing up to clear the table, the great platters of vegetables and meat had somehow been removed and the table was now laden with pots of steaming tea and plates of Sabbath pastries, miniature honey-cakes and tiny apple dumplings. The men sang as they drank their tea and ate their cakes; Yudel wasn't at all surprised to notice a bottle of Crown Royal making its way around the table, but there were no shot glasses in evidence. Instead, each of the diners poured a healthy dose of the whiskey into his tea cup and kept singing.

"Don't mind the boys," Zelig said as though he had read his guest's mind. "These are the boys from my little *shtibl* who don't have wives to go home to. Some haven't married yet and some won't ever marry and some were once married, but I take them home with me on Friday nights so they can have a decent meal at least once a week." Even in the years Zelig and Yudel had belonged to the Queens Hebrew Congregation, neither had actually felt comfortable attending services there and both had ended up as members of tiny prayer-rooms elsewhere in the neighborhood.

"And what do the boys think of eating beneath the Pudenziana?"

"What do they know? I told them this used to be an art gallery and they all bought it. They're all good boys," Zelig continued, "but none of them knows anything about this kind of *goyish* art, if you know what I mean."

Yudel knew just what he meant. His own *shtibl*, a tiny prayer-room just off Austin Street a few blocks to the east of the Wolfzahns' apartment, was also filled with dozens, perhaps scores of pious Jews who had somehow managed to grow up and even old with little or no knowledge of any culture at all other than their own.

He could have told most of the guys from *his* place, Yudel thought, that the mosaic was supposed to portray Walt Disney and the twelve dwarfs and they wouldn't have known the difference.

In a sense, the lovely silver box that the Pope may have sent to Saint Ambrose in the late fourth century was a masterpiece of late Roman metalwork. But in the context of Zelig Kropf's collection, it was merely another piece, albeit an exceptional one.

The Kropf collection, after all, consisted of over one hundred pieces. Some few, like the apsidal mosaic that hung in its gigantic grandeur over the Kropf dinner table and the enormous reproduction of the fresco from the Catacomb of Santa Cecilia that was suspended over the lintel of the front door, were mere copies of greater works—but these copies were limited to those works on which The Face appeared.

The other works—the vast bulk of the collection—consisted of the treasures of lost ages which Kropf had managed to purchase.

These were the secret faces, as Zelig Kropf had taught Yudel Wolfzahn to call them—the faces no one could see, the hidden faces of the hidden man. Lost in his momentary reverie, Yudel suddenly heard the voice of his old *melamed*, the ancient rabbi who had given him religious instruction in the tiny *cheder* on the Schäferkampsallee in the years leading up to his bar mitzvah in the great synagogue on the Oberstrasse.

It seemed so long ago!

The rabbi, ancient even when Yudel was young, was deported first to Theresienstadt and then to Auschwitz, where he was gassed upon arrival.

The synagogue itself had managed to resist all Nazi efforts to blow it up and now, Yudel had once read, belonged to the German Radio Network.

What had eventually happened to the tiny, wooden building on the Schäferkampsallee in which the rabbi's lessons had been given to armies of bored young boys, Yudel could hardly guess. Probably, the building had been destroyed with most of Hamburg during the allied bombing raids; it occasionally surprised Yudel just how little he cared about the fate of any of his childhood haunts.

When the Hamburg City Council had invited former residents of the city to return on what the brochure had baldly called a mission "of reconciliation and forgiveness," Yudel hadn't given the matter even a moment's thought; he liked to think of the city of his birth as a pile of smoking ruins and he knew himself well enough to understand how little pleased he would be to see the bustling, modern city Hamburg had undoubtedly become.

But even now, more than four decades after he last set foot on the Schäferkampsallee, Yudel could hear his rabbi's sing-song voice reading from some oversized, ancient tome. "*Ein hobrocho nimtzo-o ele basomui min ho-oyin*," he could hear the man intone even so many years later, following his rendition of the original, as he always did, with its immediate German translation, "*Die Gottessegnung befindet sich nur im Verborgenen, im Verschollenen...*"

Yudel recalled having no idea at all what his rabbi was speaking about—whatever could it mean that the blessing of God can only be found in that which is hidden? It had taken years, but eventually Yudel had found out.

His friendship with Zelig Kropf had made it clear what the rabbi had meant and his old rabbi's ancient lesson hadn't been the only strange thing about Yudel Wolfzahn's life that had become intelligible as a result of his first encounter with Zelig Kropf.

Fifteen

$\mathcal{Y}$udel Wolfzahn was born on Christmas day in 1910. His childhood was privileged, pleasant and unremarkable. As a teenager, he attended the Adolphus Lenz Gymnasium in the Altona section of Hamburg from which he was graduated in the summer of 1929.

After Gymnasium, he attended classes at the law faculty of the University of Hamburg until 1933, when it was no longer possible for Jewish students to pursue their studies there and he was rudely, summarily and unapologetically dismissed. When he asked his favorite professor how a faculty of law, of all things, could knuckle under to the barbaric pressure being exerted by Nazi hooligans and fascist thugs, he was told that there were things about Germans a Jew could never understand. The unstated corollary—that German Jews were Jews and not Germans and that they had, therefore, somehow brought all their misfortune upon themselves by imagining the opposite to be the case—was not lost on the young Yudel.

With nary a whimper, he packed the few belongings he kept in his carrel at the Law Library and went home.

Upon leaving the Law Faculty, Yudel worked for a Jewish printer down the road from his father's linen shop on the stately Rothenbaumchaussee until both shops were destroyed by Nazi supporters— hooligans, Yudel's father said dismissively—on *Kristallnacht* in 1938. Only three weeks later, Yudel Wolfzahn emigrated to the United States on the *S.S. Manhattan*, arriving in New York Harbor a few days short of his twenty-eighth birthday.

Yudel arrived in New York alone, the elder Wolfzahns having chosen to ride out the storm in their native land, secure in their belief that the lunatic fringe could never really carry out its openly espoused policies of extreme, violent anti-Semitism. Heinrich and Bertha Wolfzahn were deported to Auschwitz in the fall of 1942; they were murdered and incinerated within hours of their arrival at the camp.

As his parents' situation in Germany was deteriorating by the hour, Yudel met Clara Hirschhorn at a concert organized by the Deutscher Gesangverein of Washington Heights. Because the concert consisted solely of light folk melodies, a garden ambience had been sought and the managers of the Glee Club had secured the use of a secluded corner of Fort Tryon Park for the evening. Yudel, whose apartment was not that far away on Wadsworth Avenue and 181st Street, walked the distance on foot. As he approached the park from the south along Bennett Avenue, a woman approached him and asked for directions.

From her subtle accent, Yudel immediately recognized a fellow German; from the look of worry and fear hiding just behind her lovely eyes, he recognized a fellow Jew. He volunteered to walk with her the rest of the way to the concert and, when they got there, they sat together.

After the concert, there was coffee and after the coffee, a kiss. Yudel and Clara were married only three months later on the first Sunday in February, 1941.

Sidney Philip Robert Wolfzahn was born on Yudel's own birthday in 1942. He was three weeks premature, but otherwise healthy, and brought great joy to his parents. Yudel took a week off from his job as a typesetter at *The Times* to prepare for the *bris* while Clara recuperated from her ordeal. When the week was up, Yudel returned to work and Clara assumed the role of mother and wife.

The Wolfzahns lived a decent life in a small space; the apartment they took on Bennett Avenue between 186th and 187th Streets after the baby was born still consisted of only three rooms. Clara thought it was romantic to live on the very street—almost on the very block!—on which they had met, but Yudel was already thinking of bigger and better things. Less than four weeks after Yudel was promoted to senior typesetter at *The Times* in 1949, the Wolfzahns abruptly notified their landlord that they had decided to leave Bennett Avenue and moved to Queens.

Life in Queens was enormously different from what the Wolfzahns had become used to in Washington Heights.

For one thing, Forest Hills was more of a village in the rustic, English sense than it was a suburb of a teeming metropolis. The shops along Austin Street, snug behind their *faux* Tudor facades and thick plate glass windows, opened at the genteel hour of ten o'clock each morning once the neighborhood men were off at their profitable jobs and their refined wives had concluded their matinal toilettes at least to the extent necessary to do the morning's shopping.

The gentle scent of laurel could often be smelt along the Wolf-zahn's new street as well, which was a significant improvement over the relentless odor of gasoline exhaust fumes that wafted over Washington Heights night and day from cars crossing the George Washington Bridge, but there was yet another difference which made an even greater impression on the young couple—everyone along Austin Street seemed to speak English!

Of course, the neighborhood housed an enormous refugee population. The refugees, who were referred to in local parlance as "emigrés" or, with just the slightest suggestion of contumely, as "newcomers" or simply as "new arrivals," could naturally all speak other languages as well and they tended to segregate themselves into smaller districts. The Germans, for example, tended to live around Austin Street, while the Polish and Russian Jews chose the great brick apartment houses along Yellowstone Boulevard and 108th Street as their homes. Smaller groups of Jews from Hungary, Lithuania, Roumania and other places found their own tiny pockets as well in the fabric of the larger neighborhood, but these were generally unrecognized by the larger population.

Perhaps because they came from so many different places or perhaps because they felt the need to express their independence from the homeland in whose farthest-flung precincts they still somehow managed to live, English became the *lingua franca* of the neighborhood. Of course, one could still buy the *Aufbau* at the newsstand at the corner of Continental Avenue and Queens Boulevard—as well as the *Novoe Russkoe Slovo* and the *Egyenlöség* and the Yiddish-language *Jewish Daily Forward* but these were read by decent people in the privacy of their own living rooms.

In the Cafe Zagreb, for example, on Union Turnpike, only English newspapers were available for the perusal of paying patrons despite the fact that days and sometimes weeks would go by without a single native speaker of English crossing the threshold of the greatest and most elegant of the emigré cafés.

The Wolfzahns' first year on Austin Street went marvelously well. Yudel did well at *The Times* and received a raise *and* a Christmas bonus. Clara adapted well to the new neighborhood and made friends with the other ladies she met on her daily round of shops and markets. Even little Sidney, now seven years old, was doing well at Public School No. 164; his teacher, Miss Helen Bishop, pasted a golden star on his report card before sending it home to his delighted parents. On his eighth birthday, which was also his father's fortieth birthday, the Wolfzahns bought their only child a new, red bicycle with a tiny, silver bell attached to the handlebars.

In addition to the acquisition of more expensive things, the new prosperity of the Wolfzahn household allowed for other luxuries as well. Chief among these, at least as far as Yudel himself was concerned, was the leisure time that was now available to ruminate, to remember and to identify those pieces of life's puzzle that remained missing.

There were, Yudel liked to remind his wife, many of life's greatest treasures that money couldn't buy. "The moon belongs to everyone," he took to crooning in the small hours of the night when they would be lying in bed under their great down comforter, "the best things in life are free."

"Is a decent night's sleep also free?" Clara would ask, her cleverness only barely masking her irritation with her musical husband and his apparent ability to survive for days on end with three or four hours' sleep.

"Yes," Yudel would say after a moment's thought, as though he had failed to recognize the rhetorical nature of the question posed, "it is."

"Well, good night then," Clara would say, whereupon they both would go to sleep.

But there were also other things in Yudel Wolfzahn's life that were as free as sleep that he discovered he missed and which money simply could not buy. Chief among these was the need for male companionship. After all he had gone through, Yudel Wolfzahn found he longed to have a friend.

Making friends is a daunting task for any man, but for Yudel Wolfzahn it was an especially great challenge. He worked all day, for example, and usually came home after seven o'clock in the evening. He would have dinner with his family, help the slightly dull Sidney with his homework, read the *Post* and the *Aufbau* ("keeping up with the competition", he called it) while Clara read the free copy of *The Times* that employees were permitted to take home, wash the kitchen floor, watch the evening news and fall into bed exhausted from a busy day.

Weekends were little better. Because Yudel had had the courage to make an issue of it in the first place, management had officially guaranteed him that he would never have to work on the Jewish Sabbath. This was an important concession because *The Times'* biggest issue was the Sunday edition and this was prepared on Saturday morning and through Saturday afternoon until at least four o'clock.

Yudel had risked his chances for advancement, but he knew he had only one choice. He wasn't, truth be told, particularly religious, but he knew he had to make a statement regarding an issue that was so precious to his parents and which he himself wished were more precious to his own family. Yudel's boss at the paper was himself a lapsed Jew who, no matter how far he himself had strayed from the fold, couldn't deny another the chance to be the Jew he himself felt vaguely guilty for not being. And so, the agreement was made.

Yudel Wolfzahn was *The Times'* first employee with a Sabbath clause in his contract, but not the last. When the Anti-Defamation League published its critically acclaimed *History of Discriminatory Labor Policy in America (1900-1960)* in 1975, Yudel was listed in the index and his feat recorded in a long footnote.

But Saturdays and Sundays were busy days for the Wolfzahns too! There was laundry to do, errands to run, Little League games to attend and all sorts of family things to do. On top of that, Yudel felt obliged to continue his ongoing correspondence with the German government until such time as he could discover with certainty what the fate of his parents and all of his uncles, aunts and cousins had been. This alone was a major undertaking and resulted over the years in thousands of hours of mostly fruitless work, hundreds of letters sent to dozens of German ministries and several dozen trans-Atlantic phone calls. It was not, finally, until 1956 that the final family member was accounted for and, by then, they had all been dead for over a decade. The research complete and the results as expected, Yudel wrapped up the entire file of correspondence, transcripts and official notices and pitched the box in the trash, knowing that he would never again wish to see even a single page of it.

Depressed by the results of his awful research and crushed under the burdens of husband- and fatherhood, Yudel's need for friendship lay dormant during the first years in Queens. But by the beginning of 1952, the need to commune with a kindred spirit was undeniable and irrepressible and the guilt Yudel experienced in acknowledging it— and its attendant corollary that Clara was not able to satisfy such an elemental need—only sharpened its gnawing presence.

It was on the eve of the great midsummer fast commemorating the destruction of Jerusalem by the Romans in the year 70 C.E.—Yudel and Clara were weak on the strict observance of the joyous festivals of Israel, but neither ever passed up a fast day or a Holocaust memorial day—that Yudel came to the surprising conclusion that he was a lonely man.

It sounded, Yudel thought to himself as he walked home from synagogue after having heard the Lamentations of the prophet Jeremiah read to him from a parchment scroll, pathetic for a man of forty-two years of age with a decent job, a loving wife and an obedient, if dull-witted son to think of himself as lonely. But lonely, once Yudel had managed to put a name to it, was precisely what he felt—lonely and alone and isolated from the world around him. It wasn't people he needed—even in the few years since the Wolfzahns had moved in, the neighborhood had become even more developed and built up—but it was the sense of kinship and common purpose that he lacked.

Years later, Yudel told Zelig Kropf that he had felt at that period in his life like a brick in a brickyard surrounded by hundreds of thousands of other bricks but without any of the mortar a mason might have used to cement any two of them together.

The solution to Yudel's problem came from two different sources, neither of them at all expected.

In Washington Heights, there had been communal bath houses in the late 1940's left over from the days when there were still buildings standing that lacked indoor plumbing. In the meantime, of course, indoor plumbing had become a *sine qua non* of residential dwelling in New York as everywhere and the general populace retreated from the baths, leaving them to serve poorer neighborhoods as a sort of social club where men could gather to socialize with people with whom they neither lived nor worked.

Yudel had frequented a bath on Laurel Hill Terrace overlooking the Harlem River Drive that was a favorite with emigré Jews from the German-speaking lands. There, he spoke German and caught up with new gossip from the Old Country and there, he felt truly at home. It was the one part of life in Upper Manhattan that Yudel began to miss as he became more acclimatized to his little village in Queens. Once or twice, he had actually made the endless journey on three separate subway trains from Forest Hills to Washington Heights for the sole purpose of visiting his former hang-out, but he found it to be changed; most of his cronies had either moved to the suburbs or fallen victim to the New World prejudice against communal bathing and stopped coming. Yudel never went back.

But in the spring of 1952, it suddenly came to Yudel's attention that the Jewish bath house had not really become as extinct as he had thought—it had merely been transformed into the synagogue gymnasium.

All over Queens, synagogues were vying with each other to attract more members by enticing them with more and more elaborate facilities. Swimming pools, steam baths, weight rooms, dry heat saunas and organized sports leagues were only some of the features developed to draw in members from the most promising pool of the unaffiliated: those with plenty of money, at least some leisure time and no particular inclination to participate in any of the traditional activities of the synagogue.

When Yudel did attend services, which was infrequently, he chose to say his prayers in a small prayer room located on one of the narrow side streets between Austin Street and Queens Boulevard on the other side of Ascan Avenue from his own apartment house. The manic, slightly loony ambience of the prayer room with its mostly unwashed, entirely uneducated and cultureless congregation appealed to some ancient avatar lurking deep within some hidden chamber of Yudel Wolfzahn's heart; despite the fact that he could not name a single aspect of his little *shtibl* that he was proud of liking, the truth was that he *did* like its atmosphere and whenever he felt moved to address his God, it was in those shabby precincts with its garish electric light, its ripped upholstery and its half-demented clientele that Yudel chose to do so.

But such a tiny conventicle could hardly build a sauna! That sort of luxury was strictly the domain of the larger synagogues, and of these, the Queens Hebrew Congregation was the acknowledged leader of the pack.

The pool alone cost over $8,000 to put in. The other appurtenances, cheap only by comparison, followed in its wake until such time as the Q.H.C. could boast not only the leading health facility of any Queens synagogue, but actually of having a facility more luxurious and well appointed than almost any Gentile athletic club in the neighborhood.

Yudel Wolfzahn was among the first to join the synagogue's swelling ranks specifically for the pleasure of sitting in the steam.

The experience was worth it, even if its annual cost was hundreds of times more than an admission to the old bath on Laurel Hill Road had been. Suddenly back in the company of Jewish men his own age at least once or twice a week, Yudel Wolfzahn felt a spirit of kinship he had lacked for as long as he could remember. Slowly, he even made a friend or two from the others who took the steam at about the same times each week that Yudel was himself free.

Some friendships were casual, inconsequential relationships based on proximity and shared background, but these eventually fell away, leaving Yudel Wolfzahn with one or two friends whose friendship he thought he could value. Of these, it eventually turned out that his friendships with Lawrence Lazar Luft and Zelig Kropf became the most profound.

Yudel's friendship with Zelig Kropf was the first to develop. On a warm Sunday morning in March, 1952, Yudel was taking the steam, sitting naked on the beige tiles with his eyes closed and thinking about the way his parents' shop had been looted the morning following *Kristallnacht* not by Nazi punks but rather by his parents' bourgeois, well-dressed neighbors. He was recalling how the stout matrons had inserted their fat arms *carefully* through the broken glass of the shop's window so as to be able to steal something worth carrying home without possibly ripping one of the woolen sleeves of their shapeless ladies' overcoats.

He had been hiding around the corner and watching the sight when he saw a gang of Nazi youths coming from the other direction. To escape the inevitable beating that would follow their discovery of a lone Jewish youth, Yudel had no choice but to walk down the street past his parents' shop. He had no desire to be beaten and he chose the path of least resistance, having at least the good taste to keep his eyes lowered as he passed by the shattered shop window.

As he reached the next corner, however, he could not resist the temptation to look back one last time. He stood for a moment then turned, but having been lost in his thoughts, he hadn't realized that someone had been walking on the sidewalk just behind him.

He turned and found himself staring directly into the face of Frau Ilse Döpp, the wife of his parents' dentist. Frau Döpp was carrying a large bundle of stolen bed linens in her evil arms, linens she had filched only moments before from the Wolfzahns' shop, secure in the knowledge that the police would never arrest an Aryan woman helping herself to Jewish merchandise.

Frau Döpp had the minimally good taste to be embarrassed. Her cheeks reddened slightly and her mouth opened for a moment and then shut as though she were about to say something and then changed her mind. Her eyes, usually almost hawkish in their beady intensity, clouded momentarily. She raised her right hand to her chin, almost as though she expected Yudel to strike her, but she quickly realized the absurdity of her gesture and allowed her hand to drop.

Summoning up whatever dignity she could, Frau Döpp greeted the son of her husband's patients in her normal respectful way. "Grüss Gott, Herr Wolfzahn," she said coldly.

Yudel looked at her and found himself wondering where his

parents would find a dentist now whom they would like as much as old Dr. Döpp. It was necessary for him to say something, but all he could think to say was to repeat an old Yiddish curse his grandmother had taught him according to which it was wished that a thorny vine take root in Frau Döpp's desiccated womb and grow upwards through her abdominal cavity until it would be positioned correctly and strong enough to strangle her evil heart with its sharp, poisonous tendrils.

Frau Döpp, who could not understand the mongrel dialect her unwished-for interlocutor was trying to speak, stepped aside and, bewildered but proud, continued to make her dark progress up the Rothenbaumchaussee towards her own home.

For reasons unknown even to Yudel himself, it was this scene which had come to symbolize the Holocaust in all its horror to the adult Yudel Wolfzahn. Something about the look of Frau Döpp's eyes as they burned with hatred and shame in their bony sockets combined with Yudel's own sense of the awful, pathetic inadequacy of his response to create a certain sense of bitter powerlessness that had come to symbolize the larger horror.

It was about the look in Frau Döpp's ugly eyes that Yudel found himself meditating as he suddenly became aware of the fact that someone had sat down on the wet tiled bench next to him. He opened his eyes and found that it was a man his own age with a number tattooed on his left forearm.

The men, who recognized each other as Sunday morning regulars in the steam, greeted each other in German, but then lapsed into English. They chatted about Korea and Eisenhower and the reparations situation and the chances for Israel's survival past its third year of existence and, when they both felt they were having trouble breathing due to the extreme heat, they walked out together into the cooler air of the shower room.

Slightly pleased by the amazing speed with which a sense of intimate friendship can develop between strangers under the proper circumstances, the men showered and walked together into the dressing area. As they left the shower room, Zelig Kropf stopped in front of a full length mirror.

"It doesn't seem possible," he said, pointing at his own reflection.

"What doesn't seem possible?" Yudel felt certain he knew, but it was impossible not to ask.

To Yudel's surprise, Zelig didn't answer at all. Instead, he took Yudel's arm in his own and led his new friend to the dressing area where their lockers were located. "It doesn't seem possible that so many died and I lived," he said, "and that one day I am going to die anyway. It doesn't seem possible to imagine that I lived through the war so that my body can eventually decay anyway and it will be as though *I shall have never existed.*"

Yudel liked his new friend more than ever. "Do your feet hurt?" he asked.

"My feet? No, my feet don't hurt," Zelig answered plainly. "Why?"

"Well," Yudel answered, using a favorite line of his late father's, "I was just thinking that if you had survived while so many died only so that one day your body can eventually turn to dust and be eaten by the worms and it will be as though you never existed *and* your feet hurt, you'd be worse off than you are now."

Zelig Kropf looked up at Yudel. He stepped closer to him now, actually standing on Yudel's feet so that their noses and knees touched and so that the tips of their penises were actually brushing up against each other. "Go to hell," he said slowly as he turned and walked to his own locker to dress.

Yudel was dumfounded. In anger, he found himself repeating, absurdly, a filthy imprecation similar to the one he had once flung at the bony face of the larcenous Frau Döpp.

"*Landsmann?*" Zelig Kropf returned to where Yudel was standing with a broad grin on his face.

"*Natürlich,*" Yudel answered politely and truthfully—he *had* somehow managed to find a friend *and* a countryman.

Yudel's introduction to Lawrence Lazar Luft was also unexpected. They met playing squash in one of the Q.H.C.'s elegantly white-washed courts when Zelig failed to show up for a game with Yudel and Lawrence Lazar's partner had also been missing. The athletic director, a fine-haired young man named Sandy Gold, matched them up and ushered them into the court he had reserved for one of them.

At the onset, it had appeared that no two men could possibly have less in common. Lawrence Lazar was a rising star, a manufacturer of venetian blinds with his own factory and his own distributorship. He was an American with American parents and even an American-born grandparent. Even Lawrence Lazar's three European-born grandparents, however, had at least ended up in America and they too had been singularly successful; it had been his grandfather on his father's side, Lemech Luft, who had first founded the factory Lawrence Lazar now ran.

Lawrence Lazar was portly, but his girth somehow managed to suggest health and satiety rather than sloth or gluttony. His size seemed in proportion both to his wealth and his slightly self-deprecating good humor; Lawrence Lazar was a man of the kind immigrants can only dream of becoming: unselfconscious, happy with his generous lot, completely at home in his own skin and rooted nowhere at all except in the very place in which he lived. He was the first man Yudel Wolfzahn ever met who had his initials monogrammed on his undershirts and he was the first man Yudel ever thought of even vaguely as a friend who followed baseball.

Poorer, thinner and brighter than his friend, Yudel Wolfzahn, on the other hand, was ten years older than Lawrence Lazar Luft and looked at least twice that. He was the antithesis of not one but many of Lawrence Lazar's most impressive points: he was ill at ease in his new country, emotionally anchored to a distant land he loathed *and* loved, highly unsure about how his variety of identities were supposed eventually to coalesce and covetous of his neighbors to a degree that would have surprised anyone who knew how successful he himself had actually become. *The Times'* first employee with a Sabbath guarantee in his contract, but not exactly a Sabbath observer, a member of two separate synagogues without particularly believing in the power of prayer, a happily married man plagued by loneliness and feelings of distinct alienation, a father obsessed with his lack of progeny—Yudel Wolfzahn was a lot of things Lawrence Lazar Luft could hardly fathom, much less actually be himself.

But, Yudel knew better than most, friendship cannot be predicted or charted and by the end of their first hour of play, Larry Luft and Yudel Wolfzahn could already detect a sense of nascent friendship growing between them. They showered together, dressed together and went for lunch together at the King Edward Luncheonette at the corner of Austin Street and Continental Avenue.

When Yudel came home that afternoon, ready for the drive into the potato fields of Suffolk County he had promised Clara and Sidney, he told his wife his remarkable news: in only half a year of trying, he had made a second friend.

Sixteen

*B*y any standard, they were an odd threesome.

In the spring of 1952, Yudel Wolfzahn was forty-one years old, Zelig Kropf was forty-two and Lawrence Lazar Luft was a mere lad of thirty-one.

But each of the three related to the other two in a specific way that was quite distinct from the way those other two related to each other.

Yudel and Zelig Kropf shared a common homeland and a common set of debilitating nightmares in which Lawrence Lazar could obviously not totally share. This commonality of past experience did, in fact, create a special link between the two men, but it also served to draw Lawrence Lazar into the magic circle by allowing them both to focus their special needs on him in much the same way.

For Zelig Kropf, Lawrence Lazar came to represent the shadow of his own life—or rather the image of which his own life was the shadow—and its other side, its silver lining, its inverse *and* its converse.

While Zelig Kropf had been a slave laborer, toiling for his Nazi masters in exchange for a daily bowl of greenish, meatless gruel and the occasional beating, Lawrence Lazar Luft had been sowing his wild oats. He had been drafted, of course, in 1942, but he had had the exceptional good fortune to be sent directly to an American base in the Philippines, where he spent his entire military career managing an ammunition depot.

His stories about the war years, in fact, were what drew Zelig to Lawrence Lazar in the first place. That Larry Luft had spent 1943 mainly worrying about whether he had gotten the clap, as he said, from some almond-eyed maiden in a Quezon City brothel was an idea Zelig Kropf found almost impossible to fathom.

He found himself contemplating Lawrence Lazar's pink, round body often as the three friends sat in the cleansing steam; it was hard to say what it was precisely about his young friend's body that fascinated Zelig Kropf, but the attraction he felt was undeniable and finally he realized that Larry Luft was the only man he thought of as a friend since the mid-1930's who hadn't either died in a concentration camp or survived one.

His friend's body was an object worthy of contemplation precisely, Zelig realized, because it had no scars on it whatsoever. No one had ever beaten Larry Luft and neither had anyone ever tried to starve him to death. He had never had dysentery or rickets or typhus, had never been malnourished, had never been dragged from his home in the middle of the night by jackbooted soldiers so distant and so totally disengaged from the very horror they were perpetrating that they didn't even have the courtesy to be rude or unfriendly towards the people they were shipping off to their untimely, unwarranted deaths.

Once, Zelig Kropf approached Larry Luft in the steam and put his hand directly on his friend's pink chest. It was soft, yet firm and felt just as Zelig had always imagined pink, healthy flesh should feel. Almost instantaneously, he realized how inappropriate it was for a naked man to walk up uninvited and touch another, even a friend, in a public steam room.

"I'm sorry," Zelig stammered, suddenly ashamed.

"It's all right," Lawrence Lazar answered kindly, "No offence taken."

Zelig Kropf removed his hand and looked at it oddly as though he wasn't sure what to do with it or where exactly to put it. The moment passed, but neither man ever forgot the exchange.

Yudel Wolfzahn constituted a sort of middle ground between his two friends, sharing the background (minus the personal experience of horror) of the one and the foreground (minus the roots and the comfort) of the other. He was an American, but neither in the sense of the home-grown Larry Luft nor in the sense of the newly arrived Zelig Kropf—a sort of *former* refugee who had nevertheless failed to become the citizen into whom the grateful immigrant was supposed by American mythology to metamorphosize after shedding the cumbersome baggage of native language, custom, allegiance and dress.

Yudel too came to idolize the young, pudgy Luft. Despite his youth, he was rich. But despite his wealth, he was generous and kind—everything Yudel had convinced himself the rich could never actually be. And he was, in his stout sort of way, an attractive man. Yudel loved Lawrence Lazar's stories about the Filipino girls he had met and often asked outright to hear this or that one yet another time.

The three men took to spending Sunday mornings together in the steam at the Queens Hebrew Congregation. The reedy voices of the children in the adjacent wing learning their Hebrew lessons were audible through the open windows of the dressing room and lent atmosphere and charm to the setting. But in the steam, all outer sound was muffled and the three could speak privately or almost so—whatever privacy they had to sacrifice by virtue of being in a public place was more than compensated for by the sense of added intimacy provided by the ambience of common nudity.

Like most Jews in Queens, the three were linked by being deeply Jewish without being especially religious. They all lived in homes with kosher kitchens, for example, without scrupling too much about the dietary laws when they found themselves at office parties or in neighborhood restaurants. Even stranger perhaps to the outside observer, they all belonged to synagogues in which they attended Sabbath services regularly without bothering actually to hew to any of the ancient Sabbath laws. Oddest of all was the common sense of freedom all three felt, albeit for entirely different reasons, from any crippling sense of inconsistency that might otherwise have existed between their Jewishness and Judaism itself.

Once, Rabbi Weissbrot referred in a sermon to some of his congregants as gastronomic Jews, by which he meant not merely people who ate *kishka* and *fees*, but people who merely *consumed* Judaism without allowing *it* to consume *them*. Lawrence Lazar quoted this remark to his friends the very next morning and it had been greeted with great respect for its insight, but with little regard for its uncomplimentary implication. For better or worse, Lawrence Lazar Luft, Zelig Kropf and Yudel Wolfzahn were linked by their common ability to *be* Jews without needing to prove it to themselves or to anyone else in any particular way. And, somehow, despite their different backgrounds and stages of assimilation into the melting pot of life in New York, the three men became fast friends.

Zelig Kropf had a secret. He had carried his secret from Munich to Theresienstadt, from Theresienstadt to Auschwitz, from Auschwitz to Bergen-Belsen and from Belsen to the D.P. camp at Flossenbürg in southern Germany, where he was briefly interned before being finally released. From Flossenbürg, he had carried his secret to Hamburg, where he had stayed in a sort of transit camp until a berth for him could be secured on a trans-Atlantic steamer, and from Hamburg to New York. The secret had burned within him but as the years passed, the flame became lower and less urgent. Zelig fully expected himself to forget the secret in time, but in the spring of 1952, the fates conspired to bring Yudel Wolfzahn into his life.

Zelig Kropf's first years in his adopted land were difficult without being unfulfilling. A druggist by profession, he had found himself in professional demand in New York, where it seemed that no young men were panting after a career in pharmaceutics. Contrary to the nightmares he had had nightly on the ship from Hamburg to New York, Zelig had found work in New York less than three weeks after arrival; the problem lay not in finding a position but in choosing the most advantageous one. Language, of course, was a problem, but not an insurmountable one; Zelig eventually became the assistant pharmacist in the very large, very successful drugstore on Broadway and 86th Street run by one Isaak Fischhaut, himself a German-speaking refugee from Vienna.

The customers spoke to Fischhaut in English and Fischhaut spoke to Zelig in German and the work was done no less quickly and efficiently than if the customers had spoken directly to the druggist who was filling their prescriptions.

The years passed. Fischhaut, an elderly man even when he first came to America, had a few branch stores in what he called "the provinces," by which he meant the Bronx, Brooklyn and Queens. As soon as Zelig's English was adequate, Fischhaut sent him out to manage the Queens store and, as a perk, he offered him the brick building's second story as living quarters.

Zelig accepted both parts of the offer with deep gratitude. He made a great success of things, catering to customers of all sorts with friendly efficiency tempered with the druggist's requisite discretion. Revenue from the Queens Boulevard store doubled within a year, then tripled after two more. Fischhaut was delighted, but childless. When he died, he left his main store to a distant cousin and his branch operations to the young men he had enlisted to run them. Zelig Kropf inherited the store he had made so successful and the building which housed it and in which he lived.

At first, every minute of every day was accounted for. There were accounts to be kept current, prescriptions to fill and endless, boring conversations to conduct with customers who were mindless enough to imagine that the druggist had nothing else to do merely because there were no other customers in the shop at that precise moment. On top of that, there were the daily chores: floors to sweep, windows to wash, price lists to update and inventory to take. If he hadn't been burdened with his refugee mentality, Zelig would have engaged someone to help him with the floors and the windows, but he was nowhere near secure enough to risk any of the his shop's profits on things he could manage, somehow, himself.

In addition to all that, there was almost daily homework from the English-for-Immigrants course he took four evenings a week at Russell Sage Junior High School directly across Queens Boulevard from his shop. There were tax forms to master and pharmaceutical journals to try to read and a daily newspaper to leaf through. And there was a local policeman on the beat to befriend and neighbors to chat amiably with and the occasional new necktie to purchase. There was, simply put, a great deal for Zelig Kropf to do.

Zelig rose at five o'clock in the morning and was rarely in bed before midnight. He lived directly over his shop and rarely went out on any but the most pressing errands except to attend his class or to shop for groceries.

But, as was the case with Yudel Wolfzahn, success bred a new category of worries. As the business flourished, it became necessary to spend less and less time involved in the daily routine of running the business. Despite his inclinations, Zelig *did* hire someone to mop the floors and, eventually, an assistant pharmacist to help three days a week with the ongoing prescriptions of chronically ill patients. The tax system became clearer in Zelig's mind and required less attention and the neighbors became friends who no longer needed such serious courting.

And now a new realization struck Zelig Kropf one day towards the end of November in 1951 as he stood for a moment to survey his modest domain: he too was lonely. He was forty-one years old and still single. His friends were mostly customers he hardly knew and neighbors whose friendship he required rather than desired. There was the occasional neighborhood woman who, after delicately inquiring about the presence or absence of a *Mrs.* Kropf, would make it clear that she wouldn't say no were the druggist inclined to be friendly, but Zelig had found himself unwilling or unable to respond appropriately.

Now that the business was secure, Zelig allowed himself the luxury of contemplating things more precisely than he had found possible earlier on.

He had had a reasonable social life in Munich and had had many a young lady back to his bachelor's flat in the dowdy Agnesstrasse, but that part of the young Kropf had apparently died during the years in Theresienstadt, Auschwitz and Belsen. Even after being liberated and sent off to his new life, Zelig found himself unable to respond romantically to any of the attractive women he found himself with from time to time. He found them attractive, to be sure. And, from time to time, he felt the stirrings of a passion he had once found so natural and taken so for granted. But the ability to translate those nascent emotions into action was what the Nazis had taken along with any other part of the inner man that could have resulted in even momentary defenselessness.

But being unable to initiate or consummate romantic interludes with Queens County ladies wasn't precisely the same as possessing some sort of immunity to the need for at least social intercourse with a soul mate of some sort. As the work lessened in the shop and the profits increased, Zelig allowed himself to seek the friend he now openly acknowledged, at least to himself, that he wished to acquire.

There were a variety of false starts, among which could be counted wasted memberships in certain literary circles, pointless registration in Latin American dance lessons, fruitless enrollment in the Lions Club and a thankless stint as a Big Brother to a larcenous, sexually precocious yet morally retarded fourteen-year-old boy from Corona.

Eventually, Zelig found his way to the Queens Hebrew Congregation. He joined the synagogue, paid the special increment over the normal dues to belong to the health club as well and, when he least expected to, met not one but two friends.

Zelig knew both Larry Luft and Yudel Wolfzahn for months before it struck him that Wolfzahn was the missing piece of the puzzle that he was still carrying around in him since the day on which he was deported to the camps.

***

There had been no time for anything at all. The S.S. man had appeared at Zelig Kropf's door early one morning in the spring of 1942 and taken him to the train station. He was given a number and told to wait for his number to be called; from the amazing number of people with numbers milling around the station, he understood that his wait was going to be long.

By 1942, none of the remaining Jews in Munich had any doubts about what fate awaited them in the East. There was a good deal of emotion, but relatively little hysteria among the people in the station. Mostly, they sat pathetically on their suitcases and waited for their numbers to be called. As a sign of the degree to which it was impossible for the detainees to accept or even fully to fathom what was happening to them, Zelig liked to tell people that he recalled being vaguely disappointed to see that the snack bar in the station was closed and was quite surprised to find no paper in the men's washroom.

The day wore on and the crowd thinned. Trains left on their mysterious journeys to unknown destinations and those left behind became used to waiting.

Zelig closed his eyes and dozed off. Suddenly aware that someone was standing over him, Zelig opened his eyes and sat up. Just as he had somehow sensed, there was a man standing directly before him looking down on his sleeping form. He rose to his feet, expecting to recognize the person who, he presumed, had apparently recognized him, but he did not recognize him at all. The man was a perfect stranger.

"You'll live through this," the man said.

"I doubt it." Zelig was trying for cynicism, but all he could manage was bitter resignation.

"You will," he repeated, "I won't but you will."

Zelig found himself intrigued. "I will? How do you know? Are you a psychic?"

The man looked as though this were an odd thought. "I didn't come over here because you're going to survive," he said calmly and clearly, as though he were speaking to a child. "You're going to survive because I've come over here." There was a smoldering fire in the man's eyes, almost as though he had glass eyes that somehow managed to glint in an invisible ray of afternoon sun.

Zelig thought the man crazy, but his words were spoken with such intensity and conviction that they were impossible to dismiss as the ravings of a lunatic.

The stationmaster was calling out lists of numbers. A hush descended on the station. The man, like everyone Zelig could see, had a white piece of paper with his number scrawled on it pinned to the front of his overcoat. The stationmaster called the man's number. He looked at Zelig Kropf with more sadness than Zelig had ever imagined could be packed into one single glance.

"You will recognize him as soon as you see him," he said quickly, anxious, Zelig thought, to finish before the stationmaster stopped reading his lists of numbers. The bearers of those numbers were expected to go to the designated platform for their journey into the night.

"Who?"

"I don't know," the man said softly. "But you'll know. And when you find him, tell him that he'll know her when he finds her."

"Her? Who?"

The man smiled now, his face more weary than sad. "I don't know that either. But you'll know him and he'll know her. Tell them to have a baby."

This was too much for Zelig to fathom. "A baby?" he said with an almost silly laugh. "The man I'll know when I find him should have a baby with the woman he'll know when he finds her?"

The man seemed to miss the irony in Zelig's voice. And the stationmaster had finished with his list of numbers. The deportees in the just enumerated transport were bidden to present themselves with their luggage at Platform Eight.

"Look," the man said hurriedly, "take this." And with that, he pulled a discarded railroad ticket out of his pocket that, Zelig surmised, he must have found crumpled up somewhere in the train station. From another pocket, he produced a small pencil and, turning the ticket over to its blank side, he drew a face. Wordlessly, he handed the ticket to Zelig. Almost before Zelig could see what had been thrust into his hand, the man had vanished into the crowds descending to Platform Eight.

Zelig looked in vain for the man in the crowd, but he had disappeared. Zelig, suddenly consumed with curiosity, went after him. He managed to squeeze past scores of people and to arrive on Platform Eight even before the train itself had pulled into the station. Turning around suddenly, he saw the man with whom he had been speaking.

"Tell me more," he said into the man's ear.

"Tell him to inquire in the Catacomb of Santa Cecilia in Rome," the man said in a hushed whisper.

"Who? Who should inquire after whom?"

"The man you'll know," the man said patiently into Zelig's ear. "The man should go to Rome and visit the catacomb. Now go!"

The crush on the platform was becoming unbelievable as deportees, each clutching a single piece of luggage, endeavored not to become separated from their families. The cold spring air seemed suddenly stale and fetid; Zelig could hardly breathe and now wished to return to the great hall where he had first spoken with the man. The man, in the meantime, had looked away from Zelig and appeared to be scrutinizing the train tracks in the distance like a commuter impatiently waiting for a late train. Zelig knew that if he didn't leave the platform immediately, he would be unable to do so. Maybe it was already impossible to get back into the Great Hall, but he could still try. Zelig looked at the man, but he had turned away and, from the side, Zelig could see he was weeping.

Zelig pushed back through the crowd and somehow managed to return to his previous spot where he sat down on his suitcase. He found he could recall every single word the man had said to him. And he had the pencil sketch of a face to contemplate if he needed to convince himself that the exchange had really taken place. He stared at the picture and tried to derive some meaning from the man's strange words and as he did so, the stationmaster began to call a new list of numbers to constitute the evening's final transport.

Zelig Kropf's number was the very first on the list.

He shoved the man's little drawing in his pocket and waited for the stationmaster to finish the list of numbers and say to which track they were to report. Relieved not to have to spend the night seated on a suitcase in the train station, Zelig hurried to the track once it was announced and found himself only slightly surprised to find a boxcar sitting on the track rather than the second-class carriage in which he would normally have traveled.

The rest of Zelig Kropf's experiences during the war were almost too horrible to relate. Shipped first to Theresienstadt and then to Auschwitz-Birkenau, where he worked as a slave laborer at the I.G.-Farben-Werke, the only positive thing Zelig ever found to say about his stay in Auschwitz-Birkenau was that he was spared actually having to witness the daily selections or having to empty the gas chambers of the corpses once the poison gas had dissipated and it was possible to transport the bodies to the crematoria. From time to time, Zelig allowed himself to ponder the stranger's prediction that he would survive, but without allowing himself to attach too much hope to it. The stranger himself, after all, had also been on a transport headed for the East and it was almost impossible to imagine that he could have survived.

Of course, Zelig reminded himself, the man had specifically indicated that he himself was *not* going to survive. Eventually, it dawned on Zelig that it was precisely because the man felt that he himself *wouldn't* live but Zelig *would* that he had confided his secret in him in the first place.

The Russians liberated Auschwitz on January 27, 1945, but by then Zelig had already been relocated by the Germans to Bergen-Belsen. Eventually, he came to New York…

***

Oddly enough, it was the contemplation of Larry Luft's pink torso that first brought Zelig Kropf back to the strange words the tall stranger had addressed to him in the Munich Bahnhof in 1942.

It was a warm Sunday morning in May, 1952. The three friends were sitting in the steam and discussing Eisenhower's election prospects. The conversation was animated, but not entirely three-sided; for some reason, Yudel and Lawrence Lazar were squaring off against each other and Zelig Kropf was sitting off to the side contributing the occasional comment, but otherwise silent.

As he sat, he found himself lost in contemplation of Larry Luft's body. It was wet from the steam and pink from the heat and almost exuded a perfume redolent of health and strength. Zelig wondered what it would be like to have such a body, to have muscular upper arms and firm, hard thighs, to have a rounded, boyish stomach and a strong back that had never felt the sting of an S.S. man's whip or a German boot.

Zelig lay back on the tiled bench as his mind began to wander. Before he knew it, he was thinking about the tall man's prediction in the Munich Bahnhof that he would survive the war. He *had*, obviously, survived, he thought, but so had a lot of others. If Europe's cities were mostly empty of their Jews, Forest Hills was filled with them. The refugee ambience was such that some witty merchants had even taken to placing "English Spoken Here" signs in their windows, withdrawing them only after having it brought to their attention how hurtful such signs were to the immigrant community and how disdainful of what most of them had gone through to get to where they now were.

But the man hadn't only said that he would survive; he had also predicted that he would eventually find someone. "*Sobald Sie ihn sehen, werden Sie ihn sofort erkennen*," the man had said, Zelig still recalled. But what that meant, Zelig could still hardly say. Whom would he recognize? And would he really tell this person that he will recognize some woman when *he* sees *her*?

The ambience of the beige tiles and the hot steam, the presence of friends, the snippets of conversation Zelig could hear clearly over the whoosh of the steam, the communal nudity and the Jewish nature of the surroundings all combined to create a sense of wonder in Zelig. He had found his place.

The presence of the tall stranger was always with Zelig, always buried somewhere within the folds and creases of his consciousness. The man himself was undoubtedly dead—his transport, Zelig later learned, had gone directly to Auschwitz without the usual intermediate stop at Theresienstadt and that, for a man his age, could only have meant the gas chamber.

But even in his absence, his presence lingered on. Even more surprising, Zelig still had in his possession the crumpled railway ticket the man had given him in the station. It was the only possession he had taken along when the Germans had forced him to walk from Auschwitz to Belsen before all of Poland fell into the hands of the Red Army and it was the sole possession he had taken with him when he finally left the D.P camp at Flossenbürg for the trip to Hamburg.

Zelig allowed himself the uncustomary luxury of becoming lost in his own thoughts. He closed his eyes tightly and thought of his bachelor flat on the Agnesstrasse. He could recall with the greatest precision the way his body had begun to shake uncontrollably when the knock on the door at dawn had come and the polite demeanor of the young S.S. man who had handed him his deportation summons. The whole incident seemed otherworldly now, as though it had happened in some strange dimension or on some other planet. Yet the whole Nazi debacle hadn't happened elsewhere, Zelig knew, but here on earth. And millions upon millions of people had died because it had. A certain familiar *frisson* of outrage, horror and grief travelled down Zelig's spine into the cleft of his buttocks and rested there.

It was a most unlikely sensation, almost as though he were sitting on a glowing coal that was cold rather than hot. Zelig actually reached around to feel between if some insect or some tiny rodent hadn't crawled under him. But even as he did so, he knew that the experience was not physical, but metaphysical—and deeply so.

The cold heat enveloped Zelig Kropf's buttocks and travelled forward to form a sort of tingly girdle around his loins. It was, Zelig later thought, a bit like the initial stages of sexual arousal without the sense of playful anticipation. It was an utterly odd feeling, but not an entirely unpleasant one. Zelig fell into an even deeper and more introspective reverie.

To his amazement, he found that he was able to recall the scene in the Bahnhof with even greater precision than ever before. He closed his eyes and remembered the pathetic surprise he had felt to discover that the little snack bar by the great front gate was closed; to Zelig's surprise, he found he could actually read the menu off the signboard posted overhead. In his mind's eye, he followed the signboard down past the snack bar into the Great Hall itself.

He could see the phalanx of S.S. men guarding the front door, collecting the deportation summonses of new arrivals and handing out numbers which the detainees were to pin to their jackets and coats. In his mind's eye, he could actually see himself coming closer to the men and, to his great amazement, he found he could actually hear their conversation. They were discussing football, Zelig realized with a sudden surge of anger. They were busy helping deport innocent babies to the ovens of Auschwitz and Treblinka, but what really interested these proud soldiers of the Reich was football.

Zelig could see himself now as though he were some sort of bird circling overhead in the enormous space of the Great Hall. He pulled his gaze away from the S.S. men and turned back to the place in which he—the real Zelig—was standing and talking to the tall stranger.

He could hear the man saying the very words he could recall him having said in real life. "*Sobald Sie ihn sehen, werden Sie ihn sofort erkennen,*" the man had said. Zelig thought of the man's words as they would have sounded in English—"You will recognize him as soon as you see him"—and decided the German words had a deeper, darker ring to them than the English would have had.

But now, suddenly, Zelig saw something he hadn't recalled before. The man, who was at least six inches taller than Zelig, had moved his eyes slightly when he had spoken.

As though he were manning the controls of some (as yet, uninvented) video tape recorder, Zelig found he could manipulate the passage of time at will; he simply willed the scene to replay and it did. He could see the man approaching him and he could see himself opening his eyes as he realized that someone was standing over him.

He could hear the conversation again, but this time he gave the full brunt of his attention to the tall man. "*Sobald Sie ihn sehen, werden Sie ihn sofort erkennen,*" the man said again. But this time, Zelig concentrated on the man's eyes. Sure enough, just as he had somehow sensed the previous time, the man's head lifted slightly on the word "*sehen*" as though he expected himself somehow to *see* the man about whom he was speaking.

Even years later, Zelig couldn't say how he knew to do so, but somehow he *had* known what to do. He played the tape a third time.

Again, the snack bar. Again, the bored S.S. men talking about football as they processed innocent babes for their trips to the gas. Again, the tall stranger standing overhead. Zelig could see himself opening his eyes and thinking for a moment he would recognize the man standing over him. The man opened his mouth to speak.

"*Sofort Sie ihn sehen...*" On the word "*sehen*", the man's eyes lifted slightly and Zelig himself opened his eyes. Standing over him was a man, just as had been the case in the train station.

Larry Luft had apparently gone off to use the toilet or to get a cool drink while Zelig had been playing his scene over and over in his mind's eye. Before him, looking down at his seated friend, stood the naked Yudel Wolfzahn.

The moment he saw him, Zelig Kropf recognized him.

Seventeen

*O*nce things began to happen, they happened quickly.

Zelig had the good sense not to start in with Yudel Wolfzahn about his crazy fantasy while the two of them were stark naked, overheated and damp. Instead, he planned to wait until precisely the correct moment to bring the matter up and then to tell the whole story to Yudel as though it were some loony dream he had once had. From Yudel's reaction to the story, Zelig figured, he would somehow be able to tell what the most appropriate next step would be.

The two friends left the steam room and found Larry Luft naked and still wet from his shower, standing by a half-open window in the locker room. He was smoking a filterless cigarette and looking pensive.

It was already almost noon. Yudel himself had to go home to his family, Zelig had the shop open from one to five on Sunday afternoons and Larry Luft had a date; everyone was in a bit of a hurry to get going.

"So we'll have dinner on Wednesday?" Larry's question was half suggestion and half confirmation—over the previous few months, the three had taken to having a late dinner together on Wednesday evenings to discuss all sorts of things that it was impolite, impractical or impolitic to discuss in a public steam bath.

"I'm in," Zelig answered immediately, pleased—it was usually *he* whom the others left in the position of confirming their weekly dinner.

"Me too," Yudel answered. "But no more Chinese this time. Let's eat in a deli."

The idea met with general approval and, the specific delicatessen chosen and agreed upon, each friend was free to shower, dress and take his hasty leave. They would reconvene on Wednesday at eight o'clock at the Boulevard Deli on 102nd Street just off Queens Boulevard.

Zelig was secretly pleased; a thick, hot corned beef sandwich washed down by a few bottles of beer would, he thought, create precisely the right ambience of genial warmth and relaxed intimacy in which to the broach the topic at hand. He would wait until the meal was over and the bill paid. As usual, Larry Luft would collect each friend's share and then go himself to the front of the store to pay the check with one of the very large bills with which he always seemed to be burdened.

As soon as Larry would make for the front register, Zelig would touch Yudel's sleeve to draw his attention. He would mouth 'Stay, I want to talk to you' or words to that effect almost silently to his friend who would understand precisely what was being asked of him.

The three would all get up to leave and go into the street, but once Larry Luft had headed off towards his home, Zelig and Yudel would go back into the restaurant. They would order hot tea and dessert and, at precisely the right moment, Zelig would tell him about the tall stranger in the Munich train station.

The plan was a good one. The friends parted, each to his own afternoon plans. An hour later, Zelig Kropf was reading a newspaper at the front desk of his pharmacy waiting for a customer.

The afternoon came and went; Zelig Kropf's few Sunday customers were served, the floor was swept, the day's take was entered into the register and the front door was locked.

Like every other Sunday evening, Zelig had every intention of going upstairs to his apartment and cooking himself a veal chop for dinner. He would eat his chop, read the Sunday *Times*, perhaps watch a program or two on his new television and go to bed.

But this Sunday evening was quite different. Zelig went upstairs and cooked his chop, but he found his usually robust appetite strangely faint. He opened the paper and closed it again. He turned on his little television only to find the Sunday night slapstick grating rather than calming. Zelig walked around his apartment pondering the source of his discontent.

It didn't take him long to recognize what it was that was bothering him—he was anxious, even perhaps worried about his plans for Wednesday evening. So many things could go wrong! Yudel might cancel, for one thing—he did that from time to time if there were the possibility of some overtime work at *The Times*. Overtime meant doubletime and Yudel was always happy to pick up a few extra dollars for doing in the evening the same work he did all day long anyway.

Then there was the possibility that he would refuse to stay after the meal to speak with Zelig privately. True, Zelig told himself, there was no obvious reason why he shouldn't agree, but it was always possible he would somehow suspect that he was about to be drawn into a mystery he would probably be happier avoiding.

On top of all that, there was the chance, slight but ominous once Zelig thought of it, that Yudel would know precisely what Zelig was speaking about. After all, the man in the train station had said that Zelig would recognize the man as soon as he would see him, but he didn't say that the man wouldn't have his own message to impart. This did seem far-fetched, but the more Zelig thought about it, the more plausible it appeared to be. Zelig, for his part he now realized, had no message at all for Yudel. He had only been told to tell the man he would know that he, the recognized man, would recognize some unidentified woman as soon as he saw her. That, Zelig knew, was not much of a message at all.

The possibility that the man he was supposed to recognize would have a message for him was something he had simply not considered previously, but the more he thought about it, the more plausible this scenario became. Perhaps, Zelig suddenly realized as he folded his newspaper and stood up in the center of his sparse living room, the point of finding the man was that there would be a message he would have *for Zelig* rather than the other way around. The possibility was alluring, but also daunting, tantalizing and threatening all at the same time.

Zelig walked around his apartment and knew he could not wait for Wednesday, especially since he had no certainty he would even *have* the chance to speak privately with Yudel then either. Zelig put on his jacket. He would see Yudel that very evening.

It was a cool evening for May in New York. The day had been warm and lovely, but the sun had taken its warm rays with it when it had set and the evening air had a distinct chill in it. Zelig left his apartment and locked the door behind him. Quickly, he walked to the corner, crossed Queens Boulevard and continued eastward on the south side of the great avenue. On the far corner of Continental Avenue, there was a public telephone.

With a strange sense of unexpected gravity, Zelig dialed the Wolfzahns' number. Yudel answered on the first ring. The sounds in the background told him that the Wolfzahns were enjoying an evening of television before retiring for the night. It was ten minutes past ten.

"Yudel, it's me," Zelig said.

"*Mazel tov.*"

"Are you doing anything?"

"We're just watching television. Do you want to come over?"

Clara Wolfzahn had long since made her peace with having to entertain some of her husband's single friends from time to time. It was, she rationalized, better than having *them* take *him* to whatever bachelor haunts Queens might have to offer.

"Come over? No, not tonight. But I need to speak to you. Can you come down?"

"Down? Where down?"

"Downstairs. I'm on the corner of Continental and the Boulevard. I'll meet you somewhere or I'll wait for you here."

There was a pregnant silence on the line. "This is important?" Yudel asked finally.

"Yes, yes it is. It is important and I need to see you. I know you have work in the morning. I wouldn't bother you this late if it weren't something important."

"This is going to be all-night important or home-by-eleven important?"

"Home-by-eleven," Zelig promised, the relief in his voice audible.

"Okay," Yudel agreed. "Addie Vallin's in ten minutes?"

"*Gemacht*," Zelig answered cheerfully. "Ten minutes."

Addie Vallin's was Forest Hills' favorite ice cream parlor for as long as it existed. Dowdy and old-fashioned in its dotage without being so in a classic or classy way, it was the height of elegance in its early years. The shop, which was open late on Sunday evenings to serve the crowds leaving the Midway and Forest Hills movie theaters when the eight o'clock shows let out, was filled when Zelig got to the front door. He gave his name and stood in line. Precisely at the moment he could see Yudel Wolfzahn coming through the thick glass doors at the front of the shop, he heard his name called for a table for two.

The friends, unaccustomed to seeing each other on a Sunday evening, exchanged a rather solemn greeting. 'He knows I'm going to give him a headache,' Zelig thought to himself.

Yudel, convinced his friend was about to announce a malignant tumor growing somewhere in his body, looked appropriately grim.

The men were seated at their tiny, round table. A waitress took their order: a chocolate ice cream soda for Yudel and a Hoboken— coffee ice cream and pineapple syrup—for Zelig Kropf.

Not wanting to be interrupted by the arrival of the drinks, Zelig decided on small talk to keep things moving until he was ready to tell the story he had summoned his friend to hear.

The service was slow. Zelig and Yudel had time to cover the

weather, the heat that morning in the steamroom, the waitress' bosom, Eisenhower's election prospects (a favorite topic for both men), the travesty of Nuremberg (another favorite) and the superiority of American, as opposed to European, ice cream before the waitress came at the perfectly appropriate moment, with her tray of sodas made with American rather than European ice cream.

The friends sipped a bit of the soda first so that the ice cream would sink beneath the lip of the tall glasses in which the sodas were served. Once it was safe to do so, they began to spoon slivers of ice cream into their mouths with the long spoons provided. For a few moments, there was no need for talk. But after a few minutes, Zelig felt compelled to begin his story.

"So," he began tentatively, "you're probably wondering what we're doing here."

"I suppose. But you know, you don't always have to have a reason to phone. You could just feel like an ice cream soda and we could just go once in a while. Luft phones from time to time and we go somewhere to drink coffee and *shmooze* for an hour."

Zelig pondered this information. He was flattered by the thought that Yudel would like to spend time with him even when he had no particularly pressing reason to do so and a bit hurt to learn that Lawrence Lazar and Yudel had gone for coffee now and then without thinking to phone and ask if he'd like to come along. The fact that he himself had phoned Yudel that evening precisely because he wanted to spend an hour together without Lawrence had nothing to do with it. Zelig had a pressing *reason* for wanting to speak to his friend alone, while Larry Luft had apparently had no particular reason at all, pressing or otherwise, to spend time alone with Yudel.

"So maybe I will," he answered lightly. "But tonight is different. Tonight, I have a story I have to tell you. Only promise to hear me out and not to interrupt until I'm done."

Yudel's eyes widened slightly. "All right," he said softly.

In the garish neon light of Addie Vallin's Ice Cream Parlor, Zelig Kropf told his story about being deported from Munich ten years earlier. He spoke quietly and without emotion. He told of the tall man and, without having known in advance that he would, he revealed the man's words.

Then, having finished the part about his own number being called, he flipped ten years into the future and took up the story that very morning.

"You remember this morning, you and Larry were talking about politics or something in the steamroom and I sort of closed my eyes and lay down?"

Yudel nodded his assent.

"And you know he went out to shower or to take a leak or to smoke or something and the two of us were left alone?"

"I remember," Yudel said quietly.

"And you remember that you had stood up and come over to me, but before you could actually say anything, I opened my eyes and you were there?"

Yudel had felt strange at that particular moment himself, which was why he had stood up in the first place, but nowhere near as odd as he was feeling at this particular moment. A sort of numbness was creeping over his legs and loins, not so much a deadening of the limbs as much as a sort of etherialization of the flesh. The soles of Yudel Wolfzahn's feet were tingling, as were the palms of his hands. He could almost feel the rest of the tables in the restaurant being wheeled by invisible stage hands into the wings at the same moment some unseen sound engineer turned down the volume at all but his own table.

The sense was of being alone in a deserted world. There were clearly people all around, but suddenly Yudel couldn't hear a single word emanating from any other table. Activity was going on all around as waiters scurried about with trays of sundaes and ice cream sodas. The neon fixtures hanging from the ceiling seemed to brighten and, as they did so, their glare somehow obscured the other tables in the restaurant. Yudel looked at his friend, half expecting him to say something about the weird ambience, but Zelig seemed as unaware of the sensations Yudel was experiencing as Yudel himself had apparently been of Zelig's experience that very morning in the steamroom.

But Zelig was continuing his story. "So it was like I was back in the Bahnhof," he was saying. "I could see myself from above as though I were a swallow that had somehow flown into the station through the open eaves and I could see the man come close."

Yudel merely nodded and indicated with a waving motion of his hands that he wished Zelig to continue.

"So I could see all sorts of things I hadn't remembered remembering. I could read the menu on the wall behind the snack bar, for example. And I could hear—*actually hear*—those Nazi bastards discussing football as they processed people arriving at the station. I don't mean I somehow knew what they were talking about either," he stressed. "I could *actually* hear their voices."

Yudel wanted to ask about the voices. Had he heard them speak, or seen them speak and merely known somehow what they were talking about? And how could Zelig suddenly remember something like that without having known all along that such an indelible scene was embedded somewhere in his memory for a decade?

These and other questions deserve to be asked, Yudel thought to himself. But he found himself physically unable to pose them. Instead, he simply listened to the story and tried to take it all in.

"So I found I could sort of see the same scene twice if I wanted," Zelig was saying.

"If you wanted?"

"Well, for instance, it was only the second time I heard the man saying "*Sobald Sie ihn sehen, werden Sie ihn sofort erkennen*" that I noticed his eyes. He was looking up, but not really looking looking, just glancing. Actually, even glancing is too much. He was only lifting his eyes slightly, just sort of opening them a bit wider than they had been a moment earlier. So as he said that I would *see* the man and recognize him, he made this weird little gesture with his eyes."

"And you didn't remember remembering that?"

"No," he said, "I didn't."

"And then what?"

"Then I watched the scene a third time and this time, when he got to the part where he told me I would recognize the man as soon as I was going to *see* him, I opened my eyes."

Yudel already knew the end of the story. "And there I was."

"And there you were."

"And you recognized me?"

Zelig moved his empty soda glass to one side of the small, round table and leaned over so that his lips were practically touching Yudel Wolfzahn's right ear. Yudel could actually feel Zelig Kropf's breath on his ear lobe as he opened his mouth to speak. "I did," he said.

There was a strange stirring in the room around the Kropf-Wolfzahn table. The sounds emanating from the nearby tables were still muffled, but they had become slightly more audible now and Yudel felt that increase in volume almost physically.

"And what else did he say? I mean, aside from that you'd recognize the man when you saw him, what did he say?"

Zelig sat back in his white, cast-iron chair and contemplated the question. Up until now, he had merely related a strange incident that had mainly involved himself.

But there was a second—and a third!—part to the man's remarks that would transform Yudel from passive object into active player. Zelig was suddenly aware that he was about to change another man's life and the sensation was slightly frightening. Zelig pondered for a moment the single rabbinic dictum Yudel had ever taught him—it was the only one Yudel himself remembered from his days in *cheder* on the Schäferkampsallee—*ein hobrocho nimtzo-o ele basomui min ho-oyin.* It suddenly seemed profoundly important that, of all things, *Yudel* had taught *him* the ancient lesson according to which the blessings of God can only be found in that which is hidden from the human eye. He could almost hear Yudel's imitation of his ancient teacher's voice reciting the hoary teaching and, almost despite himself, Zelig found himself wondering if his friend's old teacher had had that very rabbinic teaching in mind as he was crammed with another few boxcar-loads of the doomed into one of the gas chambers at Auschwitz and asphyxiated.

All this musing, of course, took only moments. Zelig knew he was going to reveal at least the second part of the man's message—this, he understood now, was the real reason he had needed to meet with Yudel alone.

"Well," he answered simply, "he did say something else."

"*Nu?*"

"He said, '*Sobald er sie sieht, wird er sie sofort erkennen*'—'As soon as he sees her, he will recognize her.'"

"I *know* what it means," Yudel responded brusquely to the unnecessary translation. "What I don't know is what it *means*."

Zelig smiled and, at that precise moment, decided to save the third part of the message for some other time.

"Well, I don't know what it means either. But then again, I didn't know what the first part meant until this morning, so why should I figure everything out in one day. Maybe things will be clear tomorrow."

"They said overcast and showers in the morning," Yudel joked.

"Very funny. But who knows? Maybe we will understand if we wait. I waited ten years for the first part, now it's your turn to wait."

"Don't overstate your case. I wouldn't say you exactly understand the first part either. I mean, you were told you'd recognize someone when you saw him. But that doesn't mean that you'd ever know that you were right. And the big question—I mean the question of whom exactly it is you are to recognize when you see him—that's a question to which you have no answer at all as of yet."

Zelig wasn't quite sure how to react. In a certain sense, Yudel was absolutely right: he had no idea what the larger picture was and he had no way to know whether or not he had recognized the right man. Still, the experience of that morning had been a profound one and Zelig found himself unable to set it aside as a mere hallucination brought on by the excessive heat in the steamroom.

The waitress brought coffee and, as she set the white porcelain cups in front of the two friends, Zelig suddenly recalled that there was not only a third part to the message—the part about the man he was to recognize having a baby with the woman the man himself would recognize—but a fourth part as well, the part about the Catacomb of Santa Cecilia.

Zelig had taken the trouble to inform himself a bit about the catacomb. He, like most people, had known well enough that there were ancient cemeteries beneath the city of Rome and that these were called catacombs. But, also like most people, he hadn't known much more. Unlike most other people, however, Zelig had not been content to acknowledge his ignorance. He had made it a priority, once he was settled in his new country, to investigate the larger picture of underground Roman burial practices.

He was hardly an expert, but he had achieved something and Zelig was now able to speak with the authority born of personal research about the differences between a lucinarium, a columbarium, a cubiculum and an arcosolium. And he was quite familiar, specifically, with the Catacomb of Santa Cecilia. In one of the first books Zelig had purchased after coming to New York, he had been delighted to find a floor plan of the famous catacomb and some color plates of its most famous frescoes. He had studied the plates and read the accompanying text with the greatest interest, making detailed notes on what he had read and composing lists of books to consult for further information.

By the time he and Yudel Wolfzahn were sitting over ice cream sodas in Addie Vallin's, Zelig felt secure that he had gone as far as he possibly could in terms of materials available through the Queensborough Public Library System. If he *had*, somehow, found the information to which the man had been referring, he had failed to understand its significance. But Zelig somehow felt that he hadn't found the relevant information. Eventually, he thought, either he or the man he was to recognize would have to undertake a journey to Rome to see what secrets, if any, the catacomb would give up to someone who came to visit in person.

"You're absolutely right," he agreed readily, content with his decision to keep the rest of the message to himself, at least for the moment. "I hardly understand anything. But the one thing you have to believe that I *do* understand is that you are the man I was told I'd recognize. I can't exactly say how I know, but I know that I have never been more sure of anything in my whole life. So either trust me or don't, but a man approached me in the Munich Bahnhof ten years ago as we were both being deported and he told me I'd recognize you as soon as I saw you. So it's true I knew you for a long time before I recognized you, but maybe I've known you all this time without really *seeing* you, at least in the way the man meant that one man can see another if he really opens his eyes. Look, I don't know what I'm talking about, but I know I'm right. So don't ask how I know because I also don't know how I know. But I know that I know and..."

"And what?" A subtle tone of belligerence in Yudel's characteristically calm voice.

"...and now you know too."

***

Wednesday evening at eight o'clock, Yudel Wolfzahn and Zelig Kropf were sitting at their semi-customary table at the Boulevard Deli. Across from them was Sandy Gold, the athletic director from the Queens Hebrew Congregation. Lawrence Lazar had phoned at the last minute and begged off; he was tied up at the factory and wasn't sure he could be free much before ten o'clock that evening. He would have dinner at the office, he said, and see his friends on Sunday morning. Sandy Gold had been seated at a table alone at the rear of the store; it had been Zelig's idea to invite him to join them. They had planned to be three anyway, he said discreetly to Yudel, and it would also be a *mitzvah* to provide Gold with a bit of genuine fellowship when he was obviously eating dinner all alone.

Directly in front of the deli's front window, the little concrete island that separated 102nd Street from Queens Boulevard had only recently been outfitted with green wooden benches. The benches were a neighborhood hit—each was filled as late as eight o'clock on a warm May evening with neighbors and friends seeking a bit of company. In the center of the cement triangle, children were playing under the watchful gaze of their parents and, in some few cases, grandparents.

The sounds of the children playing and the parents chatting in Polish, French, Yiddish and German came wafting pleasantly through the open front door of the Boulevard and combined with the deeply evocative smell of smoked meat, coleslaw and sharp mustard laced with horseradish to create an atmosphere of cordiality. Often the men ate Chinese at their Wednesday night dinners, but although all three liked Chinese food, the ambience in any of Forest Hills' several Chinese restaurants couldn't compare with the atmosphere that prevailed at the Boulevard Deli.

The formica tables, the stainless steel bowls of sour tomatoes with their dainty, curved lips and sturdy, round bases, the plastic greenery that surrounded the meat counter itself, the great brass-and-plastic chandeliers that hung at regular intervals from the front to the back of the narrow restaurant—all these together conspired to create a unique Jewish atmosphere.

A buxom waitress in a white uniform appeared at the table, distributed menus and awaited the orders. Sandy Gold and Yudel chose corned beef and Zelig, the hard salami. In a few minutes, the waitress re-appeared with an enormous tray of food. The sandwiches, each of which was at least one and a half inches thick, were served with a side of fried potatoes and a mound of fresh coleslaw and, for a few minutes, no one spoke.

Once everybody's initial hunger had been assuaged, the pace of the meal slowed and conversation took place. The topics were the same as they always were—Eisenhower, Nuremberg, baseball, business and the waitress' ample bosom. Despite the fact that the very same ground had been covered just a few days earlier, there were always new angles to explore: new developments to report, new information to share, new insights into the same old subject matter to offer and new observations to make. The conversation was especially animated and enjoyable, Zelig thought.

Yudel too was enjoying the evening immensely. He had found the friends he had so sorely lacked and he liked the whole casual experience of dining out in a deli with them. The room was long and narrow, a lay-out that provided an unexpected bit of privacy for all the diners. Other tables were occupied, but one could hardly hear a single word being said by any other customer.

Yudel had been feeling strangely tired all day. He hadn't slept too well the previous evening and he had spent an especially difficult day at work. By three in the afternoon, he had seriously considered asking his supervisor for twenty minutes or so to lie down in the employees' lounge area, but he had thought better of doing so and had persevered until the end of the day.

When he came home, he had felt better. Yudel had showered and changed his clothing, looked briefly at the mail, spoken a bit with Clara and hurried out to join his friends. As he had rushed down Austin Street, he had thought to himself how invigorating his shower must have been—he hardly felt tired at all!

But now the old lassitude had returned. Yudel had drunk only half a bottle of beer and was feeling suddenly very tired and not quite able to keep up with his friends' conversation.

Zelig and Sandy Gold had drifted onto the topic of trade unions. Gold, the son of a factory owner, loathed even the thought of his father's workers being unionized. He was good to them, he provided for them, he cared for them *and* about them and he didn't need somebody from outside the plant coming in to tell him how to do his business.

Zelig Kropf, druggist, felt differently. Although he was an employer himself, he felt strongly that workers needed to organize. Organization was hardly necessary for people, he conceded, who worked for benign despots like himself or Sandy Gold's saintly father. But, he asked, what about those millions of Jewish people who must work for anti-Semitic maniacs? Certainly an organized factory can guarantee that no one will have to suffer for reasons of race or religion, Zelig insisted.

Sandy responded and Zelig retorted and Sandy answered and Zelig came back with yet another argument in favor of unionization. Zelig was enjoying the row—he and Lawrence Lazar usually agreed to avoid this topic precisely because each knew how strongly the other felt and how dangerous such an argument would be to their friendship.

In the heat of the conversation, neither Sandy nor Zelig noticed that Yudel was apparently lost in his own thoughts. His eyes had closed and he appeared either to be deep in a moment of introspection or, more likely, asleep.

His head dropped until his chin nearly touched his chest. He had told himself that he would close his eyes only for a brief moment, but once he had actually shut his eyes, they remained closed.

Yudel felt himself being drawn into some sort of trance from which he could not awaken. In this state, somehow, he was back in the Faculty of Law in Hamburg. Specifically, he was seated in his carrel in the library, studying some oversized volume of Hanseatic sea law. Vaguely, Yudel could remember that he must have been preparing for an examination on that very material when he was expelled from the university in 1933.

The library was dark and quiet, almost as though Yudel were the only person there. The light was indirect and pleasantly diffused by amber glass shades that shielded the naked light bulbs that hung from the ceiling at regular intervals. The work, which Yudel recalled as being dull and difficult to learn, was actually, he was surprised to find, quite interesting.

Both able to watch himself from a distance and also to be himself seated in the carrel, Yudel could somehow feel the pages beneath his fingers as he saw himself turning them. He was finding each word to be utterly fascinating and could barely tear himself away from each page as he reached its end.

Suddenly, there was the sound of someone approaching. Yudel looked up to find a man wearing a Nazi armband and a brown shirt standing over him.

"Are you the Jew Wolfzahn?" he asked.

"*Jawohl*," answered Yudel, just as he recalled having done in 1933.

"You are to come with me immediately. We've finally gotten permission to cleanse our school of Jewish vermin."

Yudel had hardly understood what the man was saying. He looked into his face, just as he had done in 1933, and saw that he didn't recognize him from the Law Faculty. Probably, he imagined, this was some punk from outside who had broken in.

"I don't have to do anything I don't want to do," he answered more defiantly than he recalled having done when he had really been expelled.

The man cleared the books off Yudel's desk with a single sweep of his arm. The books, especially the big tome of sea law, went flying onto the floor and when Yudel stood up and bent down to pick his book up, the man's arm crashed down on the back of his neck.

Looking on the scene from above, Yudel could simultaneously feel the sharp pain on the back of his neck and see himself sprawled on the floor. As he stood up, the man grabbed his arm and carried him off to the office of the school's rector.

Yudel could recall his relief at being brought to the rector's office. The rector, a man who had trained for the Lutheran clergy only to decide at the last minute on a career in law and who was still known for his devout religious beliefs, would undoubtedly stand up for one of his own students!

The man practically dragged Yudel along the endless corridors of the Law School. They went down long hallways Yudel could hardly even recall being in and up long flights of stairs where Yudel was sure there hadn't previously been any. They went through offices and offices and finally, Yudel was relieved to see himself standing in front of the real rector's office.

The Nazi thug who had been dragging him along the corridors left Yudel in a heap in front of the outer door to the rector's office and went inside.

Yudel could clearly hear the man announcing him, rather in the manner of medieval court heralds. "The Jew Wolfzahn," the man called out as though the rector were somewhere distant and would otherwise be unable to hear his voice.

"Bring him in," came the reply, but it was from so far away that Yudel couldn't decide if he did or didn't recognize his rector's voice. Unable to turn away now, he did as the voice bade him and went inside the room.

The rector's office was as he had remembered it being in 1933, except instead of being roughly square in shape, it was a long rectangle, so long that Yudel could hardly even see the rector's desk at the far end. Unsure of what to do, Yudel stepped forward. The brownshirt who had summoned him was nowhere to be seen.

Yudel walked and walked towards the rector's desk. It seemed unbelievably far away, he thought, and the strange thing was that it didn't appear to become closer no matter how far he walked. But eventually, there was *some* progress and the distant end of the office appeared more and more in focus.

Eventually, Yudel got to the rector's desk, but instead of the saintly Joachim Schmidt, there was a different man standing before him. The new rector was a Jew.

Yudel knew he was a Jew because he was wearing a skull cap and a great black and white *tallis,* the traditional prayer shawl Yudel wore on the rare occasions he went with his father to synagogue.

Yudel could hardly believe his eyes—as far as he could recall, he had been summoned to Joachim Schmidt's office in 1933 only to find the office occupied by a new rector, a petty functionary of the nascent Hamburger NSDAP with no training at all in law. The man, a butcher by trade, had looked at him with the greatest contumely and told him he had one hour to gather his things and get out or else he would be arrested for trespassing.

On the way out, Yudel could recall running into the school's contingent of Jewish professors, themselves scurrying to gather their personal effects from their offices rather than risk arrest for trespassing.

One of the professors, the one whose examination in maritime law Yudel had been preparing to take the following day, was wandering in the hall dazed, apparently so shocked by his abrupt dismissal from the faculty that he could not even find his office, much less empty it of his belongings in a single hour.

In 1933, Yudel had given almost his whole hour up to helping his teacher and had run to the library only at the end of the allotted time to gather his own few possessions.

But the butcher didn't seem to be in the rector's office in Yudel's vision and, in his place, there was clearly a Jewish man. The man looked sad, more deeply unhappy than Yudel could ever recall seeing anybody look. He had tears in his red eyes and seemed to be observing the laws of the Jewish mourner—he was unshaven and barefoot and had been seated on a low wooden stool rather than at Joachim Schmidt's desk.

The man approached Yudel and gently took his hand. Yudel, although he was primarily watching the scene from above, could actually feel the cold grasp of the man's hand as it took his own.

He looked up at the Jewish man and waited for him to speak. The man had obviously been weeping before Yudel had come in and was now trying to compose himself. With great difficulty—but also, Yudel thought, with great dignity—the man stood directly before Yudel Wolfzahn and opened his mouth to speak.

"*Sobald Sie sie sehen, werden Sie sie sofort erkennen,*" he said quietly.

"As soon as you see her, you will recognize her," Yudel translated for no particular reason into English.

Yudel felt he should say something, but he could hardly decide what to say. He needed to ask any of a dozen questions, but he found he could hardly formulate any.

Finally, ashamed of his own inability to speak, Yudel forced a single question from his lips. "What?" he asked.

"*Sobald Sie sie sehen, werden Sie sie sofort erkennen,*" the man repeated. This time, Yudel thought he noticed a slight movement in the man's eyes, a slight widening almost as though the man expected to see the woman about whom he was speaking come through the door at the very moment he was speaking about seeing her.

"What did you say?" Yudel asked again, knowing somehow that he had come to his last chance to ask.

But the man did not answer and Yudel was hurtled back into reality. The vision was over, there was nothing at all to see but the customary darkness one sees with closed eyes. As disappointed as he was, Yudel could suddenly hear that Sandy Gold and Zelig had shifted gears and were discussing baseball.

He was about to open his eyes, when he suddenly, unexpectedly, heard the man's voice one final time. "*Sobald Sie sie sehen...*" the man was saying a third time.

As the man spoke the word meaning 'to see', Yudel somehow knew to open his eyes.

Before him, there stood the waitress who had taken their orders and who was now standing again at the table. She was holding Sandy Gold's and Zelig's empty plates and contemplating Yudel's own plate which he had hardly touched. "You want me to wrap that stuff up?" she asked, politely gesturing towards Yudel's uneaten sandwich and cold fries.

Yudel found he couldn't take his eyes off the waitress. "What's your name?" he said, ignoring her question.

Sandy Gold and Zelig both smiled at their married friend's forward question. The waitress smiled as well.

"For someone who's been staring at my chest all night, you don't read too well," she said with a barely squelched laugh.

Yudel lowered his eyes to his waitress' bosom and there, embroidered directly over her right breast was, in fact, her name.

"Your name is Bunny?" he asked.

"No," she answered, her grin broad now, "my right tit is named Bunny. You want to know what I call the left one?"

Yudel took a wild guess. "Honey?" he suggested.

The waitress, far from being offended, laughed out loud. "I like that," she said, "Honey and Bunny. Good names for Jewish bosoms, I'd say."

"Better than Frumma and Shtuma," Zelig volunteered, pleased to have the chance to discuss a woman's bosom in public.

"So tell me, we've met before? My name is Falk. Bunny Falk." Bunny was addressing her question to Yudel Wolfzahn.

"Met before? I don't think so, unless you've served us here before," he answered honestly. "Why do you ask?"

"Well," she answered, "I'm only here for the week. I work as a secretary in the city, but I get two weeks off a year and I work as a waitress during one of them to pay for a trip during the other. So you don't know me from here, but you were looking at me like you recognized me from somewhere."

"I do recognize you," Yudel said simply. "I recognized you as soon as I saw you."

Zelig Kropf looked up instantly from the dessert list. He tried to catch Yudel Wolfzahn's eye, but he couldn't as it was fixed, apparently magnetically, on Bunny Falk's bosom.

Eighteen

*Y*udel Wolfzahn raised his right hand to shield his eyes from the glaring sunlight. From the air, he had been able to see the Mediterranean, but from the ground, all he could see were the hangers and terminal building at Fiumicino. He descended the movable aluminum staircase, feeling stiff and awkward after his overnight flight.

The Italians, to be sure, had been Hitler's allies during the war, but Yudel was somewhat surprised by the degree to which he found himself able to overlook that momentary lapse of Italian civility and culture. Despite his powerfully mixed feelings about returning to Germany, Yudel found himself quite able to plan a visit to Italy without pain or conflict.

As the passengers disappeared into the terminal building to reclaim their luggage, Yudel paused for a moment in the strong Italian sunlight to contemplate the bizarre circumstances that had brought him to Rome.

***

Once he had been able to tear his eyes away from Bunny Falk's bosom, Yudel had managed to remain discreet. He knew that Zelig Kropf must have understood that he had recognized Bunny as the woman to whom the man in the Munich train station had referred, precisely as Zelig himself had recognized Yudel not four days earlier.

But he had determined, almost on a whim, to say nothing to Zelig before he could contemplate the complicated situation first on his own. Zelig, for his part, had apparently decided not to ask any of the several obvious questions.

Bunny had mentioned that she was working at the deli for the entire week and so it was not necessary for Yudel to embarrass himself further by actually allowing his dinner companions to hear him make plans to meet a woman other than his own Clara for a date. Besides, Yudel reasoned, he had hardly made up his mind even whether he was *going* to pursue the matter in the first place. Perhaps he would simply allow the issue to drop and avoid the complications that would undoubtedly arise once he began sneaking around with other women.

It wasn't, Yudel told himself as he walked home, as though he had any particular business with Waitress Bunny! He had no secret message, no private instructions, no deep, dark mystery into which he might otherwise have looked forward to initiating the buxom waitress. If he made a date with her, she would presume that his motives were purely amorous.

Yudel had caught Bunny looking at his hand, presumably to check for a wedding band. Clara had wanted Yudel to wear a wedding band, but he had refused without having any particular reason for doing so. His own father, he had told Clara, hadn't worn a wedding band and he felt no urge to do so himself. Clara had been a bit miffed, but she made her peace with the situation and that had been that. Yudel Wolfzahn wore no wedding band.

As Yudel walked home in the cool May air, he found himself wondering whether his motives were as pure as he had wished to imagine. Bunny Falk was, after all, a very attractive woman. She had a large, prominent bosom and appealing, soft features. She had shown herself, even in the few minutes he had spoken with her, to have a good sense of humor and to be at ease with the kind of Jew Yudel was. She was probably herself the daughter of refugees, possibly even German ones, Yudel guessed. Or perhaps she herself had been born in Europe, but brought to the States at such a young age that her English had no trace of a foreign accent at all.

Yudel was shocked by the line his thinking was taking. Could he be attracted romantically to Bunny Falk? Yudel had considered himself quite happily married. His relationship with Clara was satisfying and Yudel was not merely content, but actually very happy with his position as husband and father.

It was true, naturally, that Bunny Falk was at least a decade younger than Clara Wolfzahn, but Yudel knew he could hardly make too much a big deal out of that. In ten years' time, Bunny would also be ten years older and Yudel could hardly keep seeking out younger and younger women for the rest of his life merely to gratify his aging male ego.

But whether or not romance was at the root of the matter, there was no denying that something profound was drawing Yudel to Bunny Falk. As Yudel walked home down Continental Avenue and turned east on Austin Street, he suddenly recalled the strange experience he had had in the deli, marvelling at once at the experience itself and at the fact that he had somehow managed not to give that experience even a single moment's thought since the second it ended.

In some strange way, Yudel was only now even recalling that he had had such an odd vision—if it *was* a vision!—in the Boulevard Deli. Now that he could recall the event, he could almost smell the musty odor that the great leather-bound legal volumes in the Hamburg University Law Library had had about them. The smell was so pronounced that Yudel turned his head to see where it was coming from, but there was no obvious source other than his own psyche.

The shops were all closed. Although it was not that unusual for Austin Street to be filled on a weekday evening with strollers out for a breath of cool air before bed, this particular evening the street was deserted. Yudel looked up and down the street, suddenly hoping to see at least a single other pedestrian, but there was none to be seen. The windows over the shops were mostly dark, but some were lighted. But even those with lights were too high up for Yudel to see into.

He was completely alone.

At first, Yudel found the aloneness a bit ominous, but the feeling passed and then he began to enjoy his solitude; it was, he imagined, rather like being on the set of a movie before the cast and crew arrive.

Overhead, the sky darkened. Stars twinkled in the distance and a golden crescent moon hung almost directly overhead as though at the end of a stage designer's invisible wire. Yudel suddenly felt possessed by the significance of the events that had been transpiring around him. A man had had a secret and had known to pass it along to one who was destined to survive when he knew that he himself would not. His prediction had come to pass: the man he had selected for survival had, in fact, survived—and that, despite the fact that of all those deported from the great cities of Germany, only the tiniest remnant had lived through the experience.

The man who had survived had kept the secret, waiting patiently for a full decade until the second of the man's predictions came to pass. But, despite the delay, it *had* come to pass; Zelig Kropf, usually the most sober of men, had not the slightest doubt that Yudel himself was the man he was supposed to recognize.

And now the third of the man's predictions had come true. Yudel had recognized the woman as soon as he had seen her. That the woman in question was a legal secretary moonlighting during one of her two holiday weeks as a waitress in a kosher delicatessen only made the whole experience more piquant, Yudel thought. Yudel found his thoughts fixed on Bunny Falk and on the possible reasons for which she had been brought into his life and he into hers.

Zelig had kept back the last of the man's predictions, the one regarding the baby that Yudel and the woman he was to recognize were to create. But even without the independent corroboration of Zelig's unknown testimony, Yudel knew that there was something drawing him to the buxom secretary-waitress.

Yudel found himself, of all things, quite physically aroused by his thoughts about Bunny Falk. In May of 1952, Bunny Falk was a nubile twenty-two years of age, while Yudel himself was forty-two, easily old enough to be her father. Yet, it was not as an errant daughter that Yudel found himself thinking of his new acquaintance, but as a mature, highly desirable lover.

For eleven years of marriage, Yudel had not been unfaithful to Clara Wolfzahn even one single time. Women he met at work occasionally indicated their willingness or their interest in an affair with Yudel, but he had never even considered discussing their tawdry offers, much less acting on them. Clara was not the world's most beautiful woman, he knew, but she was a faithful wife, a wonderful mother and a dedicated *Hausfrau* of the German-Jewish variety—a combination already deep into its untimely obsolescence by 1952.

The thought of cheating on his wife with a girl young enough to be his daughter was absolutely abhorrent to Yudel, yet the more he dwelled on the absurdity of the idea, the more he found it appealing. After a decade of the greatest turmoil in the outer world, Yudel's home had been a sanctuary and an oasis of peace and Clara, Yudel knew all too well, was personally responsible for that. Betraying her trust by repaying Clara's own unquestionable fidelity with an adulterous fling with a delicatessen waitress was simply too much for Yudel to take seriously. As he crossed 71st Road, he laughed out loud at the very thought of his even contacting Bunny Falk.

It was complete absurdity! An utterly ridiculous idea that was undignified to consider even if the ultimate decision *was* not to proceed in any untoward way. It was an embarrassment even to think about behaving like a teenager with overly active hormones; Yudel's mind was absolutely firm.

By the time he came home, it was almost eleven o'clock. Clara was sitting in the living room reading a book. The kitchen was completely spotless and Yudel could see through the open bedroom door that the bed was turned down.

On the coffee table were a white teapot, a shallow dish of sugar, two cups, two saucers and a plate of the florentines Clara liked to buy at the Café Zagreb on Union Turnpike.

"You're home," Clara said as Yudel walked into the room.

"Apparently."

"You had a good time?"

"I did have a good time," Yudel said simply, hoping to head off any further questioning with a forthright answer.

"Luft phoned after you left to say he wasn't coming at all." Lawrence Lazar had left open the possibility he might come to the Boulevard later on in the evening when he had spoken to Yudel earlier.

"Sandy Gold was there and he ate with Zelig and me."

"What a stroke of fortune!" Clara said with a chuckle. Yudel knew Clara couldn't stand Sandy Gold and could probably not think of anyone with whom she would have liked less to dine.

"He's okay. Not too smart, but okay. He has a good heart," Yudel added.

"He has a thick head," Clara said succinctly as she turned back to her book.

Yudel sat down on the couch and began to leaf through that afternoon's *Post*.

"You already read the paper."

"So I'm reading it again."

"So if you're so bored, why don't you wash the kitchen floor?"

Yudel washed the floor and tidied up the apartment. By half past the hour, they were in bed with the light off. Yudel slipped his hand into his wife's nylon nightgown and cupped her left breast; to his horror, he found himself comparing it to Bunny Falk's massive bosom. The horror, however, passed, whereas the barely squelched desire engendered by the brief encounter with the waitress remained in full force. The Wolfzahns made love that evening with unusual passion.

Yudel could hardly believe he was as excited as he was by making love to his own wife, but the vague sense of impropriety engendered by that very thought only served to excite him further. His passions seemed to him to be almost out of control, but to his amazement Clara seemed more pleased than horrified; in fact, she seemed to like the work-out and was herself clearly in a state of deep arousal.

Afterwards, Yudel decided not to retrieve his pajamas from their tangled heap on the floor but rather to sleep naked in his wife's arms. Clara, unprepared for signs of even dormant sensuality in her sober husband, was first intrigued and then very pleased by the new developments. She gathered him to her and stroked the side of his head until he slept.

They slept the entire night in each other's arms and when they awoke in the morning, they were still intertwined in their post-coital embrace. While the 10-year-old Sidney slept peacefully in the next room, Yudel rose naked from his bed and shamelessly went into the kitchen to put up the water for his and Clara's morning coffee before retrieving his bathrobe.

Clara rose moments later and found Yudel seated at the kitchen table reading the previous day's *New York Post* yet again.

"You've really got something for that newspaper," she observed. "You usually hardly read it even once and now you're on your third reading. *The Times* you don't read with such interest."

"I know," Yudel admitted, "but I keep feeling like there is something here I should find. I know it sounds silly, but I keep thinking there is something I'm supposed to know that is written in the paper."

Clara looked at her husband as though he had finally gone mad. "Well, let me help," she said pleasantly as she took the paper from her husband and opened it to a center page chosen at random.

They both looked down at the paper as it lay open on the kitchen table to see what magic Clara had been able to work, but at that very moment, the kettle began to whistle. "I'll make the coffee," Clara said. "You find the secret treasure in yesterday's paper."

As Clara left the room, Yudel looked carefully at the page that lay open before him. It was a section of the classified advertisements, a part of the paper that Yudel never bothered even to leaf through, much less to read carefully. It was, therefore, with all the greater sense of growing amazement that Yudel read the advertisement that was printed in the center of the page before him.

It was an advertisement from the New York City Department of Social Services. The James Walker Agency, one of the city's agencies that dealt with adoption and the placing of foster children, was in need of a new staff person to fill a position that had been specially created to help the city deal with the enormous number of refugees who had moved into the city in the years following the end of the war. The qualified candidate, the advertisement said, would speak either German, Polish, Yiddish or French, would have at least some legal training and would have to be prepared to enroll in an M.S.W. program, would be able to pass an examination based on the laws and procedures relating to adoption in New York State within six months of accepting the job and would be a home-born or naturalized citizen of the United States with strong ties to the refugee community.

By the time Clara served the morning's coffee, Yudel had made up his mind. He composed his letter of formal application during his lunch hour and posted it before he was needed back at work.

Not three full days later, a letter arrived at the Wolfzahn's home inviting Yudel for an interview. The letter suggested a time and a place for the meeting, gave instructions as to how Yudel should proceed if the suggested time were not convenient and announced that correspondence addressed to the agency as of August 1, 1952 should bear the new name it had been given in celebration of the city's Dutch heritage: The Peter Stuyvesant Agency.

Nineteen

*I*t took Yudel weeks to decide to act.

Overwhelmed with incipient guilt at the same time he was becoming obsessed with the idea of contacting Bunny Falk, Yudel responded to the various pressures building up inside him by ignoring the issue for as long as he was able.

By the first week of June, however, it was no longer possible simply to defer the matter. His intimate life with Clara infused with an almost absurdly vigorous vitality, Yudel found he could carry on with his wife only when his fantasies were firmly fixed on Bunny Falk. And the greater the degree to which Clara found herself rather unexpectedly able to respond to her husband's newly discovered sexual vigor, the greater was Yudel's guilt over what he knew to be the source of his uncharacteristic libidinal vitality.

Yudel found himself obsessed with the idea of making love to Bunny Falk. He allowed himself to sit alone in the employees' cafeteria at *The Times* and draw little stick-figure bunnies all over the margins of his complimentary newspaper.

When no one was looking, Yudel set the name Bunny in different typefaces and printed it over and over as an act of private homage to an unknowing muse. Taking his treasures surreptitiously into the men's washroom, Yudel would lock himself in one of the stalls and admire his work before destroying it.

Yudel's relationship with his friends Larry Luft and Zelig Kropf was also affected by his new-found infatuation. More than once, Yudel found himself sitting with his friends in the steam and thinking about Bunny Falk. Looking over casually at Luft's great pink body through the cleansing mist, it seemed unfair—unfair *and* wrong— that society would consider Luft's union with Bunny Falk to be a wonderful success for them both, while the married Yudel Wolfzahn's own much longed- and hoped-for union with that very same woman would be thought of as sinful, corrupt, adulterous and morally and ethically wrong, wrong, wrong.

But wrong or not, Yudel knew that he was not going to be able to carry on forever dreaming about one woman while he made love to another! There would have to be a breaking point, a moment at which honesty would require admitting his passion to the world and taking whatever consequences would inevitably ensue.

The thought of losing Clara and Sidney, however, was simply too devastating to contemplate. Yudel constantly resolved to carry on as the loving father and faithful husband he had always been. But in the next moment, his resolve to behave responsibly and decently would begin to melt away. The image of Bunny Falk, naked between the sheets of some love-nest Yudel would rent for them in some out-of-the-way quarter of Manhattan, would rise up to haunt him, a specter deeply desired *and* totally unwanted *and* capable of sending shivers down Yudel's spine at the same moment it sent massive jolts of testosterone into his system.

Even finding Bunny Falk was not as simple a task as Yudel might have wished. Having finally resolved to act, it was necessary first to locate the object of his illicit desires. During their single meeting, Bunny had said that she was a secretary who spent one of her vacation weeks working as a waitress to earn the money for a holiday during the other.

She would be long gone from the Boulevard, then, but precisely where she would be found was impossible to know. Yudel knew that his only avenue of approach lay through the narrow dining room of the Boulevard Deli, yet it seemed impossible to travel *that* of all paths. The owner of the delicatessen, one Isadore Pollack, was Sandy Gold's uncle and himself made an occasional appearance in the steam at the Q.H.C. Yudel could hardly phone him up and casually inquire where he might look to locate Miss Bunny Falk, recently temporarily employed as a waitress at Pollack's restaurant.

On the other hand, it was obvious that no other approach would yield such immediate results, and the fact of the matter was that there *were* no other approaches that occurred to Yudel. He had checked in the Queens white pages and found, to his chagrin, that there were two full columns of Falks, none of them named Bunny. As Yudel would have expected in any event, she obviously lived with her parents in whose name her telephone was listed.

Finally, Yudel took his best shot. Bribing a colleague typesetter at *The Times* with two evenings of overtime that would otherwise have properly fallen to Yudel himself, he talked his friend into phoning Isadore

Pollack at his office. Trying to sound entirely plausible, the friend explained that he had eaten at the Boulevard several weeks earlier and had become smitten with a young waitress he had encountered there.

Since he was a single man—Yudel had insisted he specifically mention that he was unmarried—he was wondering if the restaurant might not give the waitress' phone number to him. He promised up and down not to pursue her in an untoward or unpleasant manner; he merely wanted to invite her out for a cup of coffee to discover if they had any future together.

"Because my whole family was killed in the war," Yudel had had him say, "it's especially important to me that I find a wife and begin a family."

Pollack, whose family had itself endured heavy losses in the camps, was deeply sympathetic. Just as Yudel knew he would, he imagined that if the Almighty had brought this young man and this young woman together and he himself refused to help the matter succeed, it would be the equivalent of murdering the children that might otherwise come from their union. He gave Yudel's friend Bunny Falk's number.

"But if she asks where you got the number, tell her I made you promise you wouldn't pester her if she says she's not interested," Pollack had specified.

"No problem," Yudel's friend had cheerfully agreed as he hung up the telephone.

"Go get 'er," he said to Yudel, grinning as he handed over the slip of paper on which he had scrawled the number.

Yudel took offence at the vulgar implication of his friend's lecherous smile, but knew better than to say so aloud.

"Wish me luck," he said instead, returning his friend's grin with a broad smile of his own.

"Good luck, man," the friend said, meaning it wholeheartedly. He would never have thought an old Jew like Yudel Wolfzahn would have had the nerve, but if he did, Clarence Bobruck thought to himself, more power to him.

"Thank you," Yudel responded simply, adding the words 'I'll need it' silently.

The friends parted. Yudel was left alone in his supervisor's office for the remaining ten minutes of his lunch hour. In his hand was Bunny Falk's phone number.

He dialed the number.

There was no one home.

Having jumped into the pool, Yudel knew that there was no reason not to swim. That evening, he excused himself after dinner and announced his intention to walk to the corner of Queens Boulevard and Continental Avenue to buy a pack of cigarettes. It had been the first thing to pop into his mind.

"I thought you were through with smoking," Clara had observed, not irrelevantly.

"I bummed one or two from Luft the other day at the gym," Yudel explained, "and I want to give him back a full pack."

His explanation apparently accepted, Yudel was out the door.

She picked up on the first ring.

"You don't know me," Yudel began, "but we met when you were working at the Boulevard Deli a few weeks ago."

"If we met, why do you think I don't know you?"

"Well," Yudel agreed, "I guess you know me in a certain sense, but…"

Yudel took a deep breath.

"…I was hoping we might meet. Maybe for dinner or just for coffee if you'd like. I'd like…"

Yudel searched frantically for the best expression.

"…to get to know you a bit better."

There was silence on the other end of the phone, presumably as Bunny mulled over the proposition. "Why would you think I'd remember you? I must have served five hundred meals during my week in the deli. You say you were one of them, but I can't be expected to recall each separate diner—no one could."

Yudel decided to jump in with both feet. "But you do remember me. Our eyes met. I was with two other guys, Pollack's nephew Sandy was one of them. I ate corned beef…" Yudel's voice trailed off in disappointment.

"Of course I remember you," Bunny said in a sort of muffled stage whisper, now that whomever she hadn't wished to hear her conversation was apparently out of hearing range.

"She must not want her parents to hear," Yudel thought.

"And I'd love to go for coffee. When and where?"

"You know Queens?"

"We live in Rego Park."

"How about Goldenberg's Deli?"

"A deli?"

"You don't like deli?"

"I do, actually. But it's a funny place for a date."

Yudel's throat constricted of its own accord as Bunny uttered the word 'date'. He had obviously intended all along to fix a date with her, but he had remained somehow convinced that this was more of a rendezvous than a plain old American date. "A restaurant isn't that funny a place to have a date," he answered plausibly. "A machine shop would be a funny place to meet. Or a garbage dump. Or a funeral chapel."

Bunny Falk laughed into the phone. "Okay, professor," she said, "you win. Where is Goldenberg's?"

"Whitestone," Yudel answered.

"You live in Whitestone?" Bunny asked in semi-amazement. Yudel simply hadn't impressed her as the kind of man to come from a section of Queens such as Whitestone.

"Forest Hills," Yudel responded honestly, biting his tongue almost before the last syllable was out of his mouth. He had resolved *not* to tell Bunny any details at all about himself and now he had already revealed that they lived in adjacent neighborhoods.

"So if you live in Forest Hills and I live in Rego Park," she asked entirely reasonably, "why are we going to Whitestone to eat deli sandwiches?"

That question, at least, Yudel had anticipated. "First of all," he said calmly, "it's a *great* deli. And second of all, I don't want to go anywhere where we'll be interrupted sixteen times a minute because I know everyone in the place."

Bunny smelled a rat, but decided to remain silent. She had indeed noticed Yudel when he and his friends had dined at the Boulevard during her week's stint working for Isadore Pollack. Their eyes had met and Bunny had experienced a strange fluttering in the pit of her stomach that she had at first attributed to indigestion, but which she had later acknowledged as the nascent stirrings of libidinal infatuation. She had had her own fantasies about the gaunt stranger and had half-considered phoning Sandy Gold—who ate at his uncle's restaurant almost every evening—to inquire about Yudel's identity.

It was only after a good deal of deliberation that she had decided to set aside that course of action. If the man was interested in her, she had concluded, he could phone Sandy Gold himself and ask him to approach his uncle for Bunny's phone number.

"It's a date," she said.

"Next Wednesday night?" Yudel *always* ate out on Wednesday nights. He'd phone Zelig Kropf or Larry Luft and beg off, then take

Bunny Falk to Goldenberg's Deli in Whitestone. Clara would never think to phone him at the Boulevard and she generally needed to be coaxed even to inquire about the events of Yudel's Wednesday evenings. There was a modicum of danger in the plan, but the possibility of Clara's finding out about this date was so small, Yudel decided, as to be worth the risk. And the slight possibility that they *would* be found out somehow added to the excitement.

"The eleventh? Okay. You'll pick me up?"

"Of course."

"Well, not at my house. I'll meet you at the subway stop at Continental Avenue. North side of the boulevard, right in front of the bank."

"I'll be there," Yudel heard himself say. "I'll be there at seven, but if you're late, don't worry. I'll just wait. The trains aren't *that* reliable."

"It's a deal," Bunny said simply and she hung up the phone.

Yudel looked at the disconnected receiver in his hand and wondered how it had ever come to this. But at the same time that he wished fervently to cancel his date, he also couldn't wait for the following Wednesday to come. It was Thursday, the fifth of June. Six days to wait until he would dine with Bunny Falk.

Eventually, the day came. Yudel was at the subway station a minute or two early, waiting in his car with enough alibis for almost anyone he thought could even remotely possibly find him there. Clara herself was no problem; he had phoned her only minutes before and told her he had been delayed at work and was only then leaving the City. He would go directly to the deli to have dinner with his friends, he had said, and come home afterwards.

Clara had appeared neither pleased nor displeased by this information, but had merely accepted it and ended the conversation. 'Maybe she has a date with *her* boyfriend on Wednesday nights and is just thrilled I won't be home until later,' Yudel thought for a moment before dismissing the thought as fanciful and so far-fetched as to be laughable.

He was still dismissing the ludicrous idea of Clara Wolfzahn having a boyfriend on the side when he saw Bunny Falk emerge from the subway. She looked lovely, far more lovely than she had looked in her waitress uniform.

Bunny was wearing a tapered white blouse cut to show off her great bosom and a simple beige skirt. Her hair was piled up on top of her head to create an effect of even greater height and she was wearing,

Yudel thought, just enough make-up to be tasteful without being vulgar.

She was carrying a small alligator handbag and wearing matching shoes. She was, Yudel concluded, dressed to make an impression and she had succeeded wildly. Even once they had greeted each other and were driving down the Van Wyck Expressway towards Whitestone, Yudel found that he still couldn't take his eyes off Bunny Falk.

The evening went well. Discussion was limited to topics both parties considered safe: politics, the weather, the integration of the refugee community into the much-vaunted American melting pot and baseball.

Bunny was clever and funny, cracking jokes and making eyes at Yudel at the same time. She obviously understood that he was married, Yudel thought. Not only had she declined to raise the question of why they had been obliged to meet in such an out-of-the-way place, but she had clearly and studiously avoided broaching the obvious topic of families during the course of their evening's conversation.

She herself had spoken briefly about her own parents, Cynthia and Moe Falk, and had dropped her eyes respectfully when Yudel had mentioned what his own parents' fate had been. But when the conversation would normally have turned to other family members and *their* fates, Bunny turned the talk to baseball.

Yudel understood that she understood and hoped that she realized that he did. In the meantime, there was nothing to do but soldier on to whatever *denouement* this strange relationship was destined to have. Yudel felt exhilarated and resigned at the same time; anticipation, guilt, passion and despair ceased grappling with each other for Yudel's soul by the time the appetizers were served and by the time the sandwiches themselves came, they had formed a cocoon that totally enveloped the hapless Wolfzahn in its protective cover.

The evening seemed to pass quickly. Before Yudel had even thought to look at his watch, the coffee had been served and it was time to go. But where *were* they to go?

Yudel could hardly bring Bunny Falk back to the subway stop in Forest Hills at which they had met and leave her there. And if she were entertaining some sort of fantasy about his wife being off for a holiday in Florida and his being in a position to invite her back to his apartment, she had not said anything at all to betray her lurid hope. She certainly had not suggested, Yudel noted with a sense of relief, that they repair to *her* apartment. And neither had she indicated whether she actually *did* live alone.

"So maybe we'll do this again," Yudel half-asked, half-stated as they were driving back down the Van Wyck in the general direction of both their neighborhoods.

"You're asking or you're telling?"

"I'm asking." Yudel had become so inured to saying things he had never imagined in his wildest dreams he would say that the words had simply rolled off his tongue as though he confirmed dates with single women all the time.

"So I'm accepting," Bunny said softly.

"So what do we do now?"

"Now? We take me home."

"You live alone?"

"A gentleman waits to hear," Bunny observed primly. "But if you have to know, no, I don't. I live with my folks, but it's a big building and they never go out at night. You can drop me off without worrying about running into them."

Yudel felt the need to be gallant. "I wouldn't say I was worried about meeting them. I'd love to meet your parents."

By way of demure response, Bunny offered the smile of one who knew Cynthia and Moses Falk to one who didn't. "Just drop me off at the corner of Queens Boulevard and 63rd Drive," she said eventually. "If there's a spot, we can walk to the house from there. If there isn't, I'll walk myself."

"Alone?"

"I'm a big girl, Yudel. I can take care of myself."

Yudel allowed himself the luxury of meditating for a delicious moment on the fact that Bunny Falk was a big girl who could take care of herself. 'And of me, too,' he thought privately.

By this time, they were at the appointed corner. There were nothing but parking spaces for blocks in every direction and Yudel slowed as he approached the curb. Reaching for reverse, his hand overshot the shift stick and landed on Bunny Falk's knee.

Far from being shocked or horrified, she simply sat there. Yudel's mind was racing—he could hardly decide what to do when Bunny put her hand on his. Finally, Yudel parked his car, leaned over and kissed Bunny Falk on the lips. The kiss was of unmistakable character and suggested nothing at all like the avuncular friendship for which Yudel's rational self would have normally wished. There was passion in Yudel Wolfzahn's kiss, passion and far more than merely nascent desire; his kiss declared his intentions far more accurately than he would have ever dared allow himself to say aloud.

Bunny was as pleased by Yudel's unstated proposition as she was little surprised. Knowing herself to be taking the first step on a slippery slope, she kissed back.

"Next Wednesday," Yudel gasped as he allowed his hand to brush up against Bunny's well-protected bosom.

"Same place, same time," she responded as she flung open the door of the car and, without looking back even once, ran off into the night towards the safety of her parents' apartment.

How Yudel managed to survive the next week, he later could never quite say. He went to work, sat in the Sunday steam, made love once or twice to Clara and counted the days. Despite all the reasons he ought to have been consumed with guilt, Yudel was quite surprised to notice that his burden was rather light; he felt bad about betraying Clara, but nowhere nearly bad enough to consider cancelling or simply not showing up for his second date with Bunny Falk.

He made some feeble excuses to his friends about dinner and was at the subway stop with time to spare.

Bunny didn't show. Yudel waited and waited and finally, at eight o'clock, he repaired to the Boulevard where he knew he would find his friends sitting over second or third cups of coffee.

"So you did come! We thought you were out with your girl-friend!" Zelig Kropf joked as Yudel sat down at the familiar table.

Yudel's face reddened slightly, but he was otherwise able to control his shock long enough to realize that Zelig was only joking.

"Or his *other* wife," Larry Luft added, laughing at the very thought a man such as Yudel Wolfzahn being a secret bigamist.

"Actually, the subway was so late, I decided to skip my appointment and come for dinner after all," Yudel said, semi-truthfully.

The conversation veered onto the topic of the New York City subway system and, for the moment, Yudel was safe.

On the way home from dinner, Yudel stepped into the subway station to phone Bunny Falk and inquire why she had failed to appear. Her mother answered the phone and Yudel immediately hung up.

Knowing that it was already too late to phone again, he went home.

The next night, Yudel tried again. Again, Cynthia Falk answered the phone and again, Yudel hung up without speaking. Yudel was becoming desperate. He was running out of excuses to leave his apartment without Clara in the evenings and was becoming more and more uneasy about having to lie to his wife.

The truth was that he had told so many lies and half-lies in the previous few weeks that Yudel felt he could hardly recall what he had said and to whom about any given evening's plans.

A few more evenings passed without Yudel having any success at contacting Bunny. Then, on his way to the synagogue Sunday morning, he decided to give her one more try. Standing in broad daylight at the intersection of Continental Avenue and Austin Street just in front of Woolworth's, he put a coin in the telephone and dialed Bunny Falk's number.

She answered on the first ring.

Recognizing her voice, Yudel plunged right in. "Where *were* you?" he asked bluntly.

"Oh, hello Lillian," Bunny said airily, her subtle sing-song lilt clearly indicating that she was being overheard as she spoke.

"I waited for an hour," Yudel said more loudly than he had wished.

"No," Bunny said, "the blue one. And the navy shoes."

"I've been calling for days and days. Sometimes no one is home and sometimes your mother answers and sometimes it's just busy and I can't call back. Don't you know how much I was hoping to see you last week?"

"The ones with the black bows," Bunny said.

"Well," Yudel said, reconciled to speaking without being spoken to, "can we meet again? Next Wednesday, same time, same place?"

Bunny appeared to be reflecting on the offer. "No," she said finally, "the whole point is that I only want to take one suitcase. I'm only going to be gone for a week and Vi says no one dresses on Cape Cod, even for dinner. So I'm going to take a bathing suit and a few dresses and one outfit for the evening and that's that."

"You mean you're going on vacation?"

"I'll only be gone for a week," Bunny said firmly. "Then I'll be back."

"And I'll be waiting," Yudel said, his heart soaring.

"You do that," Bunny said clearly. "And tell Robert he can use my desk while I'm gone if he has any typing."

Bunny hung up and Yudel, elated, went to sit in the steam with Larry Luft and Zelig Kropf.

Twenty

*T*he taxi dropped Yudel in front of his ancient hotel on the narrow Via del Pantheon in the heart of Rome's oldest quarter. The Pantheon itself sparkled in the near distance directly across the Piazza della Rotunda, but Yudel stood on the curb for only a moment to admire its hoary grandeur; he had more important things to do in Rome and only three days in which to do them. The combination of cool October air and dazzling sunlight gave an almost preternatural feeling to the scene as Yudel turned to enter the hotel.

He registered and allowed a bellhop at least thirty years his senior to carry his single suitcase up to his room.

As the two of them waited for the wrought-iron lift to take them up to the third floor, Yudel reviewed the events that had somehow led him from the fateful dinner at the Boulevard Deli during which he had first laid eyes on Miss Bunny Falk to this moment less than six months later in the lobby of a tiny hotel in the heart of Vecchia Roma.

***

Yudel and Bunny's second date had been quite similar to their first except that they ate in a different delicatessen (the Tuv Taam in Douglaston) and spent about twice as long pawing each other before Bunny once again jumped from the car and fled into the night. Far from being dejected, Yudel found that it was more than possible to interpret her behavior in an optimistic sense: if Bunny were not feeling as consumed with passion as he himself was, then there was hardly any reason for her to flee. Yudel's own sense of guilt was hardly extinguished, but somehow Bunny Falk's intoxicating presence managed to lull it into dormant calm.

The relationship continued. Every second Wednesday night, Bunny and Yudel had dinner. For the sake of what Yudel euphemistically called 'security,' they changed venues after every meal.

"We should be posing as editors of a new guide to Queens delicatessens," Yudel had joked, but Bunny's grimace made it clear that she found the situation distinctly less amusing than did he. She knew well why it was that they didn't eat twice in the same place and that knowledge shamed and chastened her, although, she noted grimly, not severely enough to coax her into ending the relationship. Gritting her teeth and resolving to follow things through to their natural conclusion, Bunny continued seeing her gaunt boyfriend, studiously refrained from asking questions about his family and knew that she would end up in bed with him sooner or later.

Wednesday night, July 30, 1952, was the evening of the great midsummer fast. The ninth day of the Hebrew month of Av, the anniversary of the destruction of Jerusalem both in the sixth century B.C.E. and the first century of this era, is one of only two twenty-five hour fasts in the Jewish liturgical calendar and one of the very few fast days aside from the Day of Atonement itself still observed outside the narrow fringes of the ultra-Orthodox communities of Jerusalem and Brooklyn.

Among the refugees whose entire families had been destroyed during the war, it had become a custom to observe the Fast of the Ninth of Av as a sort of generalized memorial day. The practice, later superseded by the Israeli innovation of a formal Holocaust Memorial Day in the late spring, was briefly widespread and had become a regular feature of Yudel and Clara Wolfzahn's ceremonial of remembrance.

"Two weeks from tonight, we're not on," Yudel had said to Bunny as they left the Deli Palace on Hillside Avenue. "It's *Tisha Be'av*—the ninth of the Jewish month of Av—and I have to be home with Clara. It's a fast day anyway, so even if I could get away, I wouldn't eat."

Bunny knew all about the Ninth of Av. "So what's wrong with Thursday night?" she asked.

"How can I get away?"

"Just tell Clara that your Wednesday night dinner was deferred because of the fast to Thursday. It won't even be a lie," she suggested pleasantly. "You *will* be deferring your dinner a day—only it will be with me instead of those guys you usually eat with."

Yudel still hesitated. The idea of going to his little prayer-room on Wednesday evening to hear the Book of Lamentations read and to participate in the chanting of the synagogue litany of dirge, threnody and jeremiad, to fast a full twenty-five hours in solemn remembrance of the ruined Holy City and also of his entire murdered family, to spend the day deeply involved in the most basic, most ancient rites and rituals of mourning, and then to rush off to some distant deli for a meal of corned beef and sour tomatoes in the company of the woman with whom he was betraying his wife's love and trust—it was just too much to contemplate.

Yudel had told Bunny about Clara on their third date and he didn't really regret having done so, feeling that he could never have kept such an important detail private for long anyway. But somehow hearing his girlfriend utter his wife's name casually, as though she were a simple obstacle to be overcome like an delayed train or an unexpected rainstorm, simply made Yudel feel even worse than he would have felt under more anonymous adulterous circumstances.

Yudel's brow was furrowed as propriety and passion wrestled just behind the wrinkled skin. But Bunny was not quite finished yet. "My folks," Bunny added demurely, "are going to Montauk for the weekend. They're leaving Thursday morning and they won't be back until Sunday night. We could…"

Yudel's eyes opened wide.

"…skip the deli route and just eat in at my place."

Yudel's defenses collapsed. "In for a penny, in for a pound," he said weakly, his throat suddenly dry.

"That's a yes?"

"It's a yes."

"So you'll come?"

Yudel hesitated only for the slightest moment. "I'll come," he said simply.

The fast was a difficult one for Yudel. The prayer-room he attended just off Austin Street on the border of Kew Gardens and Forest Hills had neither rabbi nor cantor; instead, the various members of the congregation took their turns leading the service and offering a homily of some sort based on the lesson from Scripture read that week as part of the worship service.

This year, it was one Srul Deutsch to whom the honor of leading the service and reading *Eicha*—the Biblical Book of Lamentations—had been given.

Deutsch was a well-known figure in the tiny prayer community. Originally from Leipzig, he and his wife and three teenaged daughters had been among the thousand Jews deported from the concentration camp at Theresienstadt to Minsk in July of 1942. The train carrying the deportees had been stopped six miles short of Minsk by the S.S., who took the Jews off the train, loaded them onto waiting trucks and drove them to a nearby forest. Srul Deutsch, who had then been a young, strapping man, was one of only thirty-five men selected for slave labor and had been forced to look on as his family had been machine-gunned at close range into pre-prepared mass burial ditches by the young Gestapo men.

Deutsch had never quite recovered from the experience and had never remarried. Despite his university training in commerce, Deutsch had chosen to work for the New York Department of Public Works where he spent his days digging ditches. It was the height of irony, but somehow the act of digging allowed him to live his life out within the confines of his own trauma and this provided him with whatever solace a man in his situation could possibly know.

Deutsch led the evening service with dignity and great emotion, but it was when he unrolled the parchment scroll to read Lamenta-tions that the full burden of his experience descended on the small congregation like a heavy pall. The five brief chapters of the ancient book seemed endless to Yudel and when towards the end of the fifth chapter, Deutsch sang out, "Gone is the joy of our hearts / Our dancing is turned into mourning / The crown has fallen from our head / Woe to us that we have sinned," Yudel felt almost faint with regret and self-loathing.

The mood passed. The reading ended, the men put their shoes back on and rose from the dusty floor on which they had sat during the recitation of the book. The electric lights were switched back on. Without taking formal leave of each other, the worshipers dispersed into the warm Queens night.

Yudel went home and went to bed. Clara was surprised, but not amazed by his behavior; the fast of the Ninth of Av often had a depressing effect on her husband and she had long since learned the folly of quizzing him on his mood in such circumstances.

Yudel fell asleep and had horrible dreams. The setting for the dream, as was often the case, was the Rothenbaumchaussee in Hamburg a little bit up the street from the elder Wolfzahns' linen shop and the neighboring print shop where Yudel had worked after being expelled from the law faculty. It was, of course, the morning after *Kristallnacht*: November 10, 1938.

The street, which contained many Jewish shops, was littered with broken glass. As usual, Yudel could see the stout neighborhood matrons grimly helping themselves to as much Jewish merchandise as they could reach in the broken shop windows and, as usual, Yudel was suddenly aware of an approaching crowd of Nazi thugs.

But in this version of the dream, the gang was not made up of Nazi thugs at all but rather of their victims. The young Srul Deutsch himself, for example, was at the head of the gang and just behind him, Yudel could clearly make out his parents and Zelig Kropf. Behind them were Joachim Schmidt, the deposed dean of the Law Faculty, and Yudel's old *melamed* from the Schäferkampsallee as well as dozens of others Yudel had once known and whom, for the most part, he presumed dead.

They were advancing on him ominously and Yudel knew they were condemning him for honoring their memory on the very eve of the greatest transgression of his life.

Yudel realized they were all staring at the yellow star sewn to the front of his coat. Suddenly overwhelmed with a strange combination of rage and shame, Yudel reached up to the front of his coat and ripped the star off in disgust. But in his dream, the star was somehow as protective as it was dangerous; as he pulled the yellow badge from his coat and cast it into the gutter, the rest of his clothing fell off as well and Yudel was left standing stark naked in the middle of the stately Rothenbaumchaussee.

Suddenly ashamed of his nakedness, Yudel tried to display some semblance of modesty by spreading out his hands and placing them over at least the crucial area of his exposed loins. Seized by panic and shame, Yudel turned on his unshod heel and found himself face to face with Frau Ilse Döpp.

Yudel woke from his dream in a cold sweat. It was just past four in the morning. He rose from his bed and went into the kitchen. 'In for a penny, in for a pound,' he thought to himself as he opened the refrigerator door and poured himself a glass of cold water. Feeling strangely free of guilt, Yudel broke his fast and drank the cool water, then rinsed the glass and dried it before putting it back in the cupboard from which he had taken it.

After the fast ended, Yudel announced that his Wednesday night dinner had been put off to Thursday and left the apartment before Clara could either approve or complain. It was ten past nine in the evening, Thursday, July 31, 1952.

Yudel drove through still streets to his appointment with sin. Drawn almost irresistibly to Bunny Falk, it later seemed odd to Yudel that he had suffered no feelings at all of regret or anxiety born of ambivalence; he felt no more responsible for what he knew was about to happen than a tiny needle need feel if it should be drawn to a powerful magnet.

He parked his car carefully a few blocks from the Falk apartment and walked quickly through the quiet streets. 'If anyone sees me, I'll say I'm picking up a package for someone from work,' he thought to himself. But he didn't see anybody he knew. By the time he had walked from his car to Bunny's house, he had hardly seen anyone at all.

Bunny buzzed him up and greeted him with a brazen kiss on the lips even before the apartment door was shut behind them. She was wearing a loose-fitting white cotton blouse, a blue skirt and dark navy pumps; Yudel could hardly imagine there even *being* a more attractive woman in the world, much less that he might ever meet her.

The dining room table was set with what Yudel instinctively recognized as Bunny's mother's best china and crystal. A tall bottle of Miller's beer sticking out of an ice bucket and a plate of sour pickles were all that Yudel could actually see, but the apartment was filled with the seductive odor of hot, smoked meat.

"What's for dinner?" he asked politely as he sat down on Bunny's parents' couch.

"Me," Bunny answered frankly, fingering the top button of her blouse and smiling.

"And then?"

"Smoked goose breasts, potato salad, sour tomatoes, hot peppers and cold beer. And black bread," she added.

Yudel felt almost faint with anticipation. His mouth was dry and he could actually feel his heart beating just inside his chest. He was already in a state of advanced arousal and Bunny had so far only unbuttoned a single button of her blouse.

'*Oz der putz shteht, flieht die sekhel in tukhes,*' Yudel thought as he rose from the couch and stepped closer to the object of his tumescent desire. For once, an old Yiddish aphorism—this one consisting of the undeniable, if vulgar, assertion that the other function of an erect penis is to force one's common sense up one's rectum—was true and Yudel was relying on its universal truth to justify the folly he was now unavoidably committed to undertaking.

Having taken almost two months to take the first momentous step, Yudel and Bunny travelled the rest of the way to adulterous transgression in a matter of twenty minutes and, when they did, their union was more than merely sexual—it was almost animal in its intensity.

Yudel lay naked on Cynthia and Moe Falk's living room carpet barely able to move. In a similar state of exhausted undress, Bunny herself lay draped over her parents' sofa like some sort of hairless bearskin throw. She could hardly believe the degree of passion that Yudel had somehow managed to unleash within her; the actual act of making love to a married man had shocked her far less than the almost scary intensity of Yudel's sexual technique.

Along with the black, curly chest hairs he had shed during their torrid embrace, beads of Yudel's sweat were still glistening on Bunny's bare chest.

"Not your first time, I see," Yudel said eventually.

"You're asking or you're telling?"

"I'm asking."

"So ask!"

"Was that your first time?"

"With a maniac," Bunny answered demurely, "yes."

"And with non-maniacs?"

"First of all," Bunny said distinctly, "a gentleman doesn't ask. And second of all, what answer can I possibly give? If I say you're the first, you won't believe me because you'll figure I'll say that to the next one too and since I'll be lying to him, why wouldn't I be lying to you? And if I say you're not the first, you won't believe me because you'll figure that I must have told that to the real first so he wouldn't think I was expecting him to *marry* me just because I gave up my treasure to him instead of to someone else and since I'd have been lying to him then, why wouldn't I be lying to you now?"

Yudel said that he understood the logic, but mistrusted it. He would settle for the fact that Bunny was a virgin as far as the world was concerned. If that was good enough for the entire world, it would be good enough for Yudel Wolfzahn as well. But in his heart of hearts, Yudel knew that Bunny had been a virgin and that he had been the first. Even an American woman, he guessed, wouldn't buy smoked goose breasts for just anyone she happened to sleep with.

***

The lift eventually came and Yudel was escorted up to his room. The bellboy unlocked the door and accepted a generous tip for laying Yudel's suitcase on the luggage stand at the foot of the bed and flinging open the balcony door.

Yudel, exhausted from his flight, lay down dressed on his bed and closed his eyes.

***

Yudel could hardly explain what had happened, but there were no repeat performances after he and Bunny made love that single time on the Falks' living room broadloom. In the course of the fateful evening itself, Yudel had merely assumed he had spent whatever libidinal forces lay buried within his psychic storehouse of unknown, uncatalogued emotion. Bunny herself had seemed quite ready to proceed with the evening after the spent lovers had lain immobile for a suitable quarter-hour of mingled post-coital lassitude and *tristesse*; less than forty minutes after Yudel had exploded in repeated paroxysms of ecstasy, he and his lover were seated at the table eating sour tomatoes and hot corned beef and drinking cold Miller's beer.

When the meal was over, they watched a bit of television; once the hour had grown late, Yudel kissed Bunny good night and left.

They had left their pattern of bi-weekly dinners intact; two weeks less a day from the fateful night of their feverish coupling, they met for dinner at yet another Queens county delicatessen, Ehrenreich's Nosh-A-Rye of Kew Gardens Hills.

Their date two weeks after that fell during Yudel and Clara's annual holiday in Atlantic Beach and had obviously to be cancelled. The next date, however, was to be a return to the Tuv Taam in Douglaston on the tenth of September and was intended to be a bit of a celebration: Yudel had gotten the job at the Stuyvesant Agency and had begun Tuesday, September 2.

For the first time, Bunny declined Yudel's offer of a lift, preferring, she said, to meet him there.

She was late, but she did eventually come in. The waiter came over immediately with her dinner and she smiled in grateful acceptance.

"You're late," Yudel said when the waiter withdrew.

"It's a theme with me these days," Bunny said sweetly.

"A theme?"

"Being late. But don't worry—I'm not going to be late again for a while!"

Yudel had the unsettling sense they were speaking about something other than Bunny's chronic tardiness. "Just for a while you're not going to be late?" he asked weakly, somehow knowing what was about to come.

– 223 –

"Just for about another seven and a half months." Bunny was looking at Yudel with a strange mixture of malice and sweetness. She smiled benignly as she waited for her news to sink in. "If I nurse the baby, probably longer than that," she added thoughtfully and for good measure.

"You're pregnant?" Yudel finally said.

"Columbus discovers America."

"You mean it?"

"No, I'm puking my brains out every morning because it's my new way to lose weight. Yes, Sherlock, I mean it. Or is it Shylock?" Instead of being consumed with shame and horror, Bunny's eyes were laughing in their painted sockets. She seemed genuinely pleased to be pregnant and not at all horrified by what was bound to be the general reaction of the public to her news.

"You want the baby?" Yudel didn't know how to broach the topic, but he did know a man from *The Times* who knew a man whose brother knew how to terminate pregnancies with, he said, little or no risk to the woman involved.

Bunny looked at him as though he were absolutely crazy. "What are you suggesting? That we *kill* it?"

"Not exactly," Yudel said quickly.

"Well, that's good. Because I'd kill *you* before I'd kill *it*. At least *it* never did anything to me!"

"Well, it takes two to tango. If you're pregnant, it's not your *or* my fault. We did it together and we'll have to figure this out together. Either we'll *undo* it or we'll figure something else out." Yudel knew he sounded vaguely irritated and regretted his tone almost immediately.

"Well, we're not undoing anything. Or let me put it another way," Bunny stated unequivocally, "if you'll agree to murder *your* Sidney, I'll agree to murder *my* baby too. You go first."

Yudel knew he had lost the argument. Bunny would have her baby and he would have to deal with that somehow. If he had to, he'd find a way to support Bunny *and* Clara and try to keep them from ever meeting. But, he suddenly thought, there might be another way.

"You know, I began already at the new place," he said calmly once the tension had lifted from the table. He popped a pale green sliver of sour tomato into his mouth and washed it down with a swig of cold beer. Bunny seemed lost in thought. "Are you listening to me?" he said to rouse her from her reverie.

"I screw, I listen, I do anything you want," she replied with a flash of irritation. "The only thing I don't do is murder babies. So what is it?"

Bunny, Yudel noted, had stopped eating. She was picking at her plate and staring off into space. The annunciation had apparently not gone quite according to the script she had obviously devised in advance.

"So I'm working for the City. A social services agency. You know what that means?"

Bunny looked up from her plate. "No, not exactly," she admitted.

"It means I work in a place that arranges *adoptions*. You understand—people have babies they can't raise and give them up to wonderful, wealthy ladies and their decent, wealthy husbands who for some reason can't manage to have children of their own and the women can rest easy knowing their babies are in good families and the families that get them are in seventh heaven because all they've ever wanted is a baby and they just couldn't manage to make one on their own and the baby is a thousand times better off too—the baby grows up in a home of love and lots and lots of money and has a wonderful life. Everybody wins!" Yudel concluded triumphantly.

"And the father of the baby, I mean the man who got the woman pregnant in the first place, does he win too?"

Yudel considered the implications of her question and decided to ignore its sarcastic tone. "Yes," he answered honestly, "he does."

The matter had been allowed to drop after that. Bunny and Yudel ate their dinner in semi-silence, discussing from time to time this or that aspect of the situation but without either party having the energy or the courage to sustain another full-blown discussion of the matter in its fullest compass. As soon as decency permitted, Yudel paid the bill and drove Bunny home.

After seeing Bunny to the door of her parents' building, Yudel went directly to Zelig Kropf's drugstore and leaned on the night bell until his friend padded downstairs. Zelig's dinner with Larry Luft and Sandy Gold, who had become Yudel's regular bi-weekly stand-in, had been over for hours. He had been in his pajamas reading an Agatha Christie novel while awaiting the beginning of the eleven o'clock news. He looked a bit surprised, but not at all displeased at his uninvited friend's unexpected presence.

"What's up?" he asked affably once the great glass door was locked behind them and they were walking back through the shop to the rear staircase that led to Zelig Kropf's apartment.

"Up? The moon is up," Yudel had responded. "And the jig as well."

"The jig?"

"It's an English expression, Zelig. The jig is up. It means that the *denouement* of some particular drama is upon the players in the play.

It means we're up shit's creek is what it means."

"Have we a paddle?" Zelig asked delicately.

"No," Yudel said simply, "we do not."

Telling Zelig the whole story was simpler than Yudel had expected it was going to be. What had begun as a sort of mid-life infatuation with a buxom waitress in a local delicatessen had ended in a catastrophe of incalculable proportions. What had felt so right and so almost pre-ordained now felt sordid and wrong. "Sordid, wrong and base," Yudel repeated to his friend in a hoarse whisper. "So you see, the wages of sin aren't death after all—they're life," he observed conclusively.

Zelig listened carefully to the entire story from beginning to end. He brewed tea and drank cup after cup as his friend talked, pouring tea for Yudel to keep his throat from becoming parched but otherwise concentrating on every word. From the far-away look in his eyes, Yudel knew that Zelig was somehow being transported back to the Munich train station and that he was communing with the memory of that dismal experience and of the tall man who had approached him as he slept.

"There were four things the man said," Zelig said finally. "Five, if you include the part about me surviving the war."

"Four other things? You told me two." Yudel felt a certain strange fluttering in the pit of his stomach.

"I told you two of the four," Zelig admitted. "The part about me recognizing the man—you, I mean—as soon as I would see him was true. And so was the part about you recognizing the woman. Those were both true things, but there were other truths as well."

Yudel drew a deep breath. "Well?"

"Well," Zelig began, "one was that you and the woman you would recognize would have a baby…" His voice trailed off as he allowed the implication of what he was saying to sink in.

"God in heaven," Yudel said more to himself than truly aloud. "Why didn't you tell me?"

Zelig thought for a moment. "I don't know," he admitted. "I suppose I ought to have, but it would have been sort of like encouraging you to betray Clara and I didn't think I wanted to be responsible for that."

"But the man told you in so many words to tell me—the man you were going to recognize, I mean—to tell him that he was to have a baby with the woman he himself was going to recognize?"

Zelig thought for a moment, then nodded slowly. "He said to tell him that he would recognize the woman as soon as he would see her and that once he did know who she was, he should have a baby with her."

"So you held that back and it happened anyway. Sort of like independent corroboration."

"You're not mad?"

"No, Zelig, I'm not mad. I'm sort of confused and amazed, but I'm not mad. Did the man say by any chance what we were supposed to do with this baby once we managed to create it?"

"No, he didn't. I wish he had, but he didn't."

There was a long pause in the conversation. "Zelig," Yudel finally said, "you said there was another part to the message."

Zelig knew the time to dissemble had long since passed. "Yes," he said, "there was."

"And what was that fourth part?"

"The fourth part was to tell you that if you had any questions, you could inquire at the Catacomb of Santa Cecilia in Rome."

"Rome?"

"Rome."

"In Italy?"

"He didn't mean in the catacombs of Rome, New York. Of course, in Italy."

"And who was I supposed to look up in a catacomb?"

"He didn't quite say. He said the man I'd know should go there if he wanted to ask for more information." Zelig paused for a long moment. "He gave me this," he added, taking a thick volume from one of his bookcases and opening it to where he had taken to leaving the yellowed train ticket, now more than a full decade old, for safekeeping. Feeling the world fall away and leave him and Yudel alone on a different cosmic plane, Zelig handed the crumpled piece of paper to his friend.

On one side, it was clearly a train ticket for a journey from Augsburg to Munich, purchased a few days before Zelig's transport left the Munich train station for Theresienstadt and, presumably, discarded by a disembarking passenger. It amused Yudel to think for a moment that at the same time the Nazis had been deporting Jews to their deaths, their train stations had also been functioning in the normal way as passenger terminals.

Yudel turned the ticket over and saw a man's head drawn hastily with what had apparently been a blunt pencil. The man looked distinctly Jewish, not entirely unlike Yudel himself but younger and more handsome.

"Who is this?" he asked.

– 227 –

"I don't know."

"The man gave you this?"

"He did, but he didn't say who it was. Or what it meant. Or what connection it has, if it has any, to the catacomb in Rome. It was all left unsaid. I'm sorry, but I don't know what else to tell you."

"You could tell me that there are no more secrets. That the man said four things only. That you aren't going to remember one final detail tomorrow morning and tell me then."

"That's it," Zelig promised. "No more secrets. The only physical proof of the whole thing is the ticket you are holding. More, I don't know."

"So what do I do now?"

"How should I know what you're going to do. But if I were you, I think I'd go to Rome."

Yudel wasn't going even to think about how he could possibly justify a trip to Rome to Clara, especially if she wasn't going to be invited. Or maybe she *should* come along—she deserved a holiday and it might be just what the doctor ordered to relieve a bit of the guilt Yudel was feeling about his infidelity.

One thing was certain, however, and that was that it was absolutely necessary to undertake the journey to Rome before Bunny had her baby. Either there would or there wouldn't be any information in the catacomb, but if such information existed anywhere in the world, it was in Rome. So far, the man was batting a thousand, dead for a decade and still three for three. So there was, Yudel realized, no reason to assume he was wrong about Rome. The only question left was how to organize the trip and how to explain his sudden desire to visit Italy to his wife.

Twenty-One

*W*hen Yudel awoke from his sleep, it was already late in the afternoon. He ate a light dinner in a tiny trattoria on the Corso Vittorio Emanuele II, then decided to visit the Pantheon.

Ignoring the royal crypts, he visited the tomb of Raphael and left the building in a pensive mood; Yudel bought some ice cream in the Via degli Orfani and headed back to his hotel.

***

In the end, it had not posed any problem at all to arrange the trip. The Peter Stuyvesant people themselves had needed someone who could speak German fluently to travel to some of the D.P. camps to assess some of the thousands of potentially adoptable war orphans, several thousand of whom were still stranded in northern and southern Germany.

The Jewish children, of course, were long gone. Those left after the war with no living relations had either gone directly to Palestine under the joint auspices of the Jewish Agency and the United Nations High Command for Refugees or had languished in British camps until the Jewish state had been proclaimed and *then* gone to Israel.

The remaining children were a diversified lot: Gypsies, Slavs of various nationalities unwilling to return to their ruined homelands, displaced Balts whose countries had disappeared entirely, and various other ethnic types with no place to go. Yudel had spent three weeks touring their camps and produced a list of several hundred children he deemed educable and relatively disease-free, the two main requirements for adoptability. It had been a relatively simple matter to convince the head of the agency that he wished, as he was going to be in Europe anyway, to visit the grave of his ancestors in the Jewish cemetery in Rome.

The agency head, a kindly man to whom all immigrants were basically from some vague place "over there", was totally unable to evaluate the likelihood of a German Jew such as Yudel Wolfzahn having ancestors buried in one of the ancient Jewish cemeteries in Rome; as far as he was concerned, Italy and Germany had been allies during the war and were probably more or less the same country anyway. Three vacation days had been tacked onto the end of Yudel's trip and the matter was resolved.

Clara, who to Yudel's amazement still seemed to suspect nothing of the various goings-on that were consuming her husband's every waking moment, was simply informed that the trip was to last three weeks and three days rather than an even three weeks and that it would include a final visit to some unspecified D.P. camp in eastern France. Clara had simply accepted what she was told and hadn't even asked where in France the alleged camp was located.

Yudel had felt a great burden lift from his shoulders as his plane lifted off from Idlewild Airport and soared eastward over the Atlantic. If there was some sort of explanation for the entirely strange series of events that had begun ten years earlier in Munich and which were apparently still unfolding as Yudel flew over the ocean, it was at least possibly to be found in one of the ancient catacombs of Rome.

As unlikely as it sounded, it was certainly no more unlikely than any other detail of the story as it had unfolded to date. Yudel closed his eyes and slept for most of his flight. On the off chance that Clara might have inspected his ticket, Yudel had actually gone to the bother of buying one round-trip ticket between New York and Frankfurt on Pan American Airlines and another, separate round-trip ticket between Frankfurt and Rome on Alitalia. The first ticket was displayed prominently in his travel wallet directly across from Yudel's passport; the other ticket, the one for Rome, Yudel carefully inserted into the lining of a sports coat he intended to pack at the very last moment.

By the time his flight touched down in Frankfurt, Yudel was wide awake and quite unexpectedly apprehensive about setting his feet down on German soil after so many long years that had elapsed.

In the end, the trip was uneventful. Yudel stayed in the least expensive hotel he could find on Frankfurt's seedy Taunusstrasse and made day trips on the train north and south.

Three weeks after arriving, his work was done and Yudel couldn't wait to leave; Germany had survived the war and Yudel

Wolfzahn had survived the war, but the link between the two had been permanently and utterly severed. If Yudel was amazed by anything during his stay, it was by how little he found himself obsessed or even bothered by the vestigial hatred for Germany he had always imagined himself to harbor. The Holocaust had ended *even* the bond of hatred that tied Yudel to the land of his birth during his first years in America.

He considered going to Hamburg to ask Frau Ilse Döpp for his parents' stolen linens or to visit his parents' old home and see who was living there, but he decided against going. There was a complicated method of extracting some sort of compensation for appropriated properties from the German government, but Yudel wanted nothing of it. For better or for worse, he had stopped being a German and had become something else.

His work complete, Yudel took the train to the airport and flew south. Four hours later, he was disembarking at Fiumicino and an hour or two after that, he was waiting for the lift in the lobby of his ancient hotel on the Via del Pantheon.

✳✳✳

Despite the fact that Yudel had been in Europe for over three weeks and that his body clock had long since completed its circadian adjustment to Middle European Time, Yudel was not at all sleepy. Although by the time he returned from his walk it was already almost ten o'clock in the evening, Yudel, for some inexplicable reason, was wide awake.

He knew what he wished to do, but he didn't know if he was quite ready to do it. It was, Yudel realized, not precisely now or never, but there *was* no time like the present—and buttressing that point of view was the reality that, come what may, Yudel was going to fly back to Frankfurt in three days where he was to connect with his flight home.

Something about the cool evening made Yudel feel optimistic about his adventure, optimistic and yet at the same time highly uncertain about the wisdom of the whole undertaking. He inquired at the hotel's night desk as to the best way to get to the Catacomb of Santa Cecilia as though he were planning a trip early the next morning. The night manager, an affable Roman who spoke English with difficulty,

– 231 –

understood precisely what Yudel wanted and directed him to the Colosseum, where he was to take the number 118 bus south to the Catacomb of San Callisto. The Catacomb of Santa Cecilia, the man explained, was just behind San Callisto and opened, not necessarily promptly, at half-past eight in the morning.

Yudel thanked the manager for his help and walked out into the cool night air.

Rome was quiet for a Monday evening. There were the usual café types lounging in their favorite establishments and the regular sprinkling of tourists out to wring the absolute most sightseeing out of each of their usually too few days in the Eternal City. Yudel walked briskly along the Via di Torre Argentina, then headed east towards the Piazza Venezia.

To the south of the great Piazza Venezia, Yudel stood for a moment to admire the immensely hideous monument to Vittorio Emanuele, then hurried along the Via dei Fori Imperiali towards the Colosseum. He felt himself drawn to the ancient arena, not so much by its immensity or its antiquity, but by some other force that seemed almost to be propelling him forward.

There was a busload of German tourists climbing into a chartered bus in the shadow of the great structure and another with Austrian license plates just behind it; Yudel surmised that the German-language sound-and-light show must have just recently ended. Perhaps, he dared hope, there would be one final bus that evening to ferry home the Romans who worked the tourist trade.

Not having any idea what he would do in the absence of a bus, Yudel simply stood on the street for a moment trying to gather his thoughts. A cold gust of wind chilled him to the bone and he gathered his jacket closer around himself.

His thoughts turned to Bunny for a moment and to the tiny embryo growing inside her. A sudden surge of emotion brought tears to Yudel's eyes and, for the first time since hearing the news of Bunny's pregnancy, he allowed himself to cry. Ashamed of the depth of his own emotions, Yudel reached for a handkerchief with which to wipe his eyes; when he lowered the white handkerchief from his face, the number 118 bus was just pulling up at a bus stop fifty feet or so farther along the street from where he was standing.

Yudel concentrated on his Italian as he dropped his fare in the tin coin box. *"Dov'è scendo per il catacombo de San Callisto?"* he asked hesitantly.

The driver, pleased to hear a foreigner at least trying to speak

Italian, smiled broadly. "I'll show you," he said in terse, but perfect English.

Yudel, more than satisfied, sat down and waited. Before long, the driver was gesticulating at Yudel from his seat. "Here," he said.

Yudel got off the bus and found himself standing in front of a large building on the Via Appia Antica. In the light of a streetlamp, Yudel made out a tiny side street; it was the Via delle Sette Chiese. A large sign pointed in the direction of the Catacomb of Santa Cecilia. Feeling guided by an unseen hand, Yudel walked hesitantly down the street.

Of course, the Catacomb was closed; it was well past eleven o'clock in the evening. The Via delle Sette Chiese was entirely deserted; not even a stray cat could be seen anywhere in the vicinity.

The catacomb, of course, is underground, but over the entrance, there was a sort of building which Yudel took to be a church. The street was entirely still and looked, Yudel thought, rather like what a Hollywood set of a narrow Roman street might resemble.

Yudel walked down the street to the great wooden entrance to the building; breathing a word of prayer to a seldom acknowledged Protector, he pushed against the door. It swung open silently as though on greased hinges.

The building was clearly a church. In the distant apse, Yudel could see something that he took to be the altar. There were thick yellow candles burning in black candlestands at either side of a table, but aside from the obvious fact that someone must have lit the candles, there was no trace of anyone anywhere.

For a moment, Yudel thought he heard footfalls coming towards him, but when he held his breath in order to listen as closely as possible, he heard nothing at all.

Too far along now even to consider backing down, Yudel knew he had no choice but to walk towards the front of the church. There was a peculiar fragrance in the building rather like the smell of fresh lemons, but Yudel saw no obvious place from which the scent could likely be emanating. There were, Yudel could see, niches along the outer walls of the sanctuary in which statues of various sorts were on display. These were invisible from the extreme rear of the room, but as Yudel advanced towards the front, he could see each clearly as he passed it.

The scenes were taken from various ancient martyrologies, one more horrendous than the next. Prominent among the scenes depicted was, of course, the execution of Saint Cecilia herself, her neck miraculously refusing to give way before the executioner's three mighty blows. But there were other scenes, all of them as horrifying as the martyrdom of the saint herself: beheadings, upside-down crucifixions, strangulations, suffocations and forced drownings. Yudel lingered a moment before each niche, marvelling at the Christian ability to feel moved to piety through the contemplation of pain.

The church seemed a good deal longer once Yudel was half-way down the nave than it had from the entrance doorway. Yudel kept walking, forgetting that he was alone in the vast stone building and wondering about the age of the structure he was in. Scene after scene of indescribable suffering began to blur in Yudel's consciousness; by the fourteenth or fifteenth group, each ensemble began to seem the same as the one that preceded it.

Finally, Yudel approached the end of the balustrade and, as he did, he saw a small sign that was tacked with thumbtacks on a small wooden door that he hadn't noticed from afar.

At the top of the crinkled paper, someone had written the words "*Haec est porta Domini iusti intrabunt in eam,*" but the sign continued in a variety of European languages; next to an incorrectly drawn and colored-in Union Jack, the sign read curtly "Catacomb through here."

Yudel recalled suddenly why he had come; summoning up his courage, he pushed the door. It opened easily.

On the other side of the small door—Yudel actually had to stoop to pass through without bumping his head—was a staircase going down to a lower level. Yudel put a hesitant hand on the bannister and began his descent.

How many flights down he went, Yudel couldn't quite say. The staircase was built as a descending spiral, so it was difficult to chart distance; the light in the stairwell was so poor that it was impossible to look straight up to see how far he had already gone. Nevertheless, despite the dank, fetid air and the gloomy ambience of the almost lightless stairwell, Yudel felt a certain sense of optimism unexpectedly welling up within him. This was going to end up all right, he thought to himself with an unjustifiable sense of relief. If the guy whom Zelig had met in the Munich train station was right about three out of four predictions, he would probably be right about the fourth one too. And that, Yudel reminded himself, wasn't even counting the stranger's prediction that Zelig, certainly almost alone among the thousands of deportees summoned that day to the boxcars, was going somehow to survive the ordeal.

Yudel felt a surge of premature optimism and, as he acknowledged the inner warmth of its encouraging glow, he came to the bottom of the stairwell.

A door stood half-open just an inch or two away from the lowest step; Yudel pushed it open and stepped into the ancient crypt. He found himself in a large, cool room, in the center of which was a large table on which stood a highly polished crucifix and a vase of wilted flowers. A forest of thin tapers burnt in the corner of the room and provided light; Yudel felt encouraged and stepped forward.

At the end of the room was a passageway; aside from the door through which Yudel had just come, it was the only way out of the room he was in. Taking four long, white tapers from among the dozens stuck into the earthen floor, he extinguished three and left one lighted as he proceeded into the passage.

It was only after a minute's progress through the dark, cool passageway that Yudel realized he was surrounded by ancient graves. There were stone plaques arranged on either side of the passageway; MA..US A...IUS VIR CLARI.S..US read one fragment that Yudel could make out at eye level.

Other inscriptions were less distinct and some were so eroded by the passing centuries as to make them nearly illegible.

Under normal circumstances, it might have struck Yudel as deeply strange to find himself in the company of the dozens, perhaps hundreds or even thousands of dead bodies that presumably lay just behind the many plaques that were displayed on the walls of the passageway. But somehow Yudel was not affected adversely by the dead; he was reassured—reassured and comforted by their nearness and their presence. It was the living, Yudel thought to himself, with whom you can never be sure where you stand; with the dead, one can feel secure and thus entirely at one's ease.

The passageway ended and Yudel found himself in another large room. A yellowed sign covered by a large, discolored piece of cracked plastic announced that the visitor had entered the burial place of one of the ancient Bishops of Rome, a third century pope. Just to the left of the yellow sign, Yudel could easily make out the simple inscription CORNELIVS MARTYR EP, which the sign interpreted as "Cornelius, martyr, bishop."

Yudel admired the simplicity of the grave marker as the taper's flame began to singe his fingers. He lit the second of his tapers and raised the candle high to see if there were another way of leaving the papal crypt other than the passage through which he had just come. It was then that Yudel saw the great fresco that adorned the doorway through which he had come.

An unlit spotlight suspended from the ceiling told the story clearly enough; Yudel had read that this particular catacomb was known for its exquisite examples of very early Christian art, most of which had been left *in situ* for visitors to admire rather than having been taken off to sterile museums. During regular visiting hours, the spotlight must have made the fresco the center of attention in the crypt. But without the light, it was the simple stele marking the grave that drew the attention, as must have been the original intent of the crypt's designers, and the fresco was mere adornment.

Yudel lifted his taper as high as possible and studied the fresco before him.

It was a picture of a man surrounded by other men. Yudel studied the picture; if this was intended as a portrait of Jesus and his disciples, it was unlike any that he had ever seen before in museums of European cathedrals. This Jesus, if Jesus indeed he was, looked like a young Jewish boy. He had a mop of curly hair and large, dark Jewish eyes. For good measure, as though to make the point even clearer, he was wearing a Jewish prayer shawl, the venerable *tallis* now in its polyester period, but once made lovingly of woven linen. The central figure appeared to be seated on, of all things, a green wing chair and held an open book of some sort in his left hand. As though he were ignoring the presence of the open tome, the figure was looking towards his right, gazing, it seemed, at his own right hand which was lifted up in some sort of declamatory gesture.

Yudel found himself hypnotized by the fresco, even in the dim candlelight of his hand-held white taper. Something about the picture was speaking directly to him, but he could hardly imagine what it might be. Suddenly inspired, he pulled out the discarded railway ticket that the tall stranger had given Zelig Kropf a decade earlier.

Holding the ticket in his own left hand and the taper in his right, he looked again at the fresco and his heart skipped a beat. To a remarkable degree, the face on the ticket matched the face of the third disciple from the left. The centuries had robbed the ancient fresco of a bit of its color, but the basic images were still remarkably clear, Yudel thought. Clear and distinct and there was no doubt about it— the face on the back of the ticket was precisely the face on the catacomb wall.

Yudel half expected the fresco to speak to him—the stranger *had* specifically said that if he were to have any questions he could ask them at the Catacomb of Santa Cecilia—but it remained silent. Yudel found to his surprise that he had apparently lost his capacity to be overwhelmed by the fact that he was alone in an ancient Christian crypt in the middle of the Roman night gazing at a wall painting where one of the figures depicted matched a hurried pencil drawing handed by a man about to be deported to his unwarranted death to another who would somehow survive. The circumstances could hardly have been more odd, but Yudel had somehow accepted them as reasonable and that too, he now suddenly realized, was part of the magic.

Yudel wondered what he should do next. The taper was burning down, but there were still two left. He decided to return to the street and contemplate the significance of the evening in the security of his hotel room. Yudel turned to go, but as he did so, he saw a tiny door in the far wall he had somehow failed to notice up until that very moment.

Drawn by curiosity and a growing sense of amazement, Yudel approached the door and pushed it. It opened silently.

The door opened onto a tunnel that was so narrow and so low that Yudel could hardly stand up straight in it. Of course, the tunnel was pitch black, but the taper cast a bit of light in front of where Yudel stood and he could see, as best he could, that the tunnel was clear.

It seemed highly dangerous to do so, but Yudel felt he had no choice. He continued along the tunnel, figuring he could always come back the same way without getting lost; there appeared to be no turn-offs, only a straight and narrow tunnel leading from Pope Cornelius' crypt to wherever the tunnel was going to end.

There was no way to see where the tunnel led and, for the first time since he had suddenly felt alone on the Via delle Sette Chiese, Yudel experienced a sudden shudder of fear. But he felt committed to his quest and he continued down the tunnel. Feeling in his pocket to make sure he still had the fourth taper, he resolved to turn around and head back before he needed to light it.

The tunnel seemed impossibly long and Yudel had no idea how far he had gone. To make calculation even less precise, the tunnel was not entirely straight, but rather had begun to curve here and there so as to destroy completely his sense of direction. After just a few minutes of walking, Yudel hadn't the faintest idea in which direction he was going, only that he hadn't left the tunnel and, because he was walking with his elbows extended so that they touched both sides of the tunnel at all times, that there had been no cut-offs or turn-offs to confuse him on the return journey.

The light of the white taper made it possible for Yudel to see and read his wristwatch. Cursing himself for having failed to notice the precise time he had begun in the tunnel, he could see that it was now almost eight minutes to midnight.

He continued to walk. Six minutes to midnight came and went. It was three minutes to the hour when it struck Yudel suddenly that he somehow expected to reach the climax of his strange drama precisely at the stroke of midnight, but midnight itself came and went and Yudel could still not see the end of the tunnel.

By ten past midnight, the third taper was almost entirely burnt down. Yudel could hardly imagine how far he had come—he was certainly somewhere deep beneath the Via Appia Antica in an endless passageway that could lead anywhere at all.

Just as he resolved to stop and turn back, Yudel found himself unexpectedly at the end of the tunnel. In the dim light of the taper, he could see a door just in front of him. Yudel reached in the dark for a doorknob, but there was none. He pushed the door and it opened.

Yudel saw easily that he was in another crypt, but a moment's observation made the difference clear; whereas he had previously been in a Christian catacomb, he had now somehow found his way into an adjacent Jewish one.

Yudel recalled reading somewhere that the Jews of Rome had, indeed, buried their dead in catacombs, but he couldn't recall when the practice had begun or ended. But the Jewish ambience of the room he was now in was unmistakable; just by the spot he was standing, Yudel could see a burial marker protruding from the wall. It had a seven-branched candelabrum scratched into it and some Greek letters Yudel couldn't read. At the bottom, though, the single Hebrew word *shalom* was clearly written, albeit in a childish hand. Yudel wondered if he were disturbing the peace of the dead, but he knew he had no choice except to go further.

The room in which he found himself was not at all like the papal crypt at the other end of the tunnel. Whereas the latter was large and stark, this room was actually more of a large corridor; to the left and the right were little niches in which Yudel could clearly see dozens, perhaps scores of burial plaques.

Recalling that Zelig once mentioned that the ancient Jews had adopted the *ossilegium*—the practice of allowing the flesh of a cadaver to rot in a stone sarcophagus for a year's time and only then interring, or rather re-interring, the bones in a subterranean burial niche—Yudel felt he understood the significance of the room in which he stood.

He walked slowly to the very end of the long room to see if there were a door that would lead him further, but there was none.

"Damn," Yudel said aloud, only to recoil at the sound of his echoing imprecation as it desecrated an ancient holy place.

Yudel was down to his last taper; feeling certain he could feel his way back along the main corridor even in the dark did not make him particularly anxious to have to do so. He turned to go and it was at that precise moment that he saw the great fresco to which the man in the Munich train station had apparently been referring when he spoke to Zelig Kropf.

The fresco was actually a triptych. The central panel was the smallest and covered the space directly over the doorway as far up as the ceiling. The left and right panels were much bigger and flanked both the central panel and the doorway itself. Yudel felt a familiar tingling in the pit of his stomach and he knew he had come to the right place.

The central panel, highest off the ground, was similar to the great fresco in the papal crypt. With one great exception, the scene was the same: a teacher seated on a green chair while his disciples listened with rapt attention. The scene was almost identical except for one detail: the face of the man who had been drawn as the third disciple to the left was now portrayed at the center of the picture and the face of the man who was the central figure in the papal fresco now occupied the spot of the third disciple to the left.

But this was somehow less important than the side panels, Yudel thought. He approached the doorway and looked carefully at the ancient paintings. Slowly, he felt himself understanding.

The left panel was actually made up of two different pictures. In the lower one, a woman sat in a green chair and suckled a naked infant. She seemed at peace and happy, secure in the knowledge that her son was being nurtured and nourished. The baby was clearly a boy and seemed blissful as he snuggled in his mother's bosom; it was a scene of total domestic peace, enchanting and tranquil.

In the upper picture, Yudel could see a figure of a woman seated on a green wing chair surrounded by several male figures, but it was clearly a different woman from the one in the first scene. Resting on the woman's breast, there was a small naked boy. Since the child in both scenes was clearly the same baby, it seemed odd that the artist had made such an obvious point of painting the women in the two scenes as distinctly different people. Just before this other woman's feet, another boy sat calmly and looked into a book. And behind the woman, a young man stood and looked out calmly at the onlooker. He was wearing a white gown and had familiar curly hair and familiar dark, Jewish eyes; it was only a moment before Yudel realized that the strength of the picture lay in the fact that the baby, the boy and the young man all had the same face—and this face matched that of the baby in the lower panel.

This, obviously, was why the figures all looked in different directions rather than at each other; they could not see each other because they *were* each other.

The tingling spread from Yudel's stomach to his loins; this was the distinct feeling he had had when he had first recognized Bunny Falk in the Boulevard Delicatessen. As Yudel expected, the strange sensation spread further until it eventually encompassed his entire body.

Stepping to the right, Yudel could see that the right-hand panel too was made up of two different pictures. On the top, Yudel could see the woman from the first panel, the one with the infant at her breast. Only now, she was depicted as having aged dramatically; her hair was longer and streaked with grey and her body was heavier than it was in the first picture in the series. She held a golden lamp before her and seemed to be leading a man who was dawdling behind her. The man looked vaguely irritated about being in the picture; the woman looked determined as she gazed forward in the yellow lamp light.

The fourth picture was the most dramatic. A Roman centurion, who bore an uncanny resemblance, Yudel thought, to himself, had his lance raised and was apparently about to plunge it into a man's breast; it was the same man who had been depicted at different stages of his life in the second picture. The man was older now as well; his hair was less intensely black and his eyes looked more tired and distinctly heavier. He seemed resigned to his fate, but between the soldier and his victim, the artist had painted the woman from the first and third pictures. She was guarding the man and had placed her own hand up against the tip of the centurion's lance. She looked defiant and angry, but most of all determined. Yudel found himself leaning closer and closer to the wall the better to see the woman's face; it was a face he could not place and then, suddenly, he did know whose face it was he was seeing. The lady in the picture bore a startling resemblance to, of all people, Bunny Falk.

The fourth taper began to sputter as it reached its bottom third. Suddenly terrified of having to find his way back to the street in the dark, Yudel practically ran out of the catacomb back into the tunnel. The passageway seemed a good deal shorter on the way back than it had on the way in; in what seemed to be a matter of mere minutes, Yudel was back in the crypt of Pope Cornelius.

The taper finally went out just as Yudel was stepping back into the nave of the church from which he had begun his descent. Another minute and he was in the Via delle Sette Chiese and then on the Via Appia Antica; before Yudel even thought to look at his wristwatch, he saw a taxi approach. He hailed the cab, jumped in and gave the name of his hotel.

It was only once Yudel was back in the lobby of his hotel on the Via del Pantheon that he thought to check the time; it hardly seemed possible, but it was not even quite one o'clock in the morning. Yudel felt he had been underground for weeks, but in reality only a single hour had passed.

Yudel Wolfzahn went up to his room and fell on the bed without even having the strength to undress. When he awoke, it was late the following afternoon and the shadows cast on the wall by the sun's rays seemed ominous and vaguely threatening.

Yudel showered and shaved and hurried out to dine alone in a restaurant that had been recommended to him in Trastevere, not far from the Ponte Sublico.

Twenty-two

Zelig Kropf's dinner guests had left shortly after the grace was recited, leaving Zelig and Yudel alone in the apartment to clear the dishes and tidy up.

There was a certain intimacy between these two old men—Zelig was already 71 years old in 1981 and Yudel would be that same age on Christmas Day—that was the product of decades of common endeavor. It hardly seemed possible that almost three decades had passed since Yudel had returned from his European trip.

***

Zelig, too curious to wait for Yudel to phone *him*, had taken the liberty of phoning Clara and offering to pick her husband up at Idlewild when his plane landed; she had agreed immediately.

When Zelig had later sat down with Yudel to listen to the story, he somehow understood more in it than he had any particular reason to think was there. It wasn't precisely a sense of *déjà vu*—Zelig had no sense that he himself had somehow already heard the story Yudel was telling—as much as it was a certain inexplicable fascination with Yudel's account for which he could find no rational explanation. Almost magnetic in terms of their attractive force, the details of Yudel's experience in the catacomb pulled at Zelig in a way that was as eerie as it was intense.

It was less than a year later that he made his first discovery of "the face" on a fifth century ivory diptych he had chanced upon in the Victoria and Albert Museum in London.

The obsession with "the face" continued unabated throughout the decades; by 1981, Zelig had assembled originals and reproductions of more than a hundred works of ancient art on which he found "the face" featured either prominently or at least in the shadows. Some of his pieces, like the great apsidal fresco from the Church of Santa Pudenziana, were enormous works of art, while others were tiny fragments of ancient manuscript leaves illuminated by knowing hands. Some were things of great value that had cost Zelig Kropf thousands, while others had been available at bargain basement prices. Some reproductions had been available for purchase, while others had to be specially ordered.

The only thing missing from the collection was a real human being bearing "the face," the man whose face *was* "the face," the man whom the deportee in the Munich Bahnhof could no longer await and whom he had charged Zelig Kropf, if not in so many words then at least in gesture and deed, to find.

More times than he could even begin to calculate, Zelig had returned to the scene in the train station. The man had told him he would recognize a certain man as soon as he saw him, and he had. He had predicted that the man Zelig would recognize would himself recognize a certain woman as soon as he saw her, and *he* had. He had predicted that they would have a child, and *they* had. There hadn't been any specific instruction about the man whose face had been hastily drawn on the back of the train ticket; it had simply been thrust into Zelig's hand without a word of explanation being spoken.

It was precisely then that the man had told Zelig to tell the man he was to recognize to inquire at the catacomb if he required further information.

That the face on the ticket and the face in the catacomb fresco were identical was clearly the point; the ticket was the key to understanding what precisely in the catacomb was to be the point of inquiry. And yet the message remained unclear even after decades of rumination; even the simplest questions defied Zelig and Yudel's attempts to find satisfactory solutions.

Because Yudel knew where he personally had placed Bunny's baby for adoption, he was in a unique position to watch from the wings during the years of Marvin Kalish's youth and adolescence.

At first it seemed like an impossible undertaking, but as the years passed, things became more and more simple. Following somebody's progress, especially somebody completely unaware of any outside interest in his life, is not as complicated a matter as one might think.

Merely by making telephone calls on his lunch hour, Yudel was able to know where Marvin went to school—he had only had to phone three neighborhood public schools before he found the right one. He knew what Little League team had accepted Marvin as a member and he had a full schedule of games. More than once, Yudel had donned his ridiculous trench coat and Tilly hat and made his way to the Fleet Street Little League field to watch surreptitiously from behind a bush as the boy stood in left field waiting, usually in vain, for a fly ball to come his way.

Yudel knew the name of the elderly Italian dame from whom Marvin took piano lessons and he knew the number of Marvin's Cub Scout Troop. In later years, Yudel often felt he probably knew more about Marvin than his adoptive father did; certainly Ike Kalish couldn't name the candy store from which the adolescent Marvin bought a single pack of cigarettes once a week to smoke with an unidentified girl as they walked along 110th Street in the early Queens morning on their way to Forest Hills High.

And all this time, the prophecy, as Yudel and Zelig had taken rather dramatically to referring to the tall man's message, was coming true before their very eyes. Marvin was handsome even as a child, slender and athletic with pitch black hair and dark, Jewish eyes. But it was only as he approached his bar mitzvah year that it had become perfectly clear that, just as Yudel and Zelig had expected would be the case, Marvin's was "the face."

There was no denying it at all—Marvin simply *was* the person the man had drawn on the discarded train ticket. The drawing was inexpert, but it was distinct and there was really no possibility that Yudel and Zelig were wrong: Marvin was the man.

But what man was that? That most vexing of all the unanswered questions remained precisely that—unanswered. And as Marvin passed through adolescence, it only became more puzzling. Yudel and Zelig considered a return trip to Rome, but decided against it. It would be hard to explain and ultimately unnecessary; in 1972, Yale University Press had published a coffee-table volume of frescos from the Roman catacombs and both the frescos surrounding the catacomb portal that featured "the face"—the one from the Jewish burial cave and the group portrait that graced the crypt of Pope Cornelius—had been reproduced in full detail and in rich color.

Zelig bought the book for Yudel and Yudel bought a copy for Zelig. Often they would sit up at night once Clara Wolfzahn had gone to sleep, each man with his own book open on his lap, and talk about the frescos on the telephone.

In the meantime, both men had informed themselves not only about catacombs in general, but about the history of the Jews of Rome, about ancient burial practices, about early Christian art and about Pope Cornelius and about any other area of scholarship that could conceivably have shed any light on the mystery at hand. All these avenues had yielded some sort of fruit, but the ultimate answers remained hidden.

Yudel recalled more and more often his ancient *melamed* on the Schäferkampsallee in old Hamburg and his favorite rabbinic dictum: *Ein habrocho nimtzo-o ele bosomui min ho-oyin*—The blessings of God are always hidden from the eye.

***

"So what's new," Zelig finally asked his friend once they were alone.

Yudel looked around, as thought to guarantee that they were alone. "A lot," he said simply.

"About the face?"

"Yes, about the face."

"Something's happened to Marvin?"

"Not exactly."

"For God's sake, you didn't shoot him, did you?"

Yudel rolled his eyes towards the ceiling. "No, I didn't shoot him. I didn't waste all that money on lessons so that I wouldn't be able to miss a man at fifty feet. He's safe enough, but I'm getting worried."

"What does Clara think?" Zelig asked quietly.

It had been a joint decision of both Yudel's and Zelig's to initiate Clara Wolfzahn in the mystery in the spring of 1966, although she had been allowed to presume that Zelig, not her husband, was the father of Bunny's child and that Yudel had merely arranged the adoption as a favor for his friend. Why Zelig hadn't married Bunny once he had learned that she was carrying his child was a question Clara didn't think to ask and which neither he nor Yudel was going to suggest to her. Both men had developed the fantasy—and it had proven to be just that—that Marvin's bar mitzvah on May 28 was going to be a watershed event in the unravelling of the mystery. Clara had listened intently and seemed quite prepared to accept the fact that her husband was quite deeply involved in some metaphysical mystery that had yet to reach its resolution.

The fact that the Scriptural lesson taken from the prophets for that particular Sabbath was the story of the birth of Samson had seemed especially significant to both men. They had studied the thirteenth chapter of Judges together before the event in great detail, leaving no medieval commentator's thoughts unexplored and no avenue or rabbinical exegesis untravelled.

They had even attended the bar mitzvah convinced that their presence would provoke some sort of revelatory event. Dressed in dark suits and wrapped in enormous white and black prayer shawls, they had chosen seats at the very rear of the synagogue balcony where Ike Kalish, who was seated with the bar mitzvah family in the very front row of the enormous sanctuary and who would definitely have recognized Yudel, would never think to look for any of his guests.

They had waited impatiently for the bar mitzvah boy to be called to read the lesson from Scripture. He looked especially handsome that day, Yudel later recalled, in his navy suit and matching blue-and-gray necktie; Marvin had already somehow made the transition from boyhood to young adulthood and was merely in the synagogue to mark that metamorphosis in the traditional manner.

Yudel waited anxiously to hear how Marvin would be called up. In traditional synagogues, it would naturally be the custom for the boy to be called both by his given name and that of his father's. But as Jewish law does not recognize the institution of adoption in the fictitious sense of Western law, whereby the adoptive father actually, magically, *becomes* the father of the adopted child, it would be odd to call the boy up as the son of his adoptive father.

Yudel's Hebrew name was Judah; although it was obviously impossible that Marvin be called up as the son of Judah, it still seemed important to Yudel that he not be called up either as the son of Yitzchak, which was Ike Kalish's Jewish name. Yudel bent over the seat in front of him with his hand cupped to his ear in order to hear how the name would be spoken.

"Let Menachem come forward," the sexton had sung out to the irritation of both the adoptive and the birth fathers, whereupon Menachem-Marvin had stood up and begun to chant his lesson.

In the end, nothing at all happened. The lesson concluded, the rabbi gave his sermon and the Kalishes sponsored a luncheon for their guests in the synagogue's sumptuous banquet hall. Zelig and Yudel had considered crashing the luncheon, but it was too likely they would encounter Ike Kalish and neither was up for *that* experience. Besides, they reasoned, anything that was going to happen ought to have happened during the actual worship service; the idea that the revelation would take place during lunch had a distinctly Jewish ring to it, but still seemed sufficiently unlikely as to make the risks of attending not equal to the danger of being identified.

The men had returned home unsatisfied and disappointed. But it was that very afternoon that Yudel told Clara his theories and begged her to forgive his silence over the previous fifteen years "out of respect for Zelig."

Yudel considered Zelig's question. "Clara thinks all we have to do is to keep going. She is very strong on our original theory, you know. She thinks all we have to do is keep going until we get to the last panel and then things will reveal themselves."

The original theory had been simple: the portal was not meant to tell a story all by itself, but rather to lay out a series of events that would have to take place before any further revelations could occur. The woman in the first panel was obviously the baby's mother, but she was apparently to be replaced by another woman while the child was still an infant.

The first woman was to search for her baby—that had been clear enough in the fresco that portrayed her holding her golden lamp aloft and shlepping her hapless husband along in her wake—and then find him.

All that had really happened. What was lacking still, however, was the fulfillment of the final fresco, the one in which the brave mother from the first and third paintings put her hand up to thwart the centurion's lance from piercing her grown son's breast. Zelig, Clara and Yudel had spent hours discussing the picture and trying to determine what it could possibly mean.

"She's got to save his life," Clara insisted over and over. "The Roman setting is just because it's an ancient painting. What should they have painted in the first century? Storm troopers? The centurion is just their idea of a bad guy, but we have our own and it doesn't make any difference. The idea is that she has to save his life."

"You think?"

"Yes, I do," Clara had stated not once but on many different occasions.

Eventually, Zelig and Yudel had come to agree. For years they had been content to wait for Bunny Falk Luft to save her baby's life.

Nothing happened. "She doesn't even know who adopted him!"

Clara had said to Yudel one warm day in the spring of 1978. "How can she save his life if she doesn't even know who he is?"

"Well," Yudel had responded, "The fresco shows a man of about twenty-seven or twenty-eight. Maybe whatever is going to happen is only *supposed* to happen now. Maybe I should just call her and tell her where to find her son. She *might* be receptive."

"That's perfect! Just phone her up after twenty-five years and say, "Hi! This is the guy who helped you ditch your kid an hour after he was born. Guess what? I'm phoning you to tell you how you can meet your son after all these years and explain to him why you dumped him before he had even dirtied his first diaper!"

Yudel saw his wife's point. "She'd be angry, maybe even she'd go nuts. But the damage would be done. She'd know who he was and she'd never be able to rest—trust me on this—until she did meet him. She'd hate me for starting up, but who cares? She probably *already* hates me and even if she doesn't, what difference does it make. These are cosmic things we are talking about! *Cosmic things!* A little interpersonal hatred hardly matters when you are dealing in *cosmic things!*"

Clara agreed that Bunny's feelings about her husband were beside the point, but she didn't feel that he could just phone her up and spring this all on her.

"Why don't *we* set things up so she figures out herself who he is *and* ends up saving his life at the same time. Don't forget, we all understand the third fresco to mean that she's supposed to *search* for him. So let's set her up to search for him, to find him *and* to save his life. Then we'll see what happens."

"I think I agree," Zelig said. "I agree with Clara. We're in this so far, we have to continue. Eventually, they'll become friends and they'll spend more and more time together. If we wait for the right moment, we'll get her to save his life yet."

"When should we try again?"

"Well," Yudel responded, "I don't shoot people on *Shabbos*." The idea that one could observe the Jewish Sabbath by refraining from shooting one's children on Saturdays made both Zelig and Yudel laugh aloud.

"How about tonight?"

"I wouldn't even know where to look for them," Yudel admitted. "But you come over and we'll figure this out together. We'll order in from Pho-Nee's."

"I'll bring the beer," Zelig offered generously.

"We accept," Yudel responded gravely. "Mr. and Mrs. Wolfzahn accept Mr. Kropf's generous offer and will expect him for post-sabbatical supper at ten o'clock p.m."

Zelig indicated his pleased acceptance with a curt bow from the waist as Yudel turned to go.

"Go home to your wife," Zelig called after him as he moved towards the stairway down into the pharmacy. "On Friday night, the rabbi says sex is worship."

"Which rabbi is that?" Yudel asked over his shoulder as he rolled his eyes towards the ceiling and opened the door into the stairwell.

"Rabbi Zelig Simchah Kropf, at your service," Zelig intoned in his deepest rabbinic baritone. "Sexual counselling, our specialty."

With a wave, Yudel was out the door and down the stairs.

Twenty-three

"*I*'ll cut that bastard's balls off and ram them down his throat," Lawrence Lazar said more to himself than to his wife as he stood stiffly against the kitchen counter at half-past seven in the morning on Saturday, March 7, 1981 squeezing oranges against the glass juicer so violently that he was actually tearing the peel on the smooth glass as he pressed down. Then, in a quieter voice, "He *betrayed* me."

Bunny Luft stood quietly to his side by the kitchen window, Rabbi Weissbrot's ancient wedding gift clutched in her right hand. She felt the burden of deep conflict as she listened to her husband sputter and moan, knowing that she had betrayed her husband only slightly less definitively than had Yudel Wolfzahn.

Yudel had, of course, lied to Lawrence Lazar in the spring of 1954 when he had introduced Bunny to her future husband as a friend of Clara's. She was no friend of Clara Wolfzahn's, of course—they had never even met—but that was the lesser sin, Bunny now realized. Far more nefarious was Yudel's convenient omission of the fact that Bunny had born him a child out of wedlock, the adoption of whom he had personally arranged. Passing Bunny off as a friend of his wife's was merely false, but omitting the fact that she had been, however briefly, his lover was more than false—it was an evil lie that all concerned should have known would eventually come back to haunt them.

But Bunny had allowed Yudel's lie to put down roots and flourish for almost a quarter of a century and so could not be considered entirely free of responsibility merely because somebody else had laid the groundwork for her own deception.

Bunny had met Lawrence Lazar under false pretenses and she allowed their relationship to develop without ever feeling the moment right to tell him that the father of her child had been his own friend, Yudel Wolfzahn. Perhaps, Bunny thought to herself, she would have had to speak up had the friendship between Yudel and

Lawrence Lazar continued, but it hadn't and it had therefore seemed wiser in every way simply to allow the matter to drop.

The baby was placed, Yudel was gone both from Bunny's life *and* from her husband's, and the whole affair seemed more like a dream than part of historical reality.

"I know you're angry," Bunny began gently, "but there's no reason to go crazy. No one is chopping anyone's nuts off, at least not for the time being. I *know* I should have told you who the father was. You remember I wanted to..."

"You *wanted* to?" Incredulity and the bitterness of friendship betrayed vied in Lawrence Lazar's angry voice.

"Well, I did want to. I asked you in the car that night—I remember it like it was yesterday—if you wanted to ask me who the father was and you said you didn't want to know. You said that if you didn't know him, it didn't matter and if you did, you were probably better off not knowing."

Lawrence Lazar closed his bloodshot eyes and recalled the evening in question. It had been the night of their engagement and he had been driving with Bunny along Queens Boulevard. She had, indeed, asked him if he was going to inquire about the identity of her baby's father and he had, just as Bunny had recalled the scene, declined to ask. "I was being goddam polite," he said after a moment's deliberation. "I didn't think it was really one of my two best friends. And you *knew* I didn't know and you must have known I would have wanted to know *a lot* that one of my two best chums was your lover. Wolfzahn *introduced* us to each other, for crying out loud."

Bunny clasped the mirror to her chest. "Let's not go overboard. One roll in the hay doesn't make anyone my lover. We had one good *shtup*, but one performance was the whole run. No encores, no hold-overs, no twofers and no national tour. Fifteen lousy minutes on my mother's broadloom..."

Lawrence Lazar's eyes opened wide. "In your parents' living room you did it? That piece of shit..." His voice trailed off in voyeuristic horror as Lawrence Lazar contemplated for a moment how many hundreds, probably thousands of times, he had stood on the very patch of faded beige broadloom on which his wife had given her virginity in adulterous union to Yudel Wolfzahn.

Bunny was not so ashamed by the revelation of the previous evening that she had lost the capacity to become exasperated by her husband's inability to seize an idea quickly. "Yes, professor," she said sarcastically, "in my parents' living room. On my parents' broadloom. Are there any *more* questions?"

Lawrence Lazar, as usual, missed the rhetorical nature of his wife's question. "Why didn't you do it on the couch?" he asked, quite seriously.

"It had one of those plastic slipcovers," Bunny answered mercilessly. "Who could do it on a plastic slipcover? Who would want to? Would you?"

Lawrence Lazar was silent, apparently lost in thought.

"No," he said eventually, "I wouldn't."

The subject was allowed to drop, but not before Lawrence Lazar was allowed to make one or two more threats against his former friend's life.

"Don't make this into such a big *tsimmes*," Bunny finally instructed. "You sound like *I* betrayed *you*. *I* didn't cheat on *you; he* cheated on *her*."

"Does she know?" Almost undetectably, a certain undertone of forgiveness crept in Lawrence Lazar's voice.

"How should I know if she knows? I've never even met her. You used to know her, didn't you?"

"We met once or twice. *She* wasn't part of the group in those days; *he* was. I mean, I must have stopped up for something at the apartment and she was there, or else she was there when I dropped him off. I mean, she never came along, but sometimes I must have seen her. I can't even remember what she looked like." As he finished his sentence, some distant chime rang somewhere in the recesses of Lawrence Lazar's consciousness. But it was only a distant ringing and his agitated state kept him from focusing on the subtle phenomenon.

"So *I* should ask *you* if she knows about Yudel's affair!"

"Well, the fact that I asked you first should tell you that I haven't any idea at all. Probably she doesn't. I'm sure he didn't tell her and I certainly didn't."

"Maybe Zelig Kropf told her." Bunny hadn't ever much liked Zelig Kropf, but she had shopped regularly in his pharmacy. Once Lawrence Lazar and Zelig had grown apart, however, Bunny had switched her allegiance to the new Drug City on 63rd Drive and hadn't set foot in Zelig's shop even one single time since.

"I doubt it."

"But maybe."

Lawrence Lazar felt a shiver come over him. "Maybe he did. But I don't think so."

The matter was allowed to drop. The day promised to be sunny and warm, an early spring day at the tail end of winter. Bunny and Lawrence Lazar drank their orange juice and coffee and decided to skip synagogue services and spend the morning instead having a walk along the boulevard.

They walked arm in arm like an elderly Jewish couple, looking in the storefront windows and discussing the days of their lives. "It's all connected," Bunny said as they headed westward along the great avenue in the opposite direction from their synagogue.

"What's connected?"

"The whole thing is connected—the maniac taking potshots at Marvin, our meeting the Kalishes, me suddenly naming the boy's father after twenty-seven years of *not* naming him, even the incident in *shul* with the lady with the handbag that got the ball rolling—it all somehow fits in together."

The day was uncharacteristically warm. A certain unfamiliar scent—the combined odors of newly thawed soil in the neighborhood's window boxes, cooking smells escaping into the street for the first time in months through newly opened kitchen windows, the collective perspiration of a million and a half overdressed citizens and the occasional whiff of boiled frankfurters already wafting across the borough from the umbrella carts of the very first of the season's licensed street vendors—these combined odors produced a strange scent that filled the Queens air and boded well for the coming season. People were walking along the boulevard with their winter coats left open, woolen scarves flapping in the spring breeze rather than wrapped securely around the necks they had been bought to keep warm.

Lawrence Lazar unbuttoned his overcoat and took his wife's hand in his. "How connected? You don't think Yudel Wolfzahn has anything to do with all of this, do you?"

Bunny thought for a moment. "No, I don't. It's not *that* simple. But it's hard for me to imagine that these are all just random events that have no connection. I keep a secret for twenty-seven years and then suddenly it's public knowledge. I manage *not* to search for my first-born son for that many years and suddenly, circumstances require that I *have* to find him. Somebody is shooting at my boy, but whoever it is either can't shoot straight or is trying to miss..." Bunny's voice trailed off in reasoned contemplation of the data.

"I thought you dismissed Abernathy's idea that the shooter was not really trying to connect."

"Well, I did. Dismiss it, I mean. But now I don't know. The guy must have been standing in the doorway of that gourmet shop. He had *plenty* of time to take aim and we were only standing across the street. Okay, let's assume he was anxious *not* to hit me, but still, we weren't standing *that* close to each other. I mean, if he wanted to hit Marvin, he could have gotten a lot closer."

"But he *could* have hit you," Lawrence Lazar insisted.

"Well," Bunny answered with a growing sense that she was approaching the right track, "if he was so afraid of hitting me, then he wouldn't have shot at all. If he couldn't get the shot at Marvin he wanted, he should have gone home and waited for another day. Why would he have bothered to risk getting caught if he knew he was shooting so high he couldn't possibly connect with his target? Something is fishy about the whole thing. Maybe Abernathy is right and maybe he's not. But I'm not so sure that he doesn't have something about the shooter not wanting simply to take Marvin out. There's something else here."

"And what might that be?"

"Well, Sherlock, I *don't know* what that might be. But just because I don't get all of something doesn't mean I'm wrong. There's something in all of this, something linking all these events together, but I just don't know what it is."

"And how are you going to find out?" Lawrence Lazar knew all too well how little point there would have been in asking *if* Bunny planned to find out, since he was sure she would manage eventually to put the pieces together successfully. The only questions were *how* and, perhaps, *when*.

"I don't know that either," Bunny admitted.

"Maybe you should work out a plan of attack with Detective Abernathy?"

Bunny looked at her husband with feigned incredulity. "Why in the world would I work out anything with him?"

"Well, for one thing, he won't like you snooping around on his turf. He's supposed to be in charge of this investigation," Lawrence Lazar observed plausibly.

"Who cares what he's supposed to be in charge of? All he does is show up when someone takes another shot at Marvin. This has to do with me as much as with the boy—I don't know if Abernathy knows that, but *I* know it and that's good enough for me—anyway, I *know* it has as much to do with me as it has to do with Marvin and I mean to find out why that is. Why that is and what precisely the whole thing means and why someone is shooting at my kid…"

The Lufts were well into Elmhurst by now. They turned right onto Van Loon Street, intending to walk first to Maurice Avenue and then back towards their home along Junction Boulevard.

"That's a lot of questions," Lawrence Lazar said softly as he dropped his wife's hand in order to clasp her arm and draw her closer to him.

"But they've all got the same answer," Bunny said no less quietly. "And I'm going to find out what it is."

The quiet of Van Loon Street contrasted pleasantly with the bustle of Queens Boulevard. Lawrence Lazar unbuttoned his collar and stood for a moment in order to ask his next question with the maximum gravity possible. "Where are you going to start?" he asked, gazing directly into his wife's eyes.

"With that piece of shit that walks. With your friend Wolfzahn, I'm going to start. Where else should I begin?"

"He's probably not going to like hearing from you."

"What's it to me if he likes or doesn't like? He'll like it or he won't like it, but he'll answer my questions or I'll rip his tongue out of his head and staple it to his forehead and he won't answer anyone else's questions for the rest of his sick life."

Bunny had also stopped to deliver her answer, but now she began again to walk at a much quicker gait than previously. "We're going now?" Lawrence Lazar asked with alarm. He had hoped for at least a day or two to prepare himself for the adventure about to be undertaken.

"Now?" Bunny seemed surprised by her husband's question. "No, we're not going now. Now, we're going home for lunch. I have a *chulent* up since lunchtime yesterday, just like you like it with those disgusting brown eggs in it and a piece of *kishka* that could kill us both."

Lawrence Lazar knew all too well that stuffed derma was pure fat, but it was simply too tasty an addition to his wife's Sabbath stew to omit. He'd just have to die a bit earlier for the privilege of having eaten Bunny Luft's *chulent*; men, Lawrence Lazar knew all too well, have died for lesser pleasures than his wife's Sabbath lunch.

"So let's go," he said, proffering his arm again as they turned onto Junction Boulevard for their walk home. "When are we going to encounter the good Mr. Wolfzahn?"

Bunny looked amazed at her husband's innocence. "Tonight," she said. "When else?"

Twenty-four

*B*unny planned her assault on the Wolfzahn's apartment like a crusader planning an attack on a Saracen stronghold.

"They might not even be home," Lawrence Lazar observed to his wife later that afternoon, after they had risen from their Sabbath naps and were seated at their dining room table over yellow slabs of pound cake and strong black tea.

"They'll be there." Bunny was apparently not willing to consider even the possibility of not finding her erstwhile lover and his wife at home when she came calling.

"He won't be happy to see you," Lawrence Lazar suggested, taking a new tack in his effort to discourage Bunny from plunging head first into a situation she hardly understood.

"Who gives a shit what makes *him* happy?"

"You don't *know* he is involved in all this business with Marvin. You could just as easily be shlepping him into something he has no business being part of."

Bunny's patience was quickly running out. "For God's sake, Larry, Yudel Wolfzahn is Marvin Kalish's *father*. He's *already* involved, not least of all because he arranged an illegal adoption to get the baby to the Kalishes in the first place. That piece of shit actually sold his own son—he took *money* from the Kalishes for the kid. I'm sure that's at least a felony and probably it's worse than that. It certainly should be—I have every mind to phone Shlonsky Monday morning and find out just how many years you can sit in the slammer for selling your own kid!"

"I'm not disputing the guy is a fiend. I mean, he's the one who knocked you up, sold your kid and then introduced you to me and stood by while we got married."

"So you wouldn't have married me if you had known?"

"I didn't say that."

– 256 –

"So what *did* you say?"

"I said, he stood by and let us get married without telling me that he had slept with the bride and that she was the mother of his child. I mean, *I* know I would have married you anyway. But *he* didn't know I would have. And *he* should have cared enough about our friendship to give me the option to change my plans. I mean, he had no way of knowing you were going to tell me, did he?"

Bunny made a point of answering without having to pause and consider what the right response to *that* question might be. "No," she said, "he didn't."

Lawrence Lazar decided to give himself one final chance to discourage his wife from reopening a wound that had scabbed over and healed, more or less, more than a quarter of a century earlier. "Just remember that there isn't a single shred of evidence that connects Yudel to any of this at all."

Before Bunny had a chance to respond, Lawrence Lazar had a thought. "Unless…" he began.

"Unless what?"

"Unless nothing. I was only wondering if the lady in *shul*, the one with the handbag that got this whole thing started, I wonder if that might not have been Clara Wolfzahn."

"Well, I certainly never met her."

"I did, but it was so long ago. It was twenty-five years ago and *then* it was only when I was in their apartment picking Yudel up or dropping him back home after dinner or after one of our famous sessions in the steamroom at the Q.H.C. I remember only vaguely what she looked like—and that's what she looked like twenty-five years ago."

Bunny was intrigued. "But it *could* have been her?"

"Yes," Lawrence Lazar answered cautiously, suddenly entirely certain that the woman was none other than Clara Wolfzahn, but momentarily unsure if he should share the certainty of his conviction with his wife. "It could have been."

Bunny wasn't fooled for a moment. "It was her, wasn't it," she said in a quiet voice, suddenly overwhelmed by this piece of possibly incontrovertible evidence linking the attempts on Marvin Kalish's life with the Wolfzahns.

Lawrence Lazar knew better than to dissemble. "Yes," he answered simply. "It was."

"You're sure."

"No, not really."

"But pretty sure."

Lawrence Lazar thought for a moment before responding. "Sure enough," he said finally and in a low voice.

The matter of how to get themselves into the Wolfzahns' apartment was another item on the Lufts' Sabbath afternoon agenda.

Bunny was all for coming in casual clothing, as though they had simply been out for a Saturday night stroll on Austin Street and had had the novel idea of dropping in on the Wolfzahns' for tea. The fact that neither Bunny nor Lawrence Lazar had seen Yudel Wolfzahn for a quarter of a century didn't have to matter all that much, Bunny observed several times in the course of the discussion.

"You don't think he'll find it a bit odd that we've suddenly stopped by after twenty-seven years of complete silence."

"Not necessarily," Bunny answered. "Maybe he'll think it's a friendly gesture. You *were* friends, you know."

"Were is right," Lawrence Lazar said curtly. "We were friends, but we aren't now and it will seem strange as hell for us to just drop by. Better we should come in with our pistols drawn, state our business and threaten to blow their kid's brains out if they don't tell the entire story from beginning to end with no funny business."

"Their kid might not be there," Bunny said, apparently taking Lawrence Lazar's proposal seriously that they extract the truth from Yudel and Clara by pointing a gun at Sidney Wolfzahn's head.

"We can say we're holding him in a warehouse in Long Island City. In fact, we can say we have him locked up at my plant. They'll believe that. We'll tell them that if they don't talk, the kid will be sliced into slats and sold as a venetian blind by morning."

"They'll burst their sides laughing," Bunny said. "Nobody would take that seriously."

"We'll bring them one of his ears like they did with that guy they kidnapped in Italy."

Even Bunny hadn't lost her capacity to be amazed by her husband. "We don't really have Sidney Wolfzahn in your factory," she explained patiently. "We can't cut off his ear and present it to his parents. Even if we could, I don't think we would. But I have another idea, just as good."

Bunny leaned over her Sabbath table and told her husband just what she had in mind for that evening's assault on the Wolfzahns' flat.

The question of whether Marvin Kalish and Dawn Kupchinsky should or should not be involved in the Lufts' surprise visit to the

Wolfzahns' flat was also in need of serious discussion.

"Eventually, he'll want to meet his father," Lawrence Lazar observed plausibly. "I mean, no matter how warmly he feels about Ike Kalish, he's still got to be dying of curiosity to meet the man who really did father him."

"So?" Bunny didn't see the point of the observation.

"So if he comes along tonight, it will mix too many ingredients together in one evening's stew. He'll be communing with his father at the same time you'll be trying to worm a story out of Yudel that he won't want to tell you anyway and which he *certainly* won't want to tell in front of Marvin."

"You could argue it the other way around," Bunny mused. "Maybe Marvin's presence will be so overwhelming for Yudel—he *is* the kid's father, after all—that his guard will be down and he'll feel obliged to answer all my questions. I mean, for God's sake— this is his son, his own flesh and blood we're talking about. He's got to have some regrets about having abandoned his own son. Maybe meeting him will just shake him loose enough from his moorings to get him to talk."

"Maybe."

"Maybe I should call him or maybe I shouldn't."

"Maybe you should *and* maybe you shouldn't."

"So should I or shouldn't I?"

"Should."

"You said shouldn't a minute ago."

Lawrence Lazar thought for a moment before responding. "I know," he said eventually, "but I was wrong. Bringing Marvin along is precisely what you *should* do. That will give us the excuse for dropping by. The only thing is…what if the wife doesn't know?"

"So who cares what she knows? Life is just filled with little sur- prises! God knows I've had enough in the last few weeks; so she'll have a little one of her own too. Besides, don't you think she has a right to know that she has a stepson?"

"No, I don't."

"Well, I do."

"You'll wreck their marriage. Do you want that on your head?"

"That *putz* wrecked his marriage twenty-seven years ago when he told his wife he was having deli with you while he was screwing me on my mother's living room floor. This is just the icing on the cake, if you know what I mean."

Lawrence Lazar knew all too well what she meant. "Look," he

said, "I didn't say I was against inviting Marvin to come along. I'm only against wrecking their marriage without even giving Yudel a chance to explain. Let's make a compromise..." Lawrence Lazar's voice trailed off as he considered the implications of the suggestion he was about to make.

"So I'm listening."

"So we invite Marvin along, but we don't say who he is. I mean, if she recognizes his name, so she knows and we don't have to be the harbingers of bad news. And if she doesn't recognize his name and doesn't know who he is, so that's okay too. What matters is that you can bet your bottom dollar *he* will recognize Marvin's name. He'll recognize his name and know within one split second who he is. If he wants to acknowledge him out loud, that's his decision. If he doesn't, who cares? What counts is that Marvin's presence should be so devastating to Yudel that he just might be rattled enough to come clean."

"Okay," Bunny said.

"Just like that, okay. Not 'Okay, but...'"

"No buts. Just okay. We take Marvin along and we don't say who he is. Actually it's better this way—Yudel will be so caught up in wanting to meet Marvin and talk to him, but at the same time without letting Clara guess what their real relationship is that he won't have any energy at all left to fend off *our* questions. It's a wonderful plan. I'll call Marvin right now."

"What about the girl?"

"The girl?"

"The girl friend. Your hairdresser."

"I forgot about Dawn. By all means, though, let's invite her too— the more the merrier. If he is the shooter, we'll only be better off the more witnesses we have. And if he isn't, so who cares if Dawn Kupchinsky comes along? Actually, it's a good idea. We can use her to divert the wife if we want a chance to speak to Yudel alone."

"And if we don't?"

"So she'll meet one of her future fathers-in-laws. Nothing wrong in that, is there?"

"She'll meet him eventually anyway," Lawrence Lazar said, downing the dregs of his tepid tea. "What real difference does it make when?"

The assault party met at the corner of Sixty-Third Drive and Queens Boulevard just in front of Alexander's Department Store at nine o'clock that very evening. Marvin, who had had an enormous fight with Manny Zryb about getting the evening off, was the first to arrive.

It was as unusually cool an evening as the day had been warm. The lights of Manhattan glowed in the western distance, but Queens Boulevard itself was strangely quiet. It was too cool for leisurely window shopping, too late for couples to be rushing to make the early show at the local movie theaters and too early for those wishing to take in the late show. And traffic, for whatever reason, was light for a Saturday night; Bunny, Lawrence Lazar, Marvin and Dawn were able to cross the twelve-lane boulevard without having to stop even once for oncoming traffic.

Bunny herself proposed that the assault party, as she herself had named the four participants in that evening's adventure, not walk on Queens Boulevard. Instead, she proposed, they go a bit out of their way and walk up Sixty-Third Drive past Saunders, Wetherole and Booth Streets to Austin Street. They could then walk through the quiet, residential streets of Rego Park all the way into Forest Hills and have the privacy that secluded, untravelled streets would afford them to discuss the evening's plans.

Her suggestion adopted, the four moved south on Sixty-Third Drive in the direction of Austin Street. Bunny took her son's arm as she had when the same group had left the Precinct House earlier that week, but instead of pulling ahead of Lawrence Lazar and Dawn, she stayed close to them so they could hear her conversation with Marvin, if not quite participate in it.

"Was this Yudel Wolfzahn fellow excited about meeting me?" Marvin's voice betrayed his nervousness as he contemplated coming face to face with the man whose genetic baggage he was either doomed or privileged to carry as his own.

"Excited? I wouldn't say he is excited, at least not yet. But he's going to be very excited right away. Very surprised and very excited." Bunny gritted her teeth as she contemplated the prospect of Yudel opening the door and suddenly finding himself in the middle of the maelstrom.

Marvin still hadn't quite seized the point. "He wasn't excited about meeting me?" he asked.

"He wasn't excited because he wasn't anything at all. He doesn't know we're coming."

"You didn't phone him first?"

"No," Bunny said simply, "I didn't. Why should I? So he could say not to come? This way, whether he's in the mood for company or not, it's already too late. But don't you worry about excited. I promise, he'll be excited. Excited is probably not even the word for what he'll be. At the very *least*, he'll be excited. And probably a lot more than that."

Marvin mulled this new information over in his mind as the party made its slow progress down Austin Street towards the Wolfzahns' home. "So what do I say? 'Hello, I'm the kid you sold to the highest bidder' or how about 'Hi, Dad, let's get to know each other! You tell me what happened to you after you sold me and I'll tell you what happened to me.'"

Bunny was not amused. "First of all, I'm the last person to defend that turd, but he didn't toss you in the trash and hope the garbage man found you before you got pitched into the truck. He selected a good family from so far down on the waiting list that he knew they would leap at the chance to cut in front of the line and he offered you to them. It's not precisely like he just abandoned you on somebody's doorstep."

"Oh, no," Marvin said immediately, "it wasn't like that at all. When you abandon a baby on somebody's doorstep, you don't walk away with thousands of dollars." Suddenly, a new thought came to Marvin. "Or did you two split the take?"

Bunny had expected this question to come eventually, but she was strangely unready for it at this particular moment. "I took six hundred to pay the hospital bill and another two to cover what I had spent on maternity clothing. But I didn't have a dime left over when I was through."

"So you took eight hundred and he got more than two grand, which I presume was a fortune in those days. Why didn't you go for an even split?"

Bunny stood still for a moment and looked Marvin directly in the eyes. "I loved you," she said. "And I wouldn't take a penny for giving you up."

Marvin looked back into his mother's eyes and saw they were wet with tears of regret. "But not enough to keep me and raise me, only enough to feel creepy about taking money for giving me away."

"I did love you."

"You should have gotten a job."

"I had a job. It wouldn't ever have been enough."

"Then you should have sued my father for child support and kept on raising me. You did what you did, but you didn't have to do it. So don't tell me you love me now and you loved me then, but somehow your hands were tied. At least admit you did what you did because you wanted to do it. I don't know what kind of relationship we're going to have, but it might as well start out with some honesty."

✳✳✳

Bunny felt herself transported back to the day of Marvin's birth. May 2, 1953, was a hot, sticky day. The windows in the hospital room were open and a warm breeze was wafting in. The woman in the adjacent bed, a thin woman named Joan whose son had been born the very same day as Marvin, had a small radio which she kept tuned to one of the many big-band stations New York still had on its airwaves. The labor had been long and intense, but in the end, the child had been born safe and sound. Bunny had been exhausted when Yudel entered her room. At the time, she hadn't seen him in over six weeks.

"I was wondering when you'd show up," she said weakly.

"I came as soon as I heard."

"Did you hear I'd been spotting for three weeks? Did you hear I almost needed a Caesarian? Did you hear that I ripped open when the baby's shoulders came out?"

"I didn't hear any of that," Yudel answered honestly. "But I heard the baby was born."

"And how did you hear that?"

"I phoned the hospital."

"How did you know to phone today?"

Yudel looked into Bunny Falk's eyes. "I've been phoning twice a day every single day for two months now. Eventually, I knew they'd tell me you were here and a baby was born."

Bunny hadn't been in the mood to hear any stories of Yudel Wolfzahn's devotion to her and her baby. "Let's talk *takhlis*," she said brusquely, using the Jewish expression to underscore her desire to come directly to the point. "You found a couple?"

"They're in the waiting room."

"And what are they doing there?"

Yudel seemed confused by the question. "They're waiting," he said. "What else would they be doing in a waiting room?"

"For the baby? Now? They're waiting for the baby right now?"

"It's really best this way. Trust me on this—this is what I do all day for other couples. If you're going to give the baby up anyway, why bond with it any more than you've already done? You'll only make yourself miserable and in the end, you'll suffer even more than you already have."

"I just want to see the baby one single time."

"You saw it once."

"I want to see it again."

"It's your right. But it's the wrong decision. Believe me," Yudel had said sincerely, "I know. I've been and I know."

"I won't change my mind, if that's what you're afraid of."

Yudel had looked directly into Bunny's eyes and when he had answered, it was in a quiet voice. "If I thought you might change your mind, it wouldn't be the wrong decision. It's only because I know you'll end up giving the kid up anyway that it's best you just let things be."

In the end, Bunny had allowed herself to be convinced. She had seen her baby a second time twenty-six years and nine months later in the Precinct House at the corner of Austin Street and Yellowstone Boulevard.

Bunny never laid eyes on Yudel Wolfzahn again. He didn't call her and she didn't call him. She waited for a note or for some sort of communication, but none came. In the end, she allowed the matter to drop from her daily thoughts and returned to her job.

A year later, Yudel phoned her out of the blue and asked her if she wouldn't like to meet a friend of his.

Bunny, startled to hear Yudel's voice, agreed. She and Lawrence Lazar Luft became engaged on Tuesday, December 12, 1954, and were married in the spring of the following year. The ache and pain connected with the whole incident became fainter and less acute as the years passed, but it never subsided entirely. Even decades after the fact, it was the rare day that would come and go without Bunny giving at least a moment's thought to the baby she gave up.

***

The assault party continued to make its slow progress down Austin Street. They detoured around a large apartment house that some crazed city planner had allowed to be built precisely in the middle of the street, but after only a block they returned to Austin Street and continued westward.

"So maybe I didn't have to give you up," Bunny said to Marvin after a period of prolonged silence. They were on the west side of Yellowstone Boulevard, passing just behind the great yellow stone facade of the back of the Queens Hebrew Congregation. "But don't assume that I wanted to. Maybe I didn't *have* to, but I know I didn't *want* to either. Sometimes we do things we don't want to do because we decide somehow they are the right things to do. Anyway, there it is. I didn't want to do it, I didn't have to do it and I did it anyway. If it makes a difference to you, I'm truly sorry I let that bastard talk me into doing it."

"You mean Mr. Wolfzahn? He talked you into giving me up?"

Bunny thought for a long moment. "Well," she said, "yes and no. Yes, he talked and he talked and finally, he talked me into it. But it was me he was talking to and it was me who made the final decision. He had his own strong opinion, but the truth is that it was my decision. And don't think I wouldn't love to pin this on him. He did a lot of talking, but in the end it was my decision. You wanted honesty? Behold," Bunny concluded with a flourish of her right hand, "honesty!"

Lawrence Lazar took Dawn Kupchinksy's arm and, turning to her, silently mouthed the word 'Bullshit'. Dawn nodded in knowing assent as the party crossed Continental Avenue for the final two or three blocks before the Wolfzahns' apartment.

When the downstairs buzzer rang, Clara Wolfzahn was pouring second cups of black tea into her and Yudel's teacups. Zelig, who had had enough tea, was preparing to take his leave.

"I'll get it," Yudel said, rising from his chair and moving over to the intercom box installed just to the right of the Wolfzahns' front door. He pushed the silver button on the left of the box and, clearing his throat, said his name into the box.

"It's Susan Cohen from apartment D-55," Dawn said distinctly into the speaker box located just to the right of the front door as she read the name of the Wolfzahns' downstairs neighbor off the buzzer board. "I went down for milk and I forgot my key. Can you buzz me in?"

"Why not?" said the chivalrous Wolfzahn as he pushed the other button on his intercom box. "How often does someone have a chance to be kind to a neighbor?"

In a few short moments, Bunny, Lawrence Lazar, Marvin and

Dawn were in the sixth floor hallway heading for the Wolfzahns' door.

It was Dawn who actually rang the bell.

"Who's there?" Yudel's voice betrayed not the slightest intimation of suspicion.

"It's Susan," Dawn answered. "You just buzzed me in and I wanted to say thank you."

"You're welcome," came the polite reply through the shut door as Dawn heard footsteps withdrawing from the foyer on the other side of the Wolfzahns' front door.

"No, wait," she called out. "I want to tell you something. Could you open the door?"

The footsteps came back to the door. For a brief moment, all four people in the hall held their breath. But after only the briefest moment of deliberation, they could all hear Yudel throwing dead bolts and unlocking cylinder locks in preparation for inviting his unknown downstairs neighbor, Susan Cohen, into his home.

The door opened. At first, Yudel saw only Dawn Kupchinsky. He had seen her before the night they had both dined at Pho-Nee's before the incident in the Korean grocery, but for a fatal moment, Yudel merely assumed she looked familiar because he must have seen her from time to time folding laundry in the laundry room or tarrying by the banks of mailboxes in the lobby while she opened her mail. "Come in, Susan," he said politely as he stepped away from the open doorway.

Before he could register what had happened, all four of his unexpected guests were standing in the foyer of his modest apartment. Yudel recognized Lawrence Lazar instantly and Bunny a moment later. Who Marvin was, he also knew immediately, although for a confused moment, Yudel wasn't certain what Susan Cohen had to do with anything. But then Yudel understood that the younger woman who stood before him wasn't too likely to be Susan Cohen either.

"Shit on a stick," Yudel said to no one in particular as he contemplated the scene before him.

"You could say that again," Bunny said with a pleasant smile. "So aren't you going to ask us in?" she added, moving quickly to secure the living room before Yudel could even begin to formulate an answer to her question.

The maneuver was a complete success. By the time Yudel found his tongue, Bunny and Lawrence Lazar were seated on the living room couch facing Clara Wolfzahn and Zelig Kropf, who had just been getting ready to leave the Wolfzahns'. Yudel hovered in the doorway, looking pale, while Marvin and Dawn sat down in large green wing chairs facing the standing Yudel Wolfzahn. Both Bunny and Lawrence Lazar found themselves staring at Clara Wolfzahn, both suddenly uncertain if Clara was or was not the woman with the handbag who had accosted them in synagogue.

"So," Bunny began with relish, "probably you're asking why we've dropped in this evening..."

Yudel scowled and remained silent, but Clara made an attempt at civil hospitality.

"Why don't I make a fresh pot of tea?" she asked rhetorically, getting up from her seat. "I have a cake, too," she added.

"That would be lovely," Bunny responded for them all. "Tea would be lovely. And cake? Even better!"

Clara was enheartened by Bunny's effusive response to her meager offer. In a moment, she was in the kitchen. The others could hear her opening and closing cupboard doors in the kitchen and running the water to fill the kettle.

Bunny realized it was time to begin in earnest. "Yudel," she said, turning to her host, "this young man is Marvin Kalish."

Yudel and Bunny both turned to face Marvin at the same moment. No one spoke. Marvin could see from the look on Yudel's face that he had certainly understood that Marvin was his son. Yudel, for his part, felt certain that words were now superfluous; Marvin clearly understood that he, Yudel, had realized what their relationship was. The silence that filled the room was almost viscous.

Dawn watched Marvin's face and Zelig watched Yudel. Lawrence Lazar was watching Bunny to see what *her* next move was going to be and she herself was moving her head slowly back and forth, trying to watch both father *and* son at the same time. For a few long moments, no one spoke and the mood remained unbroken.

Bunny turned suddenly to Zelig Kropf. "Who are *you*?" she demanded baldly of her own former pharmacist.

"After all these years, we meet again. Zelig Kropf, at your service! I was just leaving, but if you don't mind, I think I'd rather like to stay now. Is that all right?"

"No. Go home, Zelig," Bunny commanded, suddenly realizing to whom she was speaking and having no time to phrase a polite answer to his vain, slightly pathetic question. "Your business here is concluded."

Zelig made no move even to get up from his seat, much less to leave the premises. "I am my hosts' guest," he said firmly. "And I have no intention of going anywhere."

Bunny opened her mouth to reply, but before she could, Larry Luft, who had recognized Zelig Kropf all too well, spoke out. "It's okay, Bunny," he said, "he's invited too. I don't know how, but this has something to do with him as well."

Zelig turned to face Bunny directly. "I remember the evening we met," he said.

Bunny was strangely moved. "I do too," she answered. "How could I forget such an evening?"

"How indeed?" Zelig turned to Marvin and Dawn and offered a brief explanation. "I was having dinner in the Boulevard with Yudel the very night your birth parents met. Sandy Gold was there as well. Larry was supposed to be there too, but isn't it lucky for you he wasn't?"

"Lucky?" Marvin couldn't imagine why it was lucky his birth mother hadn't met her future husband that fateful evening instead of this creepy Yudel Wolfzahn.

"I'd say lucky," Zelig continued. "After all, if he hadn't cancelled at the last moment, your birth parents might never have begun the relationship that led directly to your existence. Maybe they would have gotten together anyway, and maybe not. So if you like being who you are, I'd say you are lucky Larry skipped dinner that evening. But whether you consider yourself lucky or not doesn't much matter. What matters is that your birth parents met and made you, whoever you are. Look," Zelig continued in a softer tone, "even I don't presume to understand the whole truth about Marvin Kalish. But whatever the truth about Marvin Kalish turns out to be, we'd certainly never have gotten anywhere if there *wasn't* a Marvin Kalish in the first place. So it's not only you who are lucky—we all are, not only all of us here, but maybe even all of us, period."

Marvin began to understand. "I *am* lucky he wasn't there," he agreed.

"Good," Zelig said, turning back to Bunny. "So you see," he continued, "we're not all enemies here. I still remember fondly the role your husband played in my life. He was a good friend and I'm sorry we grew apart. I can't even say why it happened. But these things *do happen*." Zelig stressed his final two words to invest them with added meaning.

Now it was Marvin's turn to ask a question. "You said you're not sure you understand the *whole* truth about who I am. Who exactly *do* you think I am?"

It was a pivotal moment. Saying too much could jeopardize the whole drama that Zelig was fully expecting to unfold that very evening. But saying nothing at all could also disturb the course of expected events, perhaps even ruinously. Crossing over to the green wing chair in which Marvin was seated, Zelig Kropf bent down low and whispered a single word into Marvin's right ear.

Marvin's eyes opened wide and it seemed he was going to say something, but before he could, Zelig positioned himself directly in front of Marvin's chair and, placing the index finger of his right hand across his own lips, shook his head slightly from side to side. The unspoken message was entirely clear: whatever the truth about Marvin Kalish, it was a secret Marvin was not to feel free to reveal.

Bunny sensed she was losing control of the situation. Realizing that Zelig was obviously a major player in the drama, she relented and told him he could stay.

"You are kind," he said politely, now back on the couch he had been sharing with Clara Wolfzahn.

Eventually, Bunny turned to Yudel. "Somebody's been trying to kill our boy."

Marvin thought to interject that he was Ike and Alice Kalish's boy and nobody else's. Being in the presence of his birth parents was a shocking experience, but not so shocking as to make Marvin forget where his true allegiance lay. He tried to find the right way to express his fidelity towards the parents who raised him without sounding ungrateful to the man and woman who had given him life, but the words didn't come easily. In the end, Marvin said nothing.

Yudel knew that he had to appear shocked. He raised his hand to his mouth and opened his eyes wide. "*Lieber Gott,*" he said in a hushed tone, "tell me the whole story."

Yudel had clearly been speaking directly to Bunny and it therefore fell to her to recount the story of the previous few months. She told the story briefly and in her usual matter-of-fact style, leaving out nothing of importance and skipping over details she deemed irrelevant.

Bunny began with the shooting incident at the Styx, then moved on to the Korean grocery. Marvin felt certain that Yudel was the man Dawn had mistaken for her French teacher at Pho-Nee's that very evening, but now that he saw him in the comfort of his own home and surrounded by his familiar things, he hesitated to accuse his father of being the shooter. It seemed too wild and too strange, but above all, Marvin could not accept even the possibility that the little man whom he now knew to be his biological father was also the maniac who was trying to kill him. He looked to Dawn for corroboration of his sense that Yudel was the man in the restaurant *and* the man in the Korean grocery, but she seemed not to recognize him despite the fact that she was staring directly at him.

Marvin kept his peace as his mother moved further into the story. She told about the experience of meeting her abandoned child in the Precinct House and she briefly outlined Detective Abernathy's various feelings about the shooting incidents, delicately leaving out the theory that Marvin had staged the whole thing as a publicity stunt.

She described the incident of that very week on Austin Street when someone had apparently shot at Marvin from within the gourmet shop and she retold, briefly, the story of the previous evening's dinner with the elder Kalishes and Marvin and Dawn.

Finally, she finished her story and fell silent.

Zelig, who hadn't laid eyes on Marvin Kalish since his bar mitzvah couldn't take his eyes off "the face" now that he could see it in living flesh. He listened intently to Bunny's tale, but without looking at her even for a single moment. Marvin's face was the precise embodiment of the drawing on the ticket and the scores of other examples of ancient art he had collected throughout the years.

There was no face in the world with which Zelig was more familiar, but somehow seeing it on a real flesh-and-blood human being was an overwhelming experience. In the silence that followed Bunny's story, it would have been natural for Yudel to pick up the cudgel and tell his own, or rather his own and Zelig's story.

He opened his mouth, apparently to begin his tale, when Clara reappeared from the kitchen carrying a large silver tray. On the tray were a large teapot, a silver creamer and sugar bowl, a stack of dessert plates, cups, saucers and dessert spoons.

She set the tray down on the dining room table and returned to the kitchen for her cake.

This is the part now that Marvin, years after the fact, would always describe in slow motion.

"So," Zelig asked Bunny, as though possessed of genuine curiosity, "tell me how you came in contact with the police in the first place? I mean, there was nothing to connect *you* and Marvin, even after the first incident at the comedy club."

For some reason, Bunny didn't answer immediately. Sensing that she was lost in thought, Lawrence Lazar answered easily. "Some lady accosted us in synagogue one Friday evening. She was a slight thing with a big handbag and at a certain point in the service, she stood up and whacked me on the head with it. When I turned to see who had hit me, she said something about Bunny's son being in danger."

"And your wife has no other sons?"

"Well, we do have another son. That's the weird part. Before we could ask any questions, the woman ran out of the synagogue and Bunny ran after her. Before she escaped entirely, she said something about the Stuyvesant Agency, which was the social services agency Bunny had used to give her baby up for adoption."

"So you assumed the lady meant Bunny's first-born son, the baby she had given up?"

Lawrence Lazar seemed puzzled by the question. "Yes, of course. What else could we have thought?"

Zelig paused for an imperceptible moment. Sitting up in his place, he raised his bony arm to shoulder level and extended the index finger of his right hand towards Lawrence Lazar. "And do you see that woman here this evening?" he asked gravely.

At that very moment, Clara Wolfzahn came back into her living room carrying a large cake plate on which there was, just as she had promised, a round yellow cake.

All heads turned directly towards her as she entered the room. "Holy shit," Lawrence Lazar intoned, almost reverentially. "It's her."

In Marvin's latter recollections, the action slows down even further here.

As though on cue, Clara dropped the cake to the floor. The white porcelain cake plate smashed on the hardwood into a thousand pieces and the cake itself bounced across the living room floor until it came to a stop at Dawn Kupchinsky's feet. Dawn bent down to pick up the cake, but just as she did Zelig jumped to his feet and approached Marvin.

In a voice one would have expected to belong to one many years younger, Zelig Kropf began to intone a familiar section of the festival liturgy. "*Ato vachortonu mikol ho-omim,*" he sang, using a weird Aeolian melody none of them had ever heard used for the "Thou Hast Chosen Us from Among the Nations" section of the synagogue service.

Like spectators at a tennis match, all heads now turned from Clara to Zelig. He sang his strange song directly to Marvin, standing over him almost as though he were positioning himself to embrace the young object of his song as soon as he finished.

Dawn was the first to see the gun. The gun—a sort of cross between a hunting rifle and a shotgun that Yudel had somehow managed to acquire as a gift from a low-level gangster for whose sister he had arranged an adoption—had been hidden behind the Wolfzahns' piano, but while the assembled guests were watching Zelig sing, it had somehow appeared in Yudel's arms.

Dawn heard an extremely soft rustling noise and turned her head just precisely as Yudel was raising the weapon to shoulder level. Suddenly, Dawn realized she was still holding Clara Wolfzahn's round pound cake in her arms and she lifted it to throw it at Yudel's head. The yellow cake, which had been baked in one of the few tin tube pans Clara's mother had brought along from Germany, was plenty heavy enough to do the job. Dawn raised the cake and threw it as forcefully as she could at Yudel's head.

In a thousand attempts, Dawn could never have missed so spectacularly. Instead of knocking Yudel Wolfzahn off balance long enough for someone to lunge at him and wrest the shotgun from his arms, the yellow cake landed directly on the barrel of the gun as though it were part of a child's ring-toss game. Yudel looked at the cake strangely impaled on his gun and smiled as he released the safety.

By now, of course, everyone had turned from Zelig, who was continuing his sad chant, to Yudel.

Yudel pointed the gun directly at Marvin Kalish's heart and appeared ready to pull the trigger when Bunny suddenly flung herself across the room onto her son. Marvin, who was apparently frozen solid in sudden terror, tipped over as though he were a statue rather than a man and fell to the floor. Bunny flung herself on top of him just as Yudel raised the gun towards the ceiling and, hoping fervently that his upstairs neighbors had gone out for the evening, pulled the trigger.

A single shot rang out.

Twenty-five

"So this proves they're right—you can get used to anything."

"Well, you don't have to get too used to getting shot at. I think that part's over. At least, I hope it is."

"I suppose. But the whole thing is just too weird to assume anything. I suppose we'll have to wait and see."

Dawn Kupchinsky snuggled closer as she glanced at the clock by their bedside; it was twelve minutes past five in the morning, Sunday morning, March 8, 1981.

Marvin was as little tired as she; they had made love upon returning home, but that had only served somehow to invigorate them. Hours had passed and neither Dawn nor Marvin Kalish felt even remotely tired.

Marvin, for his part, gathered Dawn into the crook of his right arm and held her tight. But his eyes were fixed on the train ticket he held in his left hand, the ticket Zelig Kropf had produced and given to him immediately after the shot had rung out.

***

The reverberations of Yudel's single shot were still ringing in the ears of the people assembled in the Wolfzahns' living room when Zelig had gotten to his feet. Wordlessly, he had fished a yellowed scrap of paper from his pocket and handed it to Marvin. It appeared to be some sort of old ticket, but Marvin didn't even recognize the language in which it was written.

"What is it?" he had asked simply, still having failed to take in the fact that his biological father had just tried to shoot him.

"Turn it over," Zelig had answered.

Marvin *had* turned the yellow scrap over and there, in faded pencil, was a drawing of himself. The drawing was a bit smudged and the paper was cracked along the centerfold, but there was no question that the drawing was of him. "It's me," Marvin said quietly.

"I know."

"You drew this?"

"No, not me."

As this brief exchange was taking place, the others had risen to their feet and Yudel had put his gun down on the coffee table. Bunny and Lawrence Lazar joined Dawn in one corner of the room, while Yudel, Clara and Zelig stood in the doorway leading back into the foyer. Marvin stood by himself in the center of the room clutching the ticket. Despite the fact that he had been shot at not five minutes earlier, he felt strangely unafraid.

Zelig took a step forward and began to speak. "In 1942, I received a notice of deportation from the Nazi government," he began. He told the whole story, from the beginning in the Munich train station to the very end; when he revealed that Yudel was the father of Marvin Kalish, he looked towards Clara, who he presumed still thought that he, Zelig, was the boy's parent.

Clara lifted her hands in a gesture that suggested Zelig need not worry about her fragile sensitivities.

"You knew all along?" he interrupted his own narrative to ask.

"I'm not as stupid as you," was all Clara said.

Zelig resumed his tale, covering the strange collection of art featuring Marvin's face that he, Zelig, had collected over the previous quarter-century and concluding, eventually, with the shot fired minutes before by Yudel into the ceiling of his own living room.

"So?" Marvin needed to hear more.

"So what?"

"So what happens now?"

Zelig looked vaguely surprised by the question. "How should I know what happens now?" he asked. "I've lived with this story for almost forty years now. You deal with it from now on. Here's your ticket," he said, standing forward and handing the yellowed pencil portrait to Marvin. "Have a pleasant journey."

Marvin surveyed the strange group. The whole story was fantastic and Marvin was hardly the kind of man given to blind faith in fairy tales, but yet for all its inherent implausibility, the story did sound right to Marvin, implausible and improbable, perhaps—but also somehow right. And yet, for all his uncharacteristic willingness to believe, the implications of Zelig's story were simply too overwhelming to consider. "Thank you," he said softly, feeling himself somehow to be signing up for a mission he neither understood nor especially wished to understand.

"Somewhere, sometime." Yudel felt the weight of decades shifting off his shoulders, but he too felt the final chapter had yet to be written. "This will yet concern us all," he concluded poetically.

"If you wanted it to concern you," Marvin said casually, "you oughtn't have sold your child for a few pieces of silver."

Yudel seemed ready to respond to Marvin's bitter remark, but for a long while, he said nothing at all. "It wasn't like that," he offered lamely.

The good-byes had been perfunctory; Marvin had finally simply taken Dawn's hand and walked out the door into the cool spring air.

"You know," Marvin told Dawn as they walked along the boulevard towards their home, "adopted children are supposed to spend their lives wondering who they are, but that was never me—I'm the one who had no interest in tracing his birth parents, the one who knew who he was. And now that I've met my birth parents and I know who I didn't become as well as who I actually became, now I find I have no idea who I am." Marvin stopped walking and stood for a moment in the garish pink light of a streetlamp. All of a sudden, the night air seemed chilly and Marvin put his arms on Dawn's shoulders. "So who actually do you think I am?" he asked pointedly. "I mean, you don't think there could actually be anything to that crazy story, do you?"

Dawn opened her mouth to respond, then apparently thought better of it and said nothing. "Whoever you are," she said finally, leaning over to whisper into Marvin's right ear, "whoever or whatever you are, I love you."

✳✳✳

The ticket looked older and significantly more decrepit in the light of Marvin's bedside lamp than it had at the Wolfzahns'. When Zelig Kropf had handed him the ticket, for example, it had appeared merely old and yellow, like an old newspaper stored for some reason over a period of decades. But now the ticket looked more like a scrap of ancient paper that had somehow managed—*barely*—not to have turned to dust over centuries of exposure to the air.

The paper was crumbling in Marvin's fingers and he wondered how Zelig had managed to keep it in as good condition as he somehow had over the decades it had been in his trust. The edges were frayed and the folds had revealed themselves under closer scrutiny to be tears in the texture of the paper. The sketch of his face was itself marred, Marvin could now see, by several holes in the forehead and cheeks; these holes, no matter how delicately Marvin held the scrap of paper, appeared to be getting bigger.

Dawn snuggled close and watched as the paper crumbled. Only twenty minutes after Marvin had begun watching, the train ticket was a pile of yellow dust in his hands.

Marvin cupped his hands to hold the dust and walked to the window. The window was open a tiny crack, but Marvin was able to open it wide by inserting his elbow between the window frame and the pane and pushing out.

A chilly March breeze came through the window into the bedroom. Dawn rose silently from the bed and wrapped the down comforter around her shoulders as though it were a regal cape of ermine. She joined her friend in the cold breeze and watched as he extended his hands outside the window and allowed the dust to blow down into the street.

The reddish haze of a Queens dawn was already visible on the distant horizon. "Dawn, meet dawn," Marvin said softly.

"I love you," Dawn answered. "And I *will* go with you on this — what did he call it? — this pleasant journey."

"Swear it!"

Dawn reached around and opened Marvin's robe, dropping her comforter to the ground as she did so. Pressing her body to his, she swore her oath of fidelity.

"Now what?"

"Breakfast," Marvin said. "Let's make coffee and then get back into bed."

––––––

From the unpublished *Midrash Eli Melekh* by Rabbi Elimelech Weissbrot:

> *I see him, but he is not coming soon; I sense him, but he is not yet close* (Numbers 24:17): The verse may be explained in the following manner: *I see him*, thus he is present among us; *but he is not coming soon*, thus he is hidden. *I sense him*: thus he is close enough to touch his skin or to feel his breath; *but he is not yet close*, perhaps even he himself doesn't realize who he is.

Epilogue

In the medieval period, it was common for Jewish libraries to be confiscated for one reason or another by secular or ecclesiastical authorities. Rarely, however, were the books that constituted these collections actually destroyed. Sometimes they were preserved inside the confiscators' own libraries as trophies, but more often these books were disassembled and their parchment leaves used for other purposes. Most of these pages are gone forever, but those which were actually used by Gentile scribes to bind their own books have, at least to a certain extent, survived.

Since the first Hebrew manuscript leaves were found embedded in the bindings of non-Jewish books towards the end of the last century, there has been a rather disorganized effort to retrieve more and more of them.

Because the procedure necessarily involves taking apart a medieval volume that itself may be of enormous value, there has been an understandably understated response to this effort on the part of the librarians to whom those books are entrusted. Nonetheless, the search for medieval manuscript leaves continues unabated.

In 1978, a young Jewish graduate student was visiting the German city of Xanten, about halfway between Cologne and the Dutch border. Although his research concerned the 1891 blood libel that was levelled against Xanten Jew Adolf Wolff Buschoff, who was falsely accused of murdering a Christian child and using his blood for religious purposes, the student managed, once in Xanten anyway, to talk his way into the library of a local monastery. Having gained entry, he set about searching for Latin manuscript volumes that appeared to have unnecessarily or unusually thick binding leaves. In the short time—roughly a quarter hour—he was allowed to wander unsupervised through the collection, the young researcher found five volumes he thought might possibly have been bound with the confiscated leaves of Hebrew books.

Three books proved merely to have been bound by maladroit hands, but two tomes yielded the desired fruit.

The first book, a Latin translation of some of the famous letters falsely attributed to Dionysius the Areopagite, yielded two leaves of Maimonides' *Laws Pertaining to the Study of Torah*, both of which differ considerably from the published text. These leaves were published three years later by their discoverer in a learned European journal devoted to Maimonidean scholarship, whereupon they were returned to the Xanten monastery in which they were discovered.

The binding of the second book, a volume of sermons by Clement of Alexandria, yielded one single manuscript leaf which has never been published and to which printed reference has never been made. This parchment leaf, the existence of which was not even made known to the monkish librarians from under whose nose it was stolen, remained for many years in the private possession of its finder. The author, who was the intimate friend of the discoverer of the Xanten leaves, believes himself to be the sole person to whom the unpublished folio was ever shown.

The young researcher died in a freak surfing accident off the coast of Maui in 1988, leaving behind an even younger widow and a single child, a boy born only a year earlier. His entire estate, naturally enough, was left to his wife. However, a secret codicil, one which the lawyer charged with executing the will was forbidden to reveal even to the researcher's widow, left the contents of a certain safety deposit box to the author of this book. On the fifth of October, 1988, the author travelled to New York from his home in British Columbia to retrieve his bequest. The appropriate documents were prepared, the key to the box was produced by the Citibank officials and the contents of the box handed over to their new owner. The box contained the single unpublished manuscript leaf filched from the Xanten monastery in 1978. Attached to the leaf was a piece of paper torn from a child's notebook on which the author's friend had written a few words. "Yours (if you're reading this in the first place)," the note read, "to do with as you please."

The author took the leaf home and deposited it in his own safety deposit box, where it remains to this day. The page, written in an antique hand highly similar to several of the so-called Dead Sea Scrolls and especially to the Temple Scroll, is of incalculable value not only because of its great age, but because of its contents. It is a page of what presumably must have been a major work of Jewish messianic speculation, the only one of its kind known to have been composed in the early rabbinic period. The only non-Hebrew words on the page are three Latin words which appear to have seeped through the outer binding page of the book in which the manuscript leaf ended up being bound; these words, *sed non modo*, appear to come from the Vulgate Latin translation of Balaam's famous messianic prophecy: I see him, but [he is] not [to come] soon / I sense him, but he is not [yet] close (videbo eum sed non modo/intuebor illum sed non prope.) Needless to say, there can be no connection between this Latin seepage and the ancient work at hand.

It is both our extraordinary good fortune and our exceptional bad luck that the page preserved is a sort of table of contents of the larger work: good fortune, in that we would otherwise have no way even of guessing at the contents, scope or orientation of the larger work, and poor luck, in that the presence of the table of contents on the surviving leaf denies the latter-day reader even the single page of text that would otherwise have been the sole extant extract of the work in question.

The table of contents, at least, is done in the ancient style and provides a brief sentence or two of summary for each chapter rather than a simple name or, even worse, number. And so we learn a number of things that ancient Jewry believed about the redeemer for whose arrival the pious daily prayed and with whose frustrating tardiness the sages tried to grapple.

Many of the traditions listed survived and eventually became standards of Jewish messianic speculation. That the messiah's personal name would be Menachem, the Hebrew word for Consoler and Comforter, for example, is clearly far older than any scholar had previously thought, as are the traditions that the messiah will be found by them who seek him in Rome, of all places, and the homey detail that the messiah will love and perhaps even eventually marry a woman hairdresser. (This latter tradition also ended up in a garbled state as part of the gospel literature of primitive Christianity.) Also in this category is the Biblical idea that the messiah will be born into the world during or immediately following a cataclysm of the greatest and most tragic proportions during which vast numbers of Jewish people will lose their lives.

Another set of traditions to which chapters in the larger work were devoted did not survive in Jewish texts, but were transmitted by Jewish apostates who apparently knew them well through the medium of Christian messianic speculation. The idea, long forgotten and eventually denied by Jewish teachers, that the messiah will be born to a young unmarried woman, for example, is not only on the list, but is expressed in distinctly Isaianic language, just as in the gospel literature.

A third set of traditions is unknown from any ancient source. Some of these are quite in the style of known traditions, but others are distinct and seem to have developed from speculational matrices that were either intentionally repressed or accidentally forgotten. Prominent among these is the notion, far more reminiscent of the mythological underpinning of the Oriental mystery cults of Roman antiquity than of Jewish messianic beliefs, that the mother of the messiah will activate his redemptive mission first by seeking her lost son, then by finding him and finally by risking her life to save his. Only when these three conditions are met, the text seems to suggest, can the ultimate salvific mission begin. Some few others of the traditions listed which fall into this third category include the strange image of a laughing messiah and the profoundly Oedipal tradition to the effect that the messiah's greatest enemy *and* most loyal supporter will be his own father.

Temple Israel
Minneapolis, Minnesota

IN HONOR OF
THE SPEEDY RECOVERY OF
HARRY BIRGER
FROM
NANCY & LARRY SHILLER